Also by Ed Levesko

At the End of the Day
A la Fin du Jour
Eddies in Life
Umbra (English)
Umbra (French)
Point of No Return
10 West to Venice
Where Justice ends
The Guitar Player
La nuit Blanche

www.edlevesko.com
edlevesko@gmail.com

Long Time Passing

Long Time Passing

ISBN: 978-0-6157-3508-5

Ed Levesko, Publisher

For information address:
Ed Levesko, Publisher.
P.O.Box 144
Culver City, CA
90232
U.S.A.

edlevesko@gmail.com
www.edlevesko.com

Printed in the United States of America

LONG TIME PASSING

It's about friendship, life, love, death,
music, women, war, and everything else
in between.

To Kathy Lockhart & Jack Pierce

Long Time Passing

Some things in life are not easy! And if those things have anything to do with your friends; well, it can drive you crazy. But because you love your friends you want to please them, you want to be accommodating; you want to spare them, and you, any embarrassment.

So the result is that you end up internalizing your sentiments and ideas as not to piss them off, or get you all pissed off. And, yet, at the same time, you want to let them know in simple words what you really think about their ideas; but, well, not totally.

"You guys are nuts," I said.

McCall and Jackson's idea was simple, so they kept saying. The three of us would drive—I own a car---from Fort Bragg, North Carolina—the Army base where we were stationed—straight through to St. Louis, Missouri, and back in three days. I was not buying it. They were convinced it was the perfect plan.

That to dismiss it showed our complete failure to live up to the highest standards of true male hounds. Furthermore, it was not worthy of our high intellect, physical prowess—our manliness.

Denying to ourselves the only worthy goal in life, the hunt for the mysterious and elusive, which to McCall meant: Women. Simply put, we were losers if we did not go to St. Louis.

They had been trying to convince me for a while that we could spend the coming weekend visiting St. Louis to check out the scene, and see about putting to the maximum test our God-given rights in the "hunt," as they put it.

Meaning, trying to get into the knickers of some strange girl whom we had never seen before, and who was not Frankenstein's daughter.

In addition to getting away from our normal, dreary, insipid Army weekends where the excitement in the barracks was as attractive as wearing red combat boots with green shoelaces and dancing the polka.

That upon our return from such a wondrous adventure, we would have something to brag about to the other GIs who had not been daring, lucky, wise, or men enough to do what McCall and Jackson had in mind.

They kept saying that a two day weekend pass, plus an extra day because Monday was a holiday, gave us plenty of time to do approximately fifteen hundred miles round trip and, according to them, have us a ball.

"We'll be in St. Louis, what, eleven minutes—tops—and then we'll be heading back. So when do we sleep?"

"Sleep? Why you want sleep when you're having the time of your life? Shee-it," McCall said, dismissively. "Come on, Hollywood, I thought you was cool," he added, pretending to be offended by my lack of interest, my narrow view of what was really important in life, but mostly by what he called: My lack of cool.

In McCall's view, one could be forgiven for just about anything but not for lacking cool. That was the ultimate sin.

"Hollywood" was their nickname for me because I come from Los Angeles. For them, Los Angeles *was* Hollywood; the land of sunshine, magic and dreams. With wide boulevards crisscrossing the city, all lined with palm trees swaying gently in the wind.

A paradise, overflowing with bikini-clad-long-legged-beauties, and all of the above leading you to pure enchantment and ecstasy. It never made any difference how many times I had explained to them that "Hollywood" was as phony as a two dollar bill.

That it was like being on drugs, except that you were not on drugs. Which, in a larger sense, made no difference, because if you were on drugs you would never know it was not Hollywood anyway. And if you were not on drugs and thought about Hollywood, you would wish the hell to be on drugs.

That the Hollywood idea had nothing to do with normal people getting old, or that beauty fades, or that we all die. Or taking out the garbage at night, or getting up in the morning to go to work, fighting the traffic after dropping the kids off at school, hoping that the schools principals and teachers knew what the hell they were doing, but doubting that they did.

My arguments always fell on deaf ears. Hollywood for them was Lotus Land and that was that. We were sitting on our bunks, in the barracks, while I tried to make them see it was insane to drive hundreds of miles one way, and as soon as we got there, just turn around and drive hundreds of miles back.

We had been going around the question for a while. Though I really was not totally opposed to the idea; nevertheless, it seemed like we were trying to do something that was not practical in terms of the time we had to do what they wanted to do.

"Shee-it, I know you gonna like it. I know it," Jackson continued, totally convinced.

"How am I going to like doing all of that driving?"

"Come on, Hollywood. Where's your sense of adventure? Of conquering unknown territories? Of dealing with strange lovely women? Of testing yourself against all odds? I thought you cats from Hollywood were the most fearless of them all! What, you chicken?" McCall asked.

"Chicken, my ass."

Amber Karl McCall. Twenty years old. As black as night. Born on a farm in Alabama with no running water and number five in a family of six kids, three

4

females and three males, of which one had died in childbirth before McCall was born.

"Amber? That's for girls, man. How does a guy get a name like Amber?" I had asked him the first time I heard it.

"Well, my mama wanted a girl and Amber was a name she liked. She was so set on Amber that when I was born and she saw my big wanger, she got so sad and disappointed I wasn't a girl, she started to cry. My daddy feeling sorry for her said, 'OK, Amber Karl McCall, it will be.' "

"The 'big wanger' is the part that I love about the brother's story. So touching ain't it?" Jackson said. He busted out laughing making fun of McCall who did not look pleased.

Leno Truman Jackson, Jr. was the son of a preacher from the south side of Chicago and blacker than McCall, if such a thing was possible. Jackson told us that his mother had made clear to him that he was not to use any vulgar language while in the Army. He was a preacher's son and such vulgarity was not permitted.

"But, mama, all of them GIs use foul language," he had argued.

"I don't care. You are your father's son and you will not use such vicious language."

Cash made fun of Jackson's promise to his mother. But, I also noticed he tried not to use foul language himself, though he failed a lot of times.

"Truman, how did you get that?" I asked Jackson.

"My old man was in the Army when Truman desegregated the military. He always thought old Harry showed great courage, so he gave me Truman as a middle name," Jackson said.

It took a long time for anybody to find out that A—McCall's first name initial—stood for Amber. We would not have known if it had not been for Jackson, the company's clerk, who spilled the beans.

He had access to everyone's personal records. McCall just about killed him when he told everyone about it, even though Jackson was taller than McCall and twice as strong. It took three of us to pull him off Jackson.

"Shee-it, isn't that your name?" I asked him.

"Yeah, but the way he told everybody, he made me look like I was some kind of sissy or somethin'."

"No, he didn't. Come on."

Now they were the best of friends. In the meantime, they had developed a comedy routine while taking a shower as to who had the blackest ass. It was the McCall and Jackson Blackest-Ass-Shower-Show, and the rest of us GIs laughed our heads off seeing these two guys acting silly.

After Jackson told us about McCall's first name, he threatened everyone in the company that if he ever heard anybody making fun of McCall's first name, he would personally take care of it. He was, after all, the company's clerk and he had access to everyone's Army records.

That he would make sure to screw up our Army records so bad they would not only end up being assigned to some dump in Alaska and freeze their butts off, but the Army would keep them in long after their military obligation had expired because there would be no personal information about them.

How could the Army release a whole bunch of non-existent bodies to the world? If they were in the Army there would be no problem, as officially they could be accounted for. If there were no records of any kind about them, they were not in the Army, and therefore the Army had nothing to do with them.

And if it had nothing to do with them, it could not possibly give out information about someone who did not exist, who was not in the books as it were.

"I mean," Jackson, said, "it'd be like trying to bury a ghost. The box is there, but inside it is all air. Shee-it, you'd be lucky if the Army would let you be a civilian again. They would deny you was ever part of the military. Who would know anything about you?

"You'd be as good as dead; NWU—Not With Us—is what the Army would say about your sorry ass. Even if your mama came by, identified you, and told the Army you was her son, shee-it, them generals would smile and tell her they'd get back to her, which they would never do. I know what I'm talkin' about."

Nobody ever made any comments about McCall's first name after that. People started calling him: A.K.

Most of us hated the Army; I know I did. Our reasons were as varied as to why some people like the color purple and others hate it. Or maybe it was because the reality of being just another GI, among hundreds of GIs, instead of bringing us together tended to isolate us from one another. Thus, the object of our hate became the very symbol that was supposed to make us equal, and united.

Of course, the U.S. Army wants all soldiers to be one big family of happy warriors. With no other idea in our heads than to go out to kill the bad guys, and thereby preserve the American Way of Life!

Or maybe it was that we were all young, some still in our teens, or barely out of our teens, and at that age the prevailing attitude always was: screw authority in general, and FTA: Fuck the Army, in particular!

Or maybe because when we got thrown together, pell-mell, into a situation where we had no control, instinctively we tended to end up attaching ourselves to those who resembled us in ways that gave us a sense of comfort and protection, in spite of our propensity to argue that we were all independent individuals, who wanted to go our separate ways.

Or maybe it was because we all had met in our previous life as cockroaches, and had made a promise that in our next time around we would get together not as cockroaches but as something else. And now we had, belatedly, discovered that in this present round we were all still cockroaches.

There was not one single reason that I can recall as to why Jackson, McCall, and I ended up as friends. Our gross sense of humor was certainly one. That we distrusted authority was another. A further reason was that we had been assigned to share the same barracks and our bunks were close to one another.

We also worked in the same building, though we were assigned to different jobs. But there were a couple of more pertinent, practical, and specific reasons why we became friends, really.

Both of them were in a larger sense more personal than the ones I have already mentioned. The first one was that on my off-duty hours, in order to have something to do so I would not go crazy, I had joined the theater group at the base.

They were looking for volunteers to help build and paint sets for the shows, and the latest was a musical show, *Carnival,* that I ended up directing. So I asked them if they would like to come by and help us out. McCall's reaction had been less than enthusiastic.

"I thought you like music." I said.

"That's just white-trash music. It ain't got no soul."

"What are you talking about? All music's got soul."

"No. See, music is jazz and the blues.. Now, if you's doing a show about that I'm in. Otherwise forget it."

McCall played the trumpet and he was quite good at it. He carried the mouthpiece everywhere he went, making sounds. He was practicing his scales in that damn mouthpiece at all times. He slept with the thing; he took a shower with it.

He was never separated from it. He had it hanging around his neck along with the dog tags. It was like some kind of talisman for him. You could tell McCall was around just by listening to the sounds he was making. He drove everyone crazy.

The Army wanted him to join the Army band, but he had turned them down. No jazz or blues; no McCall. He was also some kind of electronic wizard, more interested in circuit boards, oscilloscopes, switches, wires, all part of his military job. He was always tinkering with electronic gear.

"If them Army guys put together a jazz gig I'd join in no time flat. Besides, I don't like playin' marchin' music. That's for old guys."

"OK, but could you lend us a hand with the sets and the other stuff for the show?"

"Man, the theater is full of fairies. I don't like hanging around them fairies," McCall said—end of the story.

"Come on," said Jackson, who seemed more amenable to the idea. "That ain't true."

"What the hell do you know about it?"

McCall's words were dismissive with no room for any further argument.

"I've been in plays before and I know," Jackson said.

"Shee-it," McCall's famous expression.

"Too bad; there are plenty of broads in the show," I said.

I knew about McCall's broad interests—no pun intended—in that department. To be around women would immediately overcome any personal reticence he might have harbored about being in an environment he considered below his manly dignity.

"Poontang? Count me in," said McCall, his spirits up, or maybe his wanger, now that he saw the situation in a different light.

"I thought you said theater's full of fairies," Jackson said.

"You take care of 'em, I take care of the poontang," McCall said, with a great cackle.

So they both eventually came to help, which led the three of us to spend more time together. The show was a great success. We had a lot of fun doing it and even though McCall did not score with any of the women in the cast, he was grateful that he could be around them in his off-duty hours.

"Poontang does my soul good," he said, when the show was over. "I get tired of hangin' around swingin' wangers all of the time. This wasn't so bad. I had a good time."

But driving to St. Louis and back, all in a period of seventy-two hours, was not my idea of a good time. On top of which there was also the problem that the three-day pass did not allow us to be so far away from our base. For McCall, of course, that was just a small detail.

They had volunteered me because I was one of the few guys in our unit who had a set of wheels, and I was perhaps as crazy as they were. The bastards knew that all they had to do was challenge me to do something crazy, and I was game.

Though, perhaps, having a car was probably a good reason why our friendship had flourished. I had a car and they did not. It was the: You will scratch my back I will scratch your back society.

I had a 1956 Chevy Impala, convertible. Cream color with bright red stripes on the sides, white wall tires, a twin set of shiny Glass Pak exhaust pipes, and the car ran like a clock. I had driven it from California to North Carolina and it was my pride and joy.

"Cash, I don't relish driving hundreds of miles one way and hundreds of miles the other way just to go spend a few minutes in St. Louis," I said.

"Cash" was my nickname for McCall. There was a movie that had come out some years ago. The movie and the name of the main character in it was: *Cash McCall.* McCall swaggered around when everybody started calling him 'Cash.' It reminded me of guys who become cops.

Once they strap a gun to their belts, they swagger around with their arms slightly bent away from their sides, their hands and fingers cool and lose, signaling to the world that they now have a gun and are ready to draw it at the first sign of trouble from the bad guys. Sort of like Gary Cooper in *High Noon.* Cash liked the nickname. It fit his personality, really.

"What, me and Jackson will take care of expenses."

"That's not it."

"Then, why?"

"For one thing, I'll be doing most of the driving and you'll sit in the back like a damn lordship and give me static that I drive the way an old lady screws."

"That's the truth ain't it?" Cash said. Both of them giggled like silly schoolgirls.

"The truth, my ass. I know you. Going at a hundred miles an hour ain't fast enough for you."

Cash's laugh was a combination cackle, hungry hyena, and the hysterical screeching of a bird about to be swallowed by the perennial hungry cat.

"Hey, Jackson, tell this fool he's risking meetin' some serious poontang in St. Louis, shee-it."

"OK, Jonathan, we'll make a deal with you," Jackson said.

"Get out of here. You and your deals. Man, you could steal someone's socks without taking their shoes off and expect the victims to say 'thank you.' "

I was by then wise enough to know I was dealing with a couple of con artists for whom there were no limits. It was always full speed ahead and damn the torpedoes. Not that I blamed them for the madness. It was probably what got them, what got all of us, through the day.

"I'm serious, we'll rent your car from you."

"Oh boy, that's a good one."

I would rent them my car and off they would go and everybody would be cool with that. I would not put it past them to sell the car, and declare it had been stolen.

"Fifteen bucks a day, plus a full tank when you get it back."

"That's close to fifty and change. Where did you get that much bread?"

That was just about what we were making as a monthly salary in the Army, so I was a bit suspicious.

"Been saving some."

"So you guys have this whole thing all figured out, haven't you?"

"Not true," Cash said.

"Not true," said Jackson.

"What's the matter with your ass? Why you always so damn suspicious?" Cash asked, pretending to be offended by my attitude.

"Cause I know you and I ain't trusting you."

"Not trust us? Shee-it, there ain't a body out there more trustworthy than me and Jackson, right Jackson?" Cash said.

"You've got that right, brother."

"Yeah, the Jessie James brothers in full living color." They both busted out laughing.

They exchanged looks. It was a signal. It was their game. When things did not go their way, they had a routine they used to shame you into doing what they wanted. I had been around these guys long enough to know their routine.

"So you's smart ass racist, man?" Cash asked.

"What the hell are you talking about?"

I knew what was coming next. Once they got started, there was no way to stop them.

9

"That's what I thought. You's afraid them white trash will start whisperin' you favor us niggers. Ain't that a bitch?" Cash said.

"Get out of here."

"You know Jackson," Cash continued, "I thought my man here was cool. I really did. Now, he don't want us ridin' in his car 'cause he's afraid of the brothers. I guess we're gonna stink up his wheels, or somethin'. Not the man I thought I knew."

Cash pretended to be highly offended by my lack of cool.

"Yeah, I know what you mean," Jackson said. "No more wheel-sit-ins allowed in his car."

"You and your sit-ins, go stick them up where the sun don't shine."

"No can do GI," Jackson said.

He and Cash started giggling again.

"Hey, Jackson," Cash said, "remember that day when we thought we was gonna get mauled by them white trash, at that restaurant in town, and my man here stood up and told those KKK thugs to shove it? Man, that was somethin', weren't it?"

"Them days are over."

"You're both full of crap. I don't know why I hang around with you. I really must be crazy, or desperate, or both."

"You love us, white boy," Cash said.

"I must, somethin'."

"So, it's a deal," Jackson said, with the satisfaction of a gambler who has a hidden ace up his sleeve and he will use it to cheat you out of your money while claiming that he won it fair and square.

And it is your fault for not knowing how to play the game, and most likely you are a real moron to think you could sit down with real pros and not risk losing your ass in the process.

"No, it ain't no deal."

Cash started to laugh his hyena's laugh. He knew what the outcome was going to be. The bastard had my number all right.

This was 1964, and the sit-ins were taking place all around us. Back in 1960, four black students went into a restaurant in Greensboro, North Carolina, sat at the counter, and ordered food.

They were denied service and told to leave, which they refused to do. The police came, arrested them, and threw them in jail. It made the headlines everywhere.

The idea of civil disobedience started with that simple act by those four students refusing to move. It grew by leaps and bounds. Before you knew it, thousands of black students, along with some white students, throughout the South, were participating in these sit-ins.

The civil rights movement was raging across the American South. Everywhere, in bus terminals, airports, hotels, public accommodations, and segregated restaurants, blacks were sitting down at counters and refusing to move until they were served—which never happened. Instead, the police were called in and the protestors were hauled off to jail.

Sit-ins were the new tactic to force the end of segregation in the South, and it was met with incredible violence on the part of whites. The reverend Martin Luther King, Jr. was the moral driving force against the entrenched bigotry, and he was instrumental in inspiring blacks of all ages, and some whites also, to fight in a non-violent way for their civil and constitutional rights.

It was pretty ugly and depressing to see the violence perpetrated against blacks by white bigots who were bent on maintaining the status quo. The only experience that I could relate to happened in Los Angeles, where some cops and some Muslim Brothers had gotten into a shootout.

The newspaper headlines theorized that the event took place because the Muslim Brothers were all black followers of Elijah Muhammad—a self-proclaimed follower of Islam—with his own version of religion, which he called the Nation of Islam.

One of their leaders, Malcolm X, accused the cops of police brutally, while the police in turn accused the Muslim Brothers of hating the white race. Nevertheless, from my distance in California the whole situation in the South, as I followed it in the newspapers, seemed to be happening in another planet.

And since I had never directly witnessed that kind of bigotry before, it never occurred to me that a few months later, after my arrival at Fort Bragg, I would find myself involved in something that I had no experience dealing with. I had been caught in it, and it was because Cash and Jackson were both simply hungry.

We had gone into a restaurant in town to get something to eat, and sat at the counter. To this day, I am not sure whose idea it was. It seemed like it just happened—a simple human act. When you are hungry you go into a restaurant, sit down at the counter, order food, they serve it, you eat it, pay for it, and you leave.

People at the restaurant had refused to serve Cash and Jackson, even though we were all wearing U.S. Army uniforms. They told us they would only serve me.

I went ape shit!

The confrontation got ugly with taunting and vicious shouting from a group of whites, most of whom were about the same age as we were. What was so depressing, at least to me, was to see white girls among them literally foaming at the mouth with their vile insults hurled at the three of us.

They used nasty and vulgar words that I usually associated with dockworkers and not with girls. And though the confrontation did not become physical, it came very close. Both Cash and Jackson kept pushing me back. There were a hell of a lot more of them than the three of us.

I had taken some boxing lessons in the past so I thought I could defend myself, or at least try to deck a couple of those pricks before they jumped all over us. The next thing I knew a paddy wagon, along with a jeep full of big burly redneck MPs, screeched to a halt in front of the restaurant and asked us to leave, which I refused to do.

They then handcuffed us, pushed us into the wagon, and hauled us off to the base jail. I could not believe what was happening. This was the first time that I had been arrested in my life.

I had never been a witness, let alone found myself involved in such a depressing situation. We were soldiers. U.S. citizens! Full-fledged members of the United States Army! We were all supposed to defend the country's ideals. We had sworn to defend the constitution and die defending it if it came to that. We were all equal.

We were citizens prepared to protect our American brothers and sisters. And yet here were our brothers and sisters acting like animals, ready to fight us just so Cash and Jackson could not sit at the counter and be served something to eat.

And because Cash and Jackson were black, none of the lofty ideals about freedom, dignity, and equality meant a thing to the people at the restaurant, and it had pissed me off to no end. Cash and Jackson had not said very much and I deeply resented them for that.

It was also confusing because I had assumed they would push the confrontation to the limit. But, of course, that was exactly what you do not do in such situations. Keeping your cool was smart. I was not being smart.

In the wagon, I was fuming. "You chicken shits. You losers. You would not fight those pigs. I thought you guys had some balls. You ain't worth a damn, both of you. You're a goddamn disgrace."

They did not say anything. I hated everyone at that moment.

The MPs, just looked at me, smiled a kind of smirk that along with their silence simply meant, "Serves you right you dumb shit for hanging around with them darkies."

The company commander of our unit, Captain Rowe, had finally come by and gotten us out. As we were driving back to the barracks Rowe said, looking directly at me, challenging me to contradict him.

"Greene, you are a U.S. Army soldier; all of you are U.S. Army soldiers. Politics is not our concern. We're military. We're guests of these people, and you will obey orders and keep away from that kind of stunt. Is that understood?"

I did not answer and he got pissed. I liked Captain Rowe. He was a decent guy. But at that moment he was giving me a lecture that I did not need. I felt that he had let me down and I hated him for it.

How in the hell, I thought, can we be soldiers, obey orders, and keep the country safe, if racist pricks were allowed to get away with such behavior? The whole thing was just ugly and depressing!

"'Greene, is that understood?" He repeated, daring for me to challenge him. This was the kind of crap that I hated about the Army. They want you to use your brains, but when you do, they are ready to knock your head off and pull rank on you.

"What the hell were you trying to prove?" he continued. "You think you can come here with your Hollywood crazy notions—I know what they call you. You think you can just waltz in here and teach these rednecks what's what?"

I did not answer his stupid question and he got pissed. "Answer me, soldier. I'm talking to you."

"No sir," I answered.

"Did you by any chance stage this? I wouldn't put it past you."

"I'm not that smart, sir," I answered, even though I did not want to answer. I thought the question was just a cheap shot and he knew it was a cheap shot.

Ignoring my answer, captain Rowe continued, "I don't have to add any comments about McCall here, but you Jackson? I thought you knew better. I can see what these two idiots would do. Why did you go there in the first place?"

"We were hungry, sir," Cash said, quietly.

There was certain finality about the way Cash sounded. It was a strength of character that I had not seen before, but which did not surprise me. It was quiet and powerful. The captain started to say something, but he checked himself.

And for the rest of the trip back to our barracks, he did not say another thing. When we got back, the sergeant major was standing with a couple of other GIs outside the company's office.

They saw the captain and saluted. Rowe saluted back but did not say anything. He just kept on walking into his office.

"Jackson, you, McCall and Greene, all three of you are restricted to the barracks until further notice. That's an order," the sergeant major said.

He was pissed. He turned around and followed the captain inside. All of the other guys looked in our direction and drifted away without making any comments.

By then my anger had been somewhat replaced by a sense of sadness and loss. I was not sure why I felt that way. I was angry more with myself for not thinking about what I was doing, but it seemed to me that to ignore what was happening at the restaurant was just too stupid, and cowardly.

I did not really think that Cash and Jackson were cowards at all. They were not. I had said it because I was pissed.

I understood that for me not being black was the difference. I wanted to understand that difference. I knew that I would never, ever, be in a position to see what they saw, felt, and had experienced in their lives. Exposed to bigotry and racism simply because of their skin color.

I was not being goody-two-shoes about it. It was just that the people at the restaurant were being such racists, and I did not like it. In the end, it had to do more with me than the fact that Cash and Jackson were black.

As we were standing outside, I saw the faces of both Cash and Jackson. For some reason I had expected them to be pissed, but all I saw was a wise smile, kind of mocking me, in fact. At that moment, the whole thing seemed too silly, so ridiculous and childish that I started to laugh. The three of us stood there laughing.

"So you gonna take on the whole friggin' town and fight 'em, are you?" Jackson said. "You think you can come here and tell them rednecks what's what? Yeah, you want to pull your Hollywood crap on them, don't you?"

"Get off my back."

Jackson had a very deep voice and he was now using it as if he were preaching. He stood there and preached to us. "The Sermon of the Barracks" is what I called it, later. Filled with images of hell and damnation.

We were all going to hell. He was trying to save our asses and them white jerks were not worth a damn, anyway, and I had better learn that.

It was making fun of the ridiculousness of the whole episode that was needed at that moment. He called Cash and himself, a pair of Negro pussies who could not defend themselves against the white oppressors.

A couple of poor lost Negro souls in debt to me, for I had tried to come to their rescue and liberate them from bigotry, racism, and tyranny, which they had failed to appreciate.

I was the missionary, come in from the revered land of Hollywood; he pronounced it: Holy—Wood. The new Mount Olympus! Where the white gods dwelled. The way he made it sound, it was a most sacred place. A shinning place on the hill. Filled with good people, honest people, people who were as pure as fresh fallen snow.

God-like people, salt of the earth people, not racists or liars or con artists or back stabbers or scumbags, or phonies, wearing blue Suede shoes and not trying to sell you snake oil. But honorable people, bent on bringing peace and harmony to the rest of the world.

People on a mission devoted to saving humankind by showing what was best in America. Keen on demonstrating to the whole world how to save poor, little, black lost souls; Americans, from them white racist scumbags.

On a sacred mission I was. Yeah. Involved in this most worthy quest. Preaching, but not only preaching but trying to show the gospel of love, tolerance, dignity, and understanding to these unworthy white trash losers.

Cash and I were laughing our heads off and, as I glanced to one side, I saw the sergeant major looking at us through the window of his office with such a stern look that, I had grabbed Cash and Jackson and pushed them toward our barracks.

The following day, the three of us were called in by the sergeant major and got a very stern lecture: If we ever pulled another similar stunt, he would personally make sure we would spend all of our free time cleaning dozens of toilets and, in between such delightful duties, we would have to do KP—Kitchen Police— as well.

And if that was not good enough to make us model soldiers and upstanding citizens, he had tons of other ideas in his head. He would be more than happy to share them with us.

The sergeant major did allow me to go back into town to get my car. But, when we visited the town again, we never went back to that restaurant. In fact, we did not go to any white-owned restaurant. The Army had put fear in our hearts and we knew they held all of the cards.

The trip to St. Louis was now a reality in their minds. I had no other choice but to get on with the program. They had my number all right.

"So what's so special about St. Louis? Why do you want to go there?"

"Why not?" Cash answered.

The drive to St. Louis and back in three days meant that we would drive like bats out of hell. Not get much sleep, and with all of the carousing we were likely to do, it did not seem such a practical idea.

It would probably mean that I would do most of the driving for the simple reason that I did not trust these guys to keep it at least within a reasonable speed, like maybe a hundred miles an hour. In addition, Cash could not drive because he had no license.

"Cash, you don't even have a driver's license, which is about as crazy as anything in life. It means me and Jackson will be doing the driving and, like I've said, you'll sit in the back like a lordship and make your caustic comments about our driving skills. I mean, why don't you have a license?"

"The pigs took it away from me."

"Why?"

"I ain't tellin' you jack."

"Shee-it, were you hauling off moonshine, you bastard? I wouldn't put it past you if you did."

"Ask him how many tickets he had before they pulled his license." Jackson said.

"OK, how many speeding tickets you got?"

Cash hesitated a moment before answering. It was almost like he was counting them in his head because he had so many of them that he had lost track. And he wanted to give me the truthful response, which, of course, I knew he would not. His act was just another way of trying to play with my head.

"I don't know."

"What the hell do you mean, 'I don't know?' "

"Well, maybe just a couple." He finally said, with a sly look.

Jackson started to laugh and Cash gave him his famous dirty look.

"A couple? Shee-it. How's about twelve tickets?" Jackson said.

"Twelve? You're kidding!" I said.

Jackson shook his head. Cash looked like he was about to hit him. "But that ain't all," Jackson continued. "He got 'em in three months' time."

"Man, that's one a week. Is that why they put you in the Army? What the hell were you doing?" I asked, not that I trusted he would answer with the truth.

"Taking care of business. And I ain't telling you jack," Cash answered.

"You're just a crazy sonovabitch, aren't you?"

"Sonovabitch I ain't; crazy, maybe." And he started to laugh his crazy laugh.

"Let's go to a civilized place, like Myrtle Beach, or something," I said.

We had been to Myrtle Beach, in South Carolina, twice and on the second occasion, we had not done so badly, though in Cash's eyes it had not been enough.

After all, he had a reputation to uphold. It would not look good to the other guys if they found out that Cash had not scored heavily, as he always claimed he did. I mean, a man has to protect his stud reputation against all odds.

"Oh, no, no more Myrtle Beach, man, them pickings was slim," Cash said.

"Slim? There's more poontang in Myrtle Beach than in the whole of St. Louis."

"Greene, you're sayin' that because you ain't never been to St. Louis."

"OK, Cash, let me ask you a question: Why is it that when you talk about poontang I understand what you're saying, but when you talk about something else, it's hard to figure out what you're saying? Why is that?"

"Hollywood, you's a riot. Everybody knows what I'm sayin', 'cept you."

"Jackson doesn't understand what you're saying half of the time."

"Hey, Jackson, is that true?"

"Shee-it, don't get me in the middle of your nonsense."

"So, Hollywood, you's comin' or what?"

"Is that an invitation or an order?"

Cash started to laugh his victorious hyena laugh reserved for those occasions when he knew things went his way.

"Outta sight," he yelled.

So that is how we ended up going to St. Louis, with Jackson and me taking turns doing the driving, while his lordship sat in the back reminding us that we drove the way old ladies screw.

Cash's brother was living in St. Louis and we went to his place. It was in the black part of town and Cash seemed to know just about everyone there. Cash's brother lived in a big, old, but well restored house.

Cash had told us that we did not have to worry about staying in a motel—his brother's house was large enough to accommodate a dozen people with no sweat.

"What is this, a cat house?" I asked him, just to give him a hard time.

"Shee-it, it's the 'House of Whispers,' " Cash said.

"Whispers? What's that? Jackson, have you ever heard so much nonsense in your life?"

"Hey, I'm cool with that."

"Yeah, you would."

"It's somethin' white hunkies don't know jack about, and you'd better not ask any more of your stupid questions," Cash said. Subject closed.

Cash's brother was a hood, lock, stock and barrel. Sleek as hell. You not only smelled and sensed that he was a hood; you knew he was, just by looking at him. But that was also what gave him a certain primitive charm. I thought he was the kind of guy, who would smile at you while sticking a long and deadly stiletto in your guts.

He never raised his voice so you had to lean over to understand what he was saying. He never seemed in a hurry. He always listened to you with his eyes half-closed, as if there was nothing more important in the world at that moment than paying attention to what you were saying. Cool and laid back.

But what was also interesting was the closeness between the two brothers. You could see that Cash had a great deal of respect for his older brother and it seemed he made it a point not to contradict him in front of other people. When I made a comment about it, Cash said their parents always insisted the younger brother had to respect the older one.

I had once asked Cash about his sisters, but he did not say much. It was almost as if he did not want to talk about them. I never insisted, but Jackson told me that one of them was born blind, and one of his brothers had died at birth before Cash was born. The blind sister and his brother's death had been major tragedies for his family.

Then, the motley crew of thugs that surrounded Cash's brother would have probably brought in armed police just to have a chat with him. These guys' attitudes could not fool anybody. They swaggered and acted as if theirs was the Kingdom and they ruled it like ancient African warlords.

The house was a beehive of activity of all sorts. Women, old men, young kids, even a few cops would stop by and have these meetings. Lots of people seemed to walk out of Cash's brother's room with happy smiles and, in many instances, clutching dollars in their hands.

"So Cash how come you're in the Army and your brother isn't?" I asked him.

"He don't want to."

"Shee-it, like he can tell Uncle Sam to shove it."

"Sure do."

"You're full of it."

"Yup, my older brother got dis-pen-sa-tion."

"What the hell is that? Dispensation from what? From being in the military? Boy, talk about being full if it, you sure as hell are."

"Now look here, Hollywood, just because we's niggers don't get the idea we don't know how to deal with the Man."

"Jackson, did you ever hear so much crap in your life?" I asked Jackson.

"The brother knows his business."

"Man, you guys don't make sense. I sure as hell would like to get 'dis-pen-sa-tion,' as Cash says. Yeah, shee-it, I wouldn't mind getting some myself."

The actual truth, which I later learned from Jackson, was that Cash's brother had been born with some kind of congenital heart problem. I understood that it was something that Cash wanted to keep quiet about it. What the hell, I thought; it was none of my business.

"You ain't smart enough to get it, Hollywood."

"I guess, I ain't. Anyway, Cash, how in the hell did your brother become a mobster? Does that run in the family? He doesn't get dispensation from that, does he?"

"He gets com-pen-sa-tion." And both Cash and Jackson busted out laughing.

I laughed with these two crazy bozos. Once they started, there was no way to stop them. I had to admit their comedy routine made life easier to deal with.

"He ain't no mobster. He's a business man," Cash added.

"Right, put that in your pipe and smoke it."

"See, that's the problem with you. Every Negro's a criminal and only whitey is the honest one around."

"I didn't say that."

"Yeah, I know your kind."

"Hey, Jackson, you're a preacher's son, what do you think of these guys?"

"They's fine."

"Why are you sounding like them? You keep saying that blacks need to speak proper English and here you're sounding like some ignoramus."

This was a sore point with him because he could not make up his mind as to why some black people, either out of being too lazy or just simply out of principle, refused to speak standard English. Preferring instead to speak in a kind of ghetto language, which, in my view, sometimes was better than standard English.

Ghetto English was more expressive, even poetic, called a spade a spade—no pun intended here—got to the heart of the matter directly, promptly, and skipped the bullshit. He was not sure about that, but he was not above using less than proper English whenever it suited his purposes. Cash used to get on his case for being two-faced about it.

"Now, look here Hollywood," Jackson said, "I didn't say do like I do but do like I say. That's what my daddy always says. And it works."

"I bet that church your father heads is probably a den of inequity. It wouldn't surprise me if he was running a numbers racket."

"Well, he ain't above cutting a few corners."

"You're just another crook passing yourself off as a preacher's son so you can rip people off. You guys are all the same, phony bastards."

"You're just jealous," Cash said.

But of course, Cash and Jackson were not crooks or dishonest or phony bastards, and I was not jealous. They were, we all were, all of us black and white, operating in a system that made us all outlaws.

That taught us from day one that cutting a few corners against the powers that be, in order to survive, was the only choice we had. And speaking in other than so called standard English was probably better in many instances.

After spending a long weekend that had started and never seemed to end, where we probably got about a half-hour of shuteye time—tops—we were driving back from St. Louis. With the top down just enjoying the scenery.

The wind rushing past us making noise like some demented monster while hearing no comments about my driving skills from Cash, who was sort of snoozing in the back.

We were keeping pretty much to ourselves. Hundreds of miles of road teeming with big, heavy-ass, trucks and me weaving in and out of such traffic. The trip had not been so bad after all.

Better than sitting in the barracks and trying to avoid some prissy-ass sergeant coming in and forcing you to go on KP duty, because everybody else had been smart enough to get out while the going was good.

"Shee-it, you know what, I think I'll ask Andy the next show we do should be *The Diary of Anne Frank*," I said, to no one in particular.

"Another show about poontang," Cash piped in.

"Man, I thought you were sleeping."

"Why would you want to do that?" said Jackson. Actually, he kind of shouted because of the noise of the wind.

"Why not?"

"You think them military guys would allow you to do a show like *Anne Frank* in an Army base, right smack in the middle of KKK country? You're crazier than I thought."

"OK, who is this bitch?" Cash asked, shouting also.

"Anne Frank?"

"Whatever. Who the hell is she? Does she put out?"

A female's name for Cash, even if he knew nothing of the woman in question, was enough for him to start thinking with what he had between his legs.

"You ignoramus, worthless piece of garbage," I said. "I ought to smack you around your ears and dump your ass off here so you can walk back. You never heard who Anne Frank was. You're just a dumb asshole, that's what you are."

"At least, I'm not a dumb, black, asshole, pimp, son of a whore, going to hell, which is what you call me all the time."

"Well, excuse me for forgetting my manners, Mr. dumb, black, asshole, pimp, son of a whore, going to hell."

"Shut up, both of you," Jackson said. "All right, Hollywood, why do you want to do this play?"

"Why not?"

"Are you crazy?"

"No, I don't see why doing this play makes me crazy."

"They won't let you do it. I'm telling you. You're asking for trouble."

"OK, you jerks, will someone tell me what this is all about?" Cash said.

"It was this girl in Germany—" Jackson started to say.

"Holland," I said.

"Yeah, Holland, anyway she was killed by the Nazis and . . . "

"What did you call the place?" Cash interrupted.

"Holland," I said.

"I've heard of the place. They've got them windmills."

"Well, I'll be go to hell. You ain't as stupid as I thought."

"Screw you, Hollywood."

"Thank you, Mr. McCall."

"You're welcome, Mr. Greene."

We had developed a routine, and nobody knew where it came from, that whenever one of us said, "screw you" the others were obliged to say "thank you" in response. We had debated using a stronger vulgar word, but in the end Jackson told Cash that his mama would not approve of any vulgar language. Cash gave Jackson a dirty look.

"OK, one more time, why do you want to do this?" Jackson asked.

"Why not? You've got something against Jews, you bigot."

"Shee-it, some of my best friends are Jews."

"Yeah, they all look alike just like we do," Cash said, and we all busted out laughing.

Then Jackson turned on the radio and it was playing the song about Kansas City, about Kansas City having the craziest way of loving.

"Man, we should go to Kansas City next," Cash said.

"On a three day pass?"

"Why not?

"Cash, you're crazy."

"They've got the prettiest little women," Cash said. End of argument.

"When it comes to poontang," Jackson said, "Cash's the man to see."

"Shee-it, I know some people there."

"What? You've got more gangster relatives there, too?"

Cash gave me one of his famous dirty looks and, as the radio blared on, we sang the song as loud as we could, at the top of our lungs. And the sun was shining. Things were good.

We were all innocent and pure, and there were no differences between people because it made better sense. And life was just a bowl of cherries and we were going to get some.

"I'm getting hungry," Cash said.

He was always hungry. He ate like there was no tomorrow and for two people, literally. He ate everything that was put on his plate. And his plate was always clean when he finished.

I always kidded him that if he turned sideways nobody would find him, and he had better put some metal weight in his shoes; otherwise, the wind would lift him up and blow him away. Skinny as a rail.

"No, you ain't," I told him, about getting hungry.

We were getting near Nashville.

"OK, "Jackson said, "Nashville is big. We'll find us a fine Negro greasy spoon joint, and we'll get us something to eat there. We don't want no sit-in incidents, right Hollywood?"

"Screw you."

"Thank you, Mr. Greene."

"You're welcome, Mr. Jackson."

"You know what I like about this country?" Cash shouted and he stood in the back of the car.

"What?" I shouted.

"Poontang!"

Cash shouted at the top of his lungs and the driver of a heavy ass truck we were now passing saw Cash standing, and the trucker blew his horn. We busted out laughing.

Yeah, life was fine and poontang was fine, and Cash, Jackson and me we were fine. And the sun along with the wind hitting you on the face was mighty fine. And if people did not have a sense of humor about life in general, or sit-ins in particular; well, tell them to go jump in the lake.

"Yeah, I'll do the *Diary of Anne Frank* play just to piss off the local KKK. And I'll even go and find me a black girl and cast her as Anne Frank, that'll teach 'em a lesson."

"Yeah, Hollywood, that's the ticket," Cash said, approvingly.

"Hollywood, the only lesson is the one you're going to get from the powers that be when they castrate you. But I got to hand it to you, you're just a dumb asshole who thinks he can change the world all by his lonesome," Jackson said.

"He's just dumb, that's for sure," Cash seconded.

"Well, boys, thank you for them kind compliments."

We had no problem finding a Negro joint, as Jackson put it, to get us something to eat once we got into Nashville, and no sit-in dramas were necessary.

The girls back in St. Louis had been fine looking. And Cash that crazy bastard did have a patter that seemed to impress those black beauties. In no time, he had them laughing and carrying on eager to do his bidding, as if he had promised to make them all beauty queens.

"It was more like you appealed to their mothering instincts that made them act, as if they were dealing with a child, shee-it," I said.

"Greene, you dirty son of a whore. How can you say that? A child don't have a wanger as big as mine," he protested.

"What are you getting so sore about?"

"Because you're always giving me crap."

"Well, if you stop acting like a child, maybe I wouldn't get on your case. Besides, you deserve it."

"Deserve it? My ass."

Jackson laughed and he and I exchanged high fives. We always liked to get on Cash's case especially because he thought of himself as the supreme ladies' man—bar none. It was one aspect of his territorial personality.

The girls made me think of ancient Nubian princesses. Tall, regal, perfect teeth, big asses, swaying and swishing to and fro probably to ancient rhythms in their heads that only they heard and understood. While we, guys, were all sex-predators, and our tongues were hanging out, and it was everyman for himself.

"Yeah, time to get me some cock," Cash had said.

"What are you talking about? Cock? Are you some kind of pervert or something? Cock's is guys."

"Jackson, tell whitey here he don't know jack."

"You never heard that expression?"

"No."

"I thought you was from Hollywood?"

"Shee-it, cock's guys."

"No, it ain't. Cock in this part of the world is poontang."

"Never heard of it."

"For once, my man here admits he don't know nothin', ah Jackson. Maybe we'll teach him somethin'."

"Dream on."

As we were coming up to an intersection, we saw a group of girls waiting for the light to change and cross the street. I accelerated to beat the red light. The next thing I knew, there was Cash standing in the back of the car waiving at the girls, and yelling at me in his high screeching, nasal, whiny voice.

"Wilrounmafuk, wilrounmafuk, wilrounmafuk . . ."

"What?"

"Wilrounmafuk, wilrounmafuk."

"What's he saying," I asked Jackson, who was laughing his head off.

"Don't you understand what he's saying?"

"No. What does he want?"

"What do you think he wants when he sees poontang?"

Jackson gave me a look that pretty much said I was just too stupid not to understand what Cash was shouting about.

"Wilrounmafuk, wilrounmafuk, wilrounmafuk."

"Why in the hell does he talk his Negro shit now?"

"Wilrounmafuk, wilrounmafuk, wilrounmafuk."

"He wants you to make a U-turn, and he's calling you a most distinguished English word," Jackson said slowly, as if teaching a young child how to be polite to his elders.

"Man, why doesn't he stop his crazy gibberish?"

"Shupanwilrounmafuk."

I slammed on the brakes and Cash almost flew out of the car. I made a fast U-turn and raced back to the intersection but, as luck would have it, just as we got there the light changed against us, and a police cruiser pulled up to the intersection perpendicular to us.

"Go through you stupid jerk, go through," Cash said, shouting, suddenly finding his normal voice and normal English.

"We've got company, you dumb ass."

"Sonovabitch. The fuzz just got here. Sonovabitch," Jackson said.

"Screw the fuzz," Cash said.

"Are you crazy? We get busted here and there ain't no captain Rowe to bail us out. We'll spend the rest of our lives in a chain gang. Besides, in case you conveniently forgot, we're not supposed to be this far away from the base."

And it was true. Our three-day pass did not allow us to be hundreds of miles from Fort Bragg. We all knew it, but we did not care. Man, we were going to live forever. What would they do to us? Draft us into the Army?

Two big burly white cops were inside the car eyeing us. Cash sat down. The light changed. I moved up across the intersection slowly. As the police sat in their car, Jackson waved at them while the cops gave us a hard, cold stare. Cash sat in the back moaning and groaning like his life was oozing out of him.

"Hollywood, you dog breath! You let 'em pigs steal my poontang, you yellow, dirty, rotten, piece of dog shit, bastard, you's lower than a snake. I'm gonna hold it against your white ass that you kept me from my beauties. I ain't never gonna forgive you. And you, Jackson?"

"Yeah, the man failed the test."

"Screw you both."

"Thank you, Mr. Greene." They answered in unison.

"You're welcome Mr. McCall and Mr. Jackson."

"Go around the block," Jackson said.

"Why?"

"Maybe we can catch them on the other side."

So I drove around the block and back to the intersection, but the girls had disappeared. We could not see them anywhere. Cash was pretending to be so disappointed, and continued with his moaning while Jackson and I laughed our heads off.

Army life for us was a pain in the ass and good at the same time. It seems weird to be saying that because Vietnam loomed inexorably larger than anything over our personal destinies, and all of us were afraid to admit it.

We knew that it was only a matter of time and we would all be shipped over there, but we kept it under wraps. No sense in making things more difficult than they were. Cash had already made up his mind that he was going to stay in the Army and be a lifer.

"I thought you wanted to go to New York and be another Miles Davis," I said.

"Shee-it. Well, actually, me and Davis wouldn't get along. New York, or Chicago, or, name it, it just wouldn't be big enough for both of us. Come to think of it, I've got me some better licks than he does. It wouldn't be fair to him." Said Cash and busted out laughing.

"No, I guess it wouldn't. I feel sorry for Davis already," Jackson said.

And Jackson and I laughed. I did not know much about music, and certainly much less about jazz or trumpet playing. But I had heard Cash play and there was no doubt he had some amazing chops.

When he was on, it was something else. It was such a pleasure to watch him play, and to hear what he was playing at a given moment was to see Cash transported into another world.

Not the crazy, gross Cash we knew, but someone with lots of musical sensibilities and talent. It did not take much to come to appreciate his musical chops. Of course, neither Jackson nor I was going to tell Cash that. He would be unbearable to live with.

Jackson was not sure what he wanted to do with his life after the Army, as he hated the idea that his old man was after him to one day take over the congregation. But for that he needed to go to bible school, get some serious studies done, and he was not keen on doing either.

As for me, I had no idea what I wanted to do.

"Stay in the Army," Cash said.

"Are you crazy?"

"And what's wrong with that?"

"I'm not a moron, that's what."

"Don't know about that. Jury's still out."

"Only morons and rednecks stay in the Army."

"Greene, that ain't true."

"What has this man's Army ever done for you? Except give you grief and have morons tell you what to do: when to go hit the sack, when to wake up, when to take a dump, how to wipe your ass, pull KP duty when you don't want to, how to dress, shine your shoes, march everywhere you go.

"Clean up the shitter for a hundred other guys, stand in line forever, send you out to get your ass killed, all for the grand total of less than sixty bucks a month, plus three hots a day and a cot. No, thanks."

"Hey, Jackson, do you like the Army?" Cash asked.

"I don't know. It really ain't so bad."

"What's the matter with you guys? The only thing the Army does is to teach you how to kill people," I said.

"Shee-it, don't need no Army to know how to kill somebody who's givin' me grief," Cash said.

"Hey, Cash, did you ever kill a guy back in them days, you know, when you was a nice and innocent young boy?"

"I ain't telling nobody."

"And you Jackson?"

"In Chi City, we do it with class. You hire one of them Polacks, pay them a couple of bucks, and that's that."

"Just pay some guys a few bucks and that's it?"

"Last time I checked."

"You're full of crap."

"OK, have it your way."

"Hey, Cash, what about your brother?"

"What about him?"

"Do you think he's ever bumped off anybody?"

"I know he has."

"Are you serious?"

"Hey, some asshole tried to double cross him on a deal that involved some money and some chick, and he told me he killed the nigger."

"Yeah, your brother looks like a regular thug."

"Now, don't get cute insulting my flesh and blood. You keep that up and I'll tell him to come by and whip your white ass silly."

"He liked me, man. I liked him, too."

"That weren't the only body you liked."

"What are you talking about?"

"Don't play your innocent crap with me, Hollywood. I saw you and Sabrina gettin' cozy."

Sabrina was a black beauty that for some strange reason had taken a shine to me as soon as we got there. I could see it and to be perfectly honest I was flattered by it. I had never been around black women before, certainly not in the sense that I was now experiencing, and the whole thing seemed filled with exotic and mysterious possibilities.

Needless to say, I did not have much trouble getting behind the program. I was not shy about it that is for sure, which was why Cash had made his comment.

"Man, can a body talk to a girl and not have the world think that somethin' is going on?"

"Talk? You called talkin' when you got a boner fric-tio-na-li-zin' it against her, puttin' your hands on her ass with the music nice and soft, while you's dreamin' of things to come and stickin' your wet tongue in her ear whisperin' sweet nothings. Shee-it. Did you promise to make her a movie star, in Holy—Wood?" And Cash cackled.

"We were just shooting the breeze."

"Shootin' the breeze," Jackson said, with a cackle of his own. "You were plannin' on shootin' somethin', that's for sure."

"I like them Hollywood types," Cash said. "They come into town like big shots U. S. Marshals, put their hands up a girl's ass and they's just 'shootin' the breeze', yes, sir, just 'shootin' the breeze,' the man says."

"Shee-it. She told me stories about you."

I knew this would get Cash, who was constantly elevating himself as the ultimate lady's man. He valued that reputation as if he were some kind of mafia don. He was willing to do and say anything to defend it.

"What'd she say?"

"I ain't telling you."

"She told you jack. I know your game."

"Yeah, yeah, yeah."

"She's a mighty fine mama. Foxy as hell and a looker, too. Tried myself a couple of times and she turned me down flat. Not interested a-tall. Never seen her wastin' her time with some white hunky, but I guess there's always the first time."

"Shee-it, the better man won."

"Better man? My ass. She felt sorry for your white ass—charity work that's all she was doin'," and Cash busted out laughing.

Sabrina was not in the Salvation Army, that's for sure. And charity work was not exactly what she and I had engaged in. But I figured no sense in getting Cash to rib me more than necessary.

"So you and Sabrina had a meetin', did you?" Jackson asked, giving me his smart aleck smirk.

"Man, we just talked."

"Isn't that what I've just said?"

"Shee-it, the way you said it sound it's as if we were committing a crime or something."

"Oh, you were committin' somethin', that's for sure. I'd say you were penetratin' her perimeter, ain't that the truth, Cash?"

"No question about it," and they both cackled at my expense seeing that I had no way of getting them to shut up. I knew it would be useless. With these guys, once they had you on the run no quarter was given.

"And you were gone for a while' Jackson continued. "In my book, a long time is very long to be havin' a con-ver-sa-tion with a foxy black woman, shee-it."

He stretched the words like he was holding a musical note that would never end.

"Hey, Hollywood, did that Negro hair scratch you some?" Cash asked me.

"You're just a sick piece of garbage," I answered.

"Yeah, Mr. Greene, had himself some black poontang and, if my hunch is correct, he's gonna be wantin' seconds, what'd you think Jackson?"

"I concur with that."

"Concur, my ass, you bastards. You just want to give me your nonsense."

"Ebony and Ivory," Jackson said.

"You know, Jackson," Cash said, "we should ask my man here to give us a blow-by-blow," and he started to laugh at his own words. "As I was sayin', we ought to have a blow-by-blow de-briefin' from Mr. Greene as to how the situation de-vel-oped?

"Shee-it, I'd figured he was getting' into somethin'—I mean that's a long time to just be shoo-t-in' the breeze. I bet 'ol Sabrina taught our boy here a couple of tricks he'll remember the rest of his livin' days. Yes, sir." Cash was laughing his hyena's laugh.

"Come on, Hollywood, own up to it. Sabrina must have been somethin' else," Jackson said, with a cackle of his own. "You know what?" Jackson continued.

"What?" Cash answered.

"I'd say we should make Greene an honorary brother. Shee-it, he's developin' a taste for mighty fine, foxy, black poontang. Yes, sir, shee-it."

"I'd be careful, Hollywood, once you go black you never come back," Cash said.

And we all laughed, because to pretend that we could keep secrets from each other about anything was as practical as trying to drink soup with your toes.

As we put more miles on the road, the landscape sameness became interminable. St. Louis now was just another image, a blurred memory, a geographical condition that had no more significance than waiting for a bus at some street corner or for the light to change so you could cross the street.

I thought these two crazy bastards were the only people I cared about in the world. The poontang was mighty fine and the hope for something, anything, that would help us get through the night to deal in the morning with the madness in our lives and of the world around us, was what kept us going from day to day.

Until the bell rang and the hooded figure with the reaper in his hands showed up to tell us our time was up.

"Hey, what you guys think of Wilson's old lady?" I said.

"Why?" Cash asked.

"I think she's just a nice kid," Jackson said.

"She ain't no poontang," Cash said.

"What are you talking about?" What's the difference?" I asked just to give him a hard time because he had his theories about women and poontang.

"Hollywood, if you don't know it, you's screwed. She ain't no poontang."

He was serious. Cash always made such a distinction. In his eyes, his own sisters were not poontang. He had once explained to me that there were women you married, like the woman his father married who became his mother.

And there were others he referred to as poontang. This duality of sentiments about women is something we men have to wrestle with in our lives. We want poontang, but our mothers are not poontang, and yet we lust after women.

"So when's a woman not poontang?"

"When you love and marry her," Cash said. End of the story.

"Like that lucky Wilson says: 'five feet of heaven in a ponytail!' " Jackson said.

"Yeah, don't make 'em like that no more," Cash said.

Wilson was a kid from Appalachia. Innocent, all smiles, tall, toothy, lanky, and tough as nails. With deep blue eyes that seemed to look at the world with a benign attitude, as if only he knew what was what. He loved the military and his whole family had been in the military since time immemorial.

He knew more about military history than a whole encyclopedia. Twenty-two years old, he had a grave sense about him, and with his slow drawl he never seemed in a great hurry. But whenever we needed muscle Wilson was there. He was as strong as an ox.

Because he was married, he was allowed to live off post and we used to go out to his place and hang around on weekends. He loved cars. He had an old 1948 Ford coupe and was always tinkering with the thing.

That is how he and I connected. He liked my Chevy. He was always telling me how I should hot rod the thing so it could run not only better but faster.

"See, Jonathan, I like your Impala, but I much prefer Fords. Chevy's fine cars and all that but nothing can beat a good Ford on any day."

"You own stock in the company or something?"

"No, all of my family has always been partial to Fords, that's all."

We were both underneath his car that day, as he was checking the crankshaft and I had helped him put the car high on bricks, while he tinkered under it. I had not met his wife and that Saturday when I came to their place, for the first time, she was out visiting a neighbor.

The next thing I knew, I was looking up at a pair of fine looking well-tanned legs and a sweet voice asking us if we wanted some cold lemonade.

"Yeah, honey, would you get us some. Emily, this is Jonathan."

"Hi Jonathan."

"Hi Emily."

Emily was lovely and as innocent as he was. And she was a beauty! A face with high cheekbones that made me think of apple cheeks. Emily was golden blonde with bright, green dancing eyes that always gave the impression that what they saw was far more amusing than what others saw.

The way she acted seemed she held a secret, and everyone wanted to find out what it was because we all wanted to share in the secret.

On that day, she was wearing shorts and she looked as delicious as only a beautiful girl can look. She had the fine features of a typical All-American girl. Perfect teeth, lovely complexion, a figure to kill, and the nicest smile, along with a winning personality—there should be a law against girls owning such great looks.

While Wilson spoke slowly, deliberately, Emily was exactly the opposite. She had been to a teacher's college and was now ready to start working at the base as a kindergarten teacher. Wilson was very proud of her. He never denied she was the one in the family who had gotten a better education than he had.

It was interesting to see how respectful and generous Cash and Jackson were with her. In fact, all of us acted toward Emily in a kind of protective way. She was very different, not vulgar or crass but natural, without pretensions. This was in sharp contrast to the girls at the restaurant where Cash, Jackson, and I had attempted to get something to eat.

Neither Wilson nor Emily seemed to be conscious that Cash and Jackson were black, even though she and Wilson came from backcountry that for ages has been and continues to be racist.

I never saw anything indicating Emily or Wilson were uncomfortable around Cash or Jackson. That we were all jealous of Wilson's good fortune in having Emily with him goes without saying. But it was not really jealousy, because deep in our hearts we all longingly wished to be that lucky—have a good woman love us.

We knew Wilson deserved to have such a beautiful girl in love with him. Cash and Jackson had sort of adopted her, and she reciprocated that sentiment. She was like their kid sister and they were her big brothers, which in a way explained why Cash did not consider Emily as poontang.

She could make them laugh, and Emily, Wilson, and Cash would end up talking about farming—raising hogs, rabbits, chickens, and how to take care of horses, and milking the cows.

"Jonathan," she asked me one day, "did you ever milk a cow?"

Cash and Jackson busted out laughing.

"The only cow he's ever milked ain't the four legged kind," Cash said.

"Now, Cash, a nice boy like you saying things like that," she said, in that sweet voice of hers along with her lovely smile.

"No, Emily, I never had the pleasure," I said.

"It's easy, right, Homer?" That was Wilson's first name.

Cash, Jackson and I used to wonder how a guy with a name like Homer ended up with such a beautiful girl.

"Names don't mean nothin'," Cash had said.

"Yeah, you should know all about that," I responded.

He gave me a dirty look but said nothing.

There were two guys in our company of horny GIs who were the envy of everyone because they both had fine looking women who loved them. One was Wilson and the other was Yoshio Hino, an American kid, who had lived most of his life in the prefecture of Nagasaki, in Japan.

He had recently returned to America and had been drafted while in his second year of college in the U.S. He did not want to ask for a student deferment, as so many other people had done to keep from being drafted into the Army.

Yoshi was the sweetest, most kind guy. Wilson was the strongest, and Yoshi was the smartest kid around. And, again, it was Jackson who told us. He had seen Yoshi's Army test results and he said that the scores were off the scale.

The Army wanted Yoshi to apply to Officers Candidate School, but he turned it down. He was an Army medic. He just wanted to be a simple soldier.

"Why do you suppose he wants to come back and live in America after what we did to his grandparents?" Jackson asked me one day.

Yoshi's grandparents had been incinerated by a U.S. atomic bomb named Fat Man, back in Nagasaki.

"Well, they attacked us first," I replied.

"True, true. Still."

"I know why," Cash jumped in.

"All right, Mr. Smarty Pants, why?"

"He wants to get himself some round-eye poontang, that's why," and he let out his crazy laugh.

"Hey, I understand Japanese women are not made the same way American women are," Jackson said, eyeing Cash whom he knew would take the bait.

"No shit," Cash said, sitting up on his bunk where he had been lazily leafing through a radio manual while blowing softly on the mouthpiece.

"Yup."

"How they're different? I mean poontang is poontang, right?"

"I'm telling you, it ain't the same," Jackson said.

Cash was all ears now. You could see that the whole idea was working its way through his brain. He was trying to picture what Jackson has just said and having a tough time dealing with whatever images his sex-crazed mind was bringing forth.

He wanted to get around the notion of Japanese women being different, but his imagination was just not helping him out. Jackson looked at me and winked.

"Get out of here," Cash said.

"Ask Yoshi," Jackson said.

"Shee-it, I ain't gonna ask him. He'll think I'm some dumb jerk or somethin'."

It was a couple of days later, while we were sitting in the mess hall having dinner, that Cash got around to bringing up the subject.

"Hey Jackson, you know what you said the other day about Japanese poontang not the same as American poontang?"

It was obvious that the subject had been on his mind for a while.

"Yeah, what about it?"

"OK, I mean, how is it different?"

"I ain't gonna tell you. Ask Yoshi. He'll tell you."

"Shee-it. Hey, Hollywood, you're the man of the world, is that true?"

"What?"

"Well, what Jackson's sayin' about Japanese poontang being different than American?"

"If Jackson says so, he's a preacher's son, he ain't no liar."

"You ever tried it?"

"Well, yes, but it was dark and I was drunk so I couldn't really tell the difference."

Cash was not sure if he should believe me because he did not really know, and he also knew that neither Jackson nor I would tell him anything. On the contrary, we would refuse to say anything just to be ornery. Therefore, the only thing he had left was to either find things out for himself or accept what we were saying.

He really did not have references about this aspect of life. The simple fact of the matter was he could not afford to appear ignorant, especially when it came to women. Jackson and I busted out laughing and Cash looked as if, had he been able to do so, he would have shown absolutely no mercy as he was slowly strangling us.

"You son of a whore," Cash said.

"Man, stop this crap, and ask Yoshi." Jackson said.

Cash looked at us for a while, trying to make up his mind about asking Yoshi and risk looking like a fool. Or not asking him simply assuming what Jackson said was true, taking it to the bank, and still end up looking like a fool. Either way, it was a losing proposition for him.

"Come on, Hollywood. Level with me. Is Jackson telling it like it is, or he's just a jive-ass nigger?"

"Look, I already told you my memory is kind of fogged up. I think Jackson's got the goods on this one. So you'd better accept it or else ask Yoshi."

"What am I gonna say? 'Excuse me, Yosh, see, it's like this. Is your girl Tamiko; well, I mean, is she different from American women, you know, like below the belt, see what I'm sayin', right?' Shee-it, I don't want to sound like an idiot."

If it were true about Japanese women, his own macho credibility would go down the toilet, and he did not relish appearing to be so ignorant, especially with the kind of reputation he had tried so hard to create among all of us.

On the other hand, if it was not true, then Yoshi would most likely look at him and for sure think that Cash was an idiot. Either way he was screwed!

Jackson and I busted out laughing, and Cash did not like it one bit.

"You pricks, it ain't true."

"Shee-it, like all of a sudden you've been gettin' plenty of Japanese poontang and you're now an expert. Get out of here," Jackson said.

"You guys make me sick," Cash said, got up and walked away from us, while Jackson and I were trying like hell to keep from falling to the floor while laughing our asses silly.

A few days later, we saw Cash and Yoshi in what appeared to be a deep and intimate discussion. Yoshi kept nodding his head and had a serious look on his face, while Cash seemed to be doing all of the talking. Cash finally walked over to us and had a big shit-eating grin on his face.

"So what did Yoshi say?" Jackson asked.

"I ain't tellin' you. He told me and it's better than you two can possibly imagine, you guys don't know jack."

"Come on, what did he say?"

"I ain't gonna tell you. Yosh said to keep it to myself and I intend to."

"So you're holding out on us, your buddies," I said, pretending to be aghast at his behavior.

"So it's better than we imagined, ah, Cash?" Jackson asked.

"You jerks don't know nothin'. I know what's what and I swore to Yosh never to tell you. So you's screwed, both of you." Cash said, ostensibly getting a kick out of trying to even the score.

The Zen man is what Cash used to call Yoshi, and it was funny because Yoshi was a Presbyterian; one of the few who existed in Japan. His grandparents had been hosts to some American missionary and they had converted.

The whole thing was crazy, ironic, and tragic in that his family had been pro-American all along, only to have the grandparents incinerated by the atomic bomb the U.S. military had dropped on their heads.

Yoshi and I used to play chess and he would checkmate me in no time. I prided myself on being a decent chess player, but he trashed my ass silly every time. It was never a contest, but a whole massacre. I never won a game against him. Never!

"Jonathan, come on, this is a game of patience, of tactics, and not one of trying to bulldoze your way through like some demented man."

"Well, that's fine for you to say. Patience is certainly not one of my virtues."

Yoshi's father was a doctor, who was in the U.S. doing post-doctorate medical studies when the war with Japan broke out. The U.S. government had not allowed him to go back to Japan, and instead he was sent to Manzanar, an intern camp, in California, where thousands of American citizens of Japanese ancestry had been interned—one of those ugly chapters in our American history—as they were all considered a national security risk to the U.S. government.

At the camp, he met Yoshi's mother and eventually through some bureaucratic miracle, they had received permission to get married. Yosh was born at the camp. His father had worked in the camp, as a doctor for the duration of the war.

After it was over, he had taken the family back to Japan where Yoshi grew up. Then his father decided to move back to the U.S.

Yoshi was engaged to a Japanese girl back in Japan, an arrangement made through his family connections. He had met her only once. Now his fiancée was coming to visit him and everyone was curious about this lovely Japanese beauty. He showed us a photo of her: A delicate butterfly.

Our male jealousy about Wilson and Yoshi because of the women they had managed to snare was understood but never really aired openly, and certainly never in an offensive way. Somehow, we all understood that to make any sexist comment was too crass.

Again, perhaps jealousy is the wrong word to use because what we questioned was our lousy luck in that we wanted to have the same luck when it came to lovely women. But it did not happen. So, the only thing we could do was complain about it.

Of course, that did not keep us from ribbing them about those very same women who were leading them by the nose. PW, which stood for Pussy Whipped, is what Cash use to call it.

The day finally came when Yoshi's fiancée arrived. She had come all the way from Japan and Yoshi's mother had accompanied the girl from California to

North Carolina. We guys had all decided we would not be on our best behavior for her. We warned Yoshi that he could not count on us being polite to his girl.

She was going to find out about the true American way of life: foul-mouthed, indifferent, tactless. We were going to gross her out like there was no tomorrow. Yoshi laughed and said that it would not make any difference to him or Tamiko. That, in fact, she was looking forward to meeting us.

Late that afternoon, we were all hanging around the basketball court when Yoshi brought Tamiko to meet us. We saw this lovely girl, like out of some dream, floating on air, as she got out of the taxi.

She was wearing an exquisite kimono that seemed incongruous in such a setting. Her steps were short and dainty. The whole thing had an air of delicacy—mysterious, magical, and incredibly ephemeral.

We were all sweaty and frazzled from a fast and tough game when she arrived.

All of a sudden, our super-macho nonsense went out the window and we found ourselves not only being polite to this total stranger, but also regretting to no end that we looked like shit and probably smelled like it, too.

She knew everyone's name and even our nicknames. Yoshi, the bastard, had told her what we were planning on doing and had cut us off at the pass. It is very hard to be a dummy and act like one when you are shaking the hand of a lovely girl with a great smile and who is polite as all get out.

As he introduced her to us, she bowed and, bigger than life, all of us bowed back. It was funny.

"Jonathan, they call you 'Hollywood.' Why? Are you a movie star?"

Everyone laughed because we thought she had grand sense of humor.

"No, Tamiko, it's just a silly nickname, that's all."

"Cash," she said, "I understand you come from a large family and have lived on a farm all of your life and know about chickens, and cows, and other things." Her soft voice and accent were charming and as mysterious as the place where she came from.

"Yes, ma'am—I mean, Tamiko."

Cash had suddenly found his good manners! The polite way he acted toward Tamiko would have made his mother happy and very proud.

Tamiko covered her mouth as she laughed. Her gesture was so incredibly natural that it seemed like we all should have been doing the same thing. Yoshi wanted to take Tamiko and his mother to a typical Southern soul-food restaurant.

Cash, Jackson and I rushed back into the barracks and took one of the quickest showers ever, and got dressed. Then, we all piled up in my car, drove by and picked up Yoshi's mother at the motel.

We went into town to a black restaurant and laughed our heads off when we saw Tamiko and Yoshi's mother delicately negotiating greasy ribs with their fingers.

After the meal, we drove Yoshi, Tamiko, and Yoshi's mother back to their motel, and Cash, Jackson and I drove back to the base.

33

"So the Zen man's gettin' some tonight," Cash said.

"With the mother around, it ain't gonna happen," Jackson said.

"Hey, did you know that the Japanese sleep on them rice mattresses?" Cash said.

"How do you know that?"

"He told me."

"Shee-it, that must be hard on your back," Jackson said.

"Yosh said it's all a matter of getting used to it. He don't like sleeping on Army bunks; too soft for his ass."

"I wonder what it would be like making love to someone like Tamiko," Jackson said, wistfully.

"I thought you knew all about Japanese women, you liar," Cash said.

"I never claimed to have slept with such beauties; I just simply told you that they're different."

"Shee-it, there ain't no difference. Yosh told me. He said that you guys were full of it."

"And you believe him?"

"Man, he knows."

"He told you that just to get you off his back."

"Well, between you two and Yosh, I prefer what the Zen man says 'cause he knows."

"Yoshi don't know jack. I bet you he's still a virgin," Jackson said.

We all busted out laughing and I imagined old Yosh, sexually hungry, as hell, trying to get Tamiko's kimono off and having a hard time. You cannot rip such a dress off a girl in a hurry. Sex in such circumstances was not so simple when you thought about it.

Maybe it was as complex as their tea ceremony, with all of their bowing, delicate choreography, and manners. I have to ask Yoshi about it, I thought. Maybe that was why the Japanese had to practice patience.

Colonel Marshall, the deputy-base commander, was not happy about the idea of doing *The Diary of Anne Frank*. Among his many duties, he was in charge of what the Army calls Special Services Division, and it had to do with the kinds of off-duty activities the Army does to keep up the morale of the troops. He did not think that the play would be a good morale booster.

I was not assigned to such a division. I volunteered during my off-duty hours just to have something to do so I would not go crazy. However, I had become good friends with the civilian guy—Andy Catz—who ran the entertainment section along with the theater, and he thought when I first proposed it to him that doing a serious show like *Anne Frank* after the musical was a good idea.

The fact that Catz was Jewish was a plus. However, the colonel was not keen on the idea of the play. He argued that GIs in general want light entertainment stuff and *The Diary of Anne Frank* was sure as hell not in that league. Andy was now singing a different tune from his original enthusiasm.

"Colonel Marshall is afraid that nobody will come and see the damn thing," Andy said, "and people will complain that it's too high brow or too depressing."

"Come on, I thought you said it was a good idea."

"Yes, but to some extent he is right. You know, GIs only want to get drunk, chase women, and enjoy a few laughs."

"Hey, nothing's wrong with that. But I also think we should challenge and expose them to view something other than fluffy stuff. I mean, I love doing musicals, but I don't think we should treat people as if they are idiots all the time. This may come as surprise to you, but people don't leave their intelligence or their sensibilities behind in some drawer back home when they join the Army."

That is what I hated about the Army, what many people hated about the military in general. The people running it never gave GIs a break in terms of allowing us to use our heads.

No, we were all stupid and to have us question things was tantamount to inciting the troops to revolt and soon, in their screwed up minds, we would end up having Caine Mutinies all over the place. I thought that Andy was above all of this, but I guess I was wrong.

"Come on, Greene, I know your game. You've got this notion of hitting people over the head with all of your ideas about social justice and against bigotry, injustice. You push this on everyone and I've got to tell you not everybody is behind it."

"Whose side are you on, anyway?"

"I think you're pushing it because we're in the South and you think that people here are so stupid they won't see the game you want to play. You know, it may come as shock to you but I happen to think *Anne Frank* is a good play, and I'm sure there are plenty of people around here who agree."

"*Anne Frank* is a great play. It's timely. And what's wrong with rubbing stupid peoples' faces in their own excrement?"

"There's nothing wrong with that if this was a civilian setting, but it isn't. You're a soldier. You obey orders. I just work here."

"OK, let me talk to Colonel Marshall."

"Are you crazy?"

"Why not?"

"He hardly has time to talk to me, and now you want me to be your secretary and set up an appointment with Marshall—you some low, shit-face GI. You think you can just waltz into his office and have a man-to-man chat with him. Son, you are dreaming."

"You're not afraid, are you?"

I knew this would get him.

"Get out of here. I'm too busy to listen to your nonsense. I'll let you know what he says."

I was not totally convinced Andy was really against the idea of doing the play. On the other hand, I knew he would get cranky, desperate, might decide not to fight the Army, would come up with a different show, and would come to ask me to help him out.

I needed to be on the alert in the event he convinced himself he had no other choice but to do what the Army wanted. I did not want him to do that. I really wanted to do a play and *Anne Frank* was my only choice. I did not want to just simply give up and find another off-duty hours activity.

That is how I initially got involved with the theater group. When I got to Fort Bragg, I wanted to do something interesting with my free time and joining the theater group was a good idea.

I am not an actor so I joined the production crew. We were in the middle of rehearsing *Carnival*, the musical, when the guy who was directing it was sent to Vietnam. We were left with nobody to take over.

I had had some experience as a stage manager in several college shows, so I went to see Andy and I told him that I was a big-time director of musicals. He did not believe a word of what I said, but he was in a bind and nobody was willing to volunteer for the job.

So by default he agreed to let me do it, but you could tell that he was afraid. At the beginning, he was always there watching me like a hawk.

What convinced him to trust me was that one day, I asked him if he liked what the other guy had done with the show so far. This was a bit of a gambit on my part, as I did not want him to be breathing down my neck all of the time. What I really wanted him to do was to leave me alone.

He told me he was not happy about what the guy had done. That was my opening. Then I asked him how he would do it, he told me and I restaged the whole thing more in the way he was suggesting. It was much more stylized. It was closer to what I had in mind for the show anyway.

"The powers that be don't like the idea of doing *Anne Frank*," I said to Jackson later.

"I told you."

"I think that Andy is being a coward. He's got nothing to lose."

"Did you tell him you want to cast a black girl for the role of *Anne Frank*?"

"No, he would have had a heart attack."

"That he would have. Anyway, that's the dumbest idea from you yet."

"Man, why are you being so reasonable? I would think of all people you would be pleased."

"Now, look here, Hollywood, I would love nothing more than rubbing these racists pricks' faces in their own caca but it ain't gonna happen. There are too many of them and not enough of us to make it possible. You've got to be smart. Just getting them to give the go ahead to do *Anne Frank* will be a big thing."

"Yeah, maybe you're right."

"I am right."

"Anyway, now I'm not sure if Andy will push hard for this."

"You never know."

"He's not military. The Army can't throw him in the brig for doing his job."

"You keep this up and you'll get thrown in the brig instead of him."

"He's a civil servant, for Christ's sake. He's secure in his job. Do they ever fire people who work for the post office?"

"You never know. He might be afraid for his job."

"If he is, he should get another job, go work for the post office."

I hated to deal with bureaucratic nonsense. And I specially hated to deal with military bureaucracy. Everything had to do with rules. It was either the Army way or the Army way. There was no in-between.

Maybe I should have fought my draft board when I got my notice, I thought. Or I should have gone to Canada or Sweden and screw them all. But I had not gone anywhere. I had accepted that it was my "duty" to serve my country. And here I was and there was nothing I could do to change it unless I went AWOL, which I was not about to do.

Thus, I found myself in the Army. I had just graduated from college and was at loose ends trying to figure out what I wanted to do with my life. While in college, I had developed a soft spot for people who were pursuing theater arts.

I took a couple of courses and discovered that I was good at telling people what to do, how to do it, and managed to get picked to be the stage manager for the shows. They trusted me—the fools.

Actually, if truth were told, the whole thing had to do with a girl that I was hot pursuing in those days. She was studying drama and was always working on the shows at school. I wonder how many guys end up doing things because there is a girl behind the whole thing.

Going on to graduate school was a possibility, but by then I was sick of school and I was not in a great financial position to continue paying for further tuition.

For four years, I had struggled trying to put myself through college while working full time. It nearly killed me. However, getting drafted in the Army was not the solution I needed or had been looking for. It was a bummer.

I was finished with my university studies, and then Uncle Sam woke up and decided to come knocking on my door. I was pissed, broke, did not have any job prospects, and I wanted a change in my life.

The Army, of course, was happy and very obliging on my behalf. There was also another reason more personal for me to want to change my life: my girlfriend and I had called it quits. It had really bummed me out.

Pamela had been a girl whom I thought I really loved, but I was never able to convey that to her. She wanted something from me that I had come to realize I could not give her because I did not know what it was.

She also came from a rather wealthy family and I was always afraid I would never be able to provide what she was used to. I was broke and I knew that poor guys are not serious material for would-be mothers-in-law who are interested in finding solid husbands for their lovely daughters.

A guy with no future was certainly not a good prospect to become a son-in-law. After we broke up, I often wondered if that was not part of the breakup. Though she never said anything about it. It was just me who was afraid and, in many ways, this fear probably became her fear as well.

It had always struck me as unrealistic to think that one person could become everything for the other. It was not that I did not want that to be the case, on the contrary.

But looking around me, all I saw were these relationships hobbling along sort of in the blind and hoping against hope, in most cases, that something, somehow would bring back to them whatever it was that had gotten them together in the first place.

Add to this the fact that I had no idea what I wanted to do; and, the mix proved to be too volatile. I hated to lose her; and, though I did not think that my loneliness and desperation would be so brutal, they were.

For many weeks, I was lost in this fog of unhappiness and a sense of loss and something—anything—was better than sitting around waiting for the phone to ring or a letter to arrive with some news from her.

The only letter I got was from my draft board advising me that my time was up and that I had better come in and do my civic duty. So I went. I had to do it sooner or later, anyway, so I thought I might as well get it out of the way.

Most of my friends were aghast at my decision because they all knew I was against the war, and I certainly never saw myself as good soldier material. But in the final analysis, it was going to be my decision and there was nothing they could do or say.

My initial weeks of basic training in the Army did wonders for my spirit and my body. I felt much better. So much better, in fact, that I decided I wanted to learn how to jump out of airplanes. Thus, I volunteered to go Airborne, which gave me a few more bucks a month.

After the training in Georgia, I was assigned to Fort Bragg, the Army base for airborne troops. However, the Vietnam War loomed larger than life over most of us, and that was the one thing that I was against.

"But if you were against this war, why didn't you claim some kind of conscientious objection, or even go back to graduate school and try for a student deferment?"

Jackson and I had talked about it one day.

"I thought about it, but it felt like I was being a phony. I didn't want to become a conscientious objector just so that I could get out of military service. I wasn't being noble or anything like that. It just didn't feel right."

"You know Greene, sometimes you surprise me."

"What do you mean?"

"You don't like the Army, yet you volunteered to go Airborne."

"Hey, that has nothing to do with it."

"What the hell are you talking about?"

"OK. First of all, I did volunteer because I wanted to know what it was like to jump out of airplanes. That has nothing to do with loving the Army. Second of all, you get a few more bucks a month to be a paratrooper, which is not bad, and you ain't a 'leg,' " a demeaning term used by paratroopers for those soldiers who did not jump out of airplanes.

"That's what I'm saying."

"What?"

"You hate the Army, so you end up here as a paratrooper which is about as loving the military as you can possibly get."

"I told you I did it because I could make a few extra bucks."

"So you're a low-class mercenary, then."

"Aren't we all?"

"I ain't."

"Yeah, keep saying that but it sure as hell ain't gonna save your ass from going to hell."

"Well, I will be in mighty fine company," he said, laughing.

"So you think that I've screwed up?"

"I don't know, man. You've got these ideas. If you believe in them, you've got to stick to them. I'm just confused. I don't really follow your logic."

"If you are confused, how'd you think I feel? What about you? How did you end up in this man's Army?"

"I volunteered."

"You volunteered? Man, that's really stupid. At least, I could argue that I was drafted."

"But you volunteered for airborne. What's the difference?"

"Big difference. I didn't join the Army. I was drafted. I only volunteered to go airborne once they got my ass, and it was only with the express purpose of learning how to jump out of airplanes and earning a few extra bucks in the process. That is it! When my time is up, I'm out of here."

"Greene, I think you're full of it."

"Maybe you're right. When you think about it, it does seem totally stupid."

"You know, I actually thought I wanted to be a chaplain's assistant. In fact, that's why I enlisted, though now I'm not sure the Army is going to keep its part of the bargain."

Jackson seemed a bit naïve as we were talking. I tried to imagine this gangly guy wanting to be a chaplain's assistant, and even though I knew that he was just as crazy as Cash or me, there was also a certain purity about him.

A great deal of inner gentleness and strength that never seemed too far away but was always ready to come forth in an instant, in a moment of crucial decision-making.

Cash had the same kind of primitive purity about him; though, his craziness over sex seemed to rob him of the same gravitas and strength that Jackson exhibited. I would also put Yoshi in that same category in terms of spiritual toughness.

They were solid. There was nothing phony about them. It made me think of what we often say about someone exceptional, that those were the kind of people you wanted around when the shit hit the fan. They would never let you down. They would always cover your back.

"So you want to save some souls, just like your old man?"

"It's not such a bad thing, is it?"

"Yeah, but what if they give you a rifle and tell you to go out and shoot people? Are you going to say, 'sorry, I didn't sign up for that? I want to save souls and not kill them.' "

"I don't know what I will do. I've talked to the chaplain and he said the Army normally does not ask people like him, like me, to go out and shoot people. Our jobs are not in that category."

"Come on, man, you can't be that naïve. You know damn well that if the Army is short of killers, they'll grab your ass and order you to shoot some crazy son of a bitch who is coming at you ready to kill you. You'll kill him because you won't have any other choice. It's all a matter of survival, man."

"Yeah, I think I know what you mean. What about you?"

"Man, I don't know. Thing is, with the guys who'd try to kill me in such a situation, if I could like talk to them we would probably discover we hate the same people, that we love our families the same way. That we don't believe in the politicians' bullshit.

"They're the same and they're all sons of bitches. They're the ones we should get rid of. But here we are, dumb-ass U.S. soldiers, about to face some dumb-ass Vietnamese soldiers, and they want to kill us and we want to kill them."

"Man, I hope I won't have to face that."

"Boy, you're a dreamer, aren't you?"

"Man, you've got to believe in something good."

"You know Jackson, as Cash would say it: 'you's as dumb as they make 'em, that's what you is.' "

"That's some crazy nigger, ain't it?"

"Yeah, he sure is. Why do you guys call each other 'nigger,' anyway?"

"Why not? Don't mean nothin'."

"I don't know about that. If I were to use it on some black guy who wasn't my buddy, I would be a dead man in no time, that's for sure."

"Yeah, that you would be."

"So why do you guys do it?"

"Man, you've got to be black to understand it. That's the only thing I can tell you."

"Well, other than coloring my skin or destroying the universe and starting over again, I'm out of luck."

"Yeah, that's true, but then again, we made you a brother the other day so now you's already a white-nigger, anyway."

"Screw you."

"Thank you, Mr. Greene."

"You're welcome, Mr. Jackson."

But of course, I was not a white-nigger like Jackson said. I could not pretend that I understood what it was like being a black person in this predominantly white society, even if these two bozos had made me a "brother."

Jackson had once told me he had not been exposed to the Southern racial discrimination Cash had suffered because he had not lived in the South like Cash did. For Jackson, coming to the South was a new experience just as it had been for me.

It was always interesting to me to talk to these two guys about discrimination, because they had experienced it in ways that were different and yet similar, which only demonstrated just how sick and insidious it was.

Jackson—even though he had been raised totally in his father's shadow in terms of his social and religious beliefs—had probably lived in some kind of bubble that in many ways protected him from the extreme racial discrimination that Cash had suffered.

This, of course, had not diminished the tension with his family due to Jackson's recent keen interest in the civil rights movement in the South. Cash, on the other, had lived all of his life in the South exposed to racial discrimination all of the time, and that was the reason why he was keenly interested in Malcom X, the Muslim leader who appeared to be fanning anti-white sentiments all over the place.

At one time, Jackson, in a fit of anger, had even threatened to join the civil right marches in the Deep South and his father had been pretty pissed about it. Though Cash had not said that he would join the Muslim Brothers, he had told his parents he was tired of the racist crap, and what he had read about Malcom X made sense to him.

"How screwed up can this be? Jackson, you, on the one hand, want to join the civil rights marches in the South. Cash, you, on the other hand, want to become a Muslim. Sheet-it, can you guys make up your minds?"

"And what's wrong with becoming a Muslim?"

"Yeah, you would like that wouldn't you? It's probably because Muslims can have many wives all at once."

"Yeah, I heard that," Cash said, "but it ain't the reason why I would consider doing it. I think the brother," and he meant Malcom X, "has some interesting ideas about us niggers, that's all. And he don't take no crap from any white racist trash."

"The only thing religion, any religion, does is to mess up people's minds," I said. "I don't believe that organized religion, and with all due respect to Jackson's father, does what it says it does.

"More people than you can shake a stick at have been killed in the name of religion. Be it Christianity, Islam, or whatever. So I don't buy it. I know you guys have your personal beliefs and that's great, but,"

"OK, what's your personal belief? Cash asked me.

"I ain't got none."

"Man, that's crazy," Cash said.

"Why is it crazy?"

"You've got to believe in something," Jackson said.

"Actually, I do now that I come to think about it."

"OK, what?" Cash asked.

"Poontang," I said, and then both of them busted up laughing.

What I also liked about these two bozos was the fact that we could talk about anything and we could call each other names, but there was a great deal of trust and respect among the three of us.

The fact that we were different, that we came from such different worlds, had not gotten in the way of how we dealt with each other and with the bullshit around us.

All of us were trying to figure out just where we stood in relation to the universe, to make sure that we would be still in one piece, and standing, when the whole madness was over.

"Hey," Jackson said, "just because I'm black doesn't mean that I've had the same experiences as Cash. I've got to hand it to him, though that muthah is tough. I've learned some things from him. You may not believe this, but I ain't no fool either and turning the other cheek isn't totally my gig, even if I'm a preacher's son."

As I have said, in many ways, discrimination for Jackson was different and to some extent was strange to him, as it was to me. Not that there had not been racial incidents in his life. There had been, he told me. But not in the brutal manner that black people in the South had suffered for so long.

He had not grown up in such dismal social and economic conditions. Jackson's father had taken him to Europe a couple of times. He went to private school. His father's social and economic standing in his own congregation, as well as in the community at large, had insulated and protected Jackson in a way that Cash had not been protected.

Or like Cash was fond of saying: "There's us niggers and there's them niggers!"

A few days later Andy said, "OK, I talked to Colonel Marshall and he, apparently, had a discussion with General Numbnuts and they're going to ask for guidelines about the idea of the show. Marshall said the general was receptive. In fact, Marshall now acts as if this whole thing was his idea in the first place."

"He is just bucking to get his first star."

"You think?"

"Come on, Andy. You know damn well that if we pull this off, Marshall will write himself a letter of recommendation and General Numbnuts will sign it. These guys kiss each other's asses all of the time. They'll probably give him a medal."

"Well, whatever they do, let's hope that we can do this thing."

"It'll be a feather in your cap as well, won't it?"

"Hey, it may not be so bad."

"What? Are you already planning to join Marshall and kiss the general's ass also?"

"Get out of here."

We put out notices all over the base for the new show, looking for talent. What most people do not get is that the Army is populated with talent galore. Just because guys are now soldiers does not mean that they put their great talents in storage, back home, to be picked up later when they went back to civilian life.

The females on any Army show were mostly military dependents, and their abilities and talent were not ordinary. Among one of my favorites in our show, *Carnival,* was a young gal who was married to some freshly-minted second lieutenant.

Her last name was Leggs and surprisingly enough, she was some long-legged-honey. She had been a dancer in Las Vegas and somehow her husband had talked her out of it. They had gotten married, and she had followed him to his Army post.

I met her because she was the choreographer for *Carnival* and she was good. But she was also bored stiff, and her own life experiences had been very different from most of the other military wives she met.

She had a sharp sense of humor about life and all of its contradictions. Her husband was a quiet guy who was also planning on making the military his life career.

"John just loves the military. I don't understand it," she said to me one night while we were sitting in the back of the theater watching the rehearsals.

"Hey, there are people like that. I don't like it, but I can see some people like it."

"All right, why?"

"For one thing, it brings them a sense of order, of belonging to something bigger than themselves. It also gives them a sense of security. They don't have to worry about getting a job and if they put in their twenty years, they can retire with a nice pension while they are still young. Also, they get to travel and see the world courtesy of Uncle Sam."

"All of that is true, but I still think it's not what I would like to do for the rest of my life."

"Why did you marry John, then?"

"It was the uniform—toy uniform—that got me all hot and bothered," she said, laughing.

"So that's what it was."

"It works every time."

"Yeah, but you knew what John wanted to do with his life so it's not as if this whole thing came out of nowhere."

"I guess I've never taken this military thing seriously. You know, it's boys playing with their toys."

"Except that this game is now for grownups, and it's real. Military people get killed exactly for playing with those toys."

"I know, but I love him."

"That's your answer. You love this guy. He loves you. No matter where he goes you go with him because you love him. It's rather simple when you look at it."

"Military life is just not my cup of tea."

"Leggs, I think you're just being difficult."

"No, I'm not. What about you?"

"What about me?"

"Would you bring your wife into this life?"

"First of all, I'm not married, secondly I'm not married, and thirdly I'm not married."

"OK, I get your point."

"I don't intend to make the military my life. I'm just here because they said I had to serve my country. I do my two years, hopefully come out in one piece, and I will kiss my military life goodbye."

"I wish John would do the same."

"As I've said, you're just being difficult."

"Listen, I want to tell you something that will make you laugh."

"OK, I'm laughing already."

"No, I'm serious," she leaned closer to me, as if afraid someone was going to hear what she was going to say.

"I know John will end up going to Vietnam and I'm scared silly. Yet, I also believe what we're doing over there is the right thing to do. How'd you figure them apples?"

"I don't know. Are you a republican or a democrat?"

"Why do you ask that? What's the difference?"

"There isn't any. I guess both parties want war."

"And you? What are you?"

"I ain't stupid."

She laughed at my words and said, "this whole war business is crazy isn't it?"

"You've said it."

She did not say anything more, just sat there all gloomy and obviously not in tune with life's dark realities. Leggs stayed with the show until it was over, then I did not see her again. I suspect that she split and went back to Las Vegas. I never saw her husband either. Military life is hard on people.

For people like me who were not interested in making the military their lives, we were both a source of amusement and a pain in the ass for those who clearly had made the choice to spend their adult lives in the military. I sure as hell did not care for it.

Wilson always got a kick out of me arguing that military life was not such a good thing. As I've said before, he loved the military and was in it for the long haul.

-III-

Then one day Wilson got his orders for Vietnam. It appeared he had volunteered to go and had told nobody. Jackson knew, of course, because he was the company clerk and had done all of the paper work. But he never told anyone. Wilson had sworn him to secrecy.

Wilson came and told me.

"You're what?"

"I'm going to Nam."

"How did that happen?"

"I volunteered."

He had a serious look on his face, as if now that he had gone ahead and done it the full reality of his act had finally come home to him.

"Are you crazy?"

"It's my job, man."

"Wilson, you're nuts. It's no good, man."

"I'll be fine."

"People are shooting over there. Have you told Emily about it?"

"She knows."

And here, again, his demeanor was not completely comfortable. The stories of the violence that was taking place in Vietnam were not benign. The intensity and ugliness had escalated and were shown on television just about every night.

Rumors the U.S. was intent on increasing its military forces assigned to Vietnam were flying everywhere, as the situation over there was getting complicated with different factions vying for political control.

Wilson, me, and lots of other guys were in the military, and the inevitability that many if not all of us would end up being shipped to Vietnam loomed over our heads day and night.

"What if, God forbid, something goes wrong? I mean, it's not worth it, man. You and Emily have your whole lives in front of you. Aren't you concerned about that?"

"She's tough."

"Nobody's that tough."

"We're all going to be shipped over there; you know that."

"OK, but why rush it? Are you trying to prove something?"

"I'm a soldier. And going to war is part of being a soldier."

"No, it ain't."

"Jonathan, I know how you feel about things, and I don't hold it against you. I know what I want to do and you know what you want to do. I'll be fine."

Wilson and I had discussed the war, and I had argued how stupid and terrible it was for people to end up shooting and killing each other. What was the point?

And while he disagreed with my position and I disagreed with his, he always made a point to listen to me, but never got upset with the fact that I had a different sentiment than he did.

"Man, this is insane."

"You're a good man, Jonathan. Thank you for your concern. You know, me and Emily come from simple but honest folks. We work the land and it's hard on us. My family has been in mining all their lives. That's all we know. Where we come from there isn't too many opportunities.

"We try and we do what we can, but it is a hard life. Mind you, I'm not complaining, but for me the Army is a better deal than going down in them mines always fearing that something may go wrong and I would not be able to come up again.

"I didn't want Emily to live like that. You know, she is the first one out of her wonderful people to get a good education. I'm proud of her. I only got myself a couple semesters, but that's enough for me. I ain't no intellectual.

"Emily is, but I don't mind and we both love the U.S. Our parents taught us to love this great country of ours. I know it ain't perfect and many faults exist. Still, I'm in the Army and when my country calls, I'm ready."

His words were simple, and there was a quiet dignity to the way he was expressing himself. There was nothing fake about his sincerity. How do people become wise?

I mean, all of these guys around me acted, as if somehow they had a handle on things in life. Even crazy Cash had something in him that made him solid, filled him with the same quiet dignity.

What had they seen, experienced, that put them in such a state of mind, or grace, really? Were they all so unaware of the reality that surrounded us, that we saw daily on our television sets, that it blinded them to the ugliness and pain that war brings? What made them the way they were?

Is that what the powers that be counted on to take advantage of people like them? The innocent and blind ignorance Wilson had that he was willing to become cannon fodder for ugly people and their grand sick designs.

It was not that Wilson or Cash or anybody else was stupid or without fear. But their fear had a limit. They knew it and somehow their desire to make things right also seemed to make them free; at least freer than I was, in spite of all that blustering education I had gotten.

They looked up to me because I had been exposed to a few more years of schooling than they had, but in reality they were far above me in what really counted: In knowing how to deal with what life had dealt them.

However grudgingly I looked at what Wilson had done, I could not help but have a deep admiration for his position. But what I feared the most was that he had not looked at the consequences of the choice he had made. And I was not being a coward or indifferent to what he thought and felt he should do.

The news of Wilson's decision was sobering to all of us. Yes, we were in the Army and had no choice but to go where it wanted to send us. And while the Vietnam War was getting uglier and more depressing, it seemed that volunteering for it was as bad of an idea as you could possibly have.

The thought of now being confronted with killing someone or being killed was just too crazy. But, of course, we had little to say because we were in the Army and its whole reason for being was to go out and kill people. With Wilson's news, there was now a kind of empty gut sentiment in me and I tried like hell to ignore it, but I could not get rid of it.

The military was Wilson's life, but it all seemed worthless, futile, with no sense at all. Yet I envied him because he had made a decision that had no ambiguity about it. The result was he was going to be facing something ultimate not only within himself but in life.

While in college, I had read both Hemingway and Camus, and others, and what their heroes had done or said about the human idea of taking such a leap into the unknown. But all that was theory and fiction. Vietnam was the real McCoy.

War and killing always seem to have a morbid curiosity for us humans. An attraction that was in many cases impossible to put away and forget, especially at this time when all we heard was how technically advanced we were in our warfare capabilities—hell, we could bomb anybody we did not like back to the stone ages.

Do wars ever solve anything at all? Yeah, it gets your ass killed and that was, perhaps, in another sense, a solution of sorts.

Strange the life of a citizen-soldier. In our company, there were about a hundred of us divided into squads and even though we had daily interaction with each other, we were also divided into clans; got close to those we liked, and felt a kinship with them that was in most cases primitive and very inexplicable.

By the force of the circumstances we faced, we lived in close proximity to each other without knowing very much about who we were, where we came from—we were close to each other because we had no other choice. We sought out people to make us feel comfortable and maybe even secure. I guess water seeks its own level.

In the Army you get assigned to a job, which may not be that different from a civilian job. But in most instances, it is a job the Army insists you need to be trained to do and not necessarily a job you already knew how to do if they would just let you do.

But, of course, the ultimate job you are to do in the Army is to learn how to kill people. You are in the Army and its reason for your being a soldier is to prepare you to go out and shoot somebody.

Jackson was in Army administration dealing with files, paper work, people's personal records, and now was the chaplain's assistant dealing with religious matters.

Yoshi was a medic, and worked in the hospital. Cash was the guy who was a fine musician, who loved jazz, but the Army had no jazz band—no jazz, no Cash. He now had to worry about electronics and radio equipment. I was assigned to a photographer's job.

When you first come into the Army, they make you take a bunch of aptitude tests that eventually gives them a profile, in theory at least, and the Army will try to match you with the jobs that need to be filled.

"Why didn't you apply for OCS?" Jackson had asked me one day.

"Are you crazy?"

"Your scores were good, not as good as Yoshi, but good."

OCS stood for: Officer Candidate School. I had been called into the company commander's office and asked if I would be willing to apply for OCS. To tell the truth, I was surprised and a bit flattered that my scores were not so shabby. On the other hand, one of the conditions for applying was that one had to extend one's tour of duty for another two years and I was not keen on the idea.

So I did not apply. Captain Rowe had said, he thought I would make a good officer. Of course, it was before the incident in town when he had to bail Cash, Jackson, and me out of the pokey.

"Hey, Jackson, can you imagine Greene a second loui—ordering you around, man. Shee-it, I'd gone AWOL in no time," Cash had said.

"Man, now I wish I had done it just to clean up your act."

"I'm sure you'd have been a real prick."

"You've got that right, especially dealing with guys like you. I'd have ripped you a new asshole."

"Screw you, Greene."

"Thank you, Mr. McCall."

"You're welcome, Mr. Greene."

So I was assigned to be an Army photographer. I had an interest in photography but it was nothing serious. I did not even own a camera. But when I was interviewed, the guy asked where I lived, and when I told him I lived in Los Angeles he asked me about Hollywood—echoes of Cash and Jackson here—and the next thing I knew, I was given a job as a photographer because I had "experience" in the "city's industry"—how stupid can the whole thing get?

They trained me to take photos. I developed a much keener interest in photography, and I realized I was good at it. I got a bunch of books and started reading about the field of photography and discovered a world fascinating and technically challenging.

I started thinking that, maybe, I could actually contribute to man's view of himself and of the world. I thought, I would investigate what it would take to become a professional photographer and, perhaps, cover events around the world working for one of those news outfits. But that was in the future.

Eventually, I was sent out to take pictures of other GIs, as they marched or stood on parade grounds, waiting for some big shot to come by and review the troops. It was not a bad gig.

At least, it kept me from just marching up and down some parade ground, waiting for some asshole general to come by, and put on a show for him. While he made mental notes to pass on later, about how this new crop of soldiers was not worth a shit; that the-country's-youth-was-going-to-hell-in-a-hand basket.

Language school is what I had really wanted to get into and I thought the fact I had studied French in college would be good, but it did not even come up. If I wanted to go to language school, I would have to apply for it later they told me. I had asked Jackson why it happened this way.

Why not try to match people's experiences, and knowledge, save time and aggravation, while making it easier for everyone involved. But he said wise men ran the Army and it was not his job to question these sages.

What was also interesting is that the Army had made Wilson a cook at first. The fact that he knew nothing about kitchen work or even how to make Army slop did not make any difference. He knew a hell of a lot about cars and mechanics but the Army had given him a job as a cook.

However, he was lucky in that he had managed to convince someone higher up he was in the wrong job, and they had transferred him to the motor pool, which was exactly what he wanted and where his skills and expertise were better employed.

There also was a kind of unseen benefit regarding Yoshi in that he was an avid golfer—at one time he had contemplated becoming a pro—quite good at it, and because of it he had met some chicken colonel who was also a golf fanatic.

Very often, Yoshi was able to get off his normal duties at the hospital, because this colonel needed a golfing partner better than he was. We all envied Yoshi for his good fortune. Yoshi did not like the idea of the colonel pulling rank so he could get him off work to be the colonel's golfing partner. But like a good soldier, Yoshi just followed orders.

He once took me golfing and I did not like it one bit. I ended up calling the game: the Great-Ball-Bitch-Equalizer in that the stupid ball does not give a damn about you, the way you feel, your eyesight, your swing, the way you stand, how much you weigh, what your religious beliefs are, whether you like American poontang or prefer Japanese poontang.

Your stomach gets tight because you know you are going to hit the trees, or the sand traps, or try to putt, and the ball just scurries by the cup totally oblivious of your heart desires and well planned strategy to sink the damn thing into the cup.

The ball goes where it wants to go and if you do not like it, too bad. Yoshi laughed and, once again, admonished me to learn to have more patience.

"Yoshi that must be a Japanese thing."

"Come on, Jonathan, patience is a universal virtue and not a Japanese thing."

"Yeah, well, I don't have it."

In the Army, you are no longer able to think for yourself because there is a regulation for everything. No independent thoughts are allowed while you are a member of the military. I suppose the logic of such attitude is practical. You cannot have a bunch of people arguing about what to do when you have bad guys coming after you.

Two questions bothered me about our present on-going war in Vietnam: where was the danger to our people, and why were we so afraid of the kind of political system the Vietnamese wanted for themselves? I could not imagine the Vietnamese had the tools to do a number on us, like the Japanese had done in Pearl Harbor.

You had to be insane and a blubbering idiot to imagine such a thing. I was not a pacifist in spite of what Andy sometimes called me. I sure as hell would not just sit by and not defend what was right to defend. But to go thousands of miles, to a foreign land, and bomb the hell out of these people was not my idea of trying to influence hearts and minds.

The second question was even more stupid than the first one. If the wise people of Vietnam desired to have a government that was different from ours, who were we to go in and try to force them to install something that we liked, but something they did not like?

I really did not know too many of my fellow soldiers who had thoughtfully considered this final question. And reading the newspapers or watching the boob tube never gave you a clear sense of what was what.

OK, I was in the Army, and there was no question it was going to ship hundreds of poor innocent GIs to the war zone. Lots of them were never going to come back alive. But it was not up to us to question what the guys running the show were doing.

As well behaved and patriotic as Americans are, we always accepted what the government told us. They knew what they were doing, did they not? Jackson, often repeated that the Army, and by extension the whole government, was run by wise men.

I knew I was not smart enough to ask the right questions. My political convictions rang hollow for the simple reason I was not into politics per se. I understood our political system on a superficial level, but I felt inadequate and argued only the most basic concepts among which going to war was not such a hot idea.

And the more I thought about it, the less convinced I became that it was the only solution available.

So why do we go to war? Since the beginning of time, men have fought wars with other men and it always seemed it had more to do with who had the sick human desire to control others—as I have said before. It was all bullshit, as far as I was concerned and said so, which was constantly getting me into trouble with the powers that be.

Was this part of the equation that led me to want to do *Anne Frank* in the first place? Yes, in a way it was, though discrimination, bigotry and putting people

51

in the gas chambers because they were different was another factor in my decision to try to do the show. So that people could see, firsthand, what terrible things human beings did to other human beings.

Was I being naïve? Yes, I suppose I was. But I could not admit it so directly because I knew I was a nobody, really, and they had the power and I had none. So other ways had to be found, and one was forced to drop back and use different tactics without calling attention to them.

I was not and I certainly fought against the idea of becoming the ultimate contrarian because, in many ways, I had not completely disavowed the notion of war, of military might, in my head, but I was working hard on it. Jackson had asked me why I had not protested by declaring myself a conscientious objector in the first place. That was, indeed, part of the problem.

I was not yet ready to make such a leap. This state of affairs caused and was causing me all kinds of contradictory sentiments. In many ways, I was hiding and not ready to face the music. Maybe it would all work out in the end. But I was not too hopeful and, like any normal human, I did have my doubts.

Because the Army has to deal with people from a multitude of backgrounds, from the poorest to the richest, from the simple-minded to the smartest, from the inexperienced to the sleekest, from the foolish to the wisest, from the uneducated to the most educated, it has to have a system to make everyone the same.

Part of their answer is to make a series of training films for just about every action a soldier is required to live through. Hell, they even have films that show new recruits how to wipe their asses clean. Well, not really, but it seemed that way.

Behind all of this, the basic idea remained the same: Kill the enemy before they kill you! It reduced the whole idea of living in this world to a simple but violent equation: Kill or be killed! To some people, such an idea gave them power and reason for being.

I could understand why Leggs, the girl who had done the choreography for *Carnival*, was both frustrated and intrigued by her husband's devotion to military life. Maybe the whole thing was as simple as boys playing with "toys" like Leggs had once told me.

Except, of course, that the "toys" they now had in their possession and control did not allow people to walk away unscathed if they happened to be caught at the receiving end of the deadly piece of metal hurling itself toward them at an ungodly speed.

I found myself not wanting to visit Wilson and Emily after I found out Wilson was going to Vietnam. I was trying to put some distance between us. I was really acting like an idiot, but I could not help it.

They did not have much time left before they were to go back to see their families, and before Wilson was shipped out. Still, I could have done a bit better but

I did not. I was scared and whenever I found myself thinking about it, it shook me up.

A bit of good news in all of this gloom and doom was that Yoshi was getting married and he was going to take his vacation to go to Japan, marry Tamiko, then bring her back with him. He spent a great deal of his free time filling out official document after official document. He got a lot of ribbing from the rest of us about getting into domestic life.

Would they eat only Japanese? What about the soul food that he was so fond of? Would Tamiko learn how to cook greasy ribs, grits, and greens with dollops of gravy on top of the whole mess? I mean it was better than raw fish, was it not?

"Raw fish? Are you kidding me?" Cash had asked Yoshi.

"No."

"Even for breakfast?"

"Even for breakfast."

"Man, you guys are somethin' else. And Tamiko eats it, too?"

"That's how we do it back in Japan."

"Man, I can't see it. Give me my chitlins of hog guts, grits, some turnip greens and I'm in heaven."

"See, Cash," Jackson said, "That's why Japanese women are different."

We all laughed and Cash gave everyone one of his famous dirty looks.

Being a soldier would eventually lead me to Vietnam; I knew that. While in college, I had studied French, spoke it fairly well, and I thought that the Army needed people who spoke French.

Vietnam had been a colony of France and the language was, at one time, officially French. So, perhaps, my French and my photographic skills would help me avoid going out and killing people.

I was waiting for an opening in the Army's Monterey language school. I was looking forward to it. I had done my basic training in Fort Ord, California, and getting back to California was what I wanted. The school's program would last for one year of intensive work, after which Vietnam would be my next military assignment.

However, the problem was that I would have had to extend my tour and I was not interested in that. Two years of actual military service was enough for me. It was nice to think of going to language school, but I knew it was not going to happen.

A GI proposes and the Army disposes.

Wilson and Emily flew back to their hometown in Appalachia to spend a couple of weeks with their families before he was to leave for Vietnam. They left their car behind, as Wilson did not want Emily to make the long drive back by herself.

We had a sad and happy get together the weekend before they left Bragg. We all wondered what was going to happen and at the same time, we all thought nothing was going to happen. We were all going to live forever!

At one time, I found myself outside the house drinking with Jackson—some near beer for him and beer for me. Jackson's drinking near beer always led me to make fun of him.

"You and your near beer. It's like having a wet dream. You haven't had any sex, and yet you think you have."

"Greene, you and your analogies. They crack me up."

Wilson came out to join us. He was quieter than normal. Perhaps the full weight of his decision had finally come home.

"I gonna miss you guys," he said.

"Man, it'll be over before you know it," Jackson said, and I knew he did not believe it. I did not believe it. Wilson did not believe it. We all hugged each other. Yet each of us tried to put on a valiant face when confronting the inevitable.

I could hear Cash and some other guys laughing inside and acting like normal twenty year olds who are going to live forever. Then they started singing the song by the Animals: *"The House of the Rising Sun"* loudly and clearly, and they all came outside.

Cash was having the time of his life, stood next to me, and was teasing me to join him. Soon all of us started to sing it and Emily came out to the door, looked at us, while shaking her head in that unmistakable sign of women who are much wiser than guys could ever hope to be.

We finished singing and the other guys started to drift back to the house while Jackson and I sort of lingered behind just a bit.

"What do you think?" he asked.

"I wish I knew."

"We won't even have to volunteer, we'll be next." He answered his own question.

"Do you think?"

"Sure do."

I did not say anything. I looked to where Cash and some other guys were standing arguing about baseball. I laughed to myself that, for once, Cash was talking about something other than women.

"This thing is really freaking you out, isn't it?" Jackson asked me.

"Yeah."

"Why?"

"I don't know, man. I'd hate it if something goes wrong."

"Let's just hope for the best."

Wilson later told us that he and Emily would both go from their home to New York, where he would pick up his military flight to Saigon via Seattle. She was coming back and would stay in Bragg at least until the end of the school year, where she was working now as a full time kindergarten teacher.

Then she would make plans as to what she was going to do. In a very strange and delusional way we were forced to treat the new situation as just another bump in the road, a change we had no control over; it was just another day in the life.

Looking at the whole thing, it seemed so incongruous and way out of proportion that our attitudes about the war were so mild and so stupid; so American, Yoshi would comment. He was also not convinced of the purpose of the war, but having recently become re-acquainted with his American roots he saw and felt that his job was to be the best medic/soldier there was and not to make waves.

"But don't you think that going to fight Asian people is kind of racist?" I asked him one day.

"Of course it is. But I'm not sure it's the only way to look at it."

"Man, you confuse me. Here you are, you were born in a prisoner of war camp in which your family had been thrown as enemies, even though your own mother was an American. Jesus. I would be pretty pissed about it, if you ask me."

"It wasn't a prisoner of war camp."

"Come on. You're just splitting hairs here?"

"Look, I'm not happy about that. But there isn't much I can do about it. Would I have preferred to be born in some other place? Of course, but that didn't happen."

"What do your parents say?"

"My mother is less understanding than my old man. He seems more detached from it. He doesn't hold it against the U.S. My mother does. What is interesting is both my parents come from what I call "exotic" families. On my father's side, there was a Samurai ancestry. On my mother's side, her younger brother, my uncle, was one of those guys who was a member of the Japanese-American battalion during World War II, you know the one I'm talking about?"

"Not really."

"Japanese-Americans who volunteered to fight the war and were sent to Europe. The 'Go for Broke,' they called themselves. It seems that whenever other American troops got trapped in some terrible situation, this battalion would be sent in to get them out and, through terrible loses, they did. My uncle was part of this group of guys."

"Are you serious?"

"Yeah, my mother has all his medals and stuff. He made me very proud to be his nephew."

"Wait a second. You mean to say that while your mother and the rest of your family were in this prison camp, your uncle was fighting in Europe for the U.S., risking getting his ass shot? Man, this is insane."

"Yeah, it was. That's why she's still sore at what happened."

"I don't blame her."

"Yeah, well. Them's the breaks."

"Wow! Is your uncle still alive?"

"No, he died not too long ago. He never married so he sort of adopted me as his own. When I was a kid, he came to visit us in Japan a few times. He told me stories about what happened during the war. Some of that stuff was pretty nasty.

"I told Wilson about it and he knew a lot of the history of these guys. He was impressed my uncle had been part of that group of soldiers. I think it made him have a little bit of respect for me, or something."

"Yoshi-san, you're something else, man."

"No, it isn't me. It's my family. You don't choose the family you're going to be born into."

"That's for sure."

"What about you?"

"I ain't got no Samurai or have 'Go for Broke' relatives."

He laughed.

"No, I guess not. But you're pretty keen on wanting to make things right."

"I try, though sometimes I think it's all for naught. I hate what's happening, man. I sometimes think I should have refused to serve in the military, declare myself a conscientious objector, like Jackson says, and I should have told them to shove it."

"Why didn't you?"

"I'm not sure really. Maybe, I'm just chicken and don't want to admit it."

"Come on."

"Anyway, the whole thing is absurd."

"So you're against wanting to help the Vietnamese?"

"I don't know, man. We have enough problems in this country we should try to solve them first, and then perhaps go out and help others with their problems."

"In a perfect world it would be a good idea, but the reality is different. We are stuck no matter how you look at it."

"So you think that meddling in other people's business half way across the world is OK?"

"I didn't say that. Maybe communism is a better deal for them. I don't know. In the meantime, there are those asking us to help them so they won't have to live under communism if they don't want to, and we have to help them."

How naïve we were.

Obviously, the only thing we grunts could do was ask questions to which we had no answers. That we did not know any better was obvious. We were wrapped in the fog of ignorance and we could not see that there could be another way. But even if we did see it, we were still grunts.

That is what happens most of the time in the world we live in. We can question, if that, but we are so far down the food chain that no matter how we feel, we have no control over our destinies. And in the present situation we were facing, Yoshi, all the others, and me, we had nothing to say, as the Army was not interested in our opinions.

Then after a proper bureaucratic delay, the Army gave us the go ahead to do *Anne Frank*. Andy was tickled pink. He could not believe it; no, actually, he believed his persuasive powers had done the job. He was proud of what he had managed to do.

He had even told Marshall that all along it had been his idea to alternate between doing a fun, light show like a musical, and a serious show like *Anne Frank*.

That it really was not a bad idea to expose GIs to something of human value, something to show the Army was not treating us like idiots after all. The bastard never gave me credit for the idea. But I did not care. I wanted to do the show and that is all that mattered.

I had managed to cast most of the parts for *Anne Frank*, except Anne. There were two young Army dependent girls who came to read for the part and whom I thought could do the part, and do it well. Andy kept on bugging me to make up my mind, pick one of them and be done with the casting, as we needed to start getting into rehearsals.

"We should double cast the part of *Anne Frank*. What do you think?" He looked at me like, once again, I was suggesting doing some kind of weird stuff.

"Why do you want to do that?"

"I think it would be a great experience for these two kids, and both girls are really good. Besides, the Army would be delighted to know we are involving as many dependents as possible."

"Since when are you interested in pleasing the Army?"

"It's not the Army I care about. It's those two girls and I don't see why you're making such a fuss over it. It should be my decision; after all, I is the director, ain't I? Shee-it."

"I hate it when you talk like some hick, you know that."

"Where is your sense of humor?"

"OK, do it your way. Actually, what you say is not so dumb about getting more dependents involved in what we do."

Andy was back into taking credit for whatever good stuff was proposed to him and making it his own. I did not care, really. I needed him to be on my side and if taking credit for something that belonged to someone else was what he wanted to do, it was right by me.

I also got Cash and Jackson to come by and help us backstage. It kept us busy and we did not dwell so much on what Wilson had done. I had also asked Yoshi if he wanted to come help us, but he was using his free time to study and finish his undergraduate work, as he wanted to go on to medical school once he was out of the Army.

Karen and Julie were thus cast for the part of *Anne Frank*. Karen's father was some colonel at the base headquarters, and Julie's father was a sergeant major, in the Special Forces. So in a larger sense I was working both sides of the street, though it is not why I decided to put both girls in the show.

Karen was natural, sleek, knew she was good, and had a tendency to take for granted that because she was talented I should cut her some slack. On top of this her father was a colonel, though she never pulled rank on me. It was just the way she was.

Julie, on the other hand, had to work hard for what she got. Things did not come easy to her and she struggled. But whereas Karen became Anne Frank, Julie *was* Anne Frank*!*

"I think she's got the hots for you," Cash said, one day.

"Who, what are you talking about?"

"Who, my ass. I'm talking about Julie."

"Are you crazy? She's just a kid."

"Well, in the South women grow up pretty fast."

"Get out of here. She's barely over sixteen-years old."

"Well, like I've said, them Southern Belles get to be women in no time. My mama was about her age when she married my dad."

"Your dad was a criminal, a child molester, that's what he was."

"Now, don't you go mouthing off bad things about my daddy."

"Hey, Jackson, did you know that Cash's father was a child molester?"

"Yeah, I knew."

"Oh, you bastards, you come from the same kind of families: Criminals and child molesters."

"Hey, Jackson, Hollywood denies Julie's got the hots for him."

Cash got a great kick out of seeing me squirm because it gave him a leg up on me. It was done, of course, in good fun, though what he had said about Julie was a little too dangerous for comfort.

"Listen, you lousy bum, you'd better keep your mouth shut before you get me into trouble."

"It's true. Don't tell me you haven't seen it." Jackson said.

And I had not. Julie and Karen, as far as I was concerned, were just a couple of kids with plenty of talent and I was very grateful to have found them to do the play.

"Oh, you bastards, what did I do that you're acting like idiots?"

It had never occurred to me that I would have any influence on Julie other than to help her with the part. I became somewhat self-conscious about it, and made sure I never found myself alone with her.

On the other hand, I was hot to get near Marcia Rice. She was another dependent whose father was no longer in the Army, and she was twenty-one. Her father had retired and both her parents were now living near the base because it provided a job and all of the other benefits the military gives ex-GIs.

Both parents now worked for the Army, as civilians, and were part of the local civilian fauna the Army was happy to employ.

Rice Pudding, is what we all called her, was a slut in the making. She was a big tease. And because of that, she had every horny GI around at her beck and call with all of us hoping to be the chosen one. She had had some experience doing lights for shows while she had attended college.

She was taking a year off from school, had come back to stay with her parents, and was on the loose in what she wanted to do with her life, so she had volunteered to do the lights for *Anne Frank*.

My secret idea, in fact, I think all of the guys' secret idea, was to one day go up with her to the rafters where all of the lights were hanging and see how things worked out. Someone had hauled up an Army mattress there; for a purpose, one could easily imagine.

Of course, the only time she went up on the rafters was with at least three other people. But we all fantasized.

Even Cash had fallen into her charm and he tried every which way to get close to her. But she was having none of it. It was also an interesting situation because Rice was white and Cash was black.

But Rice was such a floozy, and I am sure had there been some forceful mutual attraction she would not have hesitated in going further with it, and not only with him.

However, she did not care for Cash in that sense. She treated him more like a kid brother she had to indulge because she was going to get paid for baby-sitting him. And, of course, this drove Cash crazy. He could not stand it.

"Hey, what's wrong with her?"

"She don't like your ass."

"She's a damn racist," he argued.

"Cash, just because she's not about to let you get into her knickers you're now calling her a racist. Come on, you know better than that."

"All she's got to do is take a peek at my wanger and she's a goner, man, I'm tellin' you, shee-it," and he started cackling in his usual manner.

"You're such a vain jerk, ain't ya?"

"When you've got it, flaunt it. Anyway, look who's talkin'."

"Get out of my face."

"Greene, I know your game. Talked to my brother who was talkin' to Sabrina, remember her? Well, it appears she remembers you's got some ideas about your own wanger, and let me tell you she was surprised you was parading around like a peacock in heat, and she had a hard time trying to find it among them feathers. Shee-it." He busted out laughing.

"Oh, you lying bastard."

"Hey, what's this?" Jackson said.

"Man, just tellin' it like it is," Cash said.

"Telling it like it is. Shee-it, a two-year-old has a bigger wanger than you. Hey, Jackson, ain't that the truth?"

"Sure is."

"Screw you, both."

And now it was Jackson and my turn to answer in unison.

"Thank you, Mr. McCall."

"You're welcome, Mr. Greene, you're welcome, Mr. Jackson.

Once we got the OK from the Army to do the play, I wanted to get an interview with the local newspaper so we could get some free publicity and support. I went to see Andy about it.

"You're going to do what?" Andy asked with some suspicion in his voice.

"Tom Sanders wants me to get together with him and do an interview about the play."

Tom Sanders was the town's newspaper editor and he was always interested in plugging any show the Army was doing for the soldiers. I had met him while we were doing *Carnival*.

He had written a nice article, in which he praised the efforts of all the participants, especially because some of the girls in the show came from the local high school. It made both the soldiers and the townspeople feel that we were all part of the big picture.

It was an easy way of saying that the community supported the Army and the soldiers. I guess it was also a way of making themselves feel less guilty about the fact that life outside the base still remained segregated, and since the Vietnam war was our present war, that also had to be supported. It was a very strange contradiction.

I had read military life was something Southern people had always respected and were very proud of. It was part of a long and great historical tradition. And it was true. This was not just the fashion of the day. It was the real thing. So much I had to learn about Southern tradition.

Since the Army also encouraged locals to come and enjoy the shows, it always made for better public relations. It was not a crazy GI going into town to get drunk and try to rape some innocent woman.

What I had failed to tell Andy was that, in fact, I had initiated the contact with Sanders. I was doing it for two reasons. On the one hand, I was a bit apprehensive we might have bitten off more than we could chew in that *Anne Frank* was a serious play not another musical.

Andy was right about GIs being only interested in sex and getting drunk, which would have meant we would not have a large enough audience for the show. It would have been a bummer, and the Army would have been pissed about it. So we needed more townspeople to come and see the show.

On the other hand, it was also risky in that the play dealt with touchy and unpleasant matters. It might put the locals off, and they would not show up. To be frank, I do not know where I got my optimism about exposing people to the pernicious things that bigotry, racism and anti-Semitism bring out, hoping people would respond with more understanding and compassion. It was all in my head, really.

Over all, though, I felt the play was worthy of being shown and my own faith in humanity had not totally disappeared. Nevertheless, I kept those apprehensions to myself. I did not want Andy to panic and drive me crazy. I was afraid he would start arguing and get it into his head to change the show and we would end up with another musical. I did not trust him that much.

I was also keen in getting local people to come see the show. Give them another view of what bigotry, and discrimination do. Not that they were ignorant of the negative impact such behavior by normal, intelligent, and otherwise reasonable people brings about. Anyway, at least that was my theory.

The other thing I had neglected to tell Andy was that, in fact, Sanders had simply agreed to publish a small blurb about the show—a nice blurb—he had said, but nothing of any controversial nature.

Sanders was no fool and he knew printing something that would exacerbate feelings all around was not a practical idea. Though in an off-hand remark, he had said a bit of controversy always increased the paper's circulation. I pretended I had not understood what he said.

"I think we ought to run it by the powers that be and see what they say," Andy said.

"Andy, what's there to run by them? I mean, we need publicity and if it's free and is done by the local Gazette, I'm sure we'll get some of the town folks to come and see the show.

"We should do it based on giving support to the troops. Maybe we could have some kind of potluck dinners where people will bring food and goodies for the GIs. You know a sort of like USO activity."

"You're such a good guy, it warms my heart." His tone of voice however was icy and cynical.

"Come on, Andy. Why are you always so suspicious?"

"Well, with a certain kind of individual it's always wiser to be a bit, shall we say, wary."

"Man, oh, man, the stuff I have to put up with just to do a decent job around here."

"Can I sit in on this interview of yours?"

"Absolutely."

My response surprised him. I could see it on his face. He had expected me to put up some kind of resistance and then he would see through the thing and shoot it down. But my answer, which I had figured I needed to have ready just in case he wanted to sit in on the interview, had deflated his balloon.

I also knew there would be no interview. I was planning to write an article for Sanders hoping he would publish it without too much editing.

Besides, even if there was going to be an interview, I was banking on the fact that Andy was always busy and intrinsically hated to be interviewed. It made him uncomfortable; I really do not know why. Maybe there was something in his past and he did not want publicity about himself. Or maybe he was just a private guy.

"OK, you let me know when you guys set it up and I'll take a few minutes off and do it."

"Sure thing."

As I came out of his office, I ran into Julie who had just been dropped off at the theater by her mother. Thus, I found myself alone with Julie. Something I had been trying to avoid since my conversation with Cash and Jackson.

"Oh, hi, Mr. Greene."

"Julie, why do you call me Mr. Greene? You make me feel like I'm as old as your grandfather or something."

"My mother says to call you Mr. Greene."

"It's very kind of your mother to suggest it, but I would feel more comfortable if you just call me Jonathan. I mean, I'm just a few years older than you, unless you think that makes me such an old man?"

"Oh, no, it's just that," she got red in the face.

An awkward silence followed. I had a chance to take a closer look at Julie. She was a very attractive girl. A little shy. At that critical moment in life's miracles when the larva will break out of her cocoon and turn into a lovely butterfly, which I did not doubt Julie would turn into once she got over this awkward stage.

A female, but not yet a woman, still a child. It brought to mind what Cash had said about Southern girls being more mature and savvy even at that age.

But there was also a kind of struggle going on within Julie. She was a child-woman at that moment in life when things are confusing and exasperating.

"Can I talk to you?" she asked.

"Sure."

It was another awkward moment in that she gave every indication she expected me to ask her to come into the now empty and darkened theater. And now I was a bit lost. Andy came out of his office which, in a sense, saved me.

"Hi, Julie."

"Hi, Mr. Catz."

"Everything OK?"

"Yes. I just came a bit early because I wanted to talk to Mr.—well, Jonathan."

"Julie, why don't we go and sit on the stage and we can talk. If it's OK with you." I said, this in front of Andy, a witness, just in case. I did not really know why I had such a fear, but I did. Better to be nice and cool about this, I thought. Keep it even, old buddy.

"That's fine."

I went in and turned on all of the lights on the stage. There were no dark corners left anywhere. We walked up and sat in the middle of an empty but well-lit stage where everybody could see us. I was being silly, I knew that.

However, now that I was alone with her, I could also sense that maybe Cash was not being a total idiot when he had told me this young, lovely girl had "something going" for me.

It was flattering to my male ego, it goes without saying. But since I had never been in this position before, it was also scary and a bit confusing. Man, why was she not just a couple of years older, then things would be different, I thought.

On the other hand, a couple more years of age for her and I would probably not represent for her then what I might be representing for her now. Even with women of Julie's age, guys are always losers.

"I've been doing a lot of reading about Anne Frank. She was very special, wasn't she?" Julie said.

"Yes, she was."

"Do you think she would have liked people to read her diary?"

"I don't know. Why do you ask?"

There was something serious in the manner in which Julie was thinking before she spoke. She was carefully searching in her mind for the thoughts and words she wanted to use. I was getting a kick out of seeing her trying to formulate her ideas.

"I have a diary. I have been keeping it for a long time. It's my friend in many ways. I'm not sure I would like others to know what I write. Some of my thoughts are very private. Having people read what I think, the way I feel, you know, stuff . . ."

"I know what you mean. On the other hand, think what we would have missed if we hadn't known what Anne wrote. She has left us an amazing human and tender legacy. It has shown the world that even under the most trying, difficult, and totally inhuman circumstances one can still remain a normal, caring human being."

"Sometimes I think I understand her and at other times I don't think I do. Is that normal?"

"I think it is."

"I have thought of what I would have done in the same spot."

"And what do you come up with?"

"I don't know. I'm not that brave," she said, and she sounded dejected, perhaps disappointed in herself.

"Oh, I think you are."

"But I'm afraid."

"Julie, all of us are afraid."

"You're not!"

I laughed. How do you keep such innocence from getting corrupted and destroyed? How do we end up with such crazy doubts about what is good and pure in ourselves?

"What makes you say that?"

"Well, you seem to know so much. I watch you and when you talk about the play and the great Greek plays, a lot of them written for women, I feel like I don't know anything, that I'll never learn anything."

"I'm a little older than you, and have experienced a few things, that's true. But I'm just as scared of things as you are, maybe even more so."

"Really?"

"Yes."

The innocence of the human heart never ceases to amaze me. Especially the heart of a young girl, innocent, pure, filled with fantasy, open to the magic of life and of love. Yet fearful of the whole thing. What makes us lose such a sense of purity, what drives us to eventually become callous, ugly, indifferent?

"I think some people are not nice," Julie said. "I wish I understood why. I see some kids at school and many times I can see they are cruel to others who are different," she said, wistfully.

"That's why we must fight against such things as bigotry, and anti-Semitism—those things are ugly. We should always oppose them."

"Kids don't like to think about these things."

"Do you think about those things?"

"Yes. I talk to my mom and my dad."

"And what do they say?"

"They think it's terrible."

"Julie, listen, if we can manage with this play to change just one person's idea for the better, we are doing a good job. I once had a teacher in college who said that to change the whole world we have to start with one person at a time."

Julie was confronting something that impacts all of us every instant of our lives. I also realized so many of us take for granted that racism and discrimination cannot be so easily erased, that we cannot get rid of them, that they are part of who we are. That we sort of ignore them because it is not as important as—what is on television tonight, or what brand of cigarettes to buy.

But I also knew that it was an attitude that was taught, that was learned and none of us is born with such negative attitudes. We learn from our parents, our peers, and the world at large.

If Julie was reflecting on the meaning of the play, then I was doing OK, and hopefully she would walk away with something far more significant than the fact she was to act the role of Anne Frank in the play.

"Do you understand people?" She asked, after a long silence.

"I don't know that I do completely. But if you really want to know the truth, sometimes I try not to understand people because I'm not sure I'm interested in some of them."

"Is that true?"

"I shouldn't say that. I'm interested in people, but I'm not curious about them. This insane curiosity that some people have about the lives of movies stars for example. I'm not too keen on that."

"Oh, I want to know about them. I mean, they seem to live such rich lives."

"Don't believe all of that stuff you read."

"You're right. It's all propaganda," she said, laughing.

"It is propaganda, of course. What is frustrating is that people can be cruel, superficial, but they can also be incredibly kind, generous, and just wonderful. Look at you. Are you not incredibly kind, generous and just wonderful?"

She got red in the face and did not know whether to laugh at my compliments or ignore them completely, but she finally laughed.

"Thank you, though my parents might not agree with that. I know my sister would not."

"Oh, I think they do."

"But why didn't Frank's family try to leave?"

"They did."

"What I mean is why they didn't try to come to America?"

"I don't know. It wasn't easy."

"Things are very confusing. People do confuse me sometimes, though I think we all seem to be confused most of the time. There are so many conflicting things going on," she said, and her tone was sad, exasperated.

"Can I tell you a story?"

"Yes, please."

"You know Jackson, right?"

"Leno?"

"Yes."

It had happened to Yoshi, Jackson and me. Cash had not yet been assigned to our barracks. Yoshi had talked us into going to New York City, on a three-day pass, to try to see *Hamlet* with Richard Burton. It was a unique production in that it was set as a kind of rehearsal for the actual play. Thus, the actors wore regular street clothes.

We had no tickets, no reservations, nothing. I figured our chances were as good as jumping off the roof of the Empire State Building without a parachute and hoping to survive the fall, but we went anyway. About the only smart thing we did was to take our uniforms with us because in the end it was what saved the day.

That Saturday evening, I had the smart idea that we should wear our uniforms as it may give us an edge. Jackson and Yoshi had argued against it, vehemently.

"It's stupid," Jackson kept saying. "It's completely stupid!"

"You're crazy," Yoshi said.

Nevertheless, they finally agreed just to keep peace in the group. We got to the theater, and at the box office they laughed in our faces. The guy behind the window took one look at us and dismissed us without further ado. Nothing doing, guys. The fact that we were wearing our military uniforms meant nothing to him.

We stood to the side dejected and enviously looking at everyone else who came by, gave their names, and had tickets handed to them. Yoshi felt pretty low because it had been his idea in the first place.

"OK, come on, let's go out, and get drunk or something," I said.

We started to walk away when we heard a man's voice behind us.

"Excuse me, excuse me . . ."

We stopped and there was this guy, in his fifties I would guess, well dressed and holding some tickets in his hand. I also saw two women standing behind him.

"You boys don't have tickets?"

"No, sir," Yoshi said.

"Where are you boys stationed?"

"North Carolina, sir," Jackson said.

"North Carolina?" His eyes opened wide in surprise. "You're very far away from home base."

"Yes, we are," I answered.

"So you came all the way to the Big Apple to see a show when you didn't even have tickets?" He started to laugh at our naiveté.

"It was my idea, kind of stupid, isn't?" Yoshi said, his voice dejected.

"Well, it was a shot in the dark," Jackson said, and started to walk away. Yoshi and I followed him.

"Wait a second," the guy said.

We stopped, and the guy was looking back at the women. They smiled at him.

"Here," and he took three tickets and handed them to us. To say that we were shocked would be the understatement of the year.

"Are you serious?" Jackson was looking at the guy as if the man had taken leave of his senses.

"Yes, please take them."

"But what about you?" Yoshi asked, then he looked at the tickets and his eyes started going wild. I glanced at the tickets and the price of one was more money than we had among the three of us.

"We can't afford them," I said.

"It's fine. Don't worry about it. It's our pleasure to give you boys these tickets. We live in the city so we can come back and see the show another time."

He turned and pointed to the two women standing behind him with what appeared to be a sort of anxious look. It was not a look of anxiety about the tickets, but seemed to be because they saw we were having trouble figuring out how to respond to their magnificent offer.

The three of us stood, speechless. One of the women took a couple of steps and said, "You'd better hurry up before the curtain goes up."

We still did not move.

"Our son is a soldier, somewhere, go, go," she continued.

We hugged the two ladies, shook hands with the man, and rushed into the theater. Yoshi kept shaking his head and had a silly grin on his face.

"Thank you, thank you so much," he shouted from the door, as we walked in.

For many weeks afterwards, that's all the three of us talked about. Even the fact that we had seen Burton do *Hamlet* did not seem to have much significance. What mortified us a lot was the fact that we had not even asked who those people were, their names, their address, their phone numbers—nothing!

In many ways, the amazing generosity of these strangers to other strangers was far more important to us than the fact that we had seen Burton do *Hamlet*. Yoshi and Jackson grudgingly accepted that had it not been for my idea of us wearing our uniforms—that night—we would not had been able to get to see the show.

"You see Julie, these people, total strangers, did something so wonderful and so kind, selfless, incredibly human. I mean, we couldn't have paid for the tickets. They were expensive. What we thought we'd do when we got to the theater was to try to buy the cheapest tickets; you know, the ones that allowed you to hang from the rafters."

Julie laughed.

"It's human nature isn't it?" She asked in total awe of something that nobody can really get a fix on.

"Inexplicable, frustrating, impossible to understand, yet quite remarkable as you can see."

"Thank you for sharing that with me. It's a wonderful story. It's very hard to understand things, isn't it?"

She had said it with quiet conviction and determination. I tried to reflect on how I had felt when I was her age, but I could not remember much of those days. It seemed I had not done much reflecting about anything then, and it really had not been that long ago now that I thought about it.

"Anne Frank was afraid, wasn't she?" Julie continued.

"Yes. She was."

"What would she be like today?"

"Good question. We'll never know the answer."

"It's our loss."

"Yes. It is."

There was a strong sense of personal intimacy between us at that moment, but it was not sexual, at least not for me. It was that questions of human destiny, the mystery of it all, are never anyone's monopoly. We all suffer from our human ignorance, and also from our curiosity, and from our fears.

Our struggles to understand the differences between our cousins—the apes—and us will probably never be settled. We are all in the same boat. Then Julie continued on a lighter note, smiling.

"So if you are not interested in others, it's normal?"

"I don't know what normal is."

"Jonathan, are you normal?"

I laughed. Her question was probing, trying to find things out about me, though I also sensed she wanted to find things out about herself.

"I think I am, but my friends have a different opinion."

She smiled and, once again, I was conscious of a young girl trying to figure out what the world was all about.

"I know what you mean. I want to ask you a question."

"OK."

"Why did you cast me in the show?"

"That's a strange question." I was not sure what she was getting at. "You wanted to be in the show, right? I mean, you try out for a part you like, and you want to be cast for that part."

"Of course I wanted to get the part. But you also cast Karen."

"Well, I thought both of you were really good for the part. So I talked to Andy and he agreed it would be a shame to cast only one of you when you both were good for the role. Are you upset that Karen was chosen as well?"

"Oh, no. I was just curious. In fact, Karen and I were just happy you did it this way. Though, I think Karen is better than me. I seem to have such a terrible time learning my lines and she just breathes through them like nothing."

"Some people are that way, Julie. It's fine. As long as when your turn comes to step into the role you will have your lines down pat."

"Oh, don't worry. I promise you I will know my lines and I'll be ready!"

"OK, that's the spirit."

An awkward silence suddenly appeared and sat between us. Julie seemed to want to say something and, at the same time, she seemed to be afraid of saying it. Once again, I reflected how mysterious females are or, at least, were for me. Her next words threw me for a loop.

"I'm writing a poem for you," she said, softly.

Her eyes were centered on me and, for that instant, I really did wish she had been older. I would have kissed her. She saw my discomfort and gave me a reassuring smile, as if to indicate I had really nothing to worry about. That it was fine. I finally found my voice.

"You are? Oh, my goodness. Julie, it's so lovely of you. I'm flattered. Actually, I'm deeply touched. I don't know what to say."

"Maybe you should wait until I finish it before you say anything."

"I'm sure it will be great. Thank you so much. I look forward to reading it."

Now, it was her turn to appear embarrassed. She got a bit red in the face and she seemed worried. I really did not know what else to say and was trying like crazy to find something to say. I was saved by the arrival of some of other cast members and the magical moment with Julie was gone. She gave me a shy smile.

"I hope you won't tell anybody," and her voice sounded pathetically desperate.

"Don't worry. It'll be our secret."

Her face lit up. I could tell I had lifted a heavy burden from her shoulders. She got up and went to meet the others. A poem, man, I had better be very careful with this lovely, sweet, and innocent girl, I thought. I sure as hell do not want to create any situation where she thinks something is going to happen when it is not.

Suddenly, I regretted I had asked her to stop calling me Mr. Greene, not that it would have made any difference, really. I should have left well enough alone.

I need to talk to someone about this, I thought, but who? I did not trust anybody, not even Jackson who may have had some experience in dealing with this kind of stuff. I did not know why I thought Jackson had some experience; maybe it had to do with the fact his father was a preacher. His father was the person I really need talk to, I thought.

-IV-

Kenny Thompson was our barracks' resident bigot. Originally from Mississippi, he was not open or friendly to blacks. He kept pretty much to himself and had a large tattoo on his right shoulder of the Confederate flag.

His biggest hero, he was fond of saying, was: Strom Thurmond, the racist senator from South Carolina. Kenny did not openly make any negative comments about blacks, but the fact of finding himself among them, sharing living quarters, obviously rankled him.

Someone had said that he avoided using the same sink or the same toilet after some black guy had used it. But since it was nearly impossible to know just which toilet a black soldier had previously used, Kenny had obviously some very serious problems when wanting to take a dump.

Talking about self-induced constipation; old Kenny was the perfect asshole. The thought made me laugh about the sheer stupidity of human beings in general, and of Kenny's in particular.

Apparently, one of his own sisters had married a black man back in Mississippi and it drove Kenny crazy. His sister and her husband were now living in Detroit. There was a lot of tension between him and Cash and, as luck would have it, they both worked with radios, and thus had to interact with each other all of the time.

"One of these days I'm gonna kill that son-of-a-bitch," Cash said.

"Cash, let it go man, it ain't worthy. This guy's a jerk. You want me to talk to him?" I said.

"What you gonna tell him? That's he's an asshole? I've already told him."

"OK, but maybe if it comes from me he'll believe it."

"Oh, he don't believe he's an asshole 'cause it comes from me? But if it comes from you, another white asshole, he'll believe it? I don't need no white trash fightin' my battles, man."

"What's the matter with you? I know you don't need me to fight your battles. But you do something stupid, and you'll get into trouble because he is acting like a typical shit-head."

"I want to kill that son-of-a-bitch."

"And then what? You'll kill him and some other asshole will take his place. Man, best thing is to ignore him. You pay attention to his crap and you've got a problem 'cause you've made him part of your life.

"Hell, you literally allowed him to control your life. You'll give him more importance and now he will have you where he wants you. Don't do that. Ignore this jerk. Don't make him part of your life, as simple as that."

69

"Sheet-it, don't tell me what do to. It ain't none of your damn business."

"You're right. It is none of my business. I'm just a white-nigger and I don't know jack."

"Leave me alone."

"Screw you, then."

He did not answer with the usual "thank you." He was pissed.

Racism and bigotry did not stop at the base's gate. It was all around us, especially given the fact that we were in North Carolina, the birthplace of the KKK. It was still infested with KKK people, though not everyone had sympathies with them.

I was very careful not to put everyone in the same basket because there were Southern white people who opposed bigotry and racism with an amazing degree of intensity, as they had lived long enough to see how insidious and destructive it was to the human spirit.

We lived in a geographical location—and among a segment of American society—where racism played an important part in their daily lives, and to believe that overnight there would suddenly be changes of heart was naïve at best. The Civil Rights struggle had been going on now for a while.

There had been so many tragedies, so many painful experiences. So much of it was in the realm of events that had taken place just outside of my own personal experience and not far from where I was now living.

The late president Kennedy had once expressed the problem of bigotry in probably one of the most simple and eloquent words; he had said, that the problem was a moral problem. Not an economic, not a social problem, but a moral problem!

The death of Kennedy had hit me pretty big. It was the first president whom I had voted for, and I believed in him. I had been in the Army for a couple of months, was still in basic training, when the news hit us. It was numbing to say the least. Then, to watch the whole thing on television and see the assassination of Lee Oswald by Jack Ruby was so surreal.

The images that remained ingrained in our collective brains were like those of an old gangster movie, where the bad guys get away with their crimes until the good guys—Jimmy Cagney among them—come into town, and clean up the whole mess and we all go back to living *Life with Riley*, or was it *Father Knows Best?*

Kennedy's killing was when America lost her innocence—if there was innocence to lose to begin with. America's internal history is not a pretty one. It has been populated by extreme violence and disregard for the rights of others, especially people of color.

This may put her beyond shame over what Europeans have done to other societies they managed to control and destroy throughout their bloody and imperial histories. What the budding American society did to the native inhabitants of this continent is unspeakable.

And by further allowing other innocent people to be brought to the country chained inside cargo holds of ships, turning them into slaves, people whose only crime was that they had a different skin color—will never be completely expurgated from our collective guilt or from our history. This whole thing is about as American as it gets.

Once American society became ensconced in this part of the world, it grew and expanded from one ocean to the other without as much as, *by your leave*, when it conquered—meaning it stole geography that did not belong to her—territories for its Westward expansion.

Thus, California, Arizona, New Mexico, and Texas, were vast expanses of land annexed to the American Dream, all of this without considering that the so-called American Dream would end up becoming someone else's nightmares.

But it was all to the good.

Kenny was the latest mini-version of that history. He was proud of it and never hesitated to inform those around him that, in his view, only the white man had rights, especially if you were a Southerner.

By golly, the rest of us would be better off, much wiser, if we got with the program and let the South resolve her problems without interference from them Northerners who did not know their assess from a hole in the ground. He certainly was not happy that I was hanging around Cash and Jackson. He thought it was beneath my dignity.

His attitude toward blacks had a kind of perverse benigness to it. It is what many people called the *plantation* mentality. Southerners argued only they knew the black man, as they had lived side by side with him for ages; thus, only Southerners were capable of solving the problems.

No strangers were welcome, thank you very much. Go back to where you came from. The rest of us, especially guys like me who come from the West, didn't know jack and all we were doing was adding more fuel to the fire without contributing anything of value as to how the issue would be resolved.

We were just visitors. When our time was up, we would leave and the problems would still be there, they argued—so get out of here.

For many white Southerners the solution was to keep the black man down, by not providing anything of value such as an education or the right to vote—problem solved

Their argument was that by giving black men rights, the next thing they would be chasing white women. It was pretty much what Kenny argued. He knew from very personal experience as one of his sisters had married a black man. But, I also knew that there were white people who fought hard to make things right.

"Cash's pissed. That Thompson is giving him grief," Jackson said, to me.

"Cash should just ignore that him. The guy ain't worth worrying about. He's always going to be an idiot and Cash knows better than getting upset about this moron."

"I told him that, but I'm afraid Cash is going to go off the deep end one of these days and some bad stuff's gonna happen."

"We can't let that happen, man."

"So what the hell you gonna do? Ask Cash to make nice with this bigot?"

"You know, Cash does something stupid and he'll be the one who'll get the shaft. It ain't worth it."

"I keep telling him to just keep away from this jerk, but how can he? They work together every day."

And that was obviously the big problem. Kenny's idea of himself was pretty well set. Being forced to be around black people, when he did not have any choice in the matter, was bound to be a major sore point with him no matter how nice black guys were to him. It would not make any difference.

Jackson was not a guy who flew off the handle. He had a good head on his shoulders and in many ways people looked up to him to diffuse any situation that could get out of control.

"Man, what I hate the most about this is that after so much heartache and suffering by so many people, bigotry and racism are still part of our daily lives. I don't believe it. There is so much crap going on. You know, my old man was part of trying to get blacks registered to vote some years ago. I know how tough it was for my mother and my sisters.

"He would be gone for weeks and we never really knew what he was doing because my mother never said a word. But I knew that something big was taking place because I could see it on her face and she was scared. It was only recently that my dad told me what he had done."

"But if your old man was helping out, how come he is not too keen when you want to do the same thing?"

"Come on, Jonathan. It's the same stuff with all parents. 'Do as I say but not as I do.' "

The Freedom Riders—a group of individuals racing across the South back in 1961 trying to instigate changes to the status quo of segregation in a nonviolent way, to change its insidious control over black people's lives—smacked of revolt against white society. Lots of Southern whites were totally against it. They believed such activities were against the basic values of the American Way of Life.

Most depressing was the U.S. government's hesitation to get involved in this action. To give protection to citizens who were simply exercising their constitutional rights. The feds did not want to stand up for what was right even though the activities were supported by black Americans and many white Americans in their nonviolent demonstrations against local segregation laws.

The U.S. government did not have a responsible attitude about this, and it had to do with politics. The Democrats were afraid to insult the Southern whites. And the Republicans wanted to cater to the Southern Democrats so they could in turn remain in power. It is the reason why so many Americans have always argued that politicians should all be shot, period.

Kenny had never confronted me directly with his bigotry. He knew that I would not have tolerated his bullshit, but, by the same token, I never made it an issue with him, as there was no way to change such a person's attitude. I had tried many times to make it clear to Cash and Jackson that they should ignore him. But, of course, they were the targets of Kenny's bigotry—I was not.

There were always snide remarks from Kenny, which I let slide. The fact that I was close to Cash and Jackson he resented even more. I figured it would have been easier to talk to the wall and have it not only understand what I was saying and answer me back, than to try to talk to Kenny and have him become sensitive to what a moron he was.

He had complained loudly about the Army allowing *Anne Frank* to be put on, and even worse, people he knew—meaning Cash, Yoshi, Jackson and me— were undermining not only the military but also the American Way of Life. His take was that it had to do with a communist conspiracy.

He would not put it above the Jews from New York, where Andy came from, to try corrupting the moral integrity of the U.S. I was not sure if he ever came to see the play. I wanted to ask him, but I was not that curious or interested, though in another sense maybe I should have asked him just to screw his mind over.

When he found out about the restaurant incident, he mumbled we had no right to go and create problems where, according to him, none existed. If there was a redeeming quality to Kenny, it was that for some strange reason he liked Yoshi. He always tried to hang around him; and Yoshi, being the nice guy he was, never refused to talk to Kenny.

"How do you figure this bigot wants to be friends with you? Jackson asked Yoshi one day.

"Maybe his bigotry has a soft spot for Japanese people—who knows?"

"Maybe he wants to find out about Japanese poontang," Cash said.

"Cash, do you ever think about anything else?" I asked.

"I'm serious. One day, when he allowed himself to say normal things to me, he mentioned it. I told him to ask Yosh but he said he respected Yosh too much to ask him such a delicate and intimate question. He said he didn't want to 'offend' Yosh. Can you imagine this racist prick saying such things?"

"Yoshi, has he?" Jackson asked.

"No."

"He won't, I'm tellin' you," Cash said.

"Actually, he did talk to me but it wasn't really about Japanese women. It was about the language," Yosh said.

"Are you serious?" Jackson asked.

"Yeah."

"What did he say?" I asked.

"He wanted to find out if there was an alphabet to it. He also said he was still pissed off at what the Japanese had done to America, but he wouldn't hold it against me because after all I wasn't even around and, besides, I was born in this country, so I'm American."

"Very big of him," said Jackson.

"What'd you say?" Cash asked.

"I told him that it was nice of him to be so understanding, and also that the Japanese language was a nice language."

"Can you believe this jerk?" I said.

"Maybe there is a good side to him," Yosh said, not really believing it.

"Yeah, there's always good sides to bigots. They love their mamas," Jackson said.

"I want to kill that son-of-a-bitch," Cash said, and he was serious.

"Forget it, man," I said. "Scumbags like him have a way of reproducing themselves at a fast rate. You'll kill one and another ten will take his place."

"Cash," Yoshi said, "the more you pay attention to him the worse off you are. You let him control your life when you make him part of your life. The guy's an idiot and you gain nothing from getting upset over this stupidity."

"That's what I'm always saying," I said.

"I still want to punch his lights out."

"And then what?" Jackson asked. "You get to spend the rest of your life in Leavenworth. That's pretty smart."

"Well, you have to admit that he likes Yoshi, so maybe he ain't so bad, after all," I said.

They all looked at me and Cash had a frown on his face that was not friendly. He knew, they all knew, that I was just trying to diffuse the situation.

"He told me the other day," Yoshi said, "he wants to visit Japan. He did say he would be honored—I swear those are his words—if I introduced him to some respectable families and maybe, maybe, some good girls over there."

"So now he thinks you're gonna pimp for him?" I asked just to give Yosh a hard time.

"I guess."

"Boy, this world never ceases to amaze me," Jackson said.

"I will kill that son-of-a-bitch," Cash said, quietly.

To say that Kenny's behavior rankled us was to understate that he was getting on our nerves.

"Look," Yosh said, "I've been insulted a few times about the fact that I'm Asian. But what you guys don't know is that, back in Japan I was also insulted for being American, even though my father is Japanese and my mother, though American, is of Japanese ancestry."

"Are you serious?" Cash asked.

"It's true. It caused me some trouble at first because the idea of being an American seemed so weird to me. I mean, I looked like everybody else around me in Japan. My parents both looked like everybody else. It was crazy."

"So what did you do?" Asked Jackson.

"What could I do?"

"So you took it in the ass and kept your mouth shut," Cash said, in his usual blunt manner.

"No, I didn't take it in the ass. Both my parents made it clear to me that there were racists among the Japanese and that I should not let them bully me. My uncle told me many times that if some of the kids were trying to mess with me, that he would come over and personally deal with them. When he said that I felt very proud of him."

"You talkin' about the guy who went to war and fought them Nazis?" Cash asked.

"Yeah."

"Shee-it, man, that would have been somethin'," Cash said, and we saw how he was imagining Yoshi's uncle coming to Japan and beating the hell out of those bullies.

"Did he ever do it?" I asked.

"No. I told mother about it. She said that she loved and respected my uncle but that she would not allow that to happen. Besides, she said, I was also a descendant of Samurai and Samurai knew how to defend themselves.

"My father thought it was silly to fill my head with these crazy ideas. But one day I asked him about someone giving me a hard time, and he said I had his permission to defend myself and he would not be upset."

"Did you ever get into a fight?" Jackson said.

"No, but I beat the crap out of them playing chess and golf," Yosh said, laughing, and we all joined him in the laughter. "Yeah, after a while the pricks couldn't do enough for me. Actually, I did make friends with a couple of good guys. And they became so pro-American that we formed a club and nobody messed with us."

"Respect," Cash said, with relish.

"Well, guys, we've got in our midst a Samurai-Chess-Golf-champion. Shee-it, never heard of anything like this before," Jackson said.

"Well, there is always the first time," I said.

"So now you gonna play chess or golf with this racist moron?" Cash asked, somewhat facetiously.

"Get out of here," Yosh said.

Bigotry did have strange and bizarre outcomes, also. And such contradictions were hard to understand. In some specific instances, the whole thing did not make any sense at all and; in fact, it seemed like children's games.

Take for instance when African diplomats visited the South, they were always treated like white people at restaurants, hotels, and airports, everywhere! They were never discriminated against. The whole thing was ludicrous to say the least. Jackson brought it up during the conversation.

"Shee-it, what about them Africans officials who come to America and are considered white? What about them?"

"You jive-ass-lying-jerk. It ain't true." Cash was shocked.

"Yes. It's true."

"Man, I don't believe it. You mean them Africans can go to any restaurant or hotel and they's cool. No white trash is gonna give 'em crap?"

"That's right."

"Man, this is crazy!"

The total nonsense and incongruity of such a situation was too hard for all of us to understand, but it was particularly hard for Cash and Jackson to understand, let alone accept.

"OK," Cash said, "I'm African, right? That's where my family was taken from and shipped over here. So I should go out and eat at any restaurant or stay in any hotel or vote, yeah, vote, and I should be cool, right? But I ain't. So what the hell gives?"

"Them's secrets only whitey knows about 'em," Jackson said, with a tone of sadness. "OK," Jackson continued, "I want to ask you guys one stupid question."

"What?" Cash said.

"Do you think that one day we'll get a brother to be president?" Jackson said.

"President of what?" Cash said.

"Of this country?" Jackson answered.

We all looked at him as if he had taken leave of his senses, but he was serious.

"Are you crazy?" Cash asked, and for an instant we all froze.

"No, I'm serious."

"No way in hell," Cash said. "Do you think whitey would allow that? No way. It would be the civil war all over again."

"It could happen," Jackson said, and I thought he was serious about such a ridiculous idea. There followed a long silence as we all pondered a question we all knew the answer to.

"I don't know what gave you the idea," Cash said. "But that'll never happen! There ain't no way a Chinaman, or a Japanese or some other non-white in this country, would ever get to be president. No way. It's whitey or civil war."

"Shee-it," Yosh said laughing. "I was hoping by coming back here I would eventually get to be the one, but Cash here says no way in hell that's going to happen."

"Jackson, you are insane to even think that crap," I said.

"I'm an Aryan, you know," said Yosh.

"Aryans, what the hell is that?" Cash asked.

"The ultimate superior race, the masters of the universe," I said.

"So I could be president," Yosh said.

"Get out of here," Cash said.

"OK," Yosh said. "You guys don't believe me. My uncle told me a story of Hitler and the Nazis when they were allied with the Japanese during the war. The Germans decided the Japanese were white. In fact, both Germans and Japanese were Aryans."

"What's Aryan?" Cash asked.

"It has to do with a supposed ancient superior race that once dominated the world," Yoshi said. "And they called themselves Aryans. Anyway, the Nazis had a problem with the Japanese difference, obviously, so they declared the Japanese were the cousins of the Aryan race or something, and that's how they got around their racist bullshit."

"Wait a minute," Cash said. It was obvious he was very intrigued by what Yosh was saying. "How can you be cousin to some white hunkey and still look Japanese? I don't get it."

"I'm just telling you what my uncle said. Actually, my uncle thought it was pretty stupid, as he never thought of himself as anything but American of Japanese ancestry, of course."

"Your uncle was a good man," Jackson said.

"He really believed in good shit," Cash said.

"I loved him," Yosh said. "He was a good guy. Sometimes, I think that I want to be more like him than even my own father. I love my old man. He's a gentle soul unable to harm anybody. On the contrary, he wants to help people all of the time.

"And that's why I want to be a doctor just like him. But I must admit I may not have the same patience he has. In many ways, I'm more like my mother. She has a tough time suffering fools."

"Boy, that's not the impression I had of her," I said, remembering the nice soft-spoken woman we had met when she came with Tamiko to visit Yosh.

"Yeah, she seemed so sweet and gentle," Jackson said.

"What you saying, Zen man, is that you don't want to fuck with her?" Cash said.

"Yeah, that's right."

Yosh answered and not without pride as Cash, in his usual blunt way, had paid Yoshi's mother the ultimate compliment that a guy can pay to his buddy's mom. And he used a word we knew Jackson's mother would not have approved of. We all understood and smiled.

"Hey, I got an idea," Cash said. "Me and Jackson will go and buy African clothes, put them on and let's go downtown and see if it works. Shee-it, that's the ticket."

"What if you get caught?" Yoshi asked, laughing, while at the same time kind of savoring the whole idea.

"What'd they gonna do? Put us in the Army? Shee-it," Cash said.

"Cash," Jackson said, "Do you want to do it?"

"Sure, do. Hey, Hollywood, what'd you think?"

"Shee-it, let's do it. Like you say, what can they do? Send you back to Africa?"

"You guys are crazy," Yoshi said, laughing.

What was not crazy and depressing all of us was the murder of three Civil Rights workers in rural Mississippi. And Kenny was gloating over it. I was afraid that Cash would really kill this moron. Jackson, Yoshi, and I kept a vigilant eye on Cash.

It would not have taken much for him to do something rash and ugly. And the state of Mississippi refused to try the men who had done it. Not a development that made you proud of this country's system of justice. No question about it, we had to keep an eye on Cash. It really was a bad time for all of us.

-V-

Then we got the terrible news that Wilson had bought the farm! It hit us like a ton of bricks. As if we needed more bad news. It was unbearable as hell. Jackson was the one who told the rest of us. He was now the chaplain's assistant and he got the news and had accompanied the chaplain to see Emily.

We were all devastated! We would never be the same. At that moment, in one instant, in a fragment of time, as miniscule as the origin of life itself, the whole idea of existence became ugly, totally absurd, and meaningless.

There was this drained feeling in my guts because nothing in my life, no experiences of any kind had prepared me for this. Nothing I had done could relate to what had taken place with the death of Wilson. I was barren of some kind of human history, some residue of having been exposed to such tragedy before.

A memory, an insight, something that could sustain and help me live through this tragedy. An experience I had lived before, in my past, where I would have seen, been part of, learned about the question of death, and what it does to the people left behind, how they cope with it?

We were all completely unprepared for it. I thought, is it like in a western movie? But this was a different movie. Where the actors never get up after the scene is over. In fact, the only thing left to do is dig a six-foot hole, dump you into it, cover it, and those left behind have nightmares about being suffocated inside such an eternal prison from which no one ever escapes.

I thought *this is ugly.* How does one flee from such an end? This is no trial and error thing where one can do it over again hoping for a different result. Eternal sleep; what the hell was that? My sense of loss could not have been greater if someone from my own family had so abruptly disappeared from my life.

So what do we, the ones left behind, what do we do? We continue with our lives, OK, but what does that mean? Do what we have been doing? Or do we change it? But change to what? OK, maybe in the case of having a dear one die due to incurable illness there might be some modicum of comfort in that we wish that the suffering come to an end.

Even though we barely understand what is taking place, in some strange and distant way, the inevitability of the cycle of life might give us some insight, however fleeting, about the nature of life and its limited time-span and that there is nothing we can do. It is still painful and fills us with despair but we stumble out of bed the next day and we continue living.

But in what had happened to Wilson and by consequence to Emily; what do we do? So brutal, so without notice, so direct we do not know what is expected of us in such a situation? The reality was we were in the Army. And the future was we would be put in harm's way with its inevitable tragic consequence. This is insane, I thought.

There were few details about Wilson's death. Three weeks out in the boonies and he had been caught in some firefight. He had tried to rescue some other guy who had been badly injured. He did not have a chance. His body was being sent directly to his hometown.

Cash, Yoshi, me, and the others stood by listening to Jackson like a bunch of zombies. It was one of the darkest moments of our young and untried existence.

Life would never be the same for any of us. This was the first time that many of us had been exposed to someone just disappearing without the chance of coming back. It was the exposure to the questions that plague us all from the moment we become aware of it: *Where do the dead go? What happens after we die?*

Jackson said that Emily had been incredibly stoic when she got the news. She kept her cool while everyone else around her was falling apart. It did not surprise me. Emily always struck me as one of those special and unique individuals older than their years.

They know and understand things in a far and clearer way than most of us do not. Some people are that way. Where does it come from? Man, only the gods knew about such things.

I did not know what to do. There was an incredible empty feeling in my guts. I went back to the crazy sentiments I had experienced when I first learned Wilson had volunteered to go. I felt guilty and sad in a way that I had never felt before. The whole thing just did not make any sense. I tried to figure it out, and I could not get a fix on it.

That night, at rehearsal for the play, the atmosphere was funereal. I went through the motions, but my heart and mind were not in the play. I, who always looked forward to the rehearsals, felt a terrible sense of loss and sheer isolation.

After we finished, everyone left and I was the last one to close the place up. Not even Cash and Jackson who normally stayed with me to close waited around.

I walked to my car and sat inside for a while. Then with a great deal of trepidation, I drove over to Emily's place. Jackson had said that she was leaving early the next morning for her long drive home to be there when her husband's body would arrive. Man, how incomprehensible can life be?

According to Jackson, Emily had not cried. Not a single tear ever came to her eyes when she was told the news. She was as clear and lucid, as if such a tragedy had happened to someone else. I parked down the street from her house and sat in the car. I could hear voices coming from her house. I did not want to go in. I was afraid of facing Emily. I was going to lose it.

What could I possibly say to her? There was not a damn thing that I could say or do to ease her pain. I even considered leaving, not seeing her at all. Wilson had been my friend, and I was completely ignorant as to what was to be done in this situation.

Eventually the people left Emily's house, and the street got very quiet. I could hear the crickets chirping away and their song offended me to no end. I did not want to talk to anybody. I thought of what I had told Wilson before he left, and now my own words came back so incredibly clear and I started to feel like shit.

I did not understand why life had to be so cruel, so sad and uncaring, the very same words that Julie had used a few days ago about how she felt. The next thing, I knew there was Emily standing by the car.

"Are you all right?" She asked, softly.

"No." I did not try to hide my tears.

"I saw your car. Come in the house, please."

She opened the door to the car and I got out. Then she did something that I never expected, she put her arms around me and held me close to her. I could smell her hair and could feel the warmth of her body against mine.

At first, I recoiled from the contact, but she would not let me go. She put her head on my shoulders, held me very tight against her, and kissed me lightly on the check.

"Oh, Jonathan, so much pain, I'm so sorry."

"No, Emily, I'm the one who's truly sorry. I wish I could change what happened. Oh, how I wish. I would give anything to reverse what happened. Why, why?"

It is a lament that comes with humans, stays with humans, and dies with humans because life can be so horrible and uncaring. Even though it was dark, I could see her eyes, with her face so close to me, with an incredible look of purity and innocence. It was a look not only of understanding, but also of something beyond.

A look of clarity, of a sense of destiny. In such a strange way, she was there to give comfort to others when her whole life was now crumbling to nothing. There were no more secrets for her.

Then in a very primitive and animal sense, I knew what was going to happen and I felt fear like I never had felt before in my life. My feelings were both desperate and without end. I wished that other people would have been around to help keep my sanity and destiny in check, but somehow fate would not give me such a break. I started to shake.

"You're shaking. Why?" She asked me, softly.

My mouth was dry and, at the moment, I wanted to be a million miles away from there. I wished that I had not come to see her. I wished it had been me who had died and that Wilson would now be holding her instead of me.

I felt guilty for having kept away from visiting them when I found out that he was going to Vietnam. I wished I were in another universe, where things were fine and nobody got hurt or suffered pain and a complete loss.

"I think I may be coming down with a cold or something."

She knew it was a lie. I knew it was a lie. Nothing, absolutely nothing, in my life, had prepared me for what I was now facing.

"Come in, please."

She started to walk ahead of me while still holding my hand. I stopped her.

"Hey, do you want to grab a coke or something?" My voice was not steady.

"No, do you?"

"Yeah, I'm kind of thirsty. If you don't mind."

"No, that's fine." I let go of her hand and walked around the car.

We got in the car and I had a tough time getting the key in the ignition. My knees were shaking and I knew I did not want to be there. I needed time to think. I am not and have never been a religious person, but that night I prayed silently that I would be strong and wise.

Boy, did I pray. *Dear God, me who does not believe in you, show me that you exist, for once tell me, and show me what I need to do. Do not leave me here like this. Please, help me . . .*

There was a drive-in not too far from the house and I drove over there. I was hoping that we would run into someone we knew and I would try to talk someone, anyone, to come with us. I was now regretting that I had decided to come and see her alone.

The fates had other plans.

Emily knew that I was trying like crazy not to be alone with her, but she seemed also like in a trance. But what I was seeing and sensing was something that I will never understand even if I live a million years. She was fully aware of who she was, where she was, what she was doing. There was clarity of being. In total control of her life.

She did not question what was going to happen and not because she was bent on destroying herself or the idea of herself. No, it was more than that. It was as complex as the birth of the universe. That is the only thing I can think of saying.

There was an amazing sense coming from her that life held no surprises and she, perhaps, for the first time had come to understand life's inner workings. I envied her because however rotten life had been to her, it had also made her free. It held no more secrets for her.

Her lovely innocence, as a human being, had now been replaced by a reality that had no ambiguities. It was ugly, unkind, revolting, and brutal. The beauty in her life, her *raison d'être* had simply been extinguished, as when we put out the flame of a candle.

The flame dies with just a tiny swish, a sound of the air that we blow over it. The only thing left is the smell of wax and small curly whiffs of smoke that hang in midair, then slowly drift away to eventually become invisible atoms, which we will never see again.

She knew of things now, and she was no longer in the dark about life and how cruel and uncaring it can be. Life had taken from her a most precious element:

the love of another human being for her. Her loss was staggering. And no matter where she went or what she did, or how many more years she lived, there would be no surprises for her anymore. No more doubts.

At that moment, she was as pure and honest as she would ever be. She was, I sensed in my own emotional turmoil, trying to show me that I did not need to be afraid. Life needed to go on because we had no other choice but to continue.

Not suffering for something over which we had no control did not make us less human. She had died emotionally and spiritually and now was being re-born out of the chaos, but innocent no longer. Her new life would hold fewer secrets. She knew too much now.

Nothing would ever bring back what she had lost. Nothing could replace it. I did not want to have memories of that night, but I knew they would never be erased from my psyche. It is not that I did not want to remember my thoughts and feelings about Emily. There was something incongruous to the whole thing. We never once talked about her dead husband..

It was both comforting and crazy, but he existed for both of us. Without him, we would not have met. In my own screwed up sense, at that moment, it seemed as if he would have approved and understood what she was doing, what I was doing. He would never have held it against her or me.

We drove back to the house from the drive-in. We got out of the car and walked into the house. No words were exchanged between us. There seemed to be no need to say anything. I cannot remember how things started. All I know is we were in a state of complete emotional and physical surrender, lost, but we were innocent—so innocent . . .

In all my experiences, I had never felt such raw emotions about what was taking place. All of our frustrations, fears, confusion, sadness, somehow made that night inexplicable, and yet blameless and pure. There was nothing ugly or vulgar about it.

Even if I get to live until the moon falls out of the sky, the reasons and the whys of what happened between Emily and me that night will always be hidden from me simply because we are merely mortal. It is and it will always be the secret of the gods.

We had connected in a way that went beyond becoming physically intimate with each other. Emily was incredible, all giving. She held back nothing. We were in this eternal embrace of hearts and souls where questions of destiny had been answered by the gods.

We had nothing to say or do other than to receive and give to each other without regrets and as innocent as the dawn follows the dark and lonely night.

Her tenderness was so overwhelming. It was as if we had met in a time dimension that was unique, and only she and I were allowed to be part of it. She understood better than anyone the need for love, for compassion, for forgiveness.

Was it a primitive survival instinct still lodged in our brains? A primeval act that went back to the beginning of time when there was little choice but to try to survive the horrors of existence? A time when there were no bullets or Agent

Orange; but a time, nevertheless, filled with fear and admonition of the unknown, where one had to be prepared to continue and make the best of it?

There were no holds barred that evening. Everything was new, and pure. I had never been exposed to something so powerful in my life before. It totally invaded me and took over and I knew that I would never, ever, be the same again.

No matter what I did, or may happen to me in the future, my night with Emily was as close to the most basic truth of my entire existence up to now. She died that night so that I would be born. I do not know how else to explain it. I do not know.

It was as if I were the bereaved person and she was there to give me the only human comfort possible, and it all came from deep within her without any ambiguities, doubts, or regrets.

Somehow, Emily had made a gift to me of human touch, human affection, human tenderness that went beyond anything I would ever be able to understand, and no judgment was necessary or called for.

It is at moments like this that your own sense of mortality becomes clear and direct. Yet I never felt that I was replacing her husband in her life. That would never be the case. It was more like that part of her previous life had no more consequences for her, and she was saying goodbye to the inexplicable.

It was over. It would never come back to the way it was. And this was a way for her to admit it, deal with it, and look at her new life with hope and more hope.

An image came to me of something that I had once seen in a movie about people leaving Hawaii by ship and how they throw leis—garland of flowers—over the railing on the water to float away with the ocean currents.

The leis drift slowly into some kind of eternal flow away from us and we never see them again. I think it is also done when someone dies. It is some kind of tribute, and also a passage honoring the spirits of the dead. There is a strange and mysterious beauty to these rituals.

At that moment with Emily, I felt caught in these mysterious currents of eternal *va-et-viens,* as the French would say it.

"Dear Jonathan, please don't leave—not just now. But don't be sad or feel guilty, please. I want you to remember that for the rest of my life I will always know deep down in my heart that I'm one of the luckiest girls in this world, because I have been loved by two of the most wonderful men in this whole, stupid universe.

"So dear heart, be happy. I will always remember you, always. Take good care of yourself. There is special girl out there, somewhere, and you will find her, I know it! And when she comes into your life, love her with all of your soul and with that wonderful, generous heart of yours that Homer appreciated so much.

"So long, dear heart . . ."

I left later, much later, but I have no recollection of many details after this. The next thing I knew, I was sitting in my car with tears rolling down my cheeks. The only reality with me was her perfume still surrounding not only my sense of smell but also my very being.

I did not go back to the barracks immediately. It was a very bad idea, as the Army conducted unscheduled bed checks just to be sure that you were in for the night. And if you were not there, there would be hell to pay, but I did not care. What could they do to me—send me to Vietnam? Yeah, well, screw them!

I drove around for I do not know how long until the sun finally came out. I had no place to go. I had no home, no family to speak of, no woman waiting for me to return from my odyssey, no children wanting my attention, no debtors; I had no credit; I had no spiritual bank; I had no life!

In the confusion of the moment, whatever existence I might have possessed seemed to have taken a direction that was just as mysterious, as why there are black holes at the center of galaxies up there in the sky.

I finally drove back to the barracks to be present for early morning roll call. Nobody paid much attention to me and no questions were asked. I guess, I was lucky that no bed check had been done the night before.

I answered "present" when my name was called and neither Cash nor Jackson said anything, even though they must have seen I had not slept in my bunk. After the roll call, we were dismissed and I told the sergeant holding the count that I was going on sick call.

I went back to Emily's street and I sat in my car just like the night before, but this time she did not walk over when she saw me. She had told me she was leaving early, for she had a long drive in front of her.

From where I was parked, I could see her going back and forth into the house doing the final loading of the car with her personal belongings.

I just sat in my car frozen with an incredible pain in my heart and guts. I wanted to go to her and ask her to stay, please stay, to tell her it's OK, we do not have to do anything. We can just be here for each other, but I did not. The situation called for something that I simply did not have—balls.

Dear Emily, I wish that it had been me and not Wilson, your Wilson. I would gladly give my life without any hesitation to change places with him. I do not count for anything. I am not worthy like he was. Nobody would miss me. I wish I could bring him back just for you. I know you have to go, and how I wish you did not. Come back. You are stronger than me. Please, come back. Stay, please. Stay. I will make it right for you. I promise you. I will . . .

She knew I was there and she glanced in my direction only once. She locked the front door of the house, walked to her car, stopped, and hesitated for a millionth of a second, which for me was a whole lifetime. At that instant, I imagined that she would walk to where I was.

In a flash, I saw the image of this beautiful, wonderful girl, walking toward me with a big smile on her lovely face. I closed my eyes for a moment and when I opened them, I saw that she got in the car.

The car backed out of the driveway and headed in the opposite direction from where I was. The last image I saw was the signal light on the car blinking, as it stopped at the corner, then the car slowly turned left and disappeared into the early morning mist.

Emily, please forgive me. Please. I have never loved anyone as much as I love you now. I try not to understand it. I do not understand it. Take care of yourself, dear heart, as you called me. Do not trust life anymore. Never trust life. She is just a fucking cow, that is what she is, a fucking cow!

Suddenly, I had this incredible urge, this mad sentiment that if I walked into the empty house Emily would come back for something she had forgotten, she would find me there, we would talk and I would understand things.

They would become clear to me. That something that I was missing would appear, I would make it my own. I would hold onto it for the rest of my life, and nothing would ever be ugly and sad.

In that very instant, I saw myself walking back into the house, going from room to room, smelling her, looking for her, desperately searching and searching. I wanted so badly to do it. I do not think that I had ever wanted to do something that badly before.

But as I looked back at the empty house, I knew I would not have the courage to get out of my car and walk over to the house.

I was torn between an incredible feeling of wanting to make something real in my lousy life, and at the same time rejecting the whole thing as being just some kind of childish thing.

I understood that I did not have the courage to do it. I was a coward. I was playing head games pretending I was going to do something I knew I did not have the balls to do.

Son of bitch, what does it mean? The total absurdity of life was never more overwhelming to me than at that instant. It was a low moment of my life. I was hurting. Even my pain when Pamela and I broke up would not compare to how I now felt. There was no place for me to hide.

We all go through life wishing for something to take us out of our humdrum existence, thinking we are ready and prepared to find the answer we are seeking. You are a man, you meet a girl, you court her, you get married, she gets pregnant, and you become a parent.

You live, work, exist, and then you will die. Nothing romantic or even complicated about that. In fact, the whole thing seems so banal, mundane, without any poetry. But love should be more than just routine, or accepted behavior. It should be something that brings you truth and beauty, something that we are all worthy of.

Later, much later, in the days that followed, Cash and Jackson intrinsically knew what had happened and I wanted in the worst possible way to talk to them. To explain it to them. To have them cut my balls off, open my chest, and rip my heart out, but they never said a word and this gave me an even greater sense of guilt and isolation.

They both knew it and it became part of who we had become. All of us, Wilson—Emily, Cash, Jackson, me—we knew we would remain attached to each other until the end of our lives. We were children who had become orphans and had nobody else but each other. Only once did Jackson, rather obliquely, make a muted reference to it.

He received a postcard from Emily a couple of weeks after she left, but he never showed it to me and I saw him burning it later. Cash was sitting at the other end of the barracks and he only glanced at me, once, then he went back to the book he was reading.

Jackson got up and, as he went by, he touched me lightly on the shoulder and said softly.

"She's pregnant," he stopped. His voice had a sound of sorrow and pity and I was afraid to look at him directly. "She was a month pregnant when Wilson left for Nam," he added, quietly.

He did not look back at me and kept on walking.

Man, I wanted to cry, and have those two crazy bastards talk to me, insult me, rip my heart out, but hold me close, hug me and tell me that I should not carry such a terrible burden with me. Tell me that it was OK to feel lost, insecure.

That life would always be a mystery, to be appreciated, to be enjoyed, to be loved, even when she kicked you hard in the balls.

The play was coming along fine and, after some rough spots, the cast was reacting in some very interesting ways to Karen and Julie. It was the same, but it was not the same. The dynamics of having two different people act the part of Anne Frank was very hard to describe, except that they all knew it was just a great experiment in creativity.

If they had some trepidation, at the beginning, with my crazy idea of having two Anne Franks, they now fell into a wonderful routine that did not allow for fear or extreme changes in what they were attempting to do with their own individual roles.

The play was merging, turning, and tuning itself into something coherent, cohesive, and their level of comfort grew and grew. We all knew what we were reaching for, and that we were about to achieve something unique and unforgettable.

On my own personal front, I found myself more and more not wanting to be alone; on the contrary, I was constantly finding excuses to be around others. Whenever the image of Emily came to me, it overwhelmed and confused me to no end.

There was no question my life had changed in a mysterious way. Whenever I thought I had a hold on it, it would become blurred, dark, and I would have a hard time keeping focused on my daily mundane existence.

I tried to find my bearings but I did not have much success. I was tied up in a knot and the more I tried to reason out my sentiments the more confusing my whole life was becoming. In many ways, it was a desperation for some answers, for something final that made me concentrate more on not only my regular Army job but also on the play.

I do not think I could have survived if I had not had something else to take my mind off how miserable my life was—the rawness of it all.

As I have said, Cash and Jackson did not ask me anything or say anything. Their attitude toward me was the same. Nothing had changed but, of course, we all knew that everything had changed!

It was one of those contradictory situations in life where what you see leads you to deny it. Not because you do not want to accept what you see, but because you want to be blind. It is an existential choice.

In a greater sense, I loved those two crazy bastards for not pushing me into a corner, though many times I wished that I could talk to them. But I found that I could not and my inability to communicate, to share my misery with them, made the whole thing even worse.

I was alone, and I was hurting. At one time, I even contemplated volunteering for Vietnam, as I saw it as my way out of my funk. That is how screwed up I was at that moment.

One evening, at the end of the rehearsal, Andy came in. This was not unusual, though he had kept away for the most part. But I knew why. The shit was about to hit the fan. I also knew that we would have it out after everyone had gone home.

I had not had the interview with Sanders. Instead, I had written an article that was critical of bigotry and racist attitudes that I saw around me. I did not try to hide my feelings. I was not interested in being nice or polite.

Sanders, bless his soul, had done very little editing to the extent that he had pretty much published the article the way it was written. I had heard caustic comments from some people—Kenny among them—but for the most part, I did not think it was so incendiary. I mean, I knew whom I was dealing with.

What I had written was not made up. It existed. However, to be honest, my article was not benign to bigots and racists, especially when I called attention to the fact that so many ugly things were happening just outside the gates of the base.

But I was careful not to blame the whole population as that would not have been fair or wise. I did, however, point out that a high percentage of the Army population was black and there was a reason for it.

It was simply that in the military, there appeared to be a high degree of equality that did not exist on the outside. I lauded the military for its progressive attitude and view.

After all, the military had been integrated back in 1948 by President Truman, and the result had not been disastrous, as so many people, especially Southern people, had feared. On the contrary, it showed that if you made an institution, such as the Army, color blind, it could teach the rest of society something positive.

I had argued that in the final analysis, an enemy's bullet did not discriminate between who was white and who was black. It just simply killed and people died the same way from such an event. We all bled the same way, with one color of blood—red.

And how could the society, at large, ask of its black citizens the ultimate sacrifice when at the same time deny them the basic rights it granted its white members? It was racist, unfair, and totally against what the country stood for, or should stand for. Prejudice had to stop.

There was no place for it in this country, and those who sought to continue to perpetrate it had to be called for what they were: Bigots and racists.

The play about Anne Frank had, in a most eloquent manner, demonstrated how insidious bigotry, anti-Semitism, and racism were. Anne Frank and millions of others had died because so many people had looked the other way and thus had revealed themselves to be sadly misinformed, or cowards. Or worse, they did not care or had not stood up and been counted. America was a hell of a lot better than that.

We could not continue to ignore that basic rights had been denied to a large section of the population and that such discrimination had to stop, period. I knew what I was writing would not endear me to lots of people. But I did not want to shade the truth. I was most definitely grateful and impressed that Sanders had published the article with clever editing.

That evening, after the rehearsal, everybody left except Jackson and me. Cash had not come with us that evening because he was the company's clerk on duty that night. So I sat and waited for Andy to do his Carmen Miranda dance number. He finally came out of his office and walked to the stage.

"Jackson," he said, "could you give Jonathan and me a few minutes alone, please."

"Jackson, you stay where you are."

"Greene, look, I can wait for you in the car."

"No. You stay here."

Jackson looked miserable, lost, and did not know what to do. Andy saw the turmoil that he was under. Jackson attempted to get out and walk away from us but I gave him such a dirty look that he just sat and waited.

"So who do you think you are?" Andy's voice was unusually quiet.

"I don't know. You tell me."

"Actually, what you wrote isn't so bad or offensive."

"So why the charade?"

"You disobeyed my wishes. I made it clear to you that you needed to run these things by me, so I could cover your ass. It's obvious you had no intention of setting up an interview. I talked to Sanders and he supported you; nevertheless, you didn't have the balls to tell me directly what your intentions were. You didn't trust me?"

"It's not that."

"What was it, then?"

"It's hard to explain."

"Hard to explain? Come on, Jonathan. Expressing yourself has never been a problem for you, as far as I can tell. You think that you're such a hero. That you, all by your lonesome, can take on the whole world and there isn't anybody out there who cares just as deeply as you do, maybe even more than you can possibly imagine."

"I don't get it, Andy. Why are you giving me the third degree? You just told me the stuff wasn't as bad as you had feared. Man, you lost me there. I'm obviously not getting what this thing is about. Please, forgive me but you seem to be forgetting that in the final analysis I'm just a dumb jerk. Isn't that what you think of me?"

"You know, Greene, if I didn't trust you and like you I would have thrown your ass out of here a long time ago. I mean, there have been times when I came close, so close, and I held back because I do understand you. I know you think I'm some dumb asshole who's worried about losing his job. Boy, you're so wrong, so wrong. I don't give a damn about this job any more than you care for this Army. Man, you've got a lot to learn from life."

"Andy, I can do without your lectures. Get to the point."

"Hey, Jonathan, take it easy," Jackson said.

He did not raise his voice but his tone was powerful and final. His looks were direct and his eyes were burning with a clear, unambiguous look that for a moment I was afraid he was going to do or say something that I could not live with.

"You know," Andy said, "sometime ago, probably way before both of you were born, I was faced with the fact that so many of my own relatives were being converted into lamp shades in Germany only because they were Jewish. And the bitch of it all was I couldn't do anything about it. I couldn't even join this damn Army due to a bad heart. Ain't that the pits?

"I was born with a tiny heart defect, something miniscule, totally ridiculous, and inconsequential the civilian doctors whom I consulted told me. I was rejected by this man's Army to serve and do something, anything. So I steeled myself to do the best I could with what I had. Yeah, I didn't complain. I didn't blame anybody. I didn't go around with a hangdog look. I took it and dealt with it. How can life be so stupid?

"But the one thing I told myself I would never do was to be second to anybody when it came to fighting for what was right, noble, and honest for my country. I'm not second to you or to any other asshole in this screwed up world who thinks that he, and only he, has a monopoly on wanting to make this a better world."

I did not know if at that moment I had enough patience left to listen to Andy. I had my own troubles and I was not too accommodating. I looked at Jackson, and he was staring at the floor.

"Look, Andy, I'm not going to apologize for what I believe. I don't want to be a phony and say that I'm sorry to have caused you grief because of the things that I believe in. I'm not about to do that. I can't. I also have to fight my wars the way I see them.

"I'm not like you, or Jackson, or any of the others who are working hard to make this show into something special and for which I'm grateful. I'm also grateful you have given me this chance, but I want to tell you that if you want to fire me I'm fine with that. I won't hold it against you or anybody else."

"Leno, your boy here is a hard ass isn't he?" Andy said.

Jackson just smiled but said nothing.

"No, I'm not going to fire you," Andy continued. "I think it would make you feel like a sacrificial lamb and I don't want to give you that satisfaction. I wouldn't put it past you that you have intended all along for me to fire you so you can walk with this victim-hood crap around your neck like some kind of trophy to show the world you stood up to the man.

"Forget it. I have no desire to make a martyr out of you and not because you cannot be replaced. If you think that you cannot be replaced, you *are* wrong."

"I never said that. I don't feel that way."

"You know, that's probably the most honest thing you have said so far. This may come as a surprise to you but I fought for you when I had to go and see General Numbnuts and argue with him that we are right in what we are doing. He wasn't happy about it, because some people are calling him and giving him a hard time.

"Not only about the choice of the play but the other things that have come with it. The funny thing is that he knows about you. That surprised the hell out of me. I mean, here is this guy running this place with thousands of people around him, and he knows personally about you."

"Don't tell me he is afraid of losing his job over this."

"Ah, Jonathan, the guy with the facile answer. Never looking at himself to see how others see him. Always trying to avoid stopping for that single moment in his life to see himself for who he is, because if it ever happens he will be confronted and discover he is only human, decent, afraid, and lost. Never wanting or needing someone to help him get over the rough spots. Soldier Jonathan Alexandre Greene, a self-made man. Doesn't need anybody. Yes, sir, indeed."

His voice was quiet. And there was a sad tone to it. He seemed distant and I felt sorry for him, for me, for Jackson, for Emily, for Cash, for Yoshi, for Wilson, for Julie, for the whole damn world. For people who had suffered and who were going to suffer no matter what they did to protect themselves.

Life never gave anybody a break. Life did not give a shit. Life was neutral and we, humans, were the poor, sorry lot that suffered because we were incapable of understanding anything. We spent so much time doing worthless things. Stupid things. Dishonest things. Shitty things.

"Another thing that has saved your ass," Andy continued, "is that Karen and Julie are so keen on doing this show that they have driven their fathers nuts. And the fact that I had such a brilliant idea"—he started to laugh for the first time that evening—"to double cast the part of *Anne Frank* with these two girls, one the daughter of an officer and the other of an enlisted man, even General Numbnuts had to admit it was just a perfect move.

"In fact, he thought it was just a brilliant move. I think if it hadn't happened you'd be on your way to some God-forsaken place. Even Vietnam would have been paradise in comparison."

"Well, your casting those two girls," I said, "I have to admit, was one of your most persuasive and as you say 'brilliant' ideas you've had lately. I always bow to superior intelligence."

The three of us laughed because we knew the truth. The tension was now less.

"OK, Greene, here's the deal," Andy continued. "I won't try to muzzle you. I think you do understand we have something much bigger going on here. Something you need to protect, and save from drowning, from being lost in a sea of prejudice and stupidity. You need to understand you're in the middle of it, that you're part of it. That you belong, that you're not just an outsider taking pot shots at an intolerable situation.

"General Numbnuts even knew about your sit-in escapade. Man, that was something else. And just to see those two young girls, but not just those two girls but to see the whole cast so much into what they are doing, giving you everything they got because they not only believe in you but you have convinced them to believe in themselves.

"To see how committed they are to really do their best, to show the world that some things are worth fighting for, especially against bigotry, racism, and especially here in this place.

"Man, standing up for what you taught them to believe is worth putting up with your nonsense. In fact, everybody else in the show has followed your lead. That this thing is happening in this godforsaken place is something else. I have never seen so many people rooting for somebody who probably doesn't deserve it, or at least seems to be so ignorant of what's at stake here.

"Greene, you are responsible for what comes out of this whole adventure. And it is an adventure. You can fuck it up or you can make it so that one day when you are sitting in an old rocking chair on some porch, telling your grandkids what you did in your hot-shot days they will be proud of you.

"And you will look back at what is now going on and wonder not only how you managed to survive but most importantly: How you conned the rest of us to follow you in your mad quest. But just keep one final thing clear in that crazy head of yours: Don't drive us over the cliff."

He got up and without further word walked back to his office. Turned the light off, locked the office, stopped, and looked back at Jackson and me still sitting on the stage.

"Good night, guys. See you tomorrow."

"Good night, Andy," Jackson said.

"Good night," I said. "And thank you . . ."

Andy stood a moment at the door not looking directly at us, and then he turned around and walked toward the exit door. Jackson and I turned all the lights off, locked the place, and walked out. It was a clear night and we could see some of the stars blinking away in the far distant sky.

"Do you want to grab a coke, or something?" I asked him.

"Sure."

We drove in silence. When we got to the drive-in, bought some drinks and we sat in the car.

"The last time I was here it was with Emily, the night before she left."

Jackson looked at me but did not respond immediately. He did not seem surprised.

"Why are you telling me this?" He asked after a long silence.

"I don't know. I have nothing to talk about, so why not?"

"Why not, indeed."

"You think that I'm a prick, don't you? You might as well say it. What the hell, tonight seems to be the night to dump on old Jonathan."

"What are you talking about?"

"Come on, man. You can say it. I can see it on your face. I see it on Cash's face."

"The brother and I have never talked about it. He doesn't want to. I don't want to. It's none of our business. You know, this may come as a surprise to you but we respect you and we love you, we loved Wilson, we love Emily. Under trying circumstances, people do strange things, say strange things, and it's not up to any of us to judge and come to conclusions that do not concern us. People should be free to make their own mistakes."

"Yeah, you're right. I'm not even sure it is my business."

"That's funny."

"What?"

"What you've just said."

And it was true. I had no idea what my life's business was. My whole life had not been the same since that night with Emily. Yet nothing had changed and everything had changed. It was almost as if I had been living in another time dimension.

It seemed like I had been sleepwalking. If someone were to ask me anything about these previous weeks, I was sure I would not be able to explain anything that would make sense. Why did it affect me so much? I mean Emily was just another piece of ass, right.

No, she was not. But what was she? What was I? And she was pregnant by another guy. Why did she have sex with me? Dear God, why?

"What did she say in that postcard she sent you?"

"Nothing."

"Why did you torch it, then?"

"Because I wanted to."

"Right. You wanted to. Right."

"I don't owe you any explanation."

He did not. I knew it. What did I want from him anyway? Some absolution? I looked at the lights, the cars, and the people in the drive-in. The place was not full. There were soldiers and civilians sitting in their cars talking, laughing, acting as if they had a whole life ahead of them, and in a much larger sense perhaps they had.

Except that Wilson was dead, and Emily was pregnant with his child. A child he probably never knew he was going to have. A child that would grow up always wondering who his father was, while I am sitting here with Jackson feeling like shit and trying to make sense of the whole thing.

"He was my friend, too, man," I said.

"I know."

"Emily and I did not betray him."

"I never said you had."

"Yeah, but why do I have this ugly feeling that you don't really believe it?"

"What the hell are you talking about?"

"What I just said."

"Oh, so now you're a mind reader?"

"I wish I knew that you believe that we didn't betray him."

"I believe it, you dumb jerk. Didn't you hear what I said? What's the matter with you, man? Are you deaf? Shee-it, you don't have to prove anything to me."

"I hope so, man, I hope so."

I wanted so badly to believe that Jackson was on my side. I did not want him to think of me or of Emily in a bad light, and especially of Emily.

"Why did he volunteer to go to Nam? Why?"

"Soldiers go to war."

"Yeah, but he didn't have to go, man. He didn't have to go. It wasn't his time. It should have been me. Nobody gives a shit whether I live or die, man."

"I do. Cash does. Julie does. Yoshi does. Andy does. Emily does. Shee-it, I bet even Sabrina does."

Sabrina . . . that was another time when innocence was sweet and the world was fine and not corrupted by pain, sadness, and things we did not understand. It was a world that was now dead.

"Yeah. But Emily, sweet Emily. You have no idea how deep she is in my soul, in my heart, in my being, in my guts. There isn't one single day, not one single moment, when I'm alone, that I don't think about her. How's she doing? What does she think? How's she feeling? How's she coping? What memories does she treasure?

"Does she even remember Wilson? What does she remember about him? His gentleness, his seriousness? How much he loved her? Does she hate herself for what she and I did that night? What can she expect out of life now? Is she ahead of life, or behind life? And what about the baby? Did Wilson know she was pregnant? Man, it's so stupid . . .it doesn't make sense."

"You'd better stop driving yourself crazy. It ain't no good."

"I can't help it. I wish I knew what was what. These past few weeks when I wasn't around here, I went over to her house and just sat in my car, waiting, and waiting. I've been like a stupid dog, just patiently waiting. And I have no idea why or what it is I'm waiting for."

I knew I was in deep shit. I did not want to be. I wanted to live a normal life, whatever in that meant. I was driving myself nuts. It was no good. I knew it.

"Do you think that Emily was just a slut?"

Jackson looked at me for a long time before answering. There was a sad look on his face.

"Come on, you know that's really screwed up. She is none of that. I think she's a very special person."

"Then, why did she do it? Why?"

"Jonathan, what she did, she did for you, you dumb jerk! That was the most unselfish thing she could have done. Don't you see it? I'm telling you. That's the absolute truth! You've got a lot to learn about people, man."

"Man, help me out. You're into that stuff. You once said something about saving souls."

"Emily was probably as honest as a person gets in such terrible circumstances. She was hurting pretty bad, yet she saw your pain and understood it. She understood it better than you, you dickhead.

"At that moment, the only thing she could do was to show you the ultimate essence of who she was, to share a human intimacy that few of us are lucky to see in our lifetimes. She gave you a gift that is beyond words and you can't see it because you are such a dumb asshole.

"It seems all the impact it had on you was that you had sex with her; yeah, just another piece of ass. I can't believe you, man. Boy, you're just a poor sorry son of a whore. Man, she is some fine broad. Maybe one of the last few great broads left on this earth."

"Then why doesn't she try to get in touch with me?"

"Shee-it. Have you tried getting in touch with her?"

"I can't"

"What do you mean you 'can't?' "

"Just like I said."

"Boy, you think you're so special. Maybe Andy was right in what he said about you tonight. Yeah, everyone has to bow down to his majesty, Jonathan Alexandre Greene. He's above everybody else. He's King Shit!"

"Get out of my face."

"I ain't in your face yet, but if you keep this up I'll be in your face and you won't like it."

Since we had known each other, I had never seen Jackson act this way. He was upset and I could see he was trying to keep his cool while I was acting like a real idiot. For a moment, I thought he was going to hit me.

"What's it to you anyway?"

"Look buster, Emily losing Wilson—that stupid jerk—is not something that you or I will ever understand. People deal with their pain in so many different ways. She saw you in a way that you could never see yourself. She saw beyond you.

"She is wise beyond her years, this girl. That makes her very special. Her dignity is beyond criticism. You have to respect her. I don't want you to be judging her in a bad way."

"I'm not. It's just that this thing is so screwed up. I wish I knew what was what."

"It ain't clear that's for sure. But don't you go judging her, that's all I've got to say to you."

It was always amazing to me the manner in which humans, all of us, regardless of sex or race end up caring for others simply because deep down in our heart of hearts we are all the same. No matter how cynical so many of us act, at the end of the day, we are all the same.

"I don't have her address. I don't even have her phone number."

"I do," he said quietly, letting his answer hang in midair and then slowly settle down. He was trying to avoid looking directly at me. It took a moment for me to realize that his response was big, huge; that something was about to happen that would change my life forever.

"Oh, you bastard. You double-crossing piece of garbage. Being a preacher's son ain't gonna to save your black ass. You're gonna go to hell for this."

"Well, like I told you once before, I'm sure I'll be in good company," and he started to laugh that wonderful and deep-sounding laugh that I had come to love and admire. And the tension was lowered considerably.

"You've been setting me up, haven't you?"

"I ain't set up jack."

"You have. You've known it all along. You son of a whore. I'm never going to trust your ass ever again."

"Cut the crap. Do you want her number or what?"

"Do I have any choice?"

"No."

He reached into his wallet, pulled out a small piece of paper and handed it to me. Her phone number and her address were listed. Her handwriting was neat, clear, delicate, a woman's handwriting. I held it and looked at it wanting to reach across such distance, such vastness, and such inexplicable human mystery.

He was looking at me and his smile was a smirk. I knew he was challenging me. He did not think I had it in me to make a decision to call her. Well, screw him. I was going to teach him a lesson he would never forget.

I opened the door of the car, walked into the drive-in, went to the public phone, and picked up the receiver. I had a few coins with me and put them in the box after the operator told me how much the long distance call would cost. I looked back at Jackson and he had an amusing smile on his face. The asshole thought I would not do it, but my hand was shaking.

I was of two minds now that I was doing it. On the one hand, I hoped that she would not answer the phone. On the other hand, I desperately wanted her to answer the phone. Boy, talk about stupid contradictions.

The phone rang several times, and finally her sleepy voice answered.

"Hello?"

"Emily?"

"Yes?"

"Emily," I swallowed very hard before continuing, "This is Jonathan."

"Jonathan, oh, my God. It's you!" There was no hesitation in her voice.

"Yes, it's me. I woke you up. I'm sorry."

"Never mind. Oh, Jonathan."

Her soft voice was wonderful to hear again. I tried to imagine her face and wanted in the most desperate way to be right next to her. The whole thing was completely crazy. If someone had said, a few minutes ago, that I was going to be talking to her, I would have told him he was insane.

"Emily, how are you?" My mouth was dry.

"Well, a few seconds ago I was just a ghost and now I'm not. But you, how are you? Where are you? Are you OK?"

"I have never felt better in my whole life."

But it was not true. I was having trouble breathing normally. I hoped she would not notice how my voice was trying not to give away the tremendous strain I was living through. My heart was racing at hundreds of miles an hour.

"I'm at the drive-in, remember?"

"Yes."

"I'm with Jackson. He gave me your phone number."

"Bless him."

"Are you sure I'm not bothering you?"

"Jonathan, please."

"I'm sorry. You're OK?"

"Yes, I feel fine, well, suddenly I'm better than fine. It's so wonderful to hear from you."

I was not sure if I should bring up that I knew she was pregnant. I mean, she had never told me. But there was really no reason to hide it any longer.

"How's the baby?"

"Oh, he's doing great. He's beginning to kick."

"So it's a boy?"

"Well, I don't know. I think it is a boy."

"Yeah, if the baby is kicking, it must be a boy."

"You think?"

"Absolutely. I'm sorry."

"Sorry, for what?"

"I should have called you sooner."

"Well, I know you're very busy with the play and stuff."

"How'd you know?"

"Jackson has kept me abreast."

"Oh, that bum. He never told me."

Once again, I was so very grateful to Jackson for seeing me through this ordeal. My man had class.

"Please, don't be angry with him. I made him promise not to say anything to you."

"Well, he didn't."

"He's the best."

"I know. I wanted to say so many things to you, and now that I'm talking to you I can't think of what they are."

And it was true. For many weeks, months, I had been having a crazy dialogue in my head. Selecting words, thoughts, ideas of the things I would say to her if I ever saw her again. But what I had not done, and thinking about it now seemed utterly ridiculous, was to make any plans to try to find her, or go see her, or even write to her. I was so completely out of it that such simple things had been out of my head totally. How stupid was that?

"Jonathan, it's fine. Don't worry about it. Just to hear your voice is enough for me."

Then the metallic voice of the operator intruded on our conversation asking me to deposit more money.

"Man, I don't have any more coins. I'll go get some more and call you back."

"No, give me the number and I'll call you back."

"Are you sure?"

"Yes."

I gave her the number, and in a minute or so the phone rang and we continued the conversation. She sounded just wonderful. Her voice was clear, with no sadness, no regrets. When the gods are on your side, are not pissed at you and, in fact, are giving you a break, everything is possible.

"I want to come and see you. Can I?"

"That would be just wonderful. Are you sure?"

"Emily, listen, I don't know what this nasty world has in store for me, for you, for anybody, but the one thing that I'm sure of is that I want to come and see you. I have some vacation coming up and as soon as the play ends I'm driving over, that is if you want me to."

"I want you to."

"That's just great. You don't mind?"

"Why should I mind?"

"I don't know. I don't want to cause you any trouble."

"Jonathan, it would be wonderful to see you, to listen to you, to have you around."

I could not believe that she had said that. There was no ambiguity in her voice. Not trying to be nice just for the sake of making conversation.

"Really?"

"Yes, please come."

"I will. I promise you."

"Thank you, I miss you, I miss all of you guys. I'm so grateful Jackson has kept me up to date with what's going on with all of you. I love the idea that you're doing the play. In fact, I read it a few weeks ago and I found it so incredibly moving, powerful. We need more stuff like that. I'm so proud that you stuck with it and that you are doing it."

"Yeah, I like doing it. Even Andy has gotten behind it. And now he tells me the powers that be running this base are also quite pleased with the project."

"Jonathan, I'm so happy for you."

"Emily, I wish I were there with you."

"Me too, but, look, in a few weeks we'll see each other so that isn't so bad, is it?"

"No, it is not. You're right."

What was happening to me? It felt so natural that I should be talking to her, making plans with her. And the other thing that also struck me was that I had no guilty feelings anymore. Was it supposed to be this way? How could it be otherwise? I had no idea why things had happened the way they did. And under another set of circumstances, perhaps I would have been more troubled by it.

But I was not any longer.

Wilson was a memory. Yes, an important memory to be sure. I wish what happened had not happened. It was an immense tragedy for everyone. But Emily's life was not over. Yes, it was true she was going to have his baby but even that was just another incident in the lives of people.

Babies are born every day.

"Are you still there?" She asked.

"Yes. I was just thinking. Have you changed a lot?"

"Well, I'm a bit bigger now. The doctor has told me that I things are on track. I feel fine. The baby is fine. I eat properly, exercise, rest, and make plans for me and my baby."

"Send me a photo. I want to see what you look like now."

"OK, I will."

"You promise?"

"Yes."

"Oh, Emily, there is so much I want to say."

"Really?"

"Yes."

"When you come you can talk to me all you want. There will be plenty of time."

"You're right. Look, I'd better let you go back to sleep, OK. Can I call you back anytime?"

"Jonathan, I expect that. I'm counting on it, now."

"You've got it."

"OK, give my love to Cash and Jackson. Tell Jackson he's the best!"

"I will. OK, bye. I love you . . ."

I was not sure if I should have said that.

"You're lovely, Jonathan. Don't forget me."

"I won't, I won't. You can take that to the bank!"

"Wonderful. Please, stay safe. Bye."

The line went dead. I held the phone to my ear for a moment with the sounds of her words still ringing in my head, my brain, my heart. I finally put the phone back and walked out to the car. Jackson was leaning against it. He was looking at me and there was a smile on his face. I could tell he was happy.

We exchanged high fives. I felt lighter, as if a great weight had been lifted off my shoulders, off my heart, off soul. And what was also clear in my head and in my heart was that I was not afraid anymore. I felt a sense of relief and it seemed that everything was possible.

This was a really strange feeling and so contradictory to my long held belief that not a single individual could make the difference. It seemed I was about to eat my words, but I did not care.

I had found her and that is all that mattered.

"I'm going to see her as soon as the play is over."

"Sounds good to me."

Then he did something that I had not expected. He pulled me toward him and hugged me. I hugged him back.

"Thank you, Jackson."

"You're welcome."

"A bit of happiness never hurt anybody."

"Amen to that."

I went around and got in the car. He got in after me. I did not want to move. I wanted this most magic moment to last forever.

"You're one hell of a man, preacher son. I owe you!"

"Glad to be of help."

"She sends you her love."

"She OK?"

"Yeah, she sounded wonderful. She said the baby is already kicking."

"Great."

"You saved my life, man. I'll never forget it. You think I can ask her to marry me?"

"Why not?"

"Maybe she won't want to."

"OK, there you go again with your negative attitude."

"Don't you think it's a little strange?"

"She's a widow. You're single. You're both young. Where is the problem?"

"Yes, but the circumstances under which we met. It's not like everyday stuff. I don't want to do anything to offend or to make her think that I don't care about her previous life. I mean, I knew Wilson and—"

"And what?"

"I don't know, man. I don't understand it. It's so strange."

"Listen, there is no formula in life. There is no code, no equation where we can plug in the numbers and have it spew us an answer."

And it was so true. We go around hoping to get our lives lined up properly and without too much fuss. We try to act, as if everything we do has a beginning, middle and an end. Sometimes the end comes at the beginning, the middle comes at the end, and the beginning never comes.

How does one get a good handle on life and its vicissitudes? Jackson said there was no formula and maybe there is not, except when we are made to suffer. Then it does appear, as if there is a formula that some demented and sick mind invented to make us go crazy, and to make us pay for things that are not our fault.

Had Emily, because of the terrible and tragic event in her young life, invented her own formula and now she knew what the deal was? I had so much to learn from her. But would she give me a chance to prove to her I was honest and willing to pair myself off with her, go out and fight our way to make our lives worth something, worthy of the child she was now carrying?

A child who, if she ever wanted me to be the father of, would unite us or pull us apart, depending on the choice we both made?

I thought back of our night together. At that moment, I felt that her pain and desire came from the need to understand her loneliness and despair. In my confused state, I had not been able to articulate any thoughts that might have made her understand something about me.

As human beings, our need for love and affection can be so overwhelming and all encompassing, especially when a dear person has been so violently taken away from us without warning, without pity, in such a brutal manner.

We all try to find a replacement even if such a replacement lasts for just a few hours. The incredible need to be given tenderness overcomes the harsh reality, because in so many instances the comfort we seek will not last more than a passing thought, and the aftermath is what gets us, for we are pushed back to face the darkness of our worst nightmares.

In a most primitive way, I understood Emily's feelings. But I also felt so inadequate to reciprocate the comfort she had given me. Our reaching out for love and tenderness knows no barriers when faced with a tragedy of the magnitude Emily had experienced. It was so cruel and implacable.

Yet Emily had done something incredibly complex; had overwhelmed me so completely that no matter how much I reflected on it, I would never be able to unravel its mystery even if I lived until the sun burned the earth into ashes. Jackson was so right.

What saves us from going insane in such situations?

What is the residue in our brains, our hearts, that composes itself, rearranges itself, in a different mode allowing us to wake up the next day and the day after, and continues to try to protect us from the pain dulling our senses until one day all we know is that the nightmare has now been replaced by a sad sense of distance, blurred, and almost impersonal? Yet it will never disappear and leave us alone.

Scars on our souls are never erased. Never! They remain etched, as are the remnants of the matter that made up our universe as it began. We still find such leftovers so many billions of years of time after the event took place. They are there. They never disappear.

Crazy thoughts were bound to start plaguing me; I could see it. But all seemed small compared to what I was now seriously contemplating doing. It was total insanity. But on the other hand, who is normal anyway? What is normal? I've yet to figure that out.

"OK, if she'll have me, I'm going to marry her."

"Go for it."

"You think she'll marry me?"

"Why not?"

"Can you marry us? I mean you're the preacher's son."

"I don't know if I can. I'll ask my dad."

"I feel like just taking off and driving over there right now."

"Well, on your way out, just drop me off at the barracks so I can get some shuteye."

"You don't want to come with me?"

"Nope. I ain't too keen on getting busted for going AWOL."

"You're a pussy, you know that. You're just some black, sorry ass, pussy. I thought you had more balls than that. I bet you Cash would have said: 'let's go.' "

"Screw you."

"Thank you Mr. Jackson."

"You're welcome Mr. Greene."

It felt good to be back with Jackson to where our friendship had always been. We drove back to the barracks and, as our luck would have it, there was a bed check round that night made by, of all the people, Cash. When he came by my bunk, I startled him by jumping on him and hugging him.

"Get out of here, what's wrong with you?"

"I love you, man," I said, and kissed him on the cheek.

"Stop acting crazy."

We were both whispering, as this was in the middle of the night and everyone was cutting the zzzs. Jackson was coming back from the latrine and Cash walked over to him and spoke in *sotto voce*.

"What's the matter with that fool?"

"Leave him alone. He's happy, that's all."

"What's there to be happy about?"

"Shee-it, this is big."

"What?"

"He's gonna ask Emily to marry him!"

"When did he talk to her?"

"Tonight."

"Tonight?"

"Yeah, he called her up."

"No shit? Are you serious?"

"That's what he did."

"That son of a whore. He finally saw the light. Well, I never thought he would do it."

"We was wrong little brother."

"Man, this calls for some serious hang over, don't you think?"

"You've got it."

Cash walked back to my bunk and, as I was just getting ready to hit the sack, he grabbed me and hugged me. Now, it was my turn to give him a hard time.

"What, are you crazy? What's the matter with you, you fool?"

"Hollywood, you ain't such a dumb jerk after all. There's still some hope for your sorry ass."

"Screw you."

"Thank you, Mr. Greene."

"You're welcome, Mr. McCall."

"Sweet dreams, Mr. Greene."

"Thank you, Mr. McCall."

I stood by my bunk, as he walked back to where Jackson was standing. They exchanged high fives and Cash walked out of the door. Jackson saluted me and we both hit our bunks. I felt light. It was true, some heavy weight had been lifted off my shoulders.

I stayed awake for a long time thinking of Emily and watching the moonlight through the window. Imagining that the moon was smiling down on us. Such sentiment brought me a great sense of comfort, until Mr. Sandman finally arrived and poured sand in my eyes.

-VII-

Julie had a great voice, and she also knew how to play the guitar. Someone had heard her sing at her church and had inquired about her singing for the officer's club in one of their weekend shows. They put on shows for the officers and their wives. She agreed, and Andy asked me if I would set up some lights for the show.

I agreed, except that at the last minute, they also asked for a spot light to be set up and someone had to work it. I told them I would do it. Not that I had much choice. When you are in the Army, you are on duty twenty-four hours a day.

Julie sang several songs and the audience was enthusiastic, very appreciative and gave her a nice, long, warm applause, especially after she finished singing a song by Pete Seeger: "*Where Have All the Flowers Gone.*"

I was rather surprised by the reaction of the audience. After all, the men were all Army officers but I was even more surprised by the fact that Julie had chosen to sing it.

The song was an anti-war song and Seeger had not been a favorite of the American government for his political criticisms not only regarding wars, but also for past government positions on many social issues he considered crucial in making American society more equitable and just.

After Julie finished the set, many people walked over, shook her hand, and complimented her on her voice and the songs she had performed.

She was beaming and pleased. After thanking me for the lights, she went outside. I took the lights down, and helped set up the dance floor. The music started, people paired off and started dancing.

I finished putting all of the material together, took it outside, and found Julie standing by the curb. For some reason I thought she had already left.

"Julie, do you have a ride home?"

"I called my mother, and I'm waiting for her to come pick me up."

"Do you want some company while you wait?"

"That would be nice."

I loaded the stuff in the back of the Army pick-up truck I had used that night. It was a warm night, and Julie in her pretty summer dress looked as angelic, innocent, and mysterious as any girl her age would look.

People always talk about Southern Belles being good looking, charming, and Julie was most definitely one of them. There was much going on within her.

Her eyes gave that away, but they also hid other things. We both stood by the truck while we waited. We were not standing close to each other but close enough that I was aware of her perfume. An awkward silence followed. I did not know if I should start a conversation. She glanced at me a couple of times and smiled.

"I think that I'm getting better with my lines."

"Yeah, I knew you would."

"I was talking to Mr. Catz the other day and he said that what happened in Germany could happen here. Is that true?"

"I don't know. I suppose it could."

"I would fight against it!"

She was serious. Her conviction was surprising but not totally. There is always hope for better things in the new generation.

"I'm sure the NAACP and the ACLU would be happy to hear you say that."

"What are they?"

"They're old institutions in this country that fight against terrible injustices done by some people to others who are different than they are."

"You know so much."

And there was both awe and approval in her voice. It humbled me that she would think I knew a lot more than I did. But it also told me how isolated and ignorant we can be about own country's historical events and legacy.

I wondered just how much of our political and social history was taught in schools in the South. I had read many negative things about the American South.

But I had also read about how simple and friendly people were in spite of my own personal negative experiences like the event that had taken place at the restaurant.

I had certainly witnessed nice and pleasant things during my stay in the South. Thus, not everything I saw was racist or stupid. Sometimes, it is hard not to make generalities about others.

Cash had told me after our escapade back in town that not every white person in the South was a racist. This surprised me at first but, upon further contemplation, I could see his attitude was a lot smarter than I had been willing to give him credit for.

In my original view, I had thought black people tended to look upon all whites with jaundiced eyes regarding their true sentiments about blacks.

"Coming from another part of the country, the impression we get is that everybody around here is a racist," I had said to him.

"Most of the time it's true. You ain't got no bigotry in California?"

"We do, but it's not so open."

"That's phony man. I'd rather have some racist scumbag be upfront about it so I know what's what."

"Maybe you are right."

"I'm right! See, if I knew you was racist, I know what to do. If you pretend in front of me that you're not, then behind my back you are, shee-it you're the worst kind of people there is."

"Would you like to live in another place and not in the South?"

"Why?"

My question took him by surprise. It was as if he never thought about it.

"I mean, why live where jerks, like you, will give me shit behind my back," and he started to cackle.

"You worthless piece of crap. How dare you say that to my face? I ought to slap you round your ears for not respecting your elders."

"Shee-it, you's a racist jerk. I seen your ass back in St. Louis with Sabrina. Only a racist a white trash would chase such mighty fine black poontang. Shee-it. Tell me, white boy, don't you want to go back to St. Louis and reclaim your throne?"

And he busted out laughing hard at his own joke.

"Cash, you're just a sore loser, you are. The best man won and you don't like it."

"The best man, shee-it. If I had wanted, I'd taken over that poontang and you'd have been left out in the cold, yeah, out in the cold. Man, I'd have beaten your ass down in no time flat."

"Shee-it. She told me she suspected your wanger wasn't big enough."

"Oh, you lousy jerk. I put my wanger up against anybody's wanger any time and them poontang would swoon over mine like over an ice cream cone, man, on a hot summer day."

"You're just a pervert, sick, jerk. Do you ever think about anything else besides poontang?"

"Shee-it, what else is there? Shee-it."

When it came to poontang, you could never win an argument against Cash as far as anyone was concerned. Our bantering was silly but, somehow, it allows us to laugh at the total stupidity of human behavior.

But in the South, bigotry had now become such an encrusted institution you could only wonder if there were rational minds left to make a difference, any difference, a better difference. I wondered how Julie dealt with this fact in her young life.

What I saw around me was so contradictory. I saw how white people held on to their social traditions. How family and church were important to them. And their sense of patriotism was very high, honored in a way that made them appear simplistic and unsophisticated.

If you were white, you would be charmed by their polite manners and the way they treated each other. Except, of course, if you were black, then everything changed and so many Southern whites when dealing with blacks turned ugly and uncaring.

At one time, I thought the whole thing had to do with their Southern accent. It was certainly different from what I grew up with. And there was a certain charm and warm quality to it.

I appreciated it because it was different, but it also drove me crazy because I had a hard time separating such an accent from the bigotry that in so many instances came with it.

I was always interested in accents because of my interest in languages. In a larger sense, my attitude was not realistic. I wanted things to get better so that we would have a better world. I tried like crazy to understand Southern culture.

And I must confess that in the final analysis, I found it perplexing and foreign. I wondered if Julie was above all of the racist nonsense. I could see it was not easy, as racism seemed to permeate many things around us.

"Julie, you say I know a lot," I said to her after her comment. "I'm not smarter or wiser. I'm a bit older than you, that's all. But still ignorant about so many things. For example, I don't know how to sing the way you do or play the guitar."

"It's easy to learn how to play. I can teach you if you want." And she gave me a shy smile.

"Thank you. By the time I figure out what to do my tour here will be over."

I could see that my words were having the opposite effect than the one I had meant.

"What's Los Angeles like?" she asked.

"Well, it's got lots of cars. Sometimes, I think the freeways are just parking lots going at sixty miles an hour. Also, the distances are vast from one neighborhood to the next. I joke that people need their cars just to go to the bathroom."

She smiled.

"Is it true that the sun shines all year around? That you have no winters to speak of? And people are kind of crazy?"

"All of the above."

"Will you go back to California?" Her voice was filled with melancholy and longing. Man, I thought, I really have to be careful here.

"Yes, that's my home."

She bit her lips and looked away from me. A long silence followed.

"Some great songs you sang tonight," I finally said.

"Thank you. They're my favorites."

"I love that song about long time passing. It's a lovely song."

"I chose it especially for tonight," she said.

"You know, this song has a kind of special meaning. The guy who wrote it, Pete Seeger, the government wasn't nice or kind to him at one time."

"What did he do?"

"Nothing really. He was just protesting what the government was doing. And they didn't like it. So they gave him a hard time. Did you know about that?"

"No, I didn't."

"Well, it is true."

"I like the song."

There was a long silence. Then, she started to sing it softly, just her sweet voice. I stood by her enthralled by what she was doing. At that moment, Julie and I were the same. We were sharing a magical moment of her making. There were no barriers and whatever she felt for me was fine, honest, and lovely.

The words seemed so sublime, floating around us and over us. Entering our hearts and souls, looking for what made us human and unique, for that which unites us in spite of the fact that we are constantly trying to separate ourselves from each other.

Searching for that which makes us alike, because we are so reluctant to show our emotions due to the fear we all carry inside like some cosmic sentence that has been handed down to all of us.

It seems to condemn us to suffer, and to dread that others will use it against us to make us feel unworthy of each other, and make us feel unwanted, not generous with our hearts. Afraid to show our vulnerabilities.

Julie's sweet and gentle voice gave me a feeling of peace and of longing. And I realized that in spite of the feelings I now understood Julie had for me, she was perhaps too young to see that what she was sharing with me, at that moment, was far more complex and just as mysterious as the vast sky above us filled with as many stars as there are grains of sand in the world's oceans.

She was sharing the infinite power of the human heart to demonstrate that there are moments of pure joy and honesty and we do not have to apologize for our most powerful and private sentiments.

That to be honest was as graceful as a simple hope. The words of the song, like a universal prayer, talked to us about things of the heart, about human emotions, about longings. I thought, once again, how terribly disconnected we are from each other.

If we could only get away from our pretenses, it would be a much better world. Less pain, less confusion, less animosity and more of the things that counted to put us in tune with what was important.

The words, softly sung by Julie, in the silence of the night around us, spoke of things of long time passing, of flowers, of young girls and young men.

But it also spoke of soldiers and graveyards now covered with flowers, asking us when we were going to learn some truth about who we were and realize that we are all the same. That the barriers we build are not worthy of us.

The fact that she had selected the song to be sung to a military audience was very intriguing, because half of the audience would one day be facing the same reality and truth in their lives that others had faced, where many of them would not be coming back. And where there would be more widows, orphans, pain, confusion, longing and regrets.

I thought of asking Julie why she had selected the song but, in the end, it would not have made any difference for whatever her reason was it should be left in her heart, I thought. In the final analysis, whether innocent or by design, it had been her own personal choice and one had to respect that.

The gentle words were quiet and, for that split second, I found myself letting my mind wonder about girls her age, and how they dealt with their feelings, with the conflicting reality of their worlds. With their budding sexuality and all of the confusion that comes with that. This, of course, was the 60s, when all of the taboos were being broken.

When the innocence of American society was beginning to come apart. When the most recent killing of a young president—Kennedy—had been a stark reminder that our world was changing, that it was never going to be the same.

When young women were claiming their rights to make their own decisions. When the social and sexual revolution was everywhere. And when the saying was: Don't trust anyone over thirty!

She finished singing the song. It had been a most magical moment, but it was also troubling because I now knew Julie did have strong feelings for me and it was impossible for me to reciprocate them in the way she wanted. How sweet and bitter the whole thing was.

"Julie, that was just wonderful. Lovely. Thank you for sharing that with me."

"I haven't finished the poem that I'm writing for you," she said, after a long silence.

"Oh, don't worry about it. I'm sure when you're ready you'll finish it and it will be great."

"I'm too young for you, aren't I?"

Her tone was sad, with a kind of longing to it. But her words also sounded like there was a final recognition of a truth that she was now fighting to accept. But her words also jolted me. I thought, oh, man, this is not what I want to get into, not here, not now, not with Julie.

"Julie, I don't understand." I was playing for time.

"Yes, you do."

"Julie, you know things at your age can be confusing."

"I'm not confused." She fell silent and I kept looking down the road hoping that her mother would show up.

"Can I tell you something?" she asked.

"Sure."

"You promise not to laugh."

"I promise."

"Jonathan, the best thing that has happened to me was to have met you. The next best thing was your choosing me for *Anne Frank*. You're right about confused feelings and stuff. But I'm certain of one thing: I'm in love with you!"

She saw my recoiling and my surprise. Boy, this was not what I expected. Her declaration so direct, and unambiguous. It was new territory for me and I was not sure how to navigate it. I thought I should say something but I did not know what to say.

"I know that it all sounds foolish and maybe arrogant," she continued. "It's the classic story of a young finicky girl who falls in love with a man and she holds onto her fantasy because it is the only thing she has. That's why I was telling you about my diary, why I don't want anybody to read what I write."

Oh, man, I thought. If she has written anything to do with me in that diary and her parents find out, I am in deep doo-doo. I knew that I had never done or said anything to encourage her. I had never made any advances and I had never been alone with her other than the night when we sat in the middle of the stage surrounded by bright lights and, of course, tonight.

Still, tongues can wag and all it would take is some incident, like me standing with her now, or if she decided to say something foolish or exaggerated, and I would be in trouble. Jesus, she was jailbait. I now regretted that I had asked her if I could keep her company until her mother came.

In fact, I was also thanking my lucky star that I had not suggested, as it had occurred to me earlier in the evening, to take her home. Boy, the gods were covering for me, I thought.

"You don't have to be afraid, please," she said plainly, and acutely aware of the situation that was not my fault. "I won't do anything foolish. Though I want to be with you, I know you'll reject me because I'm not old enough."

"Dear Julie, you have your whole life in front of you. I'm overwhelmed by what you have said. It's not wrong or dishonest to have strong feelings about others. I have been in that position myself.

"But I want to be sure you understand I admire and respect your honesty, but it is totally out of the question for me to have any kind of relationship with you, other than the one we now have."

"I know," she said. "I'm trying to make sure I don't make a fool of myself."

"You're not. I think it's so pure and wonderful that you have told me all of this. I'll always remember it."

"I would just like to ask you for one thing."

"Sure."

"I would like you to kiss me, just once."

"Julie. You're making it very tough on me, please."

"Just once."

"Julie, I can't."

"Or you don't want to."

"OK, it's both."

"That's what I thought."

"I'm sorry, Julie."

"Jonathan, do you think that I'm foolish?"

"No."

"I'm not. I don't want to be like girls who had strong feelings for a boy and never say anything."

"Julie, you are wonderful."

And I leaned over and kissed her on the cheek. She was surprised, and touched her cheek softly and held her hand there for a while.

"But if I'm wonderful, as you say, why do you reject me?"

"Julie, I am not. I know that in many instances for reasons we don't understand, we find ourselves developing strong emotions for other people. I don't know why or how it happens. It just happens. It's not wrong. It's not immoral. It's not silly. It's not limited to just one group of people. But I would like to think you understand that nothing can happen between us. It cannot be."

"Well, maybe when I'm older?"

Her face had a look of expectations and disappointment at the same time.

"You *are* beautiful, Julie."

And she was. And the madness of what was happening with her, her feelings for me, I did not for a moment doubt that they were true and real.

"Do I have any hope, then?"

"Julie, you overwhelm me. I cannot keep you from feeling whatever it is you are now feeling. But I cannot and I will not encourage those feelings. I just cannot. You know, I sometimes wish you and I had met in a different set of circumstances."

"Is that true?"

"Yes, it is, but that is not what we have today. So I don't wish to engage in things that aren't true."

"Well, you can't keep me from loving you."

"No, I cannot. But I want you to be clear that I'm in no way, shape or form suggesting or encouraging our relationship to be more than what it is."

"I know. I understand. When you are older, don't you have more control on what you can do?" she asked, quietly.

"Julie, being older isn't such a hot thing sometimes."

"Yes, but you get to do things that you want to do."

"Not always."

"I have a friend and she tells me she never wants to grow up. She wants to always remain a kid."

"What do you think?"

"No, I want to grow up so I can do what I want to do."

She smiled a wan smile and I hoped deeply that Julie would find some way of dealing with her most intense feelings. It was scary to have a beautiful, young girl express such sentiments for me. It had never happened before. Boy, the secrets of the human heart are as mysterious as our physical origins.

"Julie, can I ask you a question?"

"Yes, of course."

"Are you always this direct?"

"It's always best to be honest about things, don't you think?"

She was challenging me. Her eyes never left my face. I could see a hint of a smile, but not in a mean way. She was holding her ground, not afraid to express a simple truth. I started to laugh. Boy, I did deserve that one, I thought.

"You're, right," I said.

We stood right next to each other, separate from each other, yet also intimately involved with each other in a way that was hard to explain let alone understand. My feelings were not confused because I really had no romantic interest in Julie. And it was not because she was not a lovely girl—she was. Also incredibly innocent and yet as wise as only women are—much wiser than men.

This has always been a great source of wonder and curiosity. You can see this attitude in girls of all ages. They know more than we guys know. I thought whoever is the guy Julie selects, when the time comes, had better know the score otherwise she will eat his lunch. Just at that moment, we saw the headlights of her mother's car.

Julie's mother was a very attractive and charming woman who radiated openness and vivacity. She had always been nice to me. She got out of the car, came over, and we shook hands.

"How are you, Jonathan? How was it?"

"Great. I think Julie made some fans tonight. They were very pleased. I was proud and happy to have been there for the occasion."

"I'm sorry I missed it."

"You didn't miss anything, really. Jonathan is being too polite."

"Come on, you know you were good tonight. They loved you in there."

The earlier tension in Julie seemed to have disappeared. There was no hint of anything being amiss and I was grateful. I shook hands with both of them, got in the truck and drove away. I am not going to tell Cash or Jackson what happened tonight, I thought. They would have a field day and I would never live it down.

But I had to admit to myself that it had not been easy. I wondered what I would have done in another set of circumstances. If she had been older? Good question. I did not think that I would have crossed the line but I would also have to accept that it was tempting, oh, boy, pretty tempting.

Yet, for some reason, I also felt that Julie had come to terms, at least in the immediate future, with whatever ideas she had been harboring about me. There seemed to be an acceptance of the present facts. I hoped the incident that had taken place tonight would not happen again. I must be very careful, in the future, when dealing with this lovely girl.

A couple of days later, I came to rehearsal a few minutes early because Andy wanted to talk to me. He had called me earlier that day.

"So what's going on?"

"Before I tell you, you've got to promise me that you won't blow your stack."

He said it with a smile on his face so I did not think it was anything serious.

"I have a strange feeling you're setting me up for something, but OK, I promise."

"Last weekend at the Officer's Club, something happened that has some people kind of upset."

My first reaction was, oh, shit, Julie said something. Oh, man I hope not. I started thinking of things to say, trying to find some excuse, something for which I was not guilty. Some way of explaining that nothing happened. If Julie had said something regarding us, that night, it had been her imagination and nothing more.

However, much to my own relief, his next words clarified the situation and gave me a great of sense that some strange and heavy burden had been lifted off my shoulders.

"Apparently, some folks were put off by one of the songs that Julie sang."

My fears evaporated and I immediately knew what song Andy was talking about.

"Man, I don't believe it! Boy, talk about fascist pigs. It's unreal."

"Did you ask her to sing that song?"

"Andy, I would no more ask her to sing a song, any song, than ask you if you want to go bar hopping with me tonight looking for some girl who would be buck naked and ready to take us both on. Come on, who in the hell do they think they are?"

"OK, you promised not to lose your cool."

I now saw why Andy had made me promise not to lose my cool. And he was right; I was pissed.

"Have we lowered ourselves to this shitty level? Julie sang the songs of her choice. I had no idea what she was going to sing. I was as surprised as anyone that evening when she started singing that song. Later, when I asked her if she knew anything about the song's history, she knew nothing. The only thing she said was that she liked the song."

"I talked to her and she said the same thing."

"Oh, you're going behind my back to see if I'm playing it straight."

"Get out of here. You know better than that."

"Andy, what the hell is going on?"

"It's just a bunch of assholes that's all. Don't worry about it."

But I could see that he was sad about the whole thing. I thought that I really did not know very much about Andy personally. He had mentioned not being able to join the Army because he had a heart problem. And how he had dealt with all of the bigotry, and anti-Semitism that took place in Germany, and how some of his relatives did not make it.

I had never tried to connect with him personally because he always gave me the strong impression that he was not interested. Yet I could see on his face that this incident was not something that he took lightly.

"Listen, Andy, I knew nothing about Julie's choice of songs. I did tell her later what I know about the song, and who wrote it. I think it's a great song and Julie managed to do an incredible rendition of it. I know that people were quite taken by it.

"I mean, here was this young, lovely girl, singing with her sweet voice about girls, young men, flowers, soldiers and death. The crowd was hushed. I'm telling you. You could have heard a pin drop. She was great. They applauded very loudly. Lots of people went up to her afterward and praised her. Man, I don't believe that people can be so ignorant, callous."

"Strange world we live in, my friend."

"You said it. Is General Numbnuts going to bust Julie or me now?"

"Come on," he laughed. "It's a few soreheads who aren't happy about *Anne Frank* and maybe still sore about your article. But screw them!"

I could see that he was serious, but also sad.

"I don't think you are going to tell me who these people are, are you?"

"In your dreams."

"Come on, be a pal. Tell me who these assholes are."

"Forget it. The main thing is that it was Julie's choice, and if they have problems there isn't a damn thing they can do or say."

"Andy, I mean, this is Fort Bragg, the base for Special Forces. I would hate to see a squad of Green Berets in combat gear getting a jump on poor Julie on her way to school one morning. Gag her, bundle her up, throw her in the stockade, and accuse her of being subversive or, a communist, or worse anti-American."

"Oh, you'd love that wouldn't you?"

"Are they now going to ask you to hold hearings about whether Julie can remain in the play? Will they court martial me for working the lights on her show? In today's world, anybody who is not with the government's program is considered an enemy of these great United States. Shee-it."

"I knew you'd have a field day with this nonsense."

"You never know with these fascists pigs."

"OK, let's just forget this crap. I don't want to discuss it any further. I also would suggest, and it is only a suggestion, that you don't say anything to Julie. It is not worth it, OK?"

"What if she asks me?"

"You say nothing. I want your word."

"Come on, Andy."

"Do I have your word?"

"Why should I give you my word?"

"Because I trust you."

"Oh, you bastard, you really know how to hit below the belt, don't you? You really know how to put a guy down."

He had me by the short hairs. He knew it, and I knew it.

"Jonathan, do I have your word?"

"Do I have any choice?"

"No."

He smiled and yet I knew that he wasn't happy about the whole incident. He knew, and I knew, that neither one of us could do very much about idiots acting; well, like idiots.

-VIII-

Thus, one day, I eventually found myself driving to eastern Pennsylvania to meet Emily after *Anne Frank* was over. The play had been a grand success. We ran it for eight performances all together and every night the auditorium was packed. I couldn't believe it. Andy couldn't believe it! General Numbnuts couldn't believe it!

Both Karen and Julie were just superb. We alternated them for each show and some people told me that they came on two different nights so they could see the difference between the two girls. And did they find any difference? Yes, both girls brought something different to the part, but were just wonderful!

Because I had more affinity for Julie with the things that had happened between us, I thought her Anne Frank was purer, much closer to the truth as I imagined the real Anne Frank was. But that is not taking anything away from Karen.

Their individual interpretations had more to do with who they were as people and not because they had missed or misunderstood the sense of the play. The two girls were outstanding! Everyone in the cast knew it. And everyone was pleased to have worked with them.

Also most remarkable, and it was Andy who mentioned it to me after the shows were over, was that no one dared to applaud at first after the curtain closed. There was this silence, as if they had not liked anything about the show, had not understood it.

Then, slowly, very slowly, the applause started and built into a loud sound so when the cast came out for their curtain calls, the audience stood and gave them a standing ovation with cat calls and whistles. And it happened every night. When it happened after the first show, Andy was shocked.

"Jesus, these are GIs, I don't believe it!"

"Are you complaining?"

"No, it's just that human beings never cease to surprise me."

"Did the powers that be show up?"

"Sure did. In fact, the General . . ."

I stopped him. "You mean, Numbnuts?"

"Shut up, yeah, he showed up with the other general and . . ."

"The other general? What other general?"

"His wife," and Andy and I started laughing trying to keep a serious face as people were filing out of the theater looking at us, and perhaps wondering if we had taken leave of our senses.

"And she told me," Andy continued, "they were very proud of the whole effort and were happy we had decided to do the play."

"Did you tell her it was *her* husband who had thought of the idea?"

"Of course. Do you think I'm an idiot? I told her that her husband was responsible for the whole thing."

"Good for you. I see you're bucking for your first star."

"The son of a bitch really believed it had been 'his' idea. You could tell. His wife seemed quite pleased. She said: 'That's my Johnny for you.' I had to fight hard not to laugh. We can do whatever we want next."

"You think?"

"Bet your ass."

"OK, how about doing *Lysistrata* next totally in the nude?"

"Is that the Greek play where the women go on a sex strike because their men are always going off to war?"

"You've got it. It'll be a great show. You know, fun, entertaining, plenty of laughs, and very apropos. Just what the GIs need."

"Are you crazy?"

"Well, you said we can do anything."

"Let's not carried away, here, shall we?"

"Why not?"

"No, it's, it's too . . . antiwar." and he busted out laughing.

"Too antiwar? My ass. It'll be perfect. Think of all of those women running around; OK, not totally naked, but half-naked on the stage. The GIs would go ape shit."

"I'm sure they would."

"Was it not General Numbnuts who said that we should try to bring fun stuff to the GIs? Man, this is a perfect fit. Sex, jokes, music, the whole stage filled with dancing half-naked broads. *Lysistrata* will be just what these crazy GIs need. I'd bet you that you would not have trouble finding guys to come and work on the show. Cash would most definitely be the first guy to sign up."

"You *are* crazy."

"OK, not totally naked, how about wearing skimpy, see through stuff, you know, sheer negligées, still wearing their undies underneath, man that's got possibilities, don't you see it?"

"You want to get our asses busted, don't you?"

"Andy, you're no fun."

"Hey, let's be happy that we got ourselves a victory."

He was right. Life sometimes is made up of small victories. Staging *The Diary of Anne Frank* in KKK country was most definitely one of them.

I am sure Cash and Jackson would have gotten a kick out of knowing and would have approved that there are numbnuts Army generals, and then there are other generals—their wives who outrank them!

After the final performance, the cast, the crew, and families of the people in the show we all went to a local restaurant downtown for a cast party. I do not know if the people at the restaurant had been warned we had two black members—Cash and Jackson—in the group, but we did not run into any problems.

116

Maybe it was because Sanders the newspaper editor had joined us. Newspapers can give your joint bad publicity.

"Let's go sit at the counter and see," I said, to Cash and Jackson.

They gave me a dirty look and pushed me toward the back where the tables had been prepared for us. It was a great evening. But as these things go, there was also a sadness and emptiness because the show was over. The work had been done.

We had accomplished something. We were all proud of it. This would be our last night together, as a group, and tomorrow we would go back to our regular, dreary lives.

Julie kept looking at me with a sad smile, and I went to sit by her and held her hand. In fact, I did it because Karen was sitting right next to her so I sat between the two of them and held their hands.

"So how do you feel, both of you?"

"Lost," Julie answered.

"Sad," Karen said. "And you?"

"Me, too. It's always a letdown after you work so hard and spend time with people you didn't know a few weeks ago, and because of the effort they become your family and you don't want the thing to end."

"So when do we do the next show?" Julie asked, her hand holding mine very tightly.

"I don't know. You'll have to ask Andy."

"Will you direct it?"

"I don't know. I may not be around. Andy and I haven't talked about it. I know he wants to do a musical, but I don't know. He's the boss."

Sanders said that he was going to write an article in the paper about the play and tell people if they had not gone to see it, they had missed something unique and meaningful. I was grateful for that.

The only complaint, if it could be called a complaint, surprisingly enough, came from Karen.

"Jonathan, it's a shame Julie and I couldn't be on stage at the same time."

"Well, maybe in the next show."

Even Cash got into the festivities. He clinked his glass and stood. Everyone looked at him. I thought, oh, boy, I hope he does not say anything stupid. Jackson looked at him and then at me with kind of like the same sentiment.

"I just want to tell y'all that it was a great show. I especially liked Julie and Karen and what they did. You girls are somethin' else."

Everyone clapped. I was not surprised at such a reaction from Cash. But, in another sense, for Julie and Karen getting such a compliment from Cash whom they knew to be just a chauvinistic character par excellence, pleased them enormously. Both girls stood and bowed. The applause was long.

"Yeah, sure was a great experience for me, even if Jonathan was the director," Cash added. Everyone laughed and clapped.

Then Julie said, "I want you all to know that it was a wonderful experience for me, too. I never thought I would learn so much and I have. I want to thank all of you, especially Jonathan because he trusted me. And Karen and I have talked and we are never going to forget what happened here . . ."

"I will second that," Karen said.

She had tears in her eyes and both girls embraced each other. Julie's mother came over and also said thank you. She deeply regretted that her husband had not been able to attend as he was on some kind of official trip in Hawaii.

"It's a shame he missed Julie's performances. They were outstanding," I said.

"I know, but I also know that when I tell him what happened, he'll be very proud of her. I do appreciate what you've done for the girls and for our community. There are still things that need to be improved . . ."

We both understood the meaning behind her simple words. I saw a glimpse of where Julie got her strength of character. Her mother gave me a lovely smile. I further saw where Julie had gotten her great smile.

As I was driving these memories and others crowded my head. They brought me a sentiment of sweetness and calm, but now my immediate concern was what I was going to be facing in a few hours. I tried to imagine what I would end up with at the end of my trip to see Emily.

I had known her husband in real life. And as a result of that, and the fact that he had been killed, I ended up spending the night with her on the day when she had received the terrible news her husband was dead.

I mean, how bizarre was that? Even under the most benign interpretation of that fact it would not pass muster with what reasonable people took to be normal behavior by normal human beings. The whole thing was about as irrational as it got.

How could one justify it? What drives people to act in such strange ways? No matter how one looked at it, it was just not what the other Emily—Emily Post— had in mind and had written about as far as proper social behavior went.

In so many ways, it was beautiful and innocent and as pure as anything; nevertheless, in regular households what had happened between Emily and me would not be considered standard fare. Things of this nature happened to "other" people, not to people like her. I felt remorseful and lost about the whole experience; there was no getting around that.

I had been trying to ignore the guilty sentiments and had pushed them way back into my own consciousness. Now that I was on my way to meet Emily, and I presumed her family, those sentiments came back strong as hell and were overwhelming me.

Nothing in my supposed "life experiences" had prepared me for what had taken place or its aftermath. About the only thing that gave me comfort was that Emily had not once, during our phone conversations we had had in the last few weeks, said anything about the circumstances and the origin of our strange relationship.

There had been moments when we would come close to starting up a discussion about Wilson but we sort of danced around it. For my part, it was simple: Fear. I suspected that it was the same thing for her, though, in many other subtle ways, Emily was far more lucid and frank than I was.

I always feared that discussing it would open up all kinds of hidden secrets and painful memories, and I was not at all sure how I would handle them in a phone conversation. The better part of valor was to ignore it, and hope that when we met we would be able to deal with it in a more direct and honest way. At least, that was my hope.

During the trip, there were moments when I had to think hard and fast because the whole thing seemed just too crazy. I did not know anything about anything. The only thing I knew was that I had developed strong feelings for this woman. But those feelings had a certain fantasy to them, like a kid waiting for his birthday present.

He does not know what it is, except he will get one. What came through the phone lines when we talked was a symphony of tender words, of mysterious images, of overwhelming sentiments, soft whispers, that in the end revealed very little and did not explain anything.

In fact, what our conversations brought me was an incredible hunger for something solid, something that I could get my mind around. The whole thing was so ephemeral, so fleeting, it almost seemed like it never really happened. But, of course, it had.

It was what also gave me a great sense of contradiction, confusion, and loss, of things not balanced. Of things that sometimes made me feel as if chaos was the element now controlling and ruling our lives. Did we know what we were doing?

And what if it turned out that she would slam the door in my face? Was I tough enough to take it, to walk away from it and have no regrets simply because I had given it my best shot? It had now been nearly five months since I had last seen Emily.

So what would I find? A woman who had been put through an ordeal that was beyond belief. Through a personal tragedy that I could not really relate to no matter how much I wanted to.

What would the encounter in person bring? Would it be the same person I had been imagining, whom I had idealized these past few months? Someone pure, sweet, wonderful, willing to find something in me that I was pretending to have when, in fact, I was scared shitless.

Would I find a flesh and blood person, human, with faults, desires, feeling abandoned by life and by what it is supposed to be—beautiful and decent? Or it would just as well turn into a kind of strange minuet, where at the end of the evening she and I would bow, maybe even shake hands, say goodnight, and that it had been "nice" meeting each other.

Did I have that something special, that something unique that could, would, touch her and make her feel that it was possible to continue with life because there were still good things, decent things in store for her, for both of us? Things that may help ease her pain and allow her to once again feel loved, wanted, and needed?

Perhaps, give me hope that she saw and understood that I could love her as I had never loved anyone before. Love her in a way that Wilson had not loved her, because there had not been such a tragedy in their young lives to bring them so much closer together.

One thing I was certain of is that I would bring Wilson in no matter how hard it was going to be. Neither his memory nor his life with her could be ignored and pushed under the rug, to be dealt with later. Either she would bring it up or I would. I knew it.

We had to begin the process and also end it at the same time. The door had to be opened and closed. We could not ignore the truth of the whole thing, and, otherwise pretend that it had not happened because it had.

There was no way of getting around such a reality. Yet at the same time, I felt a sense of morbidity about the whole thing. If her family or friends knew what had happened between Emily and me, wow, how would they react when they finally met me? Had she said anything to them?

I did not think that people could be that liberal about such things. Even though I knew deep down in my guts that what happened that evening had not, as far as I was concerned, been planned or premeditated in any way, shape, or form.

It just happened. Before there was nothing, and suddenly a new universe had been born. A universe that now was real, that existed, and belonged not just to the two of us but to the baby she was carrying. I also had to assume that Emily had the same sentiments that I had.

To imagine that she had had some kind of secret physical attraction for me since we first met, and that she had put it aside until the time was right was just unthinkable.

The one thing I understood was that even though I had never been in such a position before, I had finally come to accept that whatever was going to happen, I could walk with my head high because I had not done anything wrong and neither had she. I wanted to make that clear to her.

Was I being some kind of Good Samaritan about this whole thing? It was not clear. I better put a stop to this nonsense, I thought. Yet, a nagging doubt had lately crept back into my head because of an incident that had taken place in my senior year of college.

I had taken a class in Greek Mythology, and the professor had asked that we all write a brief résumé and hand it in because he was looking for a teaching assistant. I did not give him a résumé. I was not interested and, furthermore, I did not think that I had what it took to become a T.A. I was working my ass off nearly forty hours a week while going to school full time and to add another obligation was not what I needed.

Thus, one late evening there was a loud knock on my door and when I opened it, there was Dr. Franck. I was surprised. He did not even say hello, he just barged in and stood in the middle of the room with a defiant look on his face, glaring at me.

"What the fuck do you mean not handing in the résumé that I asked for?"

Those were his exact words! For a moment, I did not know what to say. But in some instinctive way, more like pure human self-preservation, I understood I was in the eye of the storm and the only thing that could save me was to tell the truth.

"I'm not interested in doing that," I managed to answer, but not out of defiance. I was just overwhelmed by his visit and his words. I think he expected that. I got that sentiment from looking at his eyes.

"And why is that?"

"To tell you the truth, I'm very busy. I work full time. I'm more interested in using the small amount of free time I have at my disposal to either sleep or to go out and chase strange women. That's about it."

He looked at me and had a smirk on his face.

"You're an honest sob aren't you?"

"I don't know about being a sob, but I do like to think that I'm honest."

"I could flunk you, you know."

"Why, because I don't give you my résumé?"

"Yeah, and for being obnoxious."

I started to laugh and he started to laugh.

"Obnoxious, now that's kind of interesting. At least, I don't go around knocking on people's doors in the middle of the night and bust in uninvited and insult them. I was taught that one had to respect other people's homes. And wait to be invited to come in. Maybe my own upbringing left a great deal to be desired."

I found myself talking to Dr. Franck, my professor, a man with degrees up the ass, as if he were someone the same age as me.

"OK, you think you're so smart. I'll make it as plain as I can. You don't give me that résumé, you'll be the only person in my class who'll end up getting an F in the course."

"An F?"

"That's what I said. Everyone else in my course gets an A, except you."

"An F simply because I don't give you a résumé?"

"No, because it is an assignment and you refuse to turn it in."

"That sounds like blackmail to me."

"Call it what you will. I know you are graduating this year and an F is going to screw up your GPA."

Suddenly I got pissed. Here was this guy, my professor, who had barged into my apartment late at night threatening me with the worst grade one could get, in essence flunking me out of the course.

"OK, I'll turn this résumé in, and then I'll drop the class. I have enough credits to graduate without going through this nonsense."

121

"That's pretty stupid."

"Well, you do stupid things when you are dealing with stupid people."

"I won't let you drop the class."

"You can't keep me from dropping the class."

"Sure as hell can."

"You're full of it. I don't need your class. I don't want your class. I'm not looking for any aggravations in my life. My GPA will be fine without having to deal with this nonsense. You know what, I think you better leave before I really lose my cool and end up saying or doing something I will regret," and I walked to the door and opened it.

"Mr. tough guy. Greene, are you Jewish?"

"What's it to you?"

"Well, my grandmother on my mother's side was Jewish, and if there is one thing she hated the most was to see a lazy tribesman. Incompetence is not one of the seven deadly sins, but she couldn't stand it. I sort of got that from her, see what I'm saying?"

"So what does that make you: An anti-Semite?"

"Greene, you're good, but not as good as I am. Now grab your jacket, you are coming with me."

I started to laugh but he was serious. In fact, he walked over to the chair, got my jacket, threw it at me, and walked toward the door. I could not believe this guy. I thought, this man is nuts. Nevertheless, I put on my jacket and followed him.

"I've got something to show you," he said, by way of explanation.

When we got to his car, which was an old beat up Plymouth, he got in and even before I had time to close the door he was already moving. He drove to Santa Monica beach like a possessed man and he parked the car by the pier. We did not say a word; he just kept on whistling and humming the song *From Me to You*" by the Beatles.

After he parked, he got out, went to the trunk of the car and I could hear him fiddling around with something. I could not tell what it was because it was dark and the thing seemed strange and a bit bulky.

We walked in the sand toward the water. It was dark and I was just following him. I had no idea what he was carrying or what he intended to do. I sat on the sand while he seemed to be putting something on him, over his head and he kept adjusting it. I saw a thing that looked like it had rods sticking out in every which way. After I got used to the dark, I could see the thing shine with the reflection of the distant beach lights.

The next thing I heard were sounds, strange sounds and Jack was blowing on something that emitted these sounds. It gave me the impression that he was tuning an instrument making sure the thing was going to work. Then he started and it was a set of bagpipes! It was crazy.

As he continued playing, he started to march up and down playing the pipes while I was rolling in the sand laughing my head off. I finally got up and started marching behind him. It was insane. If anybody saw us that night they might have seen two guys—past midnight in Santa Monica beach—dark as hell, going around, marching, with the sounds of bagpipes filling the night air. The only things missing were kilts. It was quite an evening!

That was the beginning of a most rewarding and amazing friendship in my life. Jack Franck is one of the most remarkable human beings I have ever met, which translates as being one of the craziest people I had ever met. He was beyond being smart. He had an incredible personal history.

He held two Ph. Ds., one in Classic Greek History and the other in Comparative Religion. He was a Fulbright scholar who had gone to Denmark and had mastered Danish, a language of some difficulty. He was a man who devoured knowledge and wanted to share it with anybody he met.

When World War II started, he had enlisted in the Canadian Merchant Marines where he lied about his age—he was only seventeen years old—so he could be part of the war effort. He spent the next two years on ships in the north Atlantic ferrying cargo to Europe, zigzagging around, trying to get away from German U-boats

After that, he quit and joined the U. S. Marines and participated in the invasion of Iowa Jima. He had been afraid the war would be over by the time he was old enough to join the Marines. Thus in February of 1945, there was Jack, the ex-Merchant Marine, now recycled as a U.S. jarhead, landing on the beaches of Iowa Jima.

"But if you really want to know the truth, I joined the Merchant Marines in Canada because I had never seen the ocean and I wanted to see it. I figured that there was no way to miss seeing the ocean if I joined the Merchant Marines."

He came from Nebraska. He had so much to say and his degree of knowledge and sensitivity were exactly what students needed. He wanted to teach. He did not want to be a professor. He just wanted to be a teacher. That had been his long-term dream.

He had been married for several years, had two kids, but his *raison d'être* was to teach. He was very passionate about it, and it was this passion that contaminated me which was why I ended up becoming one of his two teaching assistants.

Jack was bright, erudite, liberal, loyal, obnoxious, well read, well-traveled, and a card-carrying member of the ACLU and the NAACP, the only two organizations worth anything according to him. He was vulgar, in private, as only an ex-Merchant Marine and jarhead can possibly be.

He was at ease with his students who simply adored him unlike the Faculty Wives Club, who hated him for his outspokenness for calling a spade a spade. Jack always wondered why they kept asking him to come back and present papers to the group on just about any subject that struck his fancy, and some that did not.

"I guess I'm the only stupid asshole who will go anywhere just so I can try teaching people something. I don't care what they say as long as they attend those lectures."

In our lives, there is always one teacher who makes all the difference in the world. One teacher who has guided us to what is important in our elusive search for insight, knowledge, self, wisdom, and understanding; well, Jack was that for me. His sense of irreverence was notorious, and he never stood on protocol. He had a large lascivious tattoo on his left shoulder that showed this Asian girl—Miranda.

"What does Mary,"—his wife—"say about it?" I asked him one day.

"I was eighteen years old when I got it. Didn't know my ass from nothing."

"Can you erase it?"

"Yeah, but first, I don't want to. And, second, I don't care for the pain it's going to bring me, plus the scars that are likely to result from its removal. As long as my old lady is fine with that, I'm OK. Besides, I think in Filipino Miranda may be Mary. Who knows and who cares? My kids think it's cool. There isn't any daddy among their friends' fathers who sports such a thing."

I worked hard in his class. The bastard had challenged me and I could not let him down. In fact, everyone in that class worked extra hard. He had told us that he would give an A at the end of the class to everyone except me, of course. We wanted Jack to be proud of us and we did everything to bring that about.

If students were lucky enough to run into a teacher like Jack many of the problems that we have about learning, about becoming good students, perhaps would become less of a burden.

I was always a bit afraid that he would still give me an F because I never turned in the résumé, but I got an A in the class. I would have killed him if he had given me an F because I really did work hard for that class of his.

I was thinking about him, as I drove to meet Emily, because through my having been his assistant I was once confronted with a situation, which though did not touch me personally; nevertheless, affected me for a long time.

Jack had asked me to read papers that the rest of the class had written as assignments. We had to write something that was important and very personal. He wanted me to sort of pre-grade the papers for him.

There was one paper, from a girl that sat in front of me, who became the subject of so many contradictory feelings in me at the time. She had written that she had had a one-night stand with some guy and, as a result, she was now pregnant.

She did not know how to tell the guy. She was afraid to tell him. She did not know him at all. She vividly described what she was now facing, how her life was going to change, and the fact that she was Catholic an abortion was not an option.

She would have to give up the baby. Her family would reject her. She had let them down. All of the sacrifices would come to nothing. But even if abortion were an option, she mused about what it would be like to have it done with a coat hanger in some back alley in Tijuana.

What she revealed in the paper was so pure and without ambiguity. She knew exactly what was in store for her. Her narrative was incredibly moving. Her lucidity was so overwhelming that for days I went around feeling that it was within my power to rectify the situation.

That the only way was for me to tell her I knew what was going on, that I would marry her, and make everything right. I held to that notion for a long time until I realized that I was trapped in a situation that was just too crazy.

My idea of reality had now become my sense of fantasy. My wanting to, somehow, rectify this girl's plight was nothing more than sheer stupidity. Even if my sentiments were noble—and they were—the simple reality was beyond any cure I could or would present to her.

On the one hand, I could not reveal I knew her secret because I had no right to know. On the other hand, because I knew her secret I wanted to believe I was in a position to help her when, in fact, I could no more help her than I could change my sex overnight. It was a losing proposition.

It was just this crazy, romantic notion that I could somehow make everything right for her. It never occurred to me that even if I had asked her, she would not have accepted my offer to marry her knowing I was doing it because I felt sorry for her. She would have seen that I was not honest.

Jack and I discussed the paper and the girl's plight, and I told him the crazy ideas in my head but he never encouraged nor discouraged me about doing anything. He felt powerless as much as I did. He finally told me that he had referred her to the school's medical counselor.

As I drove to see Emily, the whole set of memories came back to me, and I realized that no matter how badly you want to change the world, to try to make it a better place, the simple truth is that good intentions are just that, good intentions. I never attempted to do anything about the girl. Often times, I have wondered what happened to her.

The simple fact of the matter was that I was in no position to make any difference. No matter how honest you want to be about things, sometimes it is just not possible to be honest and hope to make things right. Life does not seem to work out that way.

I had called Jack before I left to see Emily and told him all about her and what had taken place and, after listening to me, he laughed as he heard my tale of woes.

"Jonathan, you're just a crazy sob. How do you get involved with these things? You wanted to save that girl in my class, remember? Are you some kind of missionary or what?"

"Man, I don't know. I can't figure this out."

"Do you love Emily?"

"I think I do. I've never had such strong feelings about any other girl."

"Then, act on your feelings."

"It's not so easy. This whole thing is too crazy, even for me."

"What's so crazy about it? You met this girl, you had a brief affair with her, and now you want to take it to the next level. Whatever happened in her past or your past is beside the point. Your deal is in the present, old buddy. Her old man is history. You want her, you go find her.

"You square things away with her. If she wants you, she'll let you know instantly. If she doesn't, you'll know without asking her. Your buddies are right. Come on, you don't need an old fart like me to tell you what do to."

"I'm not asking you for that. It's just that I'm scared. I may end up being a father and I know nothing about that. That scares me to no end."

"What are you worried about? That you won't know how to change diapers? I thought the Army taught you that," he laughed at his own joke.

"Come on, Jack, you know what I'm talking about."

"I know what you're feeling and there is nothing wrong with having all of these crazy thoughts."

"I'm scared she'll throw me out of her house. And I'm scared that she'll say yes. How screwed up can that be?"

"If you're scared it's good. That means your senses are up, old buddy. You're controlling your destiny. Listen, when I first thought of getting married, I was scared shitless, too. I mean, I had dashed through German U-boats in the middle of the Atlantic totally convinced that I was going to get it. I had dodged Japanese bullets coming at me with such deadly and terrifying intent looking to kill poor Mrs. Franck's baby.

"I had seen the worse that humans can do to other humans. I thought I was tough, but those things did not prepare me for anything. Let me tell you those experiences failed me miserably when the time came and I asked Mary to marry me. Man, it was something else. I couldn't believe that it would freak me out, but it did."

"What about Mary?"

"Nothing. Women know this shit, man. She let me go through the ordeal and sat there like some Mona Lisa with that damn grin on her face, that Leonardo captured so incredibly well, while I'm shaking in my boots. We men are the innocent assholes in this world, certainly when it comes to women. They control the outcome. You love Emily, you go find her and do whatever you have to do. You're making it complicated. It's simple."

"Maybe to you it is."

"Listen, what Emily did was uncorrupted! We can never imagine that some people are blessed with such wholesomeness, such grace, such innocence because it's almost inhuman and when it happens, it scares the hell out of us. We're not prepared for such acts of the heart. Life should always be this basic and innocent. It should be filled with magic and beauty!

"The heart should never be used other than to love. You're at a great disadvantage because you're thinking in terms of reason and endings; in our existence, we want to be rational. She didn't do that. And life very often ain't rational. You've got to understand that what she did, she did in a most primitive, human and beautiful level—pure.

"She went far deeper within her than any of us ever gets a chance to do in our entire lives. It doesn't get any better. You're some lucky bastard but you don't even know it. You've got to take the leap, man. You had better not lose her! Emily not only told you to listen to your heart, she showed you how.

"My friend, you could live until the universe disappears and the chance of it happening again is almost nonexistent. It could, but I doubt it. The problem with so many of us humans is that we don't listen to our hearts; we don't trust. Jonathan, just listen to your heart and trust."

Listen to my heart and trust. How does one do that?

This is crazy, I thought. I am going to meet a girl who for all practical purposes is a total stranger to me. I had not courted her, spent time getting to know her, had not ever intended or desired to have any interest in her. Yet through some strange twist of life, I ended up spending a night with her; a night that over time had taken on a significance that even I could not understand completely.

It was if as I had fallen in love with a ghost. I knew very little about Emily. I certainly knew nothing about her family, who she was, really. I had come to know her not because of any particular interest, but because she was married to a guy who had been a fellow soldier and to whom I had become a friend.

The whole thing did not seem to make any sense at all. I had never had this kind of experience, any kind of experience I could relate to. I was on my way to meet someone who had become real not through my direct interaction with her, but through what I had imagined.

What about her? What did she expect from me? What was she hoping to find in me? Would she accept what had happened without any further thought as to how it had come about? What were her plans? Her thoughts? But most importantly, her feelings about me? Did she have any regrets, or was she ashamed for herself, and maybe too embarrassed to tell me on the phone?

Was I forcing something on her, on me, on both of us, something that would be better left alone? The last thing I wanted was to create illusions for both of us about each other. We had some reality that we had to deal with and it sure as hell was damn confusing.

As the peaceful countryside streamed by me, I tried to find some comfort in accepting that there are so many things in life we do not understand. My lack of experience was too scary. Yet, through the many phone conversations that Emily and I had these past few weeks, there was a growing awareness on my part, at least, of a strange feeling of love that I did not know I could have for her.

When I thought of my feelings for Pamela, my ex-girlfriend, which had been strong and true, they paled in comparison to what I was now feeling about Emily.

Man, I thought, I wish I could have talked to Jack longer. He had been a big help when I had talked to him. He had said to trust my heart. I was not used to such ideas. I always prided myself on being a rational person when it came to matters of the heart.

But the fact was rather simple: I had become absorbed in my relationship with Emily these past months, though there was really no normal relationship between us. Had Jackson more or less pushed me to do it?

No, he had not pushed me, really. He just happened to be the bridge, which I needed to cross. Come on, Jonathan, that is a poor excuse, I thought. You wanted to talk to her. You had been thinking about her.

She had become one of the most powerful elements in your whole existence. Admit it. For a reason that you did not really understand, you had managed to ignore some very powerful feelings in your heart for this lovely woman.

You had pushed those sentiments way down, tried to ignore them, and dismissed them as if that was really possible. You knew what the score was. Cash and Jackson, knew it.

You had been dancing around this idea as if the reality of it all was not so obvious to you. Man, do I not have the right to question my own feelings? Am I doing the right thing? Should I, point blank, ask her as soon as I get there just what her position was?

That way if no reciprocity existed, like civilized people, we would present our excuses, accept that there had been a misunderstanding, and quietly without histrionics say good-bye, good luck, and leave trying to keep the dignity of both parties from being destroyed.

But what if she felt about me the same way I felt about her? Then, there is no problem is there? And then the issue of the baby? Was I ready to become a father, a father to another man's child? Was that OK? Could I handle it? Would I handle it?

Parenthood was not something that had occurred to me before. I sure as hell did not know anything about it. I laughed remembering what Jack had said about changing diapers.

Did I have a big heart? Man, nothing is easy anymore. Jackson thought that I was making it more difficult than it was.

"If you love her and she loves you, you marry her and accept whatever baggage she brings with her, and that's it."

"But how can she love me, man? I mean, what happened between us was due to what she was going through."

"You don't think that she has had true feelings for you since then? You think she's been faking it?"

Jackson, as is his usual bent, had come to the crux of the matter without ambiguity. But I did not have an answer for him.

"Man, I don't know what to think. Sometimes, I feel like an idiot when I think about it because when I think about it, it doesn't appear normal."

"So, what's normal?"

"You know, like what happens to everybody else."

"And what happens to everybody else?"

"Come on, you know what I'm talking about."

"No, I don't know what you're talking about."

"Man, you just want to give me hard time."

"No, I'm not. I'm asking you what you mean by 'normal?' "

"So you think it is 'normal' that I spent one night with her, a night that was filled with pain and more pain, confusion, despair and God knows what else. Was I being a jerk who took advantage of her suffering? And, somehow, that makes it right.

"So, that now I can go to her and say: 'OK, babe, no problem, marry me and we'll be fine and whatever happened before forget about it, and let's just go out and continue with a new life and everything will be hunky-dory.' Shee-it."

"See, what you're looking for is some kind of specific thing, a kind of cast, like some well-manufactured gizmo where everything is well designed, well thought out, no sharp edges, or rough surfaces, where the texture is as smooth as silk, where nothing is out of line. Yeah, you're looking for an assembly-line feeling. As if the heart is some machine programmed to mathematically feel in a certain way."

"Come on, that's not what I'm talking about."

"Greene, I don't think you know what you're talking about."

"You're right. I don't know. I'm just trying to figure things out."

"You know what, you're afraid this thing is getting out of hand and you have no control over it. Well, guess what, there ain't no way that one can control certain things in life. And you'd better get used to it."

"Man, I think you're right. I'm scared. And I don't want to pretend that I'm not. I try to imagine just what I'm supposed to be for Emily and it's all in a kind of fog. I don't have clarity in this thing.

"And I'm afraid it's all in our heads, that there is this veil over our eyes because the reality of where we are and who we are just don't match."

"Shee-it, if there was someone who in this whole friggin' world can make something as simple as falling in love as complicated as the theory of relativity, you're the perfect asshole to do it."

"So how can I make it simple?"

"You can't. You sound like this is a mathematical formula, you know one plus one makes two. Well, guess what, when it comes to the affairs of the heart, one plus one does not necessarily make it two."

"See, it ain't simple."

"It's not that it isn't complicated. It is, but you have to deal with it. If you are looking for easy answers, I suggest that you take up basket weaving and stop this nonsense of torturing yourself.

"Either she is going to tell you that she digs you and wants to be with you and you are cool with that and that you dig her also, or she'll tell you to get lost. So you'll just have to forget about the whole thing, lick your wounds, and go back to St. Louis and Sabrina."

"Oh, you bastard, you would have to bring that up."

"Shee-it," and Jackson started to laugh out loud, "Hollywood, stop acting like a dummy and go find Emily and try to start living a normal life, whatever in the hell that means. And stop bugging me with your nonsense."

So here I am on my way to try to build a "normal life" with absolutely no idea what that means. Screw Jackson, he thinks he knows everything.

-IX-

Emily and I we were sitting on a swing in the small backyard looking toward the hills late in the evening, quiet, peaceful, the lights in the house off and we could see the distant stars in the sky. The night shadows loomed large and distorted our surroundings.

"Do you want to talk about Homer?" I asked her.

"Why?"

"It feels like we should talk about him."

"He was my love since I was a small girl living not far from his house. In many ways, it was so simple and natural we would end up getting married. I have no regrets. We both knew going into the Army at this time was dangerous. But he loved the Army. I know now that wives of military guys are the ones left behind to deal with the aftermath if something goes wrong.

"When he told me that he had volunteered to go to Vietnam, I was upset, and I was scared, so scared. Not that I would have interfered with what he wanted to do, what he saw as his duty. Do I hate the Army for what has happened to him, to me, to the baby? I don't hate it, though to be honest with you there have been many long nights when my anger boiled over and I was desperate for something, some kind of revenge, perhaps . . .

"But I'm also a rational person. I know there are many secrets around me, in my life, that I won't ever know. All I know now is that he'll always be part of my life, how can he not be when I'm carrying his child? But my life as it was is over. There is nothing I can do to make it the way it was. Even if I wished it with all of my being, it isn't going to happen.

"You may think that makes me hard and uncaring, but it isn't so. I want to live my life to the fullest. I want to see things. I want to experience things. I want to love again. I want to be loved. I have no desire to stop and spend the rest of my days stuck with longings and regrets. No, that's not what I want, that's not what I need."

Even though it was dark, I could see her eyes and they were bright, open and looking directly at me. Her tone was soft but lucid; her words were simple and direct.

"You suddenly appeared and that was that," she continued. "You became part of my life and I have no idea why. I'm not interested in finding out why because there is no sane explanation for it. I could elaborate on it, but there is no reason. I accept it because I believe it was meant to be. Don't ask me why I think that, except that it is."

"Do you have any regrets?"

131

She did not answer immediately. At that moment, I finally realized it was obvious that the whole experience had affected her in pretty much the same way it had affected me. Neither of us really understood why, but there was a kind of comfort in such mystery.

"I thought about it, but I have no regrets. Do you?"

"No."

"I refuse to let what happened to Homer drag me down for the rest of my life. Does that mean that I have not suffered, that I won't suffer in the future because of what happened? No, it doesn't. My kid brother, Billy, said to me the other day that both my pain and suffering can't be dismissed lightly.

"But, by the same token, I shouldn't stuff myself in the house, lock the door, wither away, and not go out to look at the stars the way I'm doing now with you. He's right. I wish I understood why things happen but I don't, and the only choice I have is to try to live as honorably as I can and as fully as I can."

Her words were expressed not with a sense of bitterness or longing, but were the words of someone who has looked at the abyss and had to make a choice. We had been talking for a while. Earlier, she had prepared dinner for us, and after it was over I had helped her wash the dishes.

The little house where she was living had a nice garden filled with flowers, which I did not know as I had stopped at a flower shop on my way in, and had bought a bunch of roses.

When she saw me arrive with the flowers, she got a wonderful smile on her lovely face. And she looked beautiful. Her apple cheeks radiating health and well-being, perhaps indicating how nature works when a woman is on her way to becoming a mother.

Her pregnancy was now showing and she seemed to radiate that mysterious look that pregnant women get. They in essence carry the secret of life and, in many instances, nature does seem to favor some women far more than others. Nature had not failed Emily.

"Thank you for the flowers, it was very lovely of you."

She kissed me on the cheek. I wanted to kiss her on the lips but I held back. I do not know if she would have refused, but I thought best to remain on my best behavior.

We had been talking for a while, sitting on the swing. I told her about my family. About Pamela, about Los Angeles, about my studies, about how I dreamed of one day going to live in Paris. She thought it was a wonderful idea. About my Army experiences.

About my friend Jack, the professor, and about what he said when I called him to tell him about her. I also told her about the girl, in the class who was pregnant, and how I had wrestled with trying to find a way to help her.

"I sometimes wonder what became of her. The only hope I have is that she found some honorable way to deal with what happened to her. That she didn't lose her human dignity."

"Do you feel guilty about not helping her?"

"Yes and no."

"Jonathan, so many things that happen in life, as you know, have absolutely no logical reason. They just happen. The only thing one can say is that we have no other choice but to continue with life. I hope this girl did find some way to continue with her own life. And I think that your sentiments were noble and just. But you can't feel guilty about not being able to help her."

"I know. Look, I told you that story because it's part of my past. Sometimes, I feel like I should have done something about it. But I do understand there was no other outcome."

"So many things are hidden from us. These past few months, I've come to the simple conclusion that life is now, immediate, and we have no other choice but to make the best of it. I know it sounds trite, but it's also the simplest truth," she said.

"Emily, you're wonderful."

"I don't feel wonderful sometimes, but thank you for saying it."

Then I told her about the play, about Julie, of her feelings for me, and the fact that Julie had told me she was writing a poem for me. Emily said, she understood those feelings, and had been moved by what this lovely and wonderful young girl had said to me back in Fort Bragg.

"I would like to meet her. She sounds like a lovely person," Emily said.

"She is. Maybe one day you will."

Then we talked about Cash and Jackson who had sent her their love and best wishes.

The night before I left Bragg, the three of us had gotten together to talk. We were sitting in my car and listening to the radio. It was playing a Beatles song. We were all crazy about their music, though Cash understood better the whole, crazy Beatle mania than Jackson and me.

"Man, these cats know their stuff. Amazing when you think they're white, and some whites don't know jack about music. Maybe it's because they're English."

"You're such a racist."

"Shee-it, the truth is the truth."

"So, now only the black brothers know how to make music. Shee-it, get out of here."

Cash always got a kick out of giving me a hard time. He did it just to be ornery. I guessed that in many ways his whole existence had been such a bummer that he would always suspect the white man was a worthless piece of garbage. Who could blame him?

And whenever he could, he would pull his nonsense on me. Since I was the only white guy around whom he seemed to trust, he could say anything he wanted because I would not judge him. But I gave him as good as I got.

"Hollywood, tell Emily that I want to be the baby's godfather," Cash had said.

"Forget it, man. You become this kid's godfather and poor Emily will end up with a kid who will be a gangster because you will teach him to drive like hell and he'll get busted for speeding, and who knows for what else."

"No, he won't. Shee-it, he'll have the best godfather money can buy."

"Yes, he will because I'm gonna ask her to make me the kid's godfather," Jackson said.

"Oh, Christ," I said, "the two biggest con artists this side of the Mississippi, boy, how lucky can this kid get?"

"You'd better make sure it's gonna be me," Cash said.

"Man, it's not my kid. She'll decide."

"He'll be your kid, won't he?"

"I haven't even asked her to marry me and you're already figuring out that I can order her to do what I want about her kid."

"Well, don't expect me to be nice and come help you with your plays unless you promise you'll put in the strongest word for me, OK?" Cash said.

"You do that," Jackson said, "and I gonna go tell Murray," the new company clerk, "to screw up your Army records."

"You guys are something else. Why don't you flip for it?"

"No, that ain't decent," Cash said.

"I'll tell her what you both have said and that's all, but I'll also tell her I don't favor anybody. It's up to her."

"You know something," Cash said, suddenly his voice going from relaxed to a worried tone, serious, too serious in my view.

"What?" Jackson asked.

"What if she says no to Hollywood? Then what?"

We all looked at each other and, for moment, the thought of something that we had not contemplated was front and center. Nobody, least of all me, had ever considered it. Man, it was a most distinct possibility. We all fell silent.

"No, she won't," Jackson said, after a while. But this time there was a sort of doubt in his voice.

"I think you're right, Cash," I said, thinking of another reality that had suddenly become part of our existence.

"Yeah," Cash said. "I mean, what if she's found some other guy in the meantime? I mean here's this pretty lady, alone, dealing with her tragedy, with a baby on the way. Who does she turn to? And you, Jonathan, ain't around, so what does she do?"

"You know what," Jackson said, "for once the brother is making sense. Shee-it."

The very wonderful scenario we had been discussing, with such free and wonderful sentiments, had suddenly crashed with Cash's words and got all three of us silent and depressed. All along, it had been me and these two guys talking about something we had taken for granted.

It had never occurred to us that Emily could have her own ideas, because in a much larger sense we had not considered that in the final analysis it is always the woman who makes the final decision.

I had not expressed directly to Emily any idea of what I had in mind regarding our relationship, which was for all practical purposes non-existent. The only thing she knew was that I was coming to visit her.

In the fog and emotion of this whole ordeal, it was the one thing that I should have thought about but I had not.

"What you gonna do if she says no?" Cash asked.

"Oh, man. What can I do?"

"It's your fault," Cash said, and suddenly he was mad at me.

"Come on, man, what did I do?"

"That's the problem. You did jack! You sat on your ass and did nothing."

I could tell by the sound of his voice that he knew he was getting very close to something that was incredibly touchy, and was not sure how to deal with it any more than I did. Jackson had remained silent with his head down.

"Shee-it, brother," Jackson finally said, "no sense in getting on Hollywood's case."

"Man, you should've said somethin'. Maybe just a hint, or somethin'," Cash said.

"What was I supposed to tell her?"

"How you felt. Come on, man, shee-it."

"I was thinking that it would be better if I told her in person."

It suddenly occurred to me that this whole situation was completely irrational and stupid and that Cash was right. In a flash, I saw how unrealistic my whole life had become. There was no way that I could make this thing work. My expectations were way out of line, really off the wall.

Who in the hell did I think I was? No matter how I wanted to look at it, the simple fact of the matter was that I was counting my chickens before they hatched. And that usually brings terrible pains to those who practice such behavior.

"You know what, I'll just forget the whole thing," and at that moment I meant it.

My voice had suddenly gotten cold, distant, and I felt the overwhelming sense of my own personal failure. I thought, why should I go just to be told, thanks, but no thanks? Cash and Jackson were surprised at my reaction. All of my ideas and thoughts up to then had never factored that Emily had a life of her own.

That I was only a cog in the wheel of her life in which she had to make decisions for herself, her baby, and that I did not figure in such decisions because I was not part of her life.

Yes, I had been thinking of nothing but her these past weeks, but in the final analysis the whole thing was a crazy, romantic quest that had no basis. I should have known better.

It was all in my head. And like any romantic notions that we invent and hang on to, they risk not becoming serious or lasting. It is the mind playing games.

Actually, it is us humans playing games with our own minds. It suddenly came to me that in many ways my love, infatuation, hunger, for Emily were based on a memory of my having spent a night with her, and the phone calls I had made since I had gotten in touch with her.

This is screwed up, I thought. How silly life is. Here I am panting after a lovely woman, who was not my woman, a woman whom I had idealized for so long partly out of guilt and partly out of a very strong emotion that she had evoked in my heart.

It did not escape me that Julie had also strong feelings for me and I had turned her down. At least Julie had taken my rejection with dignity and honesty. Would I react the same way if Emily said no to what I wanted to propose to her?

"Greene, you're good at this crap you know," Cash said. "It's your own goddamn fault and now you don't want to go through with it, you won't fight for her. You're a worthless piece of human scum, that's what you are."

He was mad and, in a larger sense, I knew he was right. I had screwed up. Cash always told it like it was. I could not get mad at him. Jackson was not happy either.

"Come on, Cash," Jackson said.

"No, man, he's right," I said, "I screwed up!."

"So, that's it then?" Now it was Jackson's turn to get upset with me. "After all of this you want to walk away from it? Man, I don't believe you," I could tell he was pissed. "Maybe the brother is right, and you're a worthless piece of human scum—a loser."

"Maybe I am."

"So, you're not gonna go through with it?" Cash was pissed, too. "You're gonna walk away from this. I don't believe it. Are you gonna even call her? And if you do, what you gonna say? Excuse me, Emily. You're not worthy enough for me to come and see you. See, all of this time, all of the phone calls I made to you were just a game.

"All my jive meant nothing. Good luck to you. I hope you find some other guy and I hope you have a great life because I'm too chicken shit to at least come and tell you to your face how I feel about you."

Cash was mad. I had never heard him so pissed. I loved Cash because he was the true thing. When stuff got hot or the shit hit the fan he was always cool. You always had to keep your eyes on the ball, he kept saying. Jackson was the same way. I always wondered where these two guys had learned that.

"Man, maybe you're right. Emily don't need, don't deserve some asshole like you," Cash finally said, with a great deal of sorrow in his voice.

He suddenly jumped out of the car and walked away.

A whole torrent of emotions unexpectedly invaded my heart, my soul. The more I thought about it, the more the unthinkable got to me. Man, Emily could say no, thank you. I mean, what could I offer her? I had no rights. The baby she was carrying was not mine.

I had known her for a few months when she was living with Wilson and it had never occurred to me that somehow through the way the fates work that I would ever find myself wanting to ask her to marry me. The whole thing was just too unreal.

Jackson also got out of the car and looked at me.

"Listen, I don't give a flying fuck if she tells you to your face to get lost."

I was not surprised that he was using language that his mother had specifically forbidden him from using.

"You ain't worth a shit," he continued "if you simply call her and tell her you're not coming because you're afraid to take a chance and face her. That's not what I expect from you.

"You get your ass over there, meet her, tell her what is in your heart, and if she slams the door in your face them's the breaks. And if you don't do it, you can't expect me to be your friend."

He turned around and walked away without closing the door. They were my friends and they had put it on the line. Even our idealistic idea of not wanting to use foul language had gone out of the window.

"What's it to you, you sons of bitches? It's none of your fucking business. Fuck you," I shouted after them. There was no response from them. I knew there would not be.

I was mad but I was also depressed. I hated those bastards for making me feel like a stupid idiot. It was a pretty low moment for me. I sat in my car for a very long time. All kinds of crazy thoughts assailed me. In fact, I even thought that I should just call and tell her I was not coming. This was supposed to be a time of great expectations, a time to think of good things about to come true.

A time to look forward to getting up the next morning and hitting the road with my heart filled with love, tenderness and good feelings. Instead, here I was overwhelmed by the most contradictory sentiments around. I finally went to bed, but I did not sleep very well that night.

The next morning, I got up and I noticed Cash and Jackson had gotten up before me. I started to shave and, as I was looking at myself in the mirror, I saw myself standing in front of Emily's house, knocking on the door, some guy opening the door.

And Emily standing behind him, for all intents and purposes no longer available, and she was telling me to get lost. I thought, this is crazy I finished shaving and walked to my bunk.

I sat on it and looked around at the empty barracks. This was my life, at least for the moment. It was clear that I was just another asshole soldier and that one day, eventually, I would no longer get up and shave with dozens of other guys around me or hear lots of toilets being flushed early in the day.

It was also obvious that my personal problems could not possibly make any difference to anybody else. At that moment, I really felt isolated and alone.

The total measure of my life consisted of a few civilian clothes that I had packed in my suitcase, my military uniforms, a few trinkets, some books, a car, and an empty feeling in my guts. Not much of anything, I thought.

Then, why are you going to meet her? What is behind all of this? Do you owe her anything? Do you owe yourself anything? Are you some crazy romantic, stupid, jerk who has nothing else to do with his life?

Who was I kidding? Should I call and cancel my trip? But what would I say to her? What reason would I give her? I could always make up some phony excuse. I was in the Army and all of us are familiar with how the military works, how it can screw up your life in no time, and that the Army does not respect personal feelings or schedules.

If I was looking for a sign, something to help me at this very moment, it sure as hell was not there. OK, I thought, you need to get your act together here. There ain't anybody, anywhere, that can hand you the answers. You need to find them yourself. There is no question the only way to find out was for me to get in my car and go find Emily.

Those two jerks were right. I walked out to the car and both of them were standing next to it. I did not say anything. I put my stuff in the trunk, opened the door, and got in. Cash closed the door for me.

"Drive carefully, man," Cash said.

"Yeah, give her our best," Jackson said, softly, and then both walked away without looking back.

I did not say anything. I felt that no matter what I would say the whole thing was doomed. OK, I thought, once again, I will go over there and if the whole thing turns sour on me that is just the way the ball bounces. I will show these pricks that I can take my medicine.

Later that day, while on the road, I was thinking how these two guys and their words were echoing in my head because they had burned not just the words in my own psyche, but because for the first time in my life they had confronted me with what was important; how a decision needed to be made; how the love that one has for another human being required no excuses and no reasons.

It was there. It was icy clear, and it was pure. But would it work for me? Would it bring me what love is supposed to bring? I had no clear idea what Emily felt for me. Our phone conversations of the past few weeks seemed to hover around this, but we never pressed each other on what we meant to say.

For my end, I did not dare. It was both a curse and a blessing. I always listened carefully for the words, the voice inflection, and the sound of something, a tiny variation that suggested more than what the words meant.

I was never able to discern anything that remotely indicated she did not care for me, or that there was a game being played by her for lack of something better to do. On the contrary, the thoughts, words, and intimacies we exchanged were those of lovers, of people who understood and appreciated each other in ways that were innocent, magical and mysterious. But man, does anybody know what is in the human heart?

It was not that there were no obstacles, there were—boy, there were—but what we had to eventually overcome was not in the realm of impossibility, hopelessness or indecency. No, it was Emily and I trying to negotiate through this maze called life, knowing the pitfalls, accepting what was in front of us and not making things up or getting ahead of the curve. It was what it was.

Later, much later, when I told Emily about Cash and Jackson wanting to be the baby's godfather, her response took away those negative sentiments. She had laughed and said that based on what her own brothers had already said to her, her baby was on the way to having several godfathers at once.

"How wonderful of Cash and Jackson."

"What if it turns out to be a girl?"

"Well, she will still have many godfathers."

We had been sitting on the swing for a while in almost total silence. I could faintly smell her perfume, and her quietness was very soothing.

The peaceful setting was marvelous. The countryside has always been both attractive to me and at the same time I had not been a great fan of it. I do not know why other than the fact that I come from a big city, and the city is my laird. I feel comfortable in the city.

I feel safe in the city, which seems a bit idiotic when you think about it because you are really never safe in a big city. There are lots of things we cannot control; too many people are angry and lost, and there are too many ugly, possible, confrontations.

"You lived here in this house long?"

"No, but I was lucky to have found it when I came back. It was up for rent and the people who own it are just wonderful. They even gave it to me furnished and I don't have to pay any extra for that. I like it. Do you like it?"

"Yes. It's lovely. It's you."

"Really? Well, I'm glad. I'm not very far from my parents and that's a big help. My two brothers come often to take care of the yard and the garden. They don't want me to do anything. I keep telling them that I'm not a cripple, but they don't want to hear about it."

"That's nice."

"I come out to the yard very often just like tonight, to sit here and look at the stars. I wonder how far they are. I have sat here many nights and I have thought about things. I have thought about you . . ."

"Good thoughts, I hope."

"The best."

"That's wonderful."

I took her hand and held it and she did not withdraw it.

"Life is such a mystery, isn't?" she said.

"Yes. It is."

"I mean look at us."

I looked at her and her eyes were very clear and bright. She had a smile that was pure and innocent. I had never in my whole life felt so close to someone whom I was not really close to. Being with her forced me to concentrate on better things than the ugly ones that always seem to pollute my life. .

My fears of the conversation I had had with Cash and Jackson, on the eve of my departure, had immediately evaporated when I first saw Emily as she opened the door. We simply embraced and held each other for a long time.

We did not kiss. We just stood pressed against each other. She looked at me and kept shaking her head, smiling and holding me. I did the same. No words were needed. They would have been irrelevant.

I stood away from the swing, turned around, leaned over and kissed her. She responded. She held my face in her hands and kissed me softly, exploring, sensing, searching, wanting, and needing. Her eyes focused on me intensely, not closing, not looking away, but looking at me directly, not questioning but accepting.

She stood, and while holding my hand she started to walk back to the house. It was a strange ritual, filled with so much mystery and significance for both of us at this moment. I just followed her. We stopped on the porch and I kissed her again, and her response was passionate, and without any hesitation.

We walked into her bedroom. It was gaily decorated in bright colors, and I noticed an easel standing in one corner holding a canvas with the beginning of a landscape painting. The colors were rich, vivid, and the combination along with the design was quite good.

"Is that yours?"

"Yes."

"I didn't know you painted. Oh, my God, I'm impressed."

"It isn't finished, but I kind of know what I'm going to do with it."

I stood looking at the painting and suddenly she came behind me, put her arms around me, and leaned her head against my back. I turned around and held her. I was not sure if I should press myself hard against her.

I was afraid that I was going to crush her. For some reason, in a fleeting second, I thought of what Yoshi always said about things in life. You must have patience and, if you do, good things will happen.

"Jonathan, do you want to make love?"

Her question took me by surprise. I had never expected her to be so direct that for a moment I was unable to answer her. She smiled and kissed me.

"Emily, are you sure?"

"Yes."

"But, I mean, are you allowed to make love when you are pregnant?"

"Jonathan, women make love when they are pregnant all of the time," she laughed and kissed me.

"Yes, but are you sure? I mean . . . "

"Dear heart, you have some weird ideas."

She started to laugh and she began to unbutton my shirt. This led me to do the same thing to her. Her breasts were larger than I had imagined but this gave her such loveliness.

However silly I had been, in a most basic and normal sense, Emily was demonstrating at the moment of perfect intimacy and surrender that what happens between a man and a woman in the act of love, that such secrets are revealed to no one else—lovers own them.

I had never made love to a pregnant woman before and seeing her naked with her growing belly, her sex hidden, mysterious and wanting, the moment of such intimacy gave me a strange sentiment of things unknown, of secrets that only people in love know and understand.

I kissed her breasts and then put my hand on her and she was wet, very wet. She gave me a wonderful smile when I did this.

For me, it was the first time I had seen a naked pregnant woman, but now looking at her I thought of the way nature had designed such a sight that was not only a wonderful surprise for me but it also showed me in rich terms the wonderful mystery of the cycle of life.

At first, I was hesitant and she could see it, but she was so tender with me. So practical that soon my own passion got a hold of me and we were one.

Our hunger for each other was real and there was so much need in me to be as open and giving as she was. Yet she sensed, in that particular and unique way that women have, that of the two of us I was the one that needed to feel more secure.

She understood that I was far more fragile than she was. And in that strange and mysterious act of love, she was showing me that I had nothing to fear, that what was important in love was to give fully and without any hesitation, and without fear.

Long afterward, she lay next to me with her back to me, holding and softly stroking my arm that I had put under her neck.

"I don't want you to be afraid," she said.

"How did you know I was afraid?"

"Pretty easy to see."

"Really?"

"Yes. I just want you to love me and to hold me, that's all I want."

"That's not a lot," I said, teasing her.

"I know. I'm not complicated."

"You're not? Oh, I think I've made a mistake. I only want to fall in love with complicated women."

"Well, you're out of luck, Mr. Greene," and she laughed that wonderful laugh of hers that had sustained me for weeks while we were separated, when the only contact we had had been those long telephone calls.

"What you said earlier about life being strange, it is, isn't it?" I said.

"Yes, but we must never stray from accepting that we have a right to be happy. That we have the right to be loved and to love. There cannot be any compromise in that," she said, with a strong conviction in her voice.

"Do you feel positive about the future?"

"Yes. And now even more so because of you."

"Oh, Emily, you leave me wordless. I never thought that anybody would say something like that to me, and I would find myself with nothing to say." She smiled.

"My life isn't over. I want to make a new life, a new beginning. I refuse to wallow in the pain and misery of what has happened. I can't let such sentiments rule what I must do now."

"You know, both Cash and Jackson think that they don't make girls like you anymore."

"Really? How sweet of them to say that."

"Well, it's true."

Then she said a few more words about Homer and about her life with him, about that previous life that I suspected she was trying to put behind her. Words she obviously needed to say, to end something in her life, because the past could no longer be her present. The words were soft but her conviction was anything but that.

"Jonathan, there is no key we can find how to unlock the vault of life, no secret combination to help us open it so we can understand such things. Life is what it is. It's me. It's my baby. It's you. Now, it's us. My responsibility is to my baby and I don't think he or she is looking to find out how we are going to live, at least not now.

"One day, I will have to explain what happened, of course, but it would only be to fill in a part that has been missing, but it's only a part. You can argue that it may turn out to be the most important part, but I'd like to think that it's part of a much larger picture."

"What about Homer's family?"

"His family understands that and, in fact, they have given me plenty of hints that I should consider a normal relationship with another man. My family, interestingly enough, seems to be of two minds about it. On the one hand, they intrinsically understand that I need to make a transition to a more normal life, yet on the other hand, they are not sure. I understand it. They loved him like their own son. Do you understand?"

"Yes, I think I do."

"I will always love him but it will be in a different way. He isn't around anymore. He will never be back," she stopped and for an instant, I thought she was not going to continue talking. "I can't wait for him like in the mythology books, where Penelope waited for Ulysses. I think I do understand this idea of waiting and waiting. What's there for me to wait for? He isn't coming back."

"OK, but what will your family say? Will they accept me as a replacement for him? What will they say when I tell them I want to marry you?"

She looked at me and, for a moment, she seemed a bit lost. It was as if the idea had never occurred to her at all. I could see that my blurting out that I wanted to marry her came as a total surprise.

"You want to marry me?"

"Yes. Why, is there something wrong with that?"

"No, are you sure?" and she smiled.

"Emily, I have never been more certain of anything in my life. I know we haven't talked about it before. I also know that maybe my asking you in this way isn't as romantic as it should be."

"Are you sure? Is this what you want to do?"

"Yes, I do."

She had an enigmatic smile on her face. For some reason, it made me think of what Jack had told me about men having no control over certain things, about the Mona Lisa's smile.

That women ran the show and we males had no other choice but to get on with the program. And for an instant, I allowed myself a moment of cheerfulness and I laughed out loud, thinking about what Jack had said.

"What are you laughing about?"

"Oh, it's nothing really. It's a secret, a private joke. I'll tell you about it one day."

"OK."

"The only thing I fear, other than your saying no, is that I don't want to appear to be wanting to replace Homer."

"Dear heart, you can't replace him. It's silly to put it in those terms. You're not replacing him. I don't want you to replace him. It's a different life, now. I want my baby and me to have a new life, to be yours. We will be yours if you will have us. Yes, I will have a child, a child that isn't your own flesh and blood, but a child that can be yours, if you want it to be, if you aren't afraid."

"I was, but I'm not anymore."

"Are you sure?"

"Yes, I'm sure now."

"That's lovely."

"Emily, I have so much to learn from you."

"We have so much to learn from each other, dear heart."

"Can we, one day, have more babies?"

"Of course. Do you want more babies?"

"Yes. I want lots of babies."

"OK, but let us have this one first," and she smiled teasingly.

I wanted her and we managed to connect and, once again, she was mine.

-X-

I was dreading meeting her family. Fear of the unknown is terrifying because we humans are always afraid of not being in control, and fear of being rejected.

"It's fine, Jonathan. I have told them about you."

"I hope that. . . "

"No," she gently interrupted, "not that part. It's none of their business."

"But what if they don't like me? What if they think that I'm just an opportunist or, you know, the equivalent of a carpet bagger or something?"

"Jonathan, come on, they won't," and she smiled and that seemed to make things easier.

"What will they think about me spending the nights here?"

"Where would you stay?"

"I don't know. In some motel in town—some other place? Is there a bridge nearby, I can sleep under it."

She laughed, and kissed me.

"No bridges, you are out of luck. Jonathan, I'm an adult. You're an adult."

"I know, but what if they don't like it?"

"Dear heart, my actions and decisions are my own. My family is wonderful. They love me. They're not going to make you feel unwelcome or offend you. I think you have a lot to learn about people who come from these surroundings. You'll find them tough, but kind. They're not superficial. They understand life in its most basic sense.

"They're used to dealing with things that aren't under their control. Yes, you have to earn their trust, but you'll also find that they are good people. Simple honest, hardworking, wonderful, and they'll tell you what they think and they won't beat around the bush. But the one thing that they'll know immediately is, if you love me. You don't have to say it. They'll know it!"

"They will? Really?"

"Yes."

"Am I permitted to at least hold your hand while in their presence?"

"Yes, and you can kiss me if you so desire."

"Emily, I'd never dare."

"Then, you would be foolish."

And she laughed that wonderful laugh of hers that I had come to love and appreciate.

"Do I tell them I want to marry you?"

"Yes, you're permitted to say that," she said, gaily.

We were driving on the way to meet her family. And, once again, I thought that in my previous relationships, I had never met the parents of any of the girls I had known and loved in the past.

Even in Pamela's case, it had never come up and part of it was the simple fact that her parents lived in upstate New York and so the opportunity had not been so easily available.

And Emily was right about her family. Her two brothers who worked in the mines and Laurie, the wife of Jimmy the older brother were just wonderful and so without pretension. Her father and mother were so impressed I came from Los Angeles.

Once again, I had to explain to them, as I had explained to Cash and Jackson, that Los Angeles was not Hollywood. I also told them "Hollywood" was the nickname that I had been given by my fellow soldiers. They got a kick out of it.

"We can call you Hollywood, then?" her father said, with a mischievous smile.

"Yes, if you want," I said.

"No, Jonathan is his name," his wife said, while giving him a loving, but stern look.

He winked at me. Emily's two brothers were impressed with my Chevy Impala, and I asked them if they wanted to take a ride around the countryside a bit while the others were preparing the meal. It was going to be a feast. I had bought a bottle of Jack Daniels, as Emily had said her father was fond of it.

The old man was impressed also, I could tell. I do not come from a well-constructed family and I could see that there was an amazing amount of love and affection among all of them and for each other. There was a kind of complicity among them. How I wished I had had that kind of family in my life.

Her brothers agreed to go for a drive. I asked who wanted to drive the car and Jimmy, the older of the two, took the keys from me and he drove us around the town. Billy sat in the back. People we passed waved and we waved back.

"It isn't often that we get to see a convertible around here and from California no less. In the winter it isn't such a hot idea," he said.

He drove to a small hill that overlooked the outskirts of the town, stopped the car, and we got out to look down the valley.

"So Jonathan, what are your intentions," Billy, the younger one, asked me, suddenly.

His older brother winced, and I could see that he was also surprised at his younger brother's question.

"Billy, it isn't polite to ask that."

"It's OK Jimmy, I understand. The truth is that I have found myself in love with your sister. I believe she's not completely neutral in her feelings toward me. I don't understand how it happened. I don't think that Emily understands it either.

"We, she and I, have found ourselves in a strange and curious world. A vortex of feelings—a total mystery. I have no experience dealing with such matters. I cannot say, oh, yeah, I know what needs to be done here.

"It is beyond my limited intelligence to even attempt to comprehend what is going on. The only thing I know, is that I would like to have Emily and her baby make me part of their lives. I'm not replacing Homer.

"It would be very presumptuous on my part to even consider it. I didn't know him for long. I had a great deal of admiration for him. We didn't always agree about the war. But he valued what I thought and I did the same for him."

"He was one of the few guys I really respected," Billy said. "From the beginning, it was always Emily and Homer. Everybody knew it. He loved Emily. She could do no wrong in his eyes. And she loved him. He was like a brother to me. He had a good heart. You needed something done he was always there. He never hesitated to lend you a hand."

He stopped and I could see that his eyes were filled with tears. Jimmy the older brother did not say anything. Billy kept looking in the distance not focused on anything.

"He didn't have to go like this. They said that he was helping one of his Army buddies. It doesn't surprise me. So typical of him. Someone needed help, he went out and tried. And now he's gone. Gone. Man, it's terrible. Just terrible. The good always die young."

Billy seemed possessed by haunting and painful memories and he wanted to get them out. I found myself wondering if he even remembered that I was there. You could see how Homer's death had affected him incredibly. His brother Jimmy put his hand on his shoulder. Billy did not seem to notice it.

"I know that Emily has been brutally hurt. She doesn't say much but I know how much she was hurt. She doesn't want to talk about it, but I know. I know she's tough and she has kept our family together. There is no one like her, but I know she has been badly hurt."

He turned and looked at me directly, so directly, that for a moment I had the impression that he was controlling his anger and pain because he did not want to lose it.

"I hope that you remember that. She's the best! She didn't deserve what happened to her. They had a life together. And now she is alone. She has to start all over again and with a baby. And Homer isn't around to protect her, to take care of things for her. I don't want her to get hurt ever again. It's no good. Man, I wish it hadn't happened."

He was quietly crying, his last words had been said in a soft and forlorn voice. Disjointed, and sad.

"You know," I said, "I have often wondered why a guy like Wilson—we all called him Wilson—had to die. When he first told me he had volunteered for Vietnam, I couldn't believe it. I must confess to you that I had a strange feeling in my guts and I hated that life had somehow made him do it.

"Then when the terrible news came, I kept asking why it wasn't me. My death wouldn't have made any difference. I don't think that I would have been missed the way you guys miss him."

146

"How long do you still have in the Army before you get out?" Jimmy asked.

"About a year."

"So what happens when they send you to Vietnam?"

"I don't know. Before I didn't care. But now I do. I don't know. I have some friends who have decided to go to Canada if they are assigned to go to Vietnam."

"Would you do that?"

"I don't know."

"That's no good, man," Billy said. "Emily cannot live through another tragedy like that. It would kill her, I know."

"Maybe it won't happen. Not everybody goes to Vietnam," I said, trying to make light of that idea, just to say something to relax the atmosphere.

"It's no good, man," Billy said, again.

"Well, why don't we hope for the best," I said.

"I want you to promise me something," Billy said, very quietly.

"If I can."

"That if you and Emily are together and you get your orders for Vietnam, that you call me first so I can tell her."

His request took me completely by surprise. Even Jimmy was taken aback by it. I did not know what to say and, suddenly, I got pissed. I understood Billy's incredible pain and loss, but he had no right to make such a request—no right.

"Billy, I would never do that! That destiny, if it happens, will belong to Emily and me. If I ever did what you're asking, I would never be able to look at myself in the mirror. It's completely out of the question."

Both brothers could hear in my voice that I was upset. Billy looked at me and his eyes were now softer not as challenging, as they had been a moment ago.

"We ought to be getting back to the house," Jimmy said.

"Jonathan, you're right," Billy said, "I'm sorry."

"No harm done."

And we shook hands.

"I know this has been a great loss for Emily, for all of you guys. I know that Homer will always have a special place in your heart. I have absolutely no desire to bump him out. I can't. What I would like to do, what I dream of doing, is to be part of your sister's life, of her baby's, that's if Emily will have me.

"And if she does, I intend to marry her, not make up for her loss because that's not possible, but try to build a life together just like other normal people do."

Billy wiped his tears with his sleeve and looked at me, still with a bit of reticence, but gave me what I considered a half smile. I felt good. A half smile was better than a punch in the mouth. We drove back to the house in silence.

The atmosphere back in the house was more relaxed and there was a great deal of joking and laughter. Emily gave me a wonderful smile and a wink. She looked lovely, warm, and mysterious. The red maternity dress she was wearing gave her a look of being at ease with herself, and where she was.

147

We sat at the table for the sumptuous banquet they had prepared, and her father said grace. When he finished and we were about to start eating, I stood, and they all looked at me. I was shaking, not sure if my voice was going to fail me.

"Mr. and Mrs. Nelson, I'm overwhelmed and deeply touched by your welcome and hospitality and I can't tell you the immense sentiment I have now. I don't know how to explain things to me or to anybody else for that matter."

I looked at Emily who had a lovely smile on her face because she knew how tough it was, and that what I was about to say was so important for both of us.

"I know Emily belongs to you and always will. I know what she has been through, though, I don't understand it. I don't think that we ever will. What I do understand, however, is that there is a pure sentiment in my heart that grows and grows immensely."

I stopped and looked at Emily. The whole room was so silent that I could hear my own strained breathing. I felt like my heart was going to explode and burst out of my chest. But it was now or never.

"I would like to ask for your permission and your blessings because I wish to marry Emily."

Emily reached over and grabbed my hand.

"I love her. No, I adore her," I continued looking directly at her. "I just hope to be worthy of her, of her baby, that she will accept my love."

The silence was deafening and, for an instant, I thought I had blown the whole thing to hell.

Billy stood, walked over, and broke into a wide smile, the first one I had seen from him on this day, and then he hugged me. I was completely taken aback by such a gesture.

I looked over to Jimmy and he had a wide smile on his face. At that moment, the two brothers and their sister all resembled each other in their smiles. No question they all came from the same set of parents.

"Well, sis," Billy said, "I believe the gentleman has made a serious proposal and what say you?"

"Yes, with all of my heart!"

"OK, you can kiss her now," Billy said.

I stood a bit lost, but when I looked around the table I could see that it was expected of me, so I leaned over and kissed her softly on her lips. Everyone cheered and clapped.

"See," she whispered, "I knew you were going to kiss me in front of the family."

"I love you!"

"I love you," she whispered back.

The rest of the afternoon went by so fast it sort of remains hidden in a kind of fog. I wanted to hang on to the moments, to the laughter, and to the memories. And there were plenty of memories especially when they talked about Homer.

But it was not with any sense of sadness or melancholy or regret. He had been part of their lives, and that was the way it was.

Emily's mother went to the attic and brought down several photo albums and I saw this skinny, blonde beauty, as she grew up. She had not changed that much. Those clear, sparkly eyes, the big apple cheeks had been there from the beginning and, needless to say, it was the most memorable lunch, which became dinner, that when we finally left I was a bit tipsy. Emily drove us back.

I promised to come back and see them before I left.

"You see, it wasn't so hard was it?"

"You didn't see or hear my knees shaking?"

"No, I didn't. I thought you were wonderful."

"I didn't disappoint you?"

"Of course not. Everyone in the family is happy for us. I can tell you that. And I know that Billy asked you many questions."

"How did you know that?"

"He told me. I'm his big sister, even though I'm only four years older than he is. He was always my baby. I took care of him. He's very protective of me."

"Yes, I saw that when we talked. Jimmy doesn't say very much."

"Jimmy is very special. He has always been quiet, reserved. In fact, there is a joke in the family that when he proposed to Laurie, that it was she who had to ask him questions about what he wanted to do?"

"Yeah, he's kind of quiet."

"He's like my dad. My dad and Jimmy can go fishing, sit in the boat, and never say a word the whole day. I know, I've been there with them and to get them to talk is like pulling teeth. My mom says they are very economical!"

When she talked about her family there was a sense of togetherness and of shared loved that was encompassing and full. I reflected back on my own family, where my brothers and I hardly kept in touch with each other.

Where my parents had gotten divorced, were now married to other people, and where family reunions were for all practical purposes relegated to more like happenstance than well thought-out plans.

"Yes, Mr. Greene. You have passed the test. You're one of us now."

"I hope I merit your love."

"You do. I hope I merit yours."

"Emily, you already have in more ways than you can imagine."

"Is that true?"

"Yes."

As I was driving back to Fort Bragg, after my week—five days actually—with Emily, all of the memories of my stay with her were as fresh and as real as the sun now shining on my face. I wanted to keep them fresh. I did not want them to just fade away, as most memories do.

I had spent five glorious days with someone whom I did not really know; yet these past few days had exposed me to emotions so intense that I was surprised I had them.

There was no question that my life had now taken a different route, not what I could have envisioned before. If truth be told, I really did not have any vision. I came into the Army ready to do my two years, finish it in one piece, get out, and face the future.

I was not sure what I had wanted to do with my life. Nothing seemed interesting or attractive. I was going back to California when my two years were up and maybe try graduate school, or get a job. Of the two options, going back to graduate school seemed far more interesting than getting a job.

On the other hand, my finances were not something to be proud of. I had a few bucks in the bank, that I had been saving, but not enough to keep me going for a long time. I needed a job far more than getting another degree.

And now, here is Emily and the baby.

Could we make it? These past few days I had experienced something that I never thought was possible in any life. Reflecting on the things that had happened in my past, I had no point of reference about what was now taking place. I could not say that I knew what I was doing. I had never been in such a similar situation.

I had committed to share my life with a lovely, wonderful person, who in many ways was still a stranger to me. A relationship that came with an incredible set of difficulties. Heavy baggage that would weigh us down for a long time to come. I was sure of that.

I had no idea, neither did she, of how long this thing would last. What if I ran out of patience with her? What if she ran out of patience with me because I had run out of patience with her?

The baby was really no problem when I thought about it. I laughed. I had never considered being a father. Hell, I had no idea what it meant or what it entailed. I knew it was more, a hell of a lot more, than just changing diapers. Love, of course, was a basic ingredient.

Could I love this baby? Good question. Yeah, I could. Why not? It was not the baby's fault that he or she would come into a world without a biological father. Jack had also said that children belong to those who raise them.

I laughed. Emily was pretty convinced that it would be a boy. But what if it is a girl? Man, oh, man. A daughter? Holy mackerel! Well, whether it was a boy or a girl I knew I could learn to love this baby. I was certain of that.

The baby would have a rather extended family when I thought about it. Though I was not close to my family, Emily's family was large and, of course, there was Homer's family.

We had gone to have coffee with his parents and they understood that things were different now. But they were charming, gracious and kind. When Emily told them that we were planning to get married, Homer's mother had tears in her eyes.

"It's a good thing, it's a good thing. The baby will have a father—a nice father," she said, and embraced me.

Emily had a wide smile on her face and both women cried and hugged each other. I sometimes think that the gate to pure human emotions is always available to all of us to walk through but we get confused and lost. But we must dare enter it.

And instead, we assume that if we enter it that it will lead us to some strange territory, dark, forbidden, and what we will find will be something sinister, desolate, so we do not enter it.

It is true that pain and suffering always hover over our lives and we do not know what will trigger them to raise their ugly heads and strike us without pity. Life, destiny, they are such mysteries and so abstract and at times indifferent to what we want or feel.

Is life, or what we think of it, not part of us; that is to say, is life, time, call them what you will, totally outside of us? Is what we call meaning just something that we obviously need to have so that we can at least pretend that we are trying to understand life?

But, nevertheless, still outside of us? Not part of us, but more like a tree or a river or the clouds. In other words, things that do not belong to us that might have no direct personal bearing on what happens to us, or why it happens to us?

Do we belong to—what? Does life belong to—us? I do not know that I belong to life because I do not know what it means. I have no idea what it may mean. I dribble every day in this court that I find myself in. I do not know where it leads me. I do not know how to keep the score.

I do not know what the rules are. I do not know anything. I search and I search and, yes, I find things, events, other people, but in strange and mysterious ways—ways that I do not totally understand. Yes, I do get glimpses of things around me but I still do not know what they mean.

Some people say they find "meaning" in the search itself. Others say, they find "meaning" in the results of such a quest. I suppose one can find meaning in anything given time and effort. But is the meaning so strong that once we sense it the whole thing will become as clear as a bell ringing in a silent room?

Thus, I continue in my search because I do not like to believe that it is futile and stupid, for that admits confusion or, maybe, simply defeat. I do not want to believe that the search is useless.

I try to find a context, a measuring stick, yeah, a spiritual measuring stick that might give me some clarification as to what are the sentiments that accost me. I want to measure such things against some standard, some yardstick, some gauge. It seems that, at best, the whole thing is just a wild guess and that is all.

"I hope to be worthy of your trust," I said, to Homer's mother.

"You will. If Emily says so, you will," she said.

She gently touched my face and I put my arms around both women and held them close to me. Homer's father had a big smile on his face. He embraced Emily, and shook my hand profusely.

I had wanted to go and visit Homer's grave. Emily told me where it was and I asked her to let me go alone. She did not argue.

The cemetery was on the outskirts of town. It was not large and I found his grave without any trouble. It had fresh flowers on it and a small American flag flapping slowly in the late afternoon breeze. I stood silently staring at his tombstone. His name, his date of birth and the date of his death. Simple. I was alone in the place.

Wilson, old buddy, I'm so sorry for what happened to you. There are no words to tell you how I felt when I heard the terrible news. I wished that it had been me and not you. Life was not kind to you or Emily. I don't know where you are and I don't know if you can hear me, but I want you to know that I will always respect who you were. I don't understand all that has happened since your death.

Even if I lived a million years, I wouldn't be able to explain it. Sometimes, the situation confuses me in a big way. I called a professor I had in college who became a great friend of mine—you would have liked him—and, when I talked to him about Emily, he said that I was damn lucky to have found her. That's probably how you felt about her, too.

Some people argue about destiny and other stuff and I must confess it seems like a reasonable explanation, but it still leaves me in the dark. But the one thing that I'm not confused or in the dark about, is that I love Emily! I think I love her just as much as you loved her. I know it may sound ridiculous to you that I'm here and that somehow I'm asking for your permission to marry her, but that's what I am now doing.

I promise you that I will take care of her and your baby! And I hope that I will be a good husband and as good of a father to your baby as you would have been. I also promise that your child will know all about you and though you won't be there to tell him or her about yourself, I will make sure that you will always be part of his or her life. Have no doubts about that.

So long old buddy, rest in peace.

I stood watching the sun slowly sinking over the horizon. I felt alone, but not separated from my life and from what I was intending to do. Yes, there were unknowns, confusion and fears, but the fact that I felt those things did not make me either special or unique.

My life was not so out of the ordinary that it somehow gave me a leg up on everybody else around me. I was a simple, average guy, who had indeed found himself in a most strange set of circumstances. Who had tried to do the right thing, whatever that was, and I had to trust my instincts or the fates to make things come out fine.

But I did find myself wondering about how we could explain things, understand things; death, for example? One day you are there, the next day you are not. Is there a program, a list with your name on it indicating how long you will be around, thus you cannot go beyond that date for your time finally ends and you are to be dismissed from the list of the living?

Or is the list made up as the cycle of life progresses, something like work-in-progress yet with a well-designed intention and destination? Or is it all purely by chance with no rhyme or reason?

Why was I assigned to Fort Bragg in the first place? What demented mind had programmed that I would find myself in the middle of some cemetery expressing my thoughts and feelings to a grave of someone whom I had known for a short period of time, and one whose widow was now the woman of my life, and whom I loved and was now planning on marrying?

And not only that, but I was also wanting to become the father of a dead man's child? I looked for a logical explanation and there was not any. Jack's words were now ringing in my head: listen to your heart and trust.

For an instant, the whole thing seemed clear, simple and, I thought, a bit exotic. I laughed, and I thought about Cash and Jackson and how simple the whole thing seemed to them.

Are things simple and complex at the same time? Is it a choice that we make? Do we have a choice? Or do we take the leap and we deal with whatever happens when confronting the result of that leap? If it is simple, we deal with it. If it is complicated, we deal with it. We have no other choice.

It had not been easy to say goodbye to Emily's family upon leaving. And it was nearly impossible to say goodbye to her. It drove me crazy. My feelings were so confused, so raw, so complex and desperate that I thought it was the worst position to be in. I knew I had to leave and I also knew that I was looking for an excuse not to leave.

I thought, screw the Army. They do not need me. She needs me here. Emily did not say much, but I could tell that she had also been struggling with the fact that we were going to be separated once again. It was tough. Man, I was bleeding inside so damn much. Boy, if that was what makes us adults, I did not want any part of it.

The night before I left, her tenderness in our lovemaking was beyond belief. She wanted so much of me and I wanted so much of her. I was so desperate to take with me everything that she was, everything that she now represented to me.

I did not want to leave her behind. I wanted to carry her with me back and forever. I wanted to savor the little things, the secrets that lovers and only lovers have for each other, which strangers are not permitted to share.

She had cried. And she kidded herself that she was now acting like some young girl experiencing love and separation for the first time.

"How could it be? I'm a pregnant woman. I've been in love before. I'm now a widow. How come I'm falling apart?"

"Maybe it's because of the baby."

"You think?"

"What else?"

"You still love me?"

"I will always love you. Put that in your secret stash of things to keep for the rest of your life."

I had also told Emily what had happened on the eve of my trip to see her. How Cash, Jackson and I had all been petrified that she was going to throw me out of her house. How upset both of them had been with me because, in their view, I had not done anything to advance my own cause, and they were ready to blame me if nothing good came out of my trip.

"How did they find out about us?"

"I never told them anything. They guessed it, which brings me to why you gave Jackson your phone number?"

"He wrote and asked me for it."

"What was his reason?"

"He just said he wanted to have it, just to keep in touch."

She stopped and started to laugh. "Now, I know why he wanted it, that sneak. He was going to give it to you eventually. It's all clear."

And Emily and I looked at each other and I started to laugh upon realizing that we had been had.

"When I think about it" she said, "Jackson made some strange reference about how one never knows when a phone number may come in handy. I didn't think much of it. And I didn't ask him what he meant."

"That bum, he should change his name to Cupid. And to think they made me go through hell blaming me for nothing."

"Jonathan, that wasn't fair for them to blame you," she said, half concerned half joking.

"I know, babe."

"What are you going to tell them?"

"I won't tell them anything."

"Oh, Jonathan, that's not nice."

"Eventually, I'll tell them but not right away. It'll drive them crazy. I'll let them suffer for a while."

And she smiled because she knew that these two guys were the best friends a person could have, and because all along they had our best interest at heart.

It seemed to me that while I was with Emily, we spent much of our time in bed, talking, making love, and making plans for the future. I treasured those moments so much. I am not one to think about the future let alone make plans for it, because I always think that to plan for something that nobody knows anything about is just an exercise in futility.

The future for me is today. Not tomorrow or the day after tomorrow. And yet Emily had become the future for me, that uncertain tomorrow that had not really made sense to me had now become real and present. I guess my ideas about many things were not as well set as I had thought.

And her ideas, plans, were clearly important. However, the one nagging doubt in my heart was of course if the Army decided to send me to Vietnam. That was the shadow that hovered over our lives not weighing us down but, nevertheless, omnipresent.

154

I was terrified to bring it up, though, I knew that like anything else in our lives we would have to discuss it sooner or later. I was just simply terrified of such a prospect.

And we were so hungry for each other. I would wake her up in the middle of the night, and we would make love.

"Emily, do you think it's OK?"

"What?"

"You know, making love and stuff?"

"Jonathan, are you complaining?"

"Who's complaining?"

"Be quiet and love me."

And I did, repeatedly. I was completely enthralled with her, seeing her getting dressed, watching her daily rituals, yet knowing that I would leave her behind, which would bring me feelings of incredible anxiety and pain. I tried in every way I could to engrave in my memory everything about her.

One day, she sat and was looking at herself in the mirror and combing her hair, when I glanced in her direction and I knew that my departure was approaching, like some fast train that was impossible to stop. Why did life have to be that way?

Do we have to suffer before we can be happy? Is this the only way? What demented mind thought this thing out? It sure as hell does not seem to be a benign mind, that is for damn certain. The realization of the inevitable fact that our idyllic time was coming to an end brought such incredible pain that I felt like I was choking.

I closed my eyes and tried not to think about such a terrible ordeal. The next thing I knew, she was right next to me and holding me close to her.

"It's OK. I know what you are feeling, dear heart. You must promise me that you won't be sad. I only want you to think of the time we have been together. You have brought me not only your love but also a desire to live fully. I now realize I have been hiding from myself these past months. You have no idea how I looked forward to your phone calls.

"I wanted so many times to reach and touch you, to see your face, to just have you hold my hand, but I also knew that if I said anything it would have driven you crazy. So I talked to my baby. I explained that my love for him—and I always think it is a he—would never change or disappear. That he was going to have a wonderful new father who would love him and me." She stopped.

"But how did you know that I loved you?"

"You told me the first time you called, remember?"

"Yeah, I did. I know. Afterward, I thought this whole thing is mad. But what I said was true."

"I know," she said. "I wasn't surprised. After the conversation was over, I went back to sleep and I had sweet and wonderful dreams about you."

"You never told me that."

"It was my secret."

Her eyes were wide open, bright, sunny, looking at me in such a manner, innocent, trusting, wanting, in full harmony with who she was. Love is so strange and mysterious. And the heart is its messenger.

In so many other ways, love is also outrageous! Is there anyone who has a handle on this thing and can explain it so that the rest of us can understand it?

We often drove up to the hills where she would show me places, secret places she had found for herself. One day we drove to a stream near her house. She took along her half-finished painting, all of her brushes, paints, easel and a small stool.

She walked by the edge of the stream and moved back and forth trying to find the angle she wanted. She set the easel down, put the stool in front of her, sat and started to paint.

She had brought a straw hat, and with her summer dress, she was more like a subject of a painting than the painter herself. I stood behind her and suddenly realized Emily was completely lost in what she was doing.

I felt like an intruder. She glanced at me, once or twice, smiled and went back to her painting. Slowly, I started to walk away from her, went to a nearby bunch of trees, and sat on the grass in the shade with my back against one of the trees.

She did not seem to notice my absence. I was slightly to her back and the whole scene was bucolic and magical. At that moment, I wished I were also a painter for I would have tried to capture the essence of this lovely woman, pregnant, painting, surrounded by nature, concentrating as deeply as if nothing else in the world mattered.

And, of course, nothing else mattered except whatever image she was trying to capture on the canvas. I do not know how long I sat on the grass against the tree and watched her. At one time, she looked in my direction, smiled, but it was almost like a reflex. For an instant, I thought she had forgotten I was there.

I felt sleepy and eventually slumber got a hold of me, and the next thing I knew there was Emily kneeling right next to me and kissing me softly on my lips.

I opened my eyes and her face was close to mine.

"Hey, I'm sorry."

"Why?" she asked.

"I don't want you to feel that I was bored."

"I never thought about that. I've been watching you sleep and you were sleeping like a baby."

I reached and pulled her toward me and she put her head on my chest.

"I hear your heart," she said.

"It's speaking to you."

"Yes, I think I can hear what it is saying."

"Well, tell me because I think it has secrets that it doesn't want to reveal to me, but I think it will reveal them to you."

"OK," and she pressed ear against my chest. "Oh, my goodness. This is very interesting, and also very serious."

The tenderness of lovers is magical and sublime. There is no way that others can penetrate such secrets, such mystery.

"So what is it saying?"

"Some very wonderful things."

"Like what?"

"Oh, no, I can't tell you. I'm being told to keep such things to myself."

"That's not fair."

"It's true. But on the other hand, your heart's secrets are now mine. So that's not so bad."

She kissed me again. I had never in my life felt such strong sentiments for a woman. The whole thing was a mystery that I had given up trying to figure it out.

"Let's make love."

"Here?"

"Yes."

"Jonathan, you're crazy. No dear heart, we'll go back and make love at home."

"Oh, you're no fun."

"That may be true, but I know that people have a tendency to come by here quite frequently and I don't want to embarrass you," and she laughed.

"Me, not me."

"All right, me, then."

We got up and walked back to the canvas and as if to prove her point, there were some kids who came by with fishing rods and they stood not very far from where we were and started to cast their lines.

Emily looked at me and laughed. I hugged her.

Her canvas was now taking shape. There were colors added to what I had first seen on the unfinished painting. I could see the contours of a pastoral scene that featured the stream and the water that ran downstream. I am not an expert on paintings, but my impression was that it was going to be a good painting.

"You know," I said, "I admire people who can paint. I can't even draw a straight line without it looking like a two-year old did it. When it comes to drawing anything I'm completely hopeless."

"Well, it is the same thing as directing a play, isn't it?"

"No, because with a play I can fake it. With a painting, it cannot be faked."

"That's not what Jackson said about you."

"What did he say?"

"Well, he said that the cast was impressed with your directions and ideas. He was also impressed."

"He told you all that?"

"Yes. I asked him."

"See, he never said anything. That bum."

"He likes you, Jonathan, and so does Cash."

"Yeah, they're good people. Still, I think the discipline in painting is far more rigorous than in directing plays."

"Perhaps you're right. It takes some discipline and yes a bit of talent. I like it. It gives me a sense of peace and you may not believe it, but it also makes me want to laugh about how ridiculous life can be."

"So it's all to the good."

"Yes."

"I have an idea."

"What?"

"When I get out of the Army we'll go live in Paris, and you can paint and one day become a famous painter, and all of our kids will grow up speaking English with a wonderful French accent."

"Paris . . . don't make me dream."

"Why not?"

"Yes, why not?" And she was beaming.

We drove past her high school and she remembered some of the girls who had been her friends. She talked about Sally, and Mary, and Kimberly, girls who had now moved to other areas of the state.

What I found incredibly touching was when she talked about her past, the delicate manner in which she brought Homer into her conversation, but did not linger there and moved on to other things.

I admired her for wanting to share her past with me and yet for trying to look to the future, a different future, that life had imposed on her in such a violent manner.

"Are you still friends with all of these people?"

She was quiet for a moment before answering.

"Yes and no. I have seen them, and of course, they all came by, but now it seems that I don't get to spend any time with them. I mean, they are busy with their own lives and the situation is new for everybody.

"I can see that what I feel is something that few people have lived with. I had a sense of guilt about what happened, though it was not my fault.

"I understand them. I don't really want to be a burden on anybody. I know if I called, they would be here in no time. They're good people, but I also know they're very private individuals. I'm not upset with them. This is how we live around here."

We took many baths together whenever the fancy struck us. It was just so intimate to be naked in the tub with her while she told me stories of growing up the middle of three kids, and a girl to boot.

"Where did you get those great high cheek bones?"

"Swedish and Ukrainian grandparents."

"So you and your brothers are mutts."

"Yes."

"So I'm going to spend the rest of my life with a bona fide mutt?"

"You have no other choice."

"Right after the baby is born you are both coming to join me. You don't come and I'm coming to get you."

"We will come."

"You promise?"

"Yes, I promise."

"Also, we have to figure out when we get married and I want to adopt the baby."

She looked at me for a long time in silence. I thought that perhaps I had said the wrong thing. We had never talked about the baby before. I was not sure if asking her to let me adopt the baby was what she also wanted.

I had just assumed that it was a given in our relationship. We got out of the tub and started drying each other. Then, we lay on the bed holding each other.

"Do you want to adopt the baby?"

"Yes."

"Jonathan, it's so strange for me to think about those things. For some reason, I had not even considered it. How foolish of me. Of course, dear heart, you will be his father. All along, I have thought of me being the baby's mother, and that his father . . ."

She stopped and she seemed to be overwhelmed by strong emotions and I did not know just how to react to her. I then realized that it was not as easy as I had thought. For me, it was another discovery of the deep and strong conflicting sentiments that Emily had to work through.

And no matter how much I wanted to help her, it was something that she literally had to do on her own. I was not sure how to help her and what I could do. It also became clear just how much Emily had to contend with.

The reality of her baby was suddenly making her face something that perhaps she unconsciously had been trying to avoid. We had talked mostly about us, and she had mentioned the baby but not in such a direct way.

"Do you really want to marry me?"

"Yes! I want to marry you. I want to be the baby's father. I know I'm going to love him, as if he were my own. He comes from you, and I love you! It's simple, really."

"Thank you, Jonathan."

"For what?"

"For being the way you are."

"I'm nothing special."

"Yes, you are. You don't know how special you are."

"OK, that's why I want you around me to remind me."

"I will dear heart, I will!"

She embraced me. Then she put her hand on me and I got hard. Slowly, somewhat awkwardly, she started kissing and took me in her mouth. I was overwhelmed by her tenderness and desire for me. Afterward, she smiled and seemed pleased.

"I have wanted to do it before, but I was afraid."

"Afraid of what?"

"I don't know. That I didn't know how to do it. That maybe it would not please you."

"Well, get those ideas out of your head," I said, and laughed. "Hey, let's go to San Francisco and get married there."

"San Francisco," she said, with a sense of wonder and mystery as if it represented a most magical place in the world.

"Why not?"

"There is so much of the world that I don't know anything about. I want to know. I want to understand it. I want to see it."

"Well, there's nothing that can keep us from doing it, is there?" I said.

"No, but the main thing is that we have each other, right?" She said.

"Absolutely!"

She looked at me and gave me a wonderful smile.

The days had floated by us lazily and full. All of the small things that we had to do took on a much greater significance because I was leaving. We had never really discussed it.

But it hovered over us like some eternal damnation, which we could never get used to no matter how much we either neglected to bring it up or hoped that it would go away. That by ignoring it, it would just disappear from our lives. But, of course, we were just kidding ourselves and we both knew it.

-XI-

Then, it happened! I had been wondering just how long it would take before the shit hit the fan? On the fourth evening, in the middle of the night, I knew or rather sensed that she was awake and restless. She got up and went to the kitchen. I opened my eyes, and when I did not see her come back, I got up and went looking for her.

She was sitting in the living room in front of her canvass and she had painted a large red streak across the painting as if it no longer mattered. There was something ugly and desperate in what she had done.

The painting with its large and long streak of red paint across its surface no longer represented something innocent and peaceful. It had now been transformed into an angry and violent response to something deep, destructive and painful.

There was something frantic, fearful, and desperate about the painting and I was afraid. Afraid for her, acutely aware of her loneliness, of her broken heart, still with a long way to go before it could try to heal the horror of such painful memories.

I knew that what we had done these past few days, the amazing idyllic moments we had shared so intimately, had been more like some children's fantasy that would shortly disappear like a dying breath. I felt so hopeless. I was not even sure if my presence did any good.

We had tried to build a moment, a castle on the hill, a dream. A short and beautiful dream in order to preserve our individual sanities because to think of the memories that surrounded us with their implacable reality was devastating.

And now we were facing another reality, which was going to separate us and we did not know for how long. Our moments together had been a *fantasy*. We both had tried, without speaking directly to each other, to ignore the obvious reality of our lives.

Having spent a few days together had given us a glimpse, a hope that good things could come to us we so desperately needed in order to face yet another day. I walked across the room, stood behind her, and saw that she was shaking.

"Hey, it's OK. It's OK."

I put my hand on her shoulder and she reacted to it as if I had tried to burn her. I did not withdraw my hand and eventually she put her hand on mine and held it there.

"I'm sorry," she said, "it's not going to work."

"What are you talking about?"

161

"About you and me."

"Why do you say that?"

"Because it's true."

"Emily, come on."

"I'm sorry," she said, again.

The voice came as if from some deep and dark hole. It sounded distant and neutral—no sentiment. A sound grounded in despair. It was guttural, disconnected, and almost inhuman. I had dreaded this happening from the very moment when I first got here. Man, how I had feared it. Now, what?

"Do you want me to leave?"

I knew I was taking a big chance for if she answered yes I would have no other choice than to pack my bags and leave at that very instant. She looked at me and her face was a horrible mask filled with pain, but she did not answer my question. The overwhelming feeling of terror that came over me was so painful.

I, who always prided myself on being able to deal with most circumstances in my life, now found myself entangled in sentiments that were so confusing and depressing. For an instant, the clarity and the enormity of what had happened to her and what was now happening to me was just too cruel to bear.

I knew that no matter what I said or did, at that moment, would only accentuate the distance between us and probably cause us more pain, and more confusion.

Taking us to a point of no return because whatever truth we were after, it would always be far and painful. I thought, how could I have been such a stupid fool to think that I could beat the odds in this struggle just to be.

And not only that, but how could I have been so incredibly insensitive toward her and her incredible pain that I could pretend things would be fine without any cost to both of us? That I could fix it? That all it took was for me to declare my love for her and that things would be back to normal?

How could I have been such an idiot? I had been so blinded by sentiments I had not connected deeply to the reality of who Emily and I were. To the depressing truth of her experience and suffering.

I had naively thought that all I had to do was tell her that I loved her and things would be OK. It was so depressing to be confronted with a sad and terrible truth that things were not OK.

Emily's life had changed so abruptly and, so brutally, drastically, so painfully and violently that no amount of words would possibly heal her broken heart.

Boy, how I had hoped that I could become that person in her life who could provide her the moral, spiritual, psychological help she so sorely needed.

I had to confront that in that department I was a damn failure. I could no more be the miracle worker for Emily than I could wave a magic wand and all of the ills and suffering in the world would disappear. I felt completely helpless.

I knew the heart always tries to heal so much sadness. But I also knew that some memories are never erased from our souls. Yes, time would dull the pain

162

but it would never disappear. I was looking at my own personal reality aware that I was not strong enough to be the person Emily needed at that moment. I thought I could do it, but it did not seem to be the case.

My grief and disappointment could not have been worse. That and the fact that my own inexperience and blindness to life's reality had made me realize for the first time how ridiculous our mutual efforts were. Who were we kidding?

At that instant, I wished that I had not come to see her. I wish I had not intruded upon Emily's life at all. I regretted everything that had happened. I felt completely lost and defeated.

It all seemed so futile and sterile. I just wanted to find a hole, crawl into it and not have to deal with what life was now showing me. I was not angry. I had taken a gamble and had lost.

I could not blame Emily for that. She was right. It probably was not going to work. She was far more lucid than I was, and I had to respect her sentiments.

"It's OK," I said.

I kneeled right next to her; she put her hand on my head and started to stroke it. I took her hand and kissed it.

"What's bothering you? Do you want to tell me?"

She shook her head. I could see tears in her eyes that slowly rolled down her wonderful apple cheeks.

I kissed them. I held her hand.

"Emily, is there anything I can do?"

She, once again, shook her head and tried to smile through her tears, but she seemed lost, disoriented, inside a world of hurt and without hope. Son of a bitch, I thought. Life can so fucking ugly. Why? Why?

"I love you, Emily. I love you, that's all I know."

She gave me a sad teary smile.

"If I could find some way to ease your pain, if I could find a way for your heart to feel whole and happy, if I could find a way to take the pain away from you and make you forget what happened, even if it meant giving up my life I would do it in a second.

"I wouldn't hesitate. But I don't know how I could do that. And the sadness in my heart because I cannot help you is so hard . . . so hard."

I was trying like crazy not to have tears in my eyes, but it was nearly impossible. I embraced her. Man, oh, man, I thought. There is no way that I can help her. I know there is not. How cruel can life be? How ridiculous and absurd?

"I wish . . . I wish . . ." she whispered.

"You wish what? Tell me, please."

"It's not fair . . . it's not fair . . ."

"My love, I don't know what's fair. I wish I could make your life wonderful again; I would give anything to be able to do that."

She saw my eyes filled with tears and tenderly she wiped them away. I had never cried in front of a woman before, and I thought that she would even be more afraid than was good for both of us now that she saw me crying.

She started to talk and her words were flat and without emotion. She was reciting a chain of events as if they had nothing to do with her.

"There was a knock on the door and when I opened it, there was the chaplain with Jackson standing behind him. I understood. I understood without knowing. Do you see? I understood but I didn't know. I didn't crumble like some people say they do when bad news comes to them. I didn't feel empty or lost. It seemed that everything was normal. Death just comes and that's it.

"I remember thinking that I needed to go out and buy some paints because I had wanted to start a new painting. I thought that the red I had was not strong enough. So I needed something darker, maybe mix it with blue to give it a hue that I had seen once when the sun went down. Yeah, all I thought about at that moment was a tube of red paint . . ."

She stopped. She seemed not to be talking to me but having some kind of dialogue with herself. The impression I had was she was not even aware I was there with her. Her loneliness was beyond measure, unreachable. It was part of a world that I could never inhabit for the simple reason that I had not been the victim of such a horrible personal tragedy.

I could not even imagine how to find the words to console her, to reach her, to convince her I so desperately wanted to change places with her. That I would gladly give my own life just so she would not have to live through this terrible ordeal. So she would not suffer, but I could not do it. I would never, ever be able to do it no matter how long I lived.

Can we be anything to anybody in this life? Yes, we are human, we are supposed to be the same, but we are not. No matter how hard I could try to see, feel, and identify with her suffering, I could no more do that than I could go to bed one night and wake up the next morning and be someone else.

At that very moment, holding Emily's hand I was completely in the dark unable to convey to her that I was trying like hell to be as sensitive as I thought I needed to be. I realized how phony my words would have been—how empty.

I did not know how to console Emily any more than I knew how to reach the other side of our galaxy. The universe Emily was condemned to live in was as foreign to me as the origin of life. Not that I would not try. I would try to find a way to help her. But in this contest there were no winners only losers.

Emily, no matter how hard she tried to make a new life for her, for her baby, even with my help, she would always be injured like a delicate bird that tries to fly when its wing is broken, and in its desperation it tries and tries but it cannot.

I so much wanted to make life better for Emily, to bring her joy, happiness, laughter. And I was so scared that the life, I had so stupidly thought I could provide for her, was out of my reach.

"And the most ridiculous thing," she continued, "is that for the past few weeks all I have done is deal with paper work. Government forms because my life seems to have been reduced to that. Official U.S. Army forms. I just wanted to throw them in the trash and forget about them.

"My mother got upset with me the other day because I told her that I wasn't going to finish them. That what I really wanted was for them to send my husband back to me all in one piece.

"Now I'm a war-widow and my child will be an orphan, that's my new status. I'm no longer a person, but a war-widow with an orphan child. I've become a label; a war-casualty. That's what the people at the veterans' office told me. I wanted to scream and call them all kinds of names, but I know that it isn't their fault. They are just doing their job."

She got up, went to small desk, and from one of the drawers she took out a whole bunch of forms, threw them on the floor and started to cry with such force and despair. Her sobs were so painful, so deep, that I became paralyzed. I could not move.

I finally got up, walked over to her, and held her in my arms. Emily seemed so fragile, so delicate, so lost, that for a moment I was afraid to leave her alone. I did not want to leave her in such a state. She seemed to have withdrawn from me and I was not sure she even remembered I was there.

She was in a world filled with pain and heartache, broken, dark, forbidden, implacable, and I wondered how someone could ever survive such an ordeal, and remain positive, hopeful, and sane.

It was incredibly painful and even more for me because I really had no way of making her life the way it had been. I could see how in such desperate moments it is not difficult for people to think that there is no other solution, and the only thing that makes sense is to commit suicide and seek relief from such a nightmare.

I got scared. She saw my face, and what she saw and sensed may have made her pull back from the abyss because she held me so close to her. Now it was her turn to be strong for both of us.

"Jonathan, I'm so sorry. I don't want you to suffer or be afraid because of me."

"You don't have to be sorry, Emily. Some things are not meant to be. It's our acceptance of them that converts us into adults. We're not children. Do I want to deal with the atrocities of life? No. There are moments when I wish I hadn't come along to complicate your life more than it is.

"Emily, I want so much to be different for you. To be the best for you and your baby. But I don't know that I'll ever be able to do it. I think that it's just out of my reach."

"Please, don't say that."

"Perhaps, you could deal with your life without me around. I think that all I do is complicate it. I'm not able to bring to you what you need."

"No, it's not true. I'm sorry Jonathan. I'm so afraid that once you are gone, I will be facing more loneliness, and I'm not sure I'm prepared to do that."

"I don't know how to change that reality. I can tell you that you are now the most important person in my life. I had never thought I could possibly have such strong and pure feelings for you. It has really come as a total surprise for me. But I have absolutely no regrets about it."

"Oh, Jonathan, I just need some time."

"OK, I do understand that."

And I did, in spite of the fact that it was nearly impossible for me to imagine what I would do without her. She embraced me and held me very close to her.

"No dear heart, please, I don't want you to go away. I belong to you and you belong to me."

"Oh, Emily, come with me, then."

"Jonathan, are we asking for the impossible? I need to stay here for the baby. How can life be so stupid? And why? Why?"

"But you can have the baby over there. I can be with you."

"No, Jonathan. I want to have the baby here. Do you understand?"

"I do and I don't. But you're right. It makes more sense for you to stay and have the baby here than to go back with me. I do see that. It isn't what I'd like to happen, but I do see it."

"My family is here. This is such a strange time for me that I need to remain here. I feel secure here. Do you see that?"

"I do, of course I do. I'm just afraid that, somehow, the fact that I'm not here with you may seem like I don't care."

"Jonathan, please, no my love, you're wrong. I have thought of you, of your kindness, of your love for me, of your amazing lack of selfishness, and I'm so touched by it. And even though we haven't been around each other but for a short period of time, you have shown me that your heart is pure and generous."

She went to get some Kleenex. She came back, sat on my lap and put her arms around me. I had never felt so close and yet so far from her. Emily and I lived in a world that was not the same, more like a parallel world than a singular world.

It was our reality and to overcome it would demand efforts that may be beyond me. Not that I wanted to walk away from her then or ever; I would never do that. But I also had to recognize that I was dealing with someone who was greatly injured by life and its ugliness, someone delicate, still innocent.

Could I make such a life beautiful, sane, happy, the way Emily deserved it? I did not know.

"Jonathan, why do ugly things happen? Why?"

"Boy, if I knew that, I would bottle it, sell it, and we would have so much money we could buy the Empire State Building."

She managed to smile at my silliness. I kissed her and started to laugh.

"Why are you laughing?"

"Because your nose is red. Does your nose get red when you cry?"

"I don't know. I look ugly, don't I?"

"No, you're still beautiful. Those high cheek bones make the difference."

She walked over to the mirror and looked at herself.

"You're right. My nose is red."

"Well, it's only red when you cry."

"OK, I won't cry. I don't like to have a red nose."

"Is that a promise?"

"Yes. I want to go back with you."

"Are you sure? I thought you said that it was better to have the baby here, close to your family?"

"Yes, I do. But I want to be with you, I want you to be there with me when the baby is born."

"I wish I could promise you that. I don't know what the Army will decide."

"I know."

"OK, no problem. Let's pack your bag and let's do it."

"And the baby?"

"He'll be born over there."

She stood, looked at the painting closely as if trying to find some new idea, some new thought, some new sentiment, then turned around and quietly walked back to the bedroom. I picked up all of the forms that she had thrown on the floor and put them back inside the drawer. I walked into the bedroom. She lay in bed in a fetal position, all curled up.

I got in right next to her and rubbed her back. She seemed so lost, so utterly alone.

"I'm sorry," she said.

"For what?"

"For not being brave, for not behaving like an adult. For making your life crazy."

"I can't imagine that I would want my life to be other than what it is now."

"Really?"

"Yes."

"I guess I'm not as strong as I think I am."

"Emily, you have lived a life that is no longer there. I can't imagine how I would have reacted if this tragedy had happened to me. It's beyond anything I know. Sometimes, I feel this thing isn't real.

"That I'm going to wake up and find it was all in my head. That you are not there, that it has been a dream; no, not a dream but a nightmare that someone invented to make us suffer for no reason.

"And there are days when I feel so small, so removed from you and it hurts me so much. Not because you have been distant from me; on the contrary, because no matter what I say it still doesn't answer why, not because I'm indifferent to your previous life or because I'm an idiot. It's that what has happened came about in a universe that I don't understand or control.

"I care deeply about your hurt, your emotions, your sentiments, about the impossibility of knowing why it happened, but even more about what's in store for us now. For the first time in my life, I see why people say take it one day at a time. I have been trying to do that.

"I want to believe that. If there is someone judging you and me, such a judge will look at us and not think that we are callous, spoiled, and indifferent. Our lives will always have this fact with us. Hopefully, with time the memories will soften and may even become just like some background noise the origin of which we know, but that does not rule what we feel, what we do, how we do it.

"I have never in my whole life experienced such beauty and innocence as I have these past few days with you, and for that I'm grateful to the gods that made it possible. I hope they don't have something bad in store for us.

"It's really the first time in my life I have looked at the future—at our future—with a sentiment of confidence and trust. Maybe I should not do that. But I do. I also know there will always be a part of you I'll never be able to reach and comfort."

She started to protest, but I put my finger on her lips.

"Listen, it's our reality. It doesn't mean that I don't trust you or your feelings toward me. Or those wonderful dreams you have about me, about the baby, about us. I'm not trying to pass myself off as someone of great experience and knowledge. I'm just a regular guy who has, by some strange twist of fate, fallen in love with you.

"And I want to do everything within my power to love you, to protect you and your baby, to respect you, to be available for you when things get tough. I never want you to feel that there are things that you can't discuss with me.

"I won't force you to tell me everything. If there are some things you don't want to tell me that's fine. But I also don't want this tragedy to overshadow my love for you because that would be terrible for me."

She touched my face, smiled, and kissed me.

"Jonathan, I don't want you to feel that my sentiments for you are just something for the moment. They are not."

I reached over and put my hand on her belly and she put her hand on mine. Just at that moment, the baby started to move and both of us watched the small ripples that the baby's movement made on her belly.

She looked at me, gave me a most wonderful smile, both of us rubbed her belly and the baby seemed to respond. It was probably my own anxiety and desire to be part of such a world that made me think that the baby was responding to us, at that moment.

It was a most magical moment for me and, I think for her, in that this was the first time that both of us had actually participated in this most human ritual. A most intimate moment when a man and a woman unite because of the magic and mystery of parenthood.

And even though I was not the natural father of this baby, the feeling that came over me was one of peace and quiet and I understood for the first time that I was going to be a father.

She seemed now more at ease, less troubled than she had been earlier. She had loved another man in her previous life. She was now getting ready to give birth to a child they had both produced.

168

However, the father of this child was no longer around, would never be around, so life had somehow made me inherit a role that was both scary and filled with magic. And of the many times when I had feared becoming a father, now the whole thing seemed natural, as if I had been in fact the progenitor of this child.

I loved Emily. She was the mother and I was going to be the father. The fates had spoken.

"Emily, there is something else that we need to talk about."

"Yes, I know."

"Look, at the moment I have no control over my life as a soldier. I'm at the mercy of a monster that does not recognize my deepest sentiments. I don't believe in this war. I think it's wrong. It's unjust not only to Americans, but to the Vietnamese.

"I have no way of knowing if the Army will send me over there. I have even considered that if they told me to go, I wouldn't do it. Instead, I would pack you and the baby and go to Canada."

"Oh, Jonathan, how terrible the choices."

"I know."

"Would do you it?"

"I would do it for you and the baby, yes!"

"No, Jonathan. I don't want you to make such a choice. Please."

I could see in her eyes the look of someone trying so hard to hang on to some sanity, not to give in to despair and fear. Trying to steel herself for what was next in our lives. Even if it meant that we had no control of the madness and the unexpected showing up and messing up our present existence with an implacable message:

Others had control and they did not give a shit what we felt and how opposed we were to their wretched designs over our destinies.

Her next words were said with a sad conviction that did not calm my frayed nerves. But I infinitely admired how she was also dealing with our present reality, with a degree of hope and more hope.

"I want you to know that if or when you get sent to Vietnam, I won't fall apart, I won't be negative. I won't consider it as another tragedy because I know deep in my heart that you'll come back to me, safe. So please dear heart, I don't want you to worry about us. We'll be fine. You must promise me that you won't worry about us."

"Emily."

"You must promise me!"

Her eyes were burning with an incredible look. It was not a look of despair or fear, but a look of total reality. She understood, she believed, and there would never be a way of making her change her mind. Her truth was the example that made the rule.

"I promise."

I turned the light off and Emily finally fell asleep peacefully. I stayed awake for a long time, a long time. I was afraid, but I never wanted to tell her. She believed in good things for both of us, that we were going to be safe and I also wanted to hold on to that belief. We had no other choice.

I fell into a kind of stupor that was dark, foreboding and unpleasant. All along, I had thought of the wonderful life that Emily and I could have. But I never expected the reality of our lives to intrude so strongly and so dangerously. I did not want to imagine that our future lives would be fraught with potential problems.

I had not considered that my dreams about Emily and me could instead become shattered and fruitless, filled with sadness and misunderstandings. But to ignore that danger was irresponsible. If Emily and I were going to make it, a certain reality had to be faced.

Emily had been wounded in such a terrible way that even though we both were trying to overcome such a deficit in our lives, the fundamental truth was that neither she nor I had any experience to draw upon as to how to deal with it. We were helpless. Even our combined life experiences were not enough to say that we could survive the ordeal.

Who was I kidding? Good intentions on the face of our reality remained that, good intentions. Love, happiness, search for your soul mate was a daydream in our present lives. In many ways, we stood naked and without any protection because our present existence was as mysterious and as bizarre as life could possibly get.

We did not have a handle on it no matter how much we thought we did. There was no sense in kidding ourselves. Yet I kept reminding myself of what Jack had said, of what Cash and Jackson believed. That in spite of everything it was possible for Emily and me to become a family. There was nothing wrong with searching for a bit of happiness in this life. Did we not all deserve it?

What was wrong in wanting to grab a bit of it while we could? Who said that we could not aspire to that? Are tragedies, such as the one that Emily had lived and was still living through, settled, final, and sealed in your heart?

And the people who suffer them had no other choice but to accept such tragedies and not really want to make a better life for themselves, after all?

Were we not allowed to demand better things from life? Who had the monopoly on inflicting such terrible ordeals on others? Was it God? Whose God? Which God?

So much of what has happened to me is still unclear and remains dark and forbidden. I look around and I see people doing things they do not want to do or need to do. I am like them. I do not know what I want to do or what I need to do.

Is this what life is all about? Emily is pregnant with a baby that I did not have anything to do with. A baby ostensibly conceived in love and tenderness. Yet the violence of life around us made it so that this baby will be born, and will live his or her life without one part of that life: The natural father.

OK, we can manage to live without limbs and even without parents. But is that OK? Is that what we should expect out of life? Is life an independent event outside of us, really, that we cannot have an impact on it or it on us? What we plan, think, or imagine is, what?

Is that outside of life? Like an event taking place out in the back yard, and we are inside the house and can only see through a window but cannot do anything about what is taking place outside—a spectator?

How are we to integrate ourselves into this cycle, this rhythm of seasons and sun rises and full moons that seem to regulate who we are, what happens to us, and at the same time, it appears not to have anything to do with us?

Does life have anything to do with us as living beings? Are we to integrate life into us, or the other way around? OK, so we get up in the morning and coast until we go to bed at night. That is all we do. We coast day in and day out.

After a few hours on the road, on my way back to Ft. Bragg, I decided to stop and get something to eat. I drove into a hamburger joint. It was not crowded. I got my stuff and sat to eat it. I had not done much traveling really, but what I had seen so far in the South was so strange and in so many ways seemed incredibly contradictory.

I thought about why so many white Southern people felt threatened by black people. Why was that? What was at the root of this shitty behavior? Fear? Ignorance? A sense of superiority? What? Given how complex human nature is, how it suffers and tries to find a way to live with itself, could one hope to find out why such hostility existed?

Was it the color of the skin? I mean, the color black is quite beautiful and it has its place in the rainbow of colors that nature has created. But not when black is the color of someone's skin, I guess.

What was the threat that Cash or Jackson or Sabrina, Cash's family or any other black person demonstrated or indicated or presented to white people? I mean, when it comes to danger it does not matter what one's color is, we are threatened and that is all there is to it.

I had read, and I had once told Cash and Jackson, that based on information about the origin of man we all had come from Africa, that mankind had started back in Africa and there was no doubt about it. It was now an established fact! But I also thought that perhaps nature had screwed up the deal, for she should have made us all look like zebras.

Stripes of every color should have been as normal on all humans as the colors of the rainbow. If from the beginning of time, we had all been like a rainbow there would not be any difference, no bigotry, and no racism; man, we would all have been the same—zebroids, that's what Cash would have said.

I wondered what stupid idiot had designed the world and had forgotten that simple and easy fact. But it was too late to correct it. We could never go back to day one and start all over again, that was certain. We were stuck, that was true, but we could change some things.

We had to fight the ignorance and stupidity, in which we all seemed immersed, so that we would become aware of how ugly and debilitating the whole issue of race was and change its reality.

Cash and Jackson had become friends with Homer and Emily. Black and white. Two sides of the human geography. I always marveled at how open and normal their relationship had become. I never saw anything indicating that Homer or Emily held any racists ideas about Cash and Jackson, or vice versa.

Their relationship was the same as the relationship that they had with me, with other white people. And now that I had met Emily's family, I saw why there was no reason to behave any differently. We were all the same, right? I had also the same impression of Homer's family.

Were they all that good at hiding their true feelings just to be polite while I was there? No, that was not the case. They did not seem to be pretending or acting. In other words, it did not make any difference.

Emily had said to her family that in addition to her two brothers wanting to be godfathers to the baby, that two other guys who were black—Cash and Jackson—had also expressed the same desire.

"Homer liked them very much. I like them very much."

Emily's mother was a bit reticent at first. I could see that. Perhaps she saw problems where none existed. Or perhaps it was a simple response to something that her own generation would not have found so easy to accept. Was it racism or just a first reaction to something new, strange, and unfamiliar?

"Honey, if Homer liked them and if you like them, it's really up to you. But you know that people talk and sometimes what they say it's not so nice."

"Mom, it's my life really. I don't know what harm could possibly be done by accepting those two guys as the baby's godfathers. They are good people."

"If you say so. Jonathan, what do you think?"

"It's Emily's decision. Those two guys *are* good people. I know how affected they were by what happened to Wilson."

The whole family smiled. They had said they got a kick out of me calling Homer by his last name: Wilson.

"I also know that when they asked me to ask Emily, it came from the heart. I don't think it occurred to them that they are black and the baby is white. For them, it was a baby from Wilson and Emily and that's all that mattered. I don't know if they are even aware of what they are asking."

"Do they know you want to marry Emily?" Her mother asked me.

"Yes."

"And how do they feel?"

"Both said that if I truly loved Emily, that was all that counted. Life had to be lived and though one doesn't understand what happened, such a tragedy could not prevent people from doing what was important in their lives. If Emily loved me back, that was all that mattered to them."

"That's nice," her mother said.

It was strange in so many ways to be discussing such things with Emily's mom. It was none of her business, but it was her business. After all, she was going to be the grandmother. Yet, through the conversation, I also gained a sentiment of

172

how contradictory life was. In all probability, Cash or Jackson would not really be part of the baby's immediate life.

Once the Army thing was over, all of us would live different lives and in different places. The whole notion of being a godfather to a child was romantic but given the reality of life, it would probably become a source of conversation, a human mystery of some kind that did not signify much.

This was not to deny that Cash and Jackson were serious. It was a way for them to remain connected, however remotely, to something in their lives that would always be there. A memory, yet one that they, as much as I, would always treasure.

What the hell, as the baby got older, he or she might get a kick out of having two black godfathers for the simple reason that I would make sure he or she would know why. And he or she would be proud because Wilson had appreciated these two guys. And yes, Emily or me, for that matter, would explain what the situation was, how it had come about.

And we would say that he or she had nothing to do with it, that it was his or her parents who had done it, but that it was cool. But it would probably be one of those facts of a person's life that would have an impact but not an impact of great significance. I did not know.

I decided to call Emily. I walked to the public phone. I had changed lots of dollar bills for quarters so I could call her at any time. She answered on the second ring.

"I miss you."

"That's lovely, really?" She sounded fine.

"Yes. I don't know if I can make it back to North Carolina. I want to come back and either stay with you or bring you back."

"I miss you, also. The house seems empty and sad without you. After you left, I sat here and I didn't know if I should get in my car and go chase you down the road. I felt lost and the whole thing seemed like some kind of dream. There was a sentiment of things lost and that I would never recover them. I don't know if I will be able to stand it."

"Oh, Emily, you don't know how terrible it was for me to leave you. It was the worst feeling that I have ever encountered in my life. I almost made a U-turn and went back. I felt like I was deserting you and the baby. That I would never see you again, that I would come back and find you gone, and nobody would know where you went and I would spend the rest of my life looking for you. How stupid is that?"

We make decisions in our lives from which there appears to be no escape or even logical, neat reasons that can help us understand what those decisions are and or why we made them.

We go through life, as part of a group, a tribe, and what we say or what we think quite often comes not from what we think or feel, but, rather, from what others say to us. It is as if we are something of an echo chamber, a thing feeding what we say or think.

Sometimes, I think we are limited in what we can say, or what we think. Nobody has a monopoly on our actions. We think we are limited and without exit because quite often we have come to a wall of either ignorance or stupidity, and we feel that we have to abandon our most precious and dear ideals.

We retreat into the mundane and expedient. We do not venture into the unknown for the simple reason that we are always afraid of losing, or making a mistake. We want for the most part to play it safe. And for good reasons.

Once we try to do something and we fail, the failure becomes part of our psyche, of our emotional make-up, of our idea of who we are. It takes over and we are no longer willing to dream. Thus, our fears become us. There is no difference between our fears and who we are. Yes, we become our fears.

And not only that, but we become uncaring, indifferent, soulless, and blind to the beauty that is all around us; that, in fact, is within us. Our capacity to dream pure and innocent dreams is taken away from us and, after a while, we no longer recognize who we are. We become strangers to ourselves and to others.

We thus end up separating ourselves from those we most need. And our lives become a giant list of regrets and more regrets. We become slaves to something that we do not really understand, and instead of being innocent, we end up vicious and corrupt.

Do we corrupt life? Or does life corrupt us? If life is corrupted then there is nothing we can do, but to try to keep away from such behavior. But if we, in fact, corrupt life, then there is no exit, no way to correct that, which is wrong. At that moment, it becomes abundantly clear how far from the ideal we have strayed.

"Where are you?"

"At a burger joint, staring at the French fries that are getting cold and soggy and I hate it that I'm not back there with you."

"Well, eat them before they get too soggy."

"Yeah, I will. Emily, I love you. I can't imagine my life without you. Do you think we're crazy?"

"Yes, but it's the good crazy."

'You know, if the Army does decide to send me to Vietnam, I'm not going. I've made up my mind that I'm not going. If you stay with me, we'll go to Canada or Europe. I have a few bucks and I think we can manage."

"Jonathan, you're beautiful but you're crazy."

"I mean it."

"I know you do. Maybe we won't have to make that choice."

"Will you go with me?"

"Yes dear heart, and wherever thou goes, I go."

"Emily, a man would die just to hear you say that."

"I love you, Jonathan."

"That's all I want to hear. OK, I'd better get back and eat my sorry fries."

"OK, and drive safely."

"I will. I promise you. OK, you hang up first."

"No, you hang up first."

"OK, let's both hang up at the same time. One, two, three—"

The line went dead. I stood holding the phone her words still ringing in my ear. I pictured Emily also holding up the phone as the conversation stopped. I hoped that she would not get depressed. I ate about half of the fries and walked out to my car. A couple of locals was looking at the car and smiled when I got in. I waved at them and they waved back.

-XII-

I got back on the road again and started thinking about Cash and Jackson, as the road on my way back seemed interminable. The song "*Stand by Me*" came on the radio. The song sounded kind of romantic, except that it was actually a gospel song. Jackson had pointed it out to me. Memories of our trip to St. Louis came back to me with the song about Kansas City running in my head.

Then I thought of how Cash and Jackson had put me through the ringer the night before I left to come to see Emily, and I also knew these two guys would be on pins and needles to find out what had happened.

I had decided to play a dirty trick on them. I was going to pretend the whole thing had been a giant bust and that Emily had rejected me; that, in fact, she had found some other guy and I was out of luck.

However, I was not sure if I could pull it off with a straight face. So I decided before I got back to the barracks to pick up a six pack, drink as much as I could reasonably hold without getting too drunk, and lie through my teeth.

I got back to the parking lot by the barracks, sat in my car, drank two cans before I finally walked to the barracks, and before the guys were through for the day. I finally heard Cash coming in. I pretended that I was getting my footlocker straight and did not really acknowledge him.

He wanted to come and say hello and I could tell from the corner of my eye he was hesitantly trying to figure out in his head some excuse, a reason to come by. Finally, he got enough courage and sort of shuffled over to my bunk. He was not comfortable.

"Hey, when did you get back?"

"A couple of hours ago."

I was using my driest tone, kept my voice low, neutral, but it was not easy. He really did not know how to start the conversation. I was not about to say anything at all. I tried not looking directly at him.

Then Jackson walked in, he saw Cash standing by my bunk and, again through the corner of my eyes, I could see Cash sort of giving him a hand signal to walk over to us. I guess the bozos needed to reinforce each other.

"Hey, Jonathan, when you get back?"

I pretended that I had not heard, and it was Cash who answered Jackson's question.

"He says a couple of hours ago."

Silence. By then I was kind of getting into the groove of the whole charade. I thought I am going to hold it as long as I can. I am going to make these two bastards go crazy with my silence. So I kept my face away from them.

176

"Everything, OK?" Jackson asked.

"Yeah, sure." Silence.

I could tell this was more than they could bear.

"Ah, how's Emily?" Cash finally asked.

"OK."

Oh, they were both hurting. I was trying like mad not to look at them directly because if I did, I would bust out laughing and blow the whole thing. I wanted to stretch it out to the max.

"The baby OK?"

"Yeah, I think so."

"Long trip, ah," Jackson said, after a long moment of silence.

"Yeah."

"So, I mean, things are OK?" Jackson stopped. I could tell that he did not know whether to shit or go blind.

"I guess."

"So you don't know?"

I shrugged my shoulders. I was still not facing them.

"Well, these things take time, man," Jackson said.

"Yeah."

The bastards had given me so much grief that I was just paying them back in kind. They were worried. I could tell just by listening to the way their voices sounded. Cash walked to the other side of the bunk and now I had to look either at him or at Jackson. Cash saw me smiling and he stood there for a moment trying to understand what he was seeing.

It did not make sense to him. Then he realized what was going on, and exploded with some pretended anger for all at once he understood I had done a number on them.

"You prick. You worthless piece of trash. You son of a whore. Dog Breath. You're gonna go straight and burn in hell for this!"

I started to laugh and the next thing I knew they jumped on me, threw me down on my bunk, and were beating me with their fists. The bastards were hitting me hard and laughing at the same time.

"You're Satan personified," Jackson said. "You bastard. You're the worst human being that's ever lived! Little Jesus won't forgive you for your stunt. You asshole."

Then, they picked me up, threw me on the floor, and jumped on me. We were all laughing and I had tears in my eyes from laughing so hard. They pinned me to the floor.

"Hey, get off me you bastards."

"I ain't moving until you tell us what happened. You bum."

"I ain't telling you jack."

"Then, you're staying here until you talk, right Jackson?"

"You've got it."

It was good to be back with these bozos.

"So, when she's moving back?" Cash asked later, as we were sitting in the car after bringing them up to date on what had happened during my trip. We were drinking the beer, which was now warm.

They wanted to hear all of the details. By listening to my description, they could live the whole experience themselves. Their sense of curiosity about what had happened was like that of a couple of kids, who are told of an adventure they could envision, savor, and in the end make their own.

In many simple ways, we had all been thrown together in this rather extraordinary but totally inexplicable event. They had been part of it and, in a much larger context, their sense of proprietary made them part time owners of what had taken place, and that included both the tragedy of Wilson's death and the aftermath.

I think when Wilson and Emily had met them, acting toward them as one set of normal human beings to another set of normal human beings, that had made a deep impression on Cash and Jackson. They had intrinsically understood in a more significant way, of course, that they were black and Emily and Wilson were white.

That same kind of rapport between two races was being decided all around us and inevitably would have a tremendous impact on who we were. Of course, it was ideal, but it is only in wishing human things, simple things, ideal things that we also find we are not so much different from each other.

The lesson that Anne Frank had left behind for the rest of us seemed naïve and perhaps simple, but it was also powerful and significant, for she had argued that deep down people were good at heart.

It was not an easy thing to live by everyday especially here in the South, but it was still a powerful feeling and one that we should keep in mind when dealing with each other.

I do not think Cash or Jackson misunderstood Emily and Wilson's behavior as paternalistic or condescending because it was neither. It was how normal human beings ought to behave toward each other.

In so many ways this search for normal behavior, for this humane behavior, that we all knew existed but against which so many obstacles were placed to complicate it or destroy it, was indeed what so many of us longed to be part of. And the saddest thing for me to reflect on was how stupid and denigrating racist attitudes were for all of us.

It made us less than human.

But Emily and I were now planning to get married, and were not interested in memories of destroyed lives or in being trodden by racism. What we wanted was something worthwhile, something new that in a much larger sense gave us some kind of hope that life regardless of how brutal it was—Wilson's death was ample proof of that—there was still something positive and good to get out of this.

It gave all of us a sentiment of good things in the offing. Maybe it was all for naught, still there was nothing wrong in hoping.

Her brothers' reaction to me had intrigued Cash and Jackson. I told them that Billy seemed to be much more emotional about Wilson's death than Jimmy.

"I understand," Cash said. "I'd have acted the way Billy done. Shee-it, I know I would of."

"So they liked your ass," Jackson said.

"I think so. I mean, I told them I wanted to be part of Emily's life and though I could not replace Wilson, I was willing to become the father to Emily's baby and I would try my best to make her happy."

"So when she's coming back?" Cash asked.

"She wants to have the baby over there. Closer to her family, which makes sense. I hope that I can get off and go back to be with her when the baby comes, but with the Army. I mean, I still have some vacation left, but I don't know if it's going to be possible."

"She's doing OK?" Jackson asked.

"She looks beautiful."

I had brought some photos with me and I showed them. Emily looked great. She was smiling at the camera and holding her belly with one hand. It was just amazing, this sense of happiness and well-being that the whole thing seemed to have brought to all of us.

There was no rational explanation for what had happened these past few months. If one could explain it to anybody, it would have taken something superhuman to recount it let alone understand it.

"Of course," Cash said, "you told her I want to be the baby's godfather, right?"

"I did. In fact, I told her you both wanted to be the baby's godfather."

"And what'd she say?"

"She agreed to have you both be godfathers, until I told her you were the biggest con artists this side of the Mississippi, after which she changed her mind."

"You lying bastard."

"Actually, it appears that this baby will have so many godfathers that he'll go crazy. Because her two brothers also want to be godfathers. So the baby will have at least four godfathers."

Cash and Jackson sat silent for a while, each savoring the idea that they were going to be the godfather to some strange baby—a white baby no less—who had not even been born yet.

"Hey, what if it's a girl?" Cash said, suddenly, with trepidation in his voice.

"What, you want to be a godfather only to a kid who has a big wanger?"

Cash started to laugh his hyena laugh and rocking back and forth so much the car started to shake.

"No, don't make no difference. And you Jackson?"

"I concur with that."

No mention of Wilson was made and in some distant way Cash, Jackson, and I knew and recognized that there was no further need to be concerned with such sad memories. What was important was the future because that is what made sense and not continue to dwell on such a tragic past. It was over.

Other facts had now replaced that previous life. It was a new life for all of us and, in our inexperienced way, we pushed aside the debris of past lives, of sad and gloomy histories, because that is what humans do, that is until the shit hits the fan, again.

I went to call Emily while Cash and Jackson sat in the car and waited for me.

"OK, I got back about a couple of hours ago. Cash and Jackson were happy for us when I told them the news. I showed them your photos and other than the fact you have a big belly, they said you haven't changed that much."

"OK, please give them my love. Tell them that I was touched they want to be the baby's godfathers. I'm delighted and honored by their request."

"They know. I love you."

"Really?"

"You mean, you don't know it?"

"Of course I know it. Please stay safe, and call me when you can."

"I'll call you every night."

"OK. I love you."

When I got back to the car Cash said, "listen, somethin' else has come up while you were gone,"

"What?"

"It's the Zen man."

"What's wrong with him?"

"He's been kind of quiet lately," Cash said.

"He's always quiet," I said.

"Yeah, but I know somethin' is bothering him."

"But what? Has he said anything to you?"

"No, but I know the Zen man. Somethin' is bothering him. I know it!"

'But what could it be?" Jackson said.

"I don't know," said Cash.

"Hey, he's got a lot of things on his mind. Maybe he is having second thoughts about marrying Tamiko," I said.

"I think that's what it is," Jackson said.

"What makes you say that?" I asked.

"I don't know. It's just a gut feeling I got. Or maybe she told him to get lost." Cash said.

"Should we ask him?" Jackson said.

"What are we gonna say: 'having problems with Tamiko, lately, Zen man?'" Cash said.

A couple of days went by and I could see that something was indeed bothering Yosh. He said he was happy that things with Emily had worked out. But he seemed withdrawn, avoiding us. Whenever we would kid with him about Japan and Tamiko he smiled, but the smile did not seem particularly honest.

What do we do when our sixth sense is telling us something is wrong with those around us? How are we to interpret those unmistakable signs in the other, telegraphing us things are not what they should be? We all lived in this glass bubble, yet most of us wanted to give Yosh whatever space he needed.

To ask him directly what was bothering him seemed to be pushy. And for the rest of us, it was something that we did not feel qualified to ask let alone be able to phrase the question properly.

We all knew that he had been preparing all kinds of documents about Tamiko. So Jackson seemed to be the logical source of anything that would help us clarify things. However, Jackson had said that he knew nothing and, so far, Yosh had said nothing about any problems in that regard.

It was Kenny who clarified the deal for us in his typical idiotic way. How he found out was a total mystery to us. Our understanding was that Kenny was not close enough to Yosh to be a confidant. It did not seem like Yosh would confide in him. It did not make any sense.

We were eating lunch one day, when Kenny approached the three of us, with a certain self-righteousness that was not out of place given his stupidity. He knew he had something over us.

In his stupid mind, it gave him an air of superiority because he had guessed, correctly, that we were in the dark about what was bugging Yosh. He had come to believe that what he knew, or guessed, gave him a morally superior position relative to us and he meant to exploit it to the max.

It is interesting how idiots are always looking for something that will make them feel superior to others, for the simple reason that in the miserable lives they have there is very little to be happy about. Thus, in their misery anything they could do to put others down was what they lived for. The world is filled with such sick minds.

He came and sat at our table, as if we had invited him. Cash looked at him and back at us.

"Did anyone invite you to sit here?" Cash said.

"Hey, since when is this Army table your personal property?"

"What the hell do you want," Jackson said.

"I know something that you guys don't know jack about."

"Who gives a shit," Cash said.

"It's about Yoshi," Kenny said, knowing fully well that we were Yoshi's friends and that whatever it was Kenny knew we would want to know it as well.

"What are you talking about?" I asked the schmuck.

"Well, seeing that you guys act like a bunch of assholes, I ain't gonna tell you."

"Stop your bullshit and get it over with. You're not welcome at this table. Get the hell away from this table," Cash said, obviously pissed. Kenny looked at him and smiled his rather condescending smirk.

"Hey, Yosh ain't going to Japan, after all," Kenny said.

Kenny's words put all three of us on our guard. We did not trust the prick.

"Why, what's wrong?" I asked.

"He just ain't, that's all."

"What the hell do you know?" Cash said.

"Well, fuck you if you don't want to believe me."

"OK, I'll go and ask him," Cash said.

"He won't tell you jack," Kenny said.

"Cash, wait until he says something," I said.

"Yeah," Jackson said.

"Good bye, ladies," Kenny said.

He had lately taken to calling us ladies. He got up from our table and walked away, a sick grin on his racist mug. He had rattled us about Yosh, no question about it.

"I wanna kill this sick bug," Cash said, livid.

"I'm beginning to think you're right about what to do to this jerk," Jackson said.

"I know how I can get rid of this prick. When we go out to target practice. If he gets in the same foxhole with me, I'll shoot him and pretend it was an accident. Who would know? The rifle just discharged accidentally."

Cash was serious.

"Come on, you're crazy." I said. "Look guys, let's not make this thing about Yoshi more complicated than it is. If he's having some problem it's better we wait until he says something. I don't want to crowd him."

"Shee-it, but if he's hurting he needs us, man," Cash said.

And the truth was the Yosh was hurting. You could see it on his face. There was something about him lately that was just too obvious to ignore. But again, the mad thing about others is that unless they want to tell you what is on their minds, one has to respect their desire to be private, and to be left alone.

But Yosh was our friend and when it came right down to it, if he needed our help and he did not know how to ask for it, then it was up to us to go to him and tell him we were there in case he needed us.

Then Yosh took me aside and told me what was going on. I could tell that he did not want to say anything, but that the whole thing had to be aired out and he needed to tell somebody or he would explode. It turned out to be what we had suspected all along. He had gotten one of those "Dear John" letters from Tamiko.

So many GIs get them and drives many of them to go AWOL quite often. Apparently, she had decided that marrying Yosh was not a good idea after all. She gave him all kinds of excuses, but the one that hurt the most was that she accused him of being indifferent to the fact that he was an Asian guy preparing to go to war against other Asian people.

She was not against marrying an American per se. She hated the idea, however, that Yosh was going to end up in Vietnam and she was a pacifist and against any kind of war. She had also, rather bluntly, reminded him that his grandparents had been killed by an atomic bomb dropped on Japan by Americans, and she wanted to find out why he seemed to be so passive about it. Did he not care at all?

"They were killed by the fat American," she had said. Actually, Fat Boy was the name given to the atomic bomb we had dropped on Nagasaki.

"And now you're going to go and kill Vietnamese babies and women and old men," she reproached him.

From what Yosh told me, she had concluded that, as a Japanese, though, born in America, Yosh had to deal with this aspect of his personal and family history and all Yosh was now doing was getting ready to go and kill Asian people.

She had told him the incredible sense of guilt about what the Japanese Army had done to the Chinese when they invaded China. She had really tried to get other people to think about this but all she got was talk about how patriotic she had to be and not to say anything against Japan. She did not agree, and she did not want to be a phony, or lie about facts that could not be denied.

"You didn't know all of this when you met her?"

"Not really."

"Yosh, it would seem your relationship didn't start off on the right foot."

"I know. What can I do? I love her. This is so stupid and crazy."

He had been devastated by what she told him. That was the reason he had been acting strange lately. I did not know why he thought we would not understand his feelings. Maybe he was simply afraid to share the bad news with us. Or maybe it was all about not losing face.

"Have you tried talking to her?"

"Yeah, but she's pretty much set against the war and my being part of it."

"So she won't marry you?"

"No, she won't."

"Jesus, Yosh, it's not your fault."

"I know, but she doesn't see it that way. For her, the fact that I'm probably going to be shipped over to Nam is the worst thing that could happen to us. I sometimes think that for her even my dying over there isn't as bad as the fact that I may end up killing Asian people."

The terrible thing was that, lately, Yosh had been dealing with pretty much the same contradictory sentiment as far as the Vietnam War was concerned. He had been drafted into the U.S. Army and was suddenly faced with a culture that was not strictly speaking his own.

Though he had been born in this country and his mother was an American, the simple fact of the matter was that for all practical purposes Yosh was Japanese in temperament, outlook, rationality, looks, and upbringing. His whole outlook was not completely American for the simple reason that he had not been raised in the U.S.

He saw America through the eyes of someone who has essentially been living in exile and though proud of his American heritage, as well as of his Japanese one, the fact was that Yosh had found himself straddling two very different cultures that were not as compatible as he would have liked them to be. Yosh was a foreigner and an immigrant in his own country of birth.

He and I had had several talks about this dichotomy in him and while he felt that he could deal with both of them without compromising what was fine with both of them, he also ran into contradictions that were proving to be more difficult than he had imagined.

"You know, sometimes I don't know just exactly where I fit in. There are moments when I fully understand what Cash and Jackson are living through, for in many ways I'm just like them. I'm just another nigger—an Asian nigger—as Cash is fond of reminding me."

"Come on, Yosh."

"Well, it's true. You know, the other day when we were talking and Jackson was shocked about people from Africa, especially the diplomats, being treated here like they were white? I know something about that."

"What do you mean?"

"I understand how conflicting such things are for them. I mean, they were both born in this country, both Americans and both black. But where do they belong? Do they belong here or back in Africa? You tell me."

"They're Americans for Christ's sake."

"Are they?"

"Of course, they are."

"Why?"

"Why? Yosh, you just want to give me a hard time on this."

"No, I'm serious."

"They're Americans because they were born here."

"So was I! But I don't feel American. In fact, I don't know what it means to be an 'American'. I'm neither here nor there. In many ways, Cash and Jackson are in a better position than me. Now here I'm in this Army and to tell you the truth I don't like the idea of me, an Asian guy, going out to fight other Asian guys. Why does it have to happen?"

"The other day when we talked, you seemed to have no problems with this."

"Well, now I do."

"What's behind all of this?"

"Been doing some thinking and I'm slowly coming to the conclusion that I shouldn't have allowed myself to be drafted into the Army. I should have told them to go and screw themselves or just simply gone to Canada, or back to Japan. I have double nationality, you know."

"It's kind of late for that, ain't it?"

"No. If I decide to split, I'll do it."

"Are you crazy?"

"No."

"Yosh, you're beginning to sound like Cash. Come on, man. You know better than that."

"Yeah, because I know better that's why I'm telling you this."

"So now you want to go AWOL?"

"It seems I've been AWOL all of my life. I don't belong here and I don't really belong in Japan."

"OK, Tamiko is against the war. In many ways, it makes sense because the Japanese are strong pacifists. It's in their constitution. But Yosh, is there something you're not telling me? Like maybe your own family is against this whole thing of your being in the Army?"

"If you want to know the truth, it's my mom who sort of agrees with me that if I want to split I should do it. She tells me to be certain as to what I want to do. That somewhere in my life there will come a time when I'll have to make a decision about what is important to me.

"My old man isn't sure what to make of my mom's attitude. In a sense, he knows that I'm torn by this duality in me. We have talked about it, but my father is also someone who does not easily give advice. He has always wanted me to look at the problem and arrive at my own decisions."

"So you think he'll be fine if you decide to split?"

"I think so. Yet, I've got to tell you my mother is also afraid of what I'll do. She has never explicitly said that I should get out of the Army and go AWOL. She has never said that. But if I ever did it, I know she would be one hundred percent behind my decision, even though she is afraid. My mother is so incredibly strong and her moral position is just amazing.

"My mom isn't a fanatic or some crazy radical and she knows better, than anyone, my own contradictions. She and my dad had big arguments about what would happen to me once I reached the draft age. My uncle, bless his soul, never argued either for or against the military even though he had suffered when he thought about fighting for this country while his whole family was behind barbed wire.

"He told me that many times he was discouraged and torn by what he felt. But he also said that many times when he saw his buddies killed, he thought that he owed them his best efforts to make sure that nothing like what they had experienced would happen again.

"It's funny, he fought not just to help those people in Europe, but he also fought for Americans, regardless of origin, who had the right not to fear because they were different. In many ways I feel like him; yet, at the same time I don't want to be part of this sick war effort."

I did not tell Cash or Jackson of my talk with Yosh. I did not want to bring more confusion to what was already a very confusing situation. Besides, I felt that the conversation I had with Yosh should be kept private. If he wanted to tell the others his feelings, he would do so. I would prefer it that way. Thus, I kept my mouth shut.

And now looking back it may have been my mistake for Yoshi, one day, he just simply disappeared! Nobody knew where he was, where he went, what had happened to him. Of course, we all knew that he had just gone AWOL. For the Army this was the ultimate crime. Especially during a time of war.

This was some rather serious stuff. No getting around that. Cash and Jackson thought that Yoshi was right. I knew how they felt and in many ways I, too, understood why Yoshi had split. Yet I was also torn by the fact that looking at what he did in the harsh light of its reality, there was no doubt that Yoshi had come to a decision that would affect everything he did for the rest of his life.

I could understand, in the abstract, that he felt no affinity for the U.S. Yes, it was the country where he was born, but other than that he had not lived here long enough to have developed some kind of American "consciousness." His connection to the country, was the fact that his mother was American and he had been born here, but that was it.

He had not grown up in the U.S. I wondered what his parents were feeling now that the reality of his actions was impossible to ignore. We all felt like shit. I did not tell any of this to Emily, however.

I had said to her that I would not stay in the U.S. or the Army if I were to be sent to Vietnam. I knew that I would do it, even though now I was scared that soon I might be facing such a choice and there was not much room to maneuver. Man, oh, man, this whole thing is just for the shits, I thought.

"Why did he do it? I mean, why? It don't make sense."

Cash was really ticked off by Yoshi's disappearance. He took it personally. He felt betrayed. Jackson was less emotional about it. I was confused, but I think that of the three of us I was more likely to intellectually accept Yoshi's decision. Not that I was not emotionally affected by it. I was, after all, against the war.

"Man, he could have argued some kind of conscientious objection. I mean, shee-it," Cash said.

"Man, to become a C.O. you have to do it from the get go. You can't do it in the middle of the deal. It don't look good and the Army is going to screw him over. I just don't understand it, either," Jackson said.

"Do you think your old man can help him?" Cash asked.

"How?"

"Shee-it, I don't know. Doesn't he have some contacts in the government?"

"Yeah, he does. But, what's he gonna say? 'Excuse me, guys, but give this kid a break.' It don't work like that."

"Do you guys know how we can contact his family? His mom?" Cash asked.

"Well, from what he said, his mom sort of agrees with what he did," I said. "He told me that she would back him up on whatever decision he made. So she probably knows where he is."

"Shee-it, this is bad. I feel like we let him down," Jackson said. "Maybe if we had talked to him, maybe we could have talked him out of it. That jerk, Kenny, he's probably laughing his head off because he told us about it and we ignored it. Shee-it."

The whole thing was pretty depressing. In another sense, there was a kind of guilty feeling that seemed to be different from the feeling we had had about Wilson's death—we could not have prevented it.

But with Yoshi, the sentiment was we could have done something about it. We could have argued with him not to do it. Or at least try to find some other help, maybe a head shrink, or someone to whom he could have gone and talked things over.

In our desire to cut him some slack, it seemed we had screwed up.

I had finally talked to Emily about it and she knew I was pretty upset. I blamed myself to some extent, but she had argued that in the final analysis it was Yoshi's decision to make.

Though Emily had met Yosh before, it always seemed that Cash and Jackson had created a better rapport with her. I do not know why it had happened that way.

"I'm redoing the painting, remember?" she said.

"Oh, wonderful. What did you do?"

"Well, I thought about what I had done to it that evening and it was clear that I had been foolish, and so I went back to the stream, sat in the same spot and literally retraced my original idea. I saw where I had made some mistakes of color, texture and images. I corrected them, and it actually looks much better.

"Also, as I was doing it the baby was kicking, which I got a kick out of. I was thinking about you and, at that moment, everything seemed wonderful and clear, perfect. And I understood what my present life is about, and it's the baby, you, and us. So I think that it'll be much more inspirational and pure because of the baby and you."

"Oh, Emily. You're amazing."

"Really?"

"Yes."

"Thank you. So are you."

"So I guess we're both amazing."

"Absolutely. I went to see the doctor and he said that everything is on target that I'm gaining the right weight and he isn't worried about anything. That we should let nature do what she does best. Isn't that great?"

"Of course. I'm sure you will have a healthy baby."

"No, we will have a healthy baby."

"You're right. It seems so strange that I'm going to be a father. And do you know something, I like it."

"Good."

Talking to her, which I did almost every night and made me rather poor—actually broke—was incredible for me. It gave me in some ways a kind of insular distance from my everyday existence. I often wondered what it would be like living every day with Emily. Would it be so romantic and magical? What if the hidden truths of our situation came out and made us sad?

I was always questioning my own peculiar position regarding her. I often wondered if among the many sentiments I had, I was simply avoiding the truth because of the pain and confusion it could bring me. However, as is the case in life, what we desire is not always provided.

Thus, it had come like a thunderbolt that hit me in the solar plexus when Yoshi just disappeared. I should have been prepared for it, but I was not. How naïve of me. I hated to think that I had not learned my lesson about pain and confusion.

Jackson came and told me that he was going to Nam. He had been selected to go and he was waiting for his orders to come in.

"What are you talking about?"

"I'm on the list, man."

"Are you serious?"

He showed me the list.

"This is totally stupid. I don't believe it."

"Well, we might as well prepare for our deployment," Cash said.

Jackson, my buddy. My man. He seemed rather cool about it. I thought I had better get used to the idea that so many of the people I knew would be going. I would be going, and there was a good chance that many of us would be coming back in body bags.

"I bet you the reason they're sending your ass over there is because they expect many dead GIs and they want to have all of the available chaplains and their assistants so they can deal with the dead. Shee-it, I bet you that's what it is."

"Come on, Greene, why are you so damn depressing?"

"He's right," Cash said.

There are things in life that prompt us to get into a melancholic sense about where we are in the scheme of things. Some of us are more prone than others to get into this mental state. I, for some reason, have always been in this category of people who are melancholic and I wish I knew why.

No getting around it. The shit was starting to hit the fan and there was no way of stopping what was coming. The fact that Jackson seemed somewhat detached from what his future would be like made it even worse for me.

A mental picture of what another loss in my life would mean made it even more depressing. What could I do? What could anyone of us do?

I called Emily and she knew instantly that something was wrong. I guess the sound of my voice gave it away. I had not wanted to share the news with her. On the other hand, if I could not talk to her, whom could I talk to?

Even the idea of talking to Jack was not the same thing. I needed Emily's love and understanding far more than I needed Jack's words at the moment.

"What's wrong?"

"Jackson is on the list for Vietnam." I could not hide it from her. That much I knew. There was a long silence at the other end of the phone.

"Emily, are you there?"

"Yes."

"I'm sorry."

"Oh, Jonathan . . ."

"Emily, I didn't want to tell you. I'm really sorry."

"Jonathan. If you can't tell me, who are you going to share it with?"

"It's funny. You are the only person I can share this with. And at the same time, you should be the last person to share this with. It's so screwed up."

"Jonathan, I love you. I want you to always trust me so that I know where you are, what you are feeling, and thinking, even the most painful things. I don't want you to hide such things from me. Do you understand?"

"I do and I don't."

"Dear heart, we must be brave. We must have courage."

"I know."

"Do you want me to come over?"

"Emily, you're something else. No, I will be fine. It's just the idea that makes it so hard to deal with."

"Are you afraid?"

"Yes."

"Jonathan, we have to believe in something good, positive. We can't dwell on negative things all the time. We'll never make it. You, me and our baby have a long life ahead of us. I don't want to sound uncaring because I'm not.

"But Jackson's life isn't controlled by us, not even by him at this moment. That's the reality. I'll pray for him. But you can't be so depressed by this. I need you. The baby needs you."

Her voice, though quiet, did not sound sad. It was the voice of a person who has seen terrible things and yet it was also the voice of hope and reason.

"You're right. You know, sometimes I fantasize about wanting to protect everybody from evil, from pain, from ugly things, only to realize that in most instances I'm just another guy, another person, and I have no magic powers to stop all of this madness."

"You're doing your best, my love."

"I'm trying. But it's frustrating because in the final analysis, I haven't got any control."

"Nobody does."

"OK. You know, just talking to you is so great. I couldn't imagine living without you. You are more than I deserve."

"Oh, Jonathan, how wonderful of you to say that."

"It's true."

"Thank you. OK, let's keep things in perspective. Nothing bad will happen. He'll go and he'll come back, and he'll be the same old Jackson we love and appreciate. OK?"

"OK."

Later, that evening, as I lay in my bunk thinking about her words, her voice, her image, it did not seem too impossible to concentrate on what she said, on what she so fervently believed.

Then, Yosh called me. It was late in the day. Fortunately, I was in the dark room developing some negatives when the phone rang. I was kind of busy and did not want to answer it. I thought it was probably the sergeant calling me to develop some of his own personal photos. I had done it in the past and it was a tradeoff. He left me alone and I developed his photos. It was mostly of his kids.

I picked up the phone.

"Greene, speaking."

"Jonathan, this is Yosh."

"Yosh? Jesus Christ, where in the hell are you?"

"I'm in San Francisco. Can you talk?"

"Yeah, sergeant smuts isn't around. What is going on, man?"

"Nothing. I'm going to Canada."

"Yosh, shit. This is no good man."

"No, it is good, man. For the first time, I feel I'm in control of my life. I went to visit my folks and though they are afraid of my decision, they said that it was my decision. Whatever I wanted to do was fine with them as long as I took total responsibility for it.

"They would back me up. So I'm going to Canada. I'm going to register at the University so I can continue with my medical studies. I'm interested in keeping people alive and not in killing them."

"So you're not coming back?"

"No, I won't?"

"Yosh, you know the military is going to screw with you. You probably will never be able to come to the U.S. unless you're wearing handcuffs . . .and that ain't no good, man."

"Hey, I've lived most of my life out of the U.S. so it isn't as if I was going to miss something that I really never had. I'm an American by accident. I'm not saying that I'm not proud of it. But what I've been asked to do I just can't do. Believe me it wasn't easy for me to do this, but I had no other choice."

"I wish you had told us about it."

"And then what? You guys would have probably tried to talk me out of it and I had made up my mind. So rather than put everyone through the ordeal, I decided not to say anything. Of course, I regret I didn't tell you guys but I thought it was better to do it this way. I hope you aren't sore that I didn't say anything."

"Come on, Yosh. You know we're behind you."

"OK, that's all I need to know."

"What about Tamiko?"

"What about her?"

"Well, is she happy with your decision?"

"I don't know. I haven't talked to her. In any event, she had nothing to do with my decision."

"Well, she wasn't happy with you going to Nam."

"No, she wasn't. But that's a small part of why I did it. Yes, it was a part but not really significant."

"Yosh, I don't know what to tell you."

"You don't have to say anything. That's how things work out. I'm not regretting what I did. I only regret that I probably won't see you guys, again. And that's the shits."

"Well, that's how the ball bounces."

"You OK?"

"Yeah. Jackson got his orders to 'Nam."

"You're kidding?"

"No."

"What's he saying about it?"

"What can he say?"

"He's gonna go?"

"Yeah. I don't think that Jackson has much of a choice, really."

"Come on, of course, he does."

"Well, it's not easy for him."

"Do you think it was easy for me?"

"I know it wasn't. In fact, this may come as a surprise to you but I told Emily that if I ever got orders to go, that I would just pack her and the baby and we would move to Canada. So, maybe we'll get to see each other after all."

We laughed. It was good to hear from Yosh. He sounded calm, controlled. He did not sound agitated or in some kind of emotional crisis. Yosh was always cool and he was demonstrating it. But I also had to wonder just how tough it was. He never struck me as being a coward, or irresponsible.

I always thought he had a good head on his shoulders so what he had done was not without forethought. I was sure he had given it a great deal of thought and his conviction, as he had contemplated what he was facing, had won the day.

In many ways, I admired him. He saw what he had to do. He saw the choices in front of him and he acted based on what he understood his situation to be. But it was a radical step, no question.

"In many ways I envy you, old buddy."

"Oh, yeah?" He seemed surprised. "But it isn't easy."

"I can imagine."

"The thing is that my parents were fine with it. It ain't easy for them. I know. But they have been wonderful. In fact, my old man has some connection at McGill University and he called and the guy promised to help me get in if that is what I want to do. My grades aren't too shabby. So I think I have a good shot at it."

"Yosh, with your shitty grades, I don't know," we both laughed, as Yosh had straight A's.

"Maybe you're right."

"Any university would be more than happy to take you in, man."

"You think?"

"Come on, Yosh."

"Man, I hope so."

Any university looking at Yoshi's grades would never hesitate to give him a berth in their medical program. Yosh was smart, period. He would make a great doctor. I had no doubt about it.

"Piece of cake, babe," I told him.

He laughed. Boy, how I secretly wished in my heart that Yosh would not only survive but succeed in what he was attempting to do. I knew that what he had done, going AWOL, was just not kosher and it might still come back and bite him in the ass.

"So when're going to tell Tamiko?"

"I don't know. It's funny but I'm kind of afraid to tell her."

"Why? Isn't that what she wanted?"

"Well, I don't know that she wanted me to go AWOL."

"But Yosh, how else were you going to get out of this? You know that declaring yourself a C.O. would not work. Your only choice was to split and that's why you did."

"I know. Still, I feel kind of strange telling her about it."

"Yosh, you're a funny guy."

"And our great racist friend?"

"Well, he hasn't said much."

"Maybe he feels let down."

"Screw him."

"Cash and Jackson doing OK?"

"Yeah. We talk about you all of the time."

I stopped. I was not sure if saying such things to him would make it harder. On the other hand, I had told Yosh that Cash, Jackson and I would constantly talk about him.

For the most part because we did not know where he was. So we imagined all kinds of things. We even thought of trying to contact his parents, but in the end we decided against it.

"What if he hasn't told them?" Cash had asked.

"Yeah, you're right," Jackson had said.

"OK," Yosh said. "Tell those two crazies that I'm going to try to keep in touch with them. That I valued their friendship to no end. And you, take care of yourself, Emily and the baby. And I'll be in touch."

"OK, buddy, you know you'll be in our thoughts. Bye and take care of yourself."

"I will."

For some reason, I felt less troubled by what Yosh had done after speaking with him. I did not really know why I felt that way. Maybe it was because I trusted him to know what he was doing.

He had not volunteered to share more information with me in terms of when he was going to Canada or anything else. I had not asked for it. I guess, we were both afraid of something happening later and we subconsciously had avoided getting into a trap.

Then, Julie sent me a note asking if I would meet her one late afternoon after school. She would come by the theater to meet me. I was not sure if that was the right thing to do. I had shared with Emily Julie's crush on me, and Emily had said she understood.

So after work that Wednesday afternoon, I went to meet Julie. The theater was empty, but later a bunch of GIs who had formed a band would be rehearsing. I had not seen her for several weeks, not since the play was over, and while Andy and I had talked briefly about what the next show would be, I told him that maybe he should get someone else to direct it, as I was not sure what the powers that be had in store for me.

"Do you want to get out of going to Nam?" Andy had asked me.

"What are you talking about?"

"Well, General Numbnuts is rather keen on doing something shortly, and I happened to mention that I thought you would be perfect to direct." He stopped.

The silence between us was pretty heavy. Andy had never intimated or had suggested that I could get out of going to Nam just by simply asking him, and by extension get General Numbnuts, to find some excuse for me not to be sent to Nam.

I remember how Yosh hated it that some bird colonel had gotten him out of his hospital's duties so he could have a partner to play golf. And now here was Andy coming out and telling me that his connection with the general was strong enough to make a deal on my behalf. I was completely taken aback by his suggestion. I really did not know what to say.

"I know this sounds a bit crazy," he continued.

"Crazy? It sounds downright subversive if you ask me."

"Come on."

"Jesus Christ, Andy."

"Look, you could do a hell of a lot more good here bringing some kind of pleasure to these poor soldiers than going over to Nam."

It really blew my mind to even consider what Andy was proposing. I could not think straight.

"Andy, Christ. Do you know what you're asking me to do? You want me to find some sneaky way of avoiding going to Vietnam. I mean, this is crazy. I can't believe we're talking about it."

"Look, I suspected that you would get upset about it. But again, people don't stop living when something bad happens to others. They don't suddenly give up who they are, who they want to be because some horrendous situation is taking place."

"Andy, wait a second. This sounds so strange to me because not too long ago, you gave me a big lecture about how you didn't serve in the military because you have some kind of heart disease, or something and you felt disappointed."

"It's not a heart disease. It's a heart murmur that I was born with. It has never bothered me. I played sports at school and there was never a problem. I was fit to go but the Army had other ideas. It wasn't my fault."

"OK, but nevertheless, it kept you from going and don't tell me that it didn't bother you."

"It did, but not for the reasons you think. But after I thought about it, I didn't try to hide the fact that this thing had kept me from going. I also realized that I could be just as effective in helping with the war effort in my own limited way. I had a long discussion with my rabbi and he said it wasn't my fault, and that life has some rather strange ways of making things happen."

"Yeah, but what you're suggesting isn't the same thing. You're telling *me* that you can get me out of Vietnam duty by going to the general and asking him to keep me here because I'm needed here far more than I'm needed over there. I just can't believe that you're saying that."

"Look, I'm not suggesting anything dishonest, subversive or disloyal. What I'm saying is that this war is going to bring misery and suffering to many people—Vietnamese and Americans. If I can keep you, or anyone, from going over there within the limitations of my job, my convictions, I'll do it."

"I never took you for a peacenik."

"Life is full of surprises."

Needless to say, the conversation with Andy had left me totally messed up. I did not know what to think. More than anything else, I resented that Andy had somehow connected me with some kind of hidden wish to try to work myself out of what until then I considered my normal military obligation.

Suddenly, the ghost of Wilson appeared and it depressed me even more. I did not know if I could talk to Emily about it. I did not know if I could talk to Cash or Jackson. Then what I had said to Emily about not going if I got orders to go to Vietnam.

What was the difference between me going to Canada just like Yosh or letting Andy sweet talk the general into letting me stay if I got orders to go? This is so incomprehensible, I thought. What Andy had said seemed to be dirty, dishonest, and even cowardly.

I hated the war and what it was doing to so many people, and what I suspected it was going to do to hundreds if not thousands of young guys. But I was also not prepared just to forget what I still considered my own military commitment, my obligation, as if it were some kind of jump rope game, easily forgotten when it was over.

I had argued against not going, and now that this thing had been dropped in my lap, I resented it very strongly. I knew Andy had been serious about it.

Suddenly, I was afraid. It was like Andy had told me something that he was feeling about me, what would happen to me, that he knew ahead of time as if he had been reading the tea leaves, and he was now warning me not to do it.

I felt the same foreboding as when Wilson found out he was going to Nam. Reflecting on it now gave me a creepy feeling and I was not sure what Andy was trying to tell me. It really threw me for a loop. I was completely baffled by what we had talked about, and about my own sentiments, which were very far from being clear.

Though I also was not going to blame Andy for what he had in mind. He was the good guy and I deeply appreciated his concerns and friendship. But, I could not agree to what he was proposing.

This had to be the strangest of feelings. I had such contradictory emotions. It suffocated me. I had left Andy's office in complete state of confusion and shock. I wanted to resent Andy for what he had told me. I wanted to hate the son-of-a-bitch, but I could not.

It was in such a state of mind that I went to meet Julie.

She seemed changed. I do not know what exactly had changed, but something had changed. I sensed a bit of tension in the air. But it seemed that she was angry with herself and not with me.

Maybe a better description would be one of disappointment. Boy, life does not get easier, I thought. I seemed to be going around in circles and I did not like it one bit.

"Julie, what did you do to your hair?"

"I had it cut."

"Why?"

"I don't know. You don't like it?"

"Actually, it makes you look more mature, more serious."

"Really?"

"Yeah, it's an interesting cut."

"Only interesting?"

"Actually, it fits you. It's a good cut. I guess it was the surprise of it that made me react that way."

"So you do like it?" And her lovely face looked anxious.

"Yes. I mean, the last time I saw you, you had a different hairdo. So now that I think about it, it does look great. I mean that."

"Well, thank you. I like it."

"So, what's been happening to you? Are you still doing some singing?"

"Yes, mostly at school assemblies."

"Oh, good. How are your parents?"

"They're fine."

It was very awkward for some reason. I decided that maybe I should be a gentleman, and leaned over and kissed her on the cheek. She was so surprised and embarrassed.

"That's how grownups greet each other."

She smiled. Then, she reached into her bag, pulled out a piece of paper and handed it to me.

"I finished the poem."

"Oh, my goodness."

I took the poem from her trembling hand. Then I leaned over a second time and gave a soft peck on the other cheek.

"Oh, twice. It must be my lucky day," she said, smiling.

"No, it's mine. What a wonderful surprise. You want to read it for me?"

"I don't know . . ."

"Yes, please." I handed her back the paper. She hesitated for a second, and then she started to read it with a clear and strong voice. But she was not actually reading it really; she was reciting it from memory while looking at me and, at that moment, Julie seemed to radiate this incredible warmth and aura.

Somehow, the sense of intimacy that she was creating by softly reciting her poem was incredibly powerful. I was with her and for a fleeting moment the world ceased to exist around us, and we were the only two people alive. It was a lovely experience.

She read:

People say there is a time and a place.
But no one knows.
Only the stars know and the moon, too.
But they don't tell us.
Trees and leaves know. The sun knows.
Even the sea knows.
The clouds, the sky, the rain, the night.
The flowers.
But they don't tell us.
But death does come and it has a time.
The heart knows, but it is quiet and only
Speaks in riddles, and it whispers softly.
And if we are lucky, we hear things, but
It is still mysterious.
We appear to be. But we are not.
Are you the essence of life?
Are you my new spring?
To see the other is to see a torrent of golden sunlight.
We want to be us and we are others instead.
To be loved is to know the time and place.
It is clear, warm and it is safe.
And to love is to find, and it is
As honest as the rainbow for it shares
The time and place.
Water droplets kissed by the sun's rays.

Those turn into beauty and nobility.
And laughter.
Still, no one tells us the time and the place.
Or when?
And to love is like a new dawn, bright, magical, and eternal
The time as well as the place.
Then we know that we are we and not others.
I am muted by fate and know my cries are in vain.
My wings have been shorn.
And flightless and worn
I turn and weep.

Jesus Christ, I thought. I was overwhelmed by what she had written. I did not know what to say. Like Andy had once said: Human beings never cease to amaze! I could see that she wanted me to say something and like a damn fool I stood speechless. She folded the paper and handed it to me after what seemed a long silence.

"Do you like it?"

"Julie, this is so beautiful. I don't know what to say. If I say something, it would sound so banal and stupid. You take my breath away."

Her eyes shone with an incredible look. The next thing I knew, she leaned over and kissed me on the lips, innocent, and soft. It was so natural and without any pretension on her part. I do not think I could have avoided the kiss.

It came and it went. I could see that for her it seemed to mean not the beginning of something, but rather the end. A whole universe had been born and had died.

She was so close to me that, for a moment, I was somewhat confused and tempted, but I held back. Not because I was afraid; no, it was a sentiment of total purity that emanated from her that I did not want to pollute it with anything vulgar or crass.

"Please, I hope I didn't offend you."

"Julie, no offense taken, please."

Boy, women have always overwhelmed me. What the hell was going on here? However, I did manage to keep my cool and did not reciprocate her kiss.

"Don't worry," she said, " It won't happen again."

"Julie, you're a beautiful person. I can only hope and pray that you'll always remain so. That life won't destroy that which you are. I will remember this moment for the rest of my life. I promise you."

"Thank you. Me, too," and she gave me a wonderful smile.

I hugged her briefly. Her young body touched mine, but again I did not do anything that I would later feel guilty about, or regret. I held her hand for a brief moment. I looked toward the front door and in some crazy way, I hoped that nobody would come just now.

I did not have any designs on her. It was that at that instant, I really did not want the spell to be broken. It was really a magical moment for me. And I think it was for her, also.

"Has Andy decided what show he will do next?"

"I don't think so."

"Will you direct it once he decides?"

"I don't know, Julie."

"It would be lovely if you did it."

"Thank you. But you know, I have no control over what happens."

"I know."

We stood awkwardly without knowing what do to next. I wanted to leave, but at the same time, I did not want to appear as if I did not want to stay there. She saved the moment.

"I have to go."

"OK."

"I hope I didn't embarrass you."

"No Julie, you didn't."

"I'm glad."

"And I love the poem. It's really something else. I will treasure it for as long as I live."

"OK."

For some strange reason, it felt as if Julie had suddenly grown up in front of me and I was now looking at someone poised, mature, sure of herself, less of the confused teenager.

Maybe this was a defining moment for her, more for her than for me. She was at that transitional moment, emerging and slowly turning into a something charming and unique. The change, though not yet obvious to her, showed there was a certain serenity and calmness that was quite striking.

Yeah, Julie was on her way into the lovely woman that I hoped one day she would become. I always thought that that was her destiny. And I was happy and reflected that maybe, just maybe, in some small way, I had contributed to such metamorphoses. We shook hands, like serious grown-ups.

"If you do another show, will you think about me?"

"You know I will."

"And I just want to say something."

"What?"

"Emily is a very lucky girl."

This took me by surprise. How did she know? Should I ask her? She saw my reaction and smiled.

"Jackson told me when I saw him the other day and I asked him where you were. He said you had gone to visit Emily."

We both stood awkwardly looking at each other. The gulf that had separated us was now growing much larger. I saw no need to justify anything to

Julie. It was really none of her concern, but I also understood her need to come to terms with her own feelings and desires.

Suddenly, she did not seem to be just a kid, but an adult. I remembered what Cash said about Southern girls who grow up very fast.

"I understand she's a lovely girl."

"Yes, she is."

"I wish you both the best."

"Thank you, Julie. And thank you for such a magnificent gift."

"I would like to ask you to please sign the program for me."

"Sure."

She took a well-preserved copy of the program.

"What do you want me to say?"

"Jonathan, you're supposed to know what to say," she said.

"You're right."

So, I wrote:

To Julie, a most wonderful human being, though she does not believe it. And to a great budding artist for the immense pleasure she brought not only to me but also to countless others by her magnificent performances. And to someone who believed in me. Thank you for being who you are. Please, please, stay that way. I wish you love, happiness, good health and a long life!

Yours truly,

Jonathan.

She smiled, when I handed her the program. She looked at it, hesitated a moment and a confused look crossed her eyes but she dismissed it. She turned around and walked out of my life, and I felt no regrets.

I stood watching her go and she never turned to look back. I do not know how long I stood there. It was a while before I was able to regain some perspective on what had taken place. I opened the paper again and looked at the poem. It was written in strong hand with no hesitation, and the handwriting was very nice.

Man, oh man, so much about people that I need to know. I wanted to call Emily and share with her what had happened. She had once said that she understood a girl like Julie having a crush on a guy, and how in retrospect the whole experience made us richer and perhaps a bit wiser. Some GIs came into the building and walked to the stage and started to set up for their rehearsal.

"I know how she feels. A young and impressionable girl, a handsome guy," Emily said, when I called her later in the evening.

"Handsome? Well, let's not exaggerate."

"I'm not."

"I'm so overwhelmed by what she wrote. I can't tell you."

"I can just by listening to the sound of your voice."

"I was trying so hard not to give her any ideas."

"You didn't. Trust me. It happens all of the time. It's natural and very human."

"Emily, I think only you can understand what I'm feeling now."

"I know. That's why I love you."

"Really?"

"Yes, you dummy."

"You're not upset?"

"Why should I be? Julie has understood something about herself. She'll be fine."

"I hope so."

"She will. With time, she will find a man worthy of her, of her love, her passion, her affections, her poetry . . . of who she is . . . it's inevitable . . . she will, trust me."

"I love you."

"I know."

"Good night, babe . . . I miss you."

"Good night, my love. The baby is moving . . . I think he's saying hello to you."

"You're amazing. OK, good night my love. I kiss you both."

I did not think Emily would have become jealous of Julie, and I wanted more than anything else to share the experience with her because I knew she would understand it, would see it for what it was worth. I knew she trusted me and my desire to tell her was not a way of excusing or justifying anything.

I wondered how long before Julie would find someone her age to fall in love with. And how much love and tenderness she would be capable of giving. And I thought that whoever the guy was, he was going to be some lucky bastard.

I laughed. I thought, what the hell, this is what life is really all about. Feelings, confusion, and through the process one hopes to find love, clarity and serenity. I certainly hoped that it would be so for Julie.

-XIII-

I stood looking down at the two graves. I read the tombstones' etchings: Homer Timothy Wilson, 1942-1964, age 22. Emily Wilson, 1943-1964, age 21. Baby, Timmy Wilson, 1964-1964. Emily and the baby were buried in one common grave.

Emily, my Emily, she had died in childbirth along with her baby!

The two graves were neatly arranged right next to each other. The cemetery was desolate. It was cloudy, late in the afternoon. The trees surrounding the place were green, and there was a soft breeze blowing that touched the leaves but did not disturb them.

The silence was heavy, as it always is in cemeteries. The flowers on some of the graves were dried up, desiccated. The flowers on Wilson's, Emily's and the baby's graves, however, appeared to be fresh.

I did not know why I was standing there. I did not know why I had come to this place. I did not know just what I was looking for. I did not know what I was supposed to do. I did not know what I was supposed to feel. I knew shit. That is all I knew.

That is all I had known for the last ten fucking, lousy, miserable, piece of shit years, since the telegram giving me the horrible news arrived while I was in Vietnam, back in 1964. I looked around me and the silent graves told me of lives, of loves, of dreams, of hopes, of death, of—of what?

The dictionary defines empty as: Having nothing in it. Vacant. Worthless. Unsatisfying. Meaningless. It defines madness as: Great anger. Fury. Insanity. It defines nothingness as: Lack of existence. Extinction. Uselessness. Insignificant.

And it defines death as: Any ending—any ending.

I had felt all of those things, and more, so much more.

Endless definitions. Off the shelf meanings we want to understand. We can spend the rest of our stinking, worthless lives, thinking about them. Studying them, as they apply to the reality around us. Or we can try to come to terms with them and—and then what? We die. Simple.

Death, as the dictionary explains it, is any ending. So what is life? The lack of any ending? There is a sense of stagnation. Neither here nor there. The dictionary may define it. It does not explain it. It just is.

Billy, Emily's younger brother, stood by the gate of the cemetery waiting, while smoking a cigarette. His police officer's uniform, neat, and clean. He was wearing dark glasses so it was hard to tell what he was thinking or feeling. He had been shocked to see me show up at the police station after so many years.

At first, he did not recognize me. And when I told him who I was, there was a kind of hesitation on his part that told me deep, way deep inside of him, he did not want to recognize me. He did not smile. His handshake was distant. In many ways, I was the unwanted visitor. The visitor from hell!

At that moment, I felt like I should not have come at all. I had avoided it for such a long time and now that I was here my presence felt tired, inadequate, and artificial. It had not been easy to get here. Not for lack of means or time. Hard to explain. Primitive fear. Beyond comprehension fear.

Not fear of the unknown, but of the known. Now, I felt like an intruder. I did not belong here. To be honest, the whole exercise felt vacant. But it was something that I had promised to offer to the vacuity of the universe not that the universe gives a damn, that is why I had never set a time to do it.

It was a fact that I woke up to and went to sleep with for so long that it had become part of my existential routine. It was like brushing my teeth after I got up in the morning, and brushing them again just before I went to bed. Automatic. Machine-like. Stagnant.

With Billy, there was no connection of any kind. I had met him ten years ago when I had come to visit Emily for the first, and for the last time. But I never tried to keep that connection going or keep it alive after her death.

In fact, I had not made the effort to keep any connection with her family. I saw no reason to do so. I was a stranger to them. They were Emily's family, but not my own.

Yes, we shared some fading memories—tiny. If there had been a connection, a vague and a spiritual connection at that, over the years, it had become dull, meaningless, and more like a wart that one cannot get rid of.

So one learns to live with it. Once in a while one touches it, but it does not disfigure the area where the wart is. It is there, that is all. Its familiarity is boring—insignificant.

While standing by the graves, I wanted to feel sad, guilty, wounded, but felt none of those things. It was as if my heart had been pounded down, burned, and shriveled nearly to cinders.

Where it had been left ticking but more from a reflex than from something being completely alive. It had been transformed into something that still worked, mechanically, bumpy, empty..

I mean, I was still breathing but my whole existence felt more like a long stretch of road that needed to be paved over. Waiting for the asphalt to be poured, and then it would dry when the sun hit it, on its way to become just another road to nowhere, irrelevant, lost in a landscape of emptiness.

For such a long time, I had lived with my pain. At first, I had counted the seconds, the minutes, the hours, the days, the weeks, the months; then, all of that had melted into years of incomprehensibility and nothingness.

For many reasons, some of which I understood most of which I did not, I had finally ended up coming to this cemetery. My voluntary absence in this part of the world had just happened.

Oh, I knew that it had always been within my power to make this pilgrimage, as it were, but I always felt like I did not belong here. That in the scheme of things, it would be offensive, unnecessary, and intrusive. I mean, what could I gain or resolve from it? What?

I did not belong here anymore than to the many forgettable places I had barreled through in the past ten years—going nowhere. I wanted to feel suffocated, asphyxiated, choked. All I felt was dullness, tiredness. I was here, that is all. Time felt like a long stretch of stupor.

My buddy Jack, back in California, had always told me that I did not have to feel guilty about the reverses of life, about Emily's death. They happen. And he was right. But it had not made things easier when dealing with her death. What makes things easier when a loved one dies?

The passage of time? Dullness of memories? Replacing the loved one with someone else? It is said that the heart is resilient, but I believe it shrinks. I knew standing here glancing at her grave would not provide any answers simply because there are none.

My spiritual landscape was flat. It stretched everywhere but went nowhere. It was lifeless. No breeze to move the grass, or the leaves from the trees. No sounds of birds flying. It was a Martian landscape.

It just stood still. Airless, empty. I had no recollection of my life these past years. I could no more say where I had been than how many seasons I had lived through.

My existence had no colors, no contrast of any kind. It was arid and it seemed to drift wherever I looked, yet stuck in some time warp. Tragedy is routine. Nothing profound about it. Feelings get disconnected. The emotional continuity is false.

There is no equilibrium about how much one suffers in life relative to a loss of a loved one. You cannot regain the balance. There is no price tag that one can compare it to. No sale specials in the store of life.

All I felt was a monotony of the spirit, as if I had just awakened from a tired and deep sleep, while sitting at the edge of the bed trying to orient myself to what I was supposed to think, to what I was supposed to feel, to what I was supposed to do next. OK, brush my teeth, pee, and shower, re-heat some cold coffee, and get some food.

Tired tasks but not essential to making me look at the sun and wonder about its majestic beauty and power. The brightness of my life had been obscured. Spiritually, I was homeless. It had been longer than I could remember. I occupied space, that was all.

Had I been that successful in pushing my pain so deep that it had now gone down this black hole of my own existence where I did not feel much, and where my life in a perverse logic of its own had refused to sink totally into oblivion?

It had frozen half way down and refused to go any further; it had not come back up. It stood midway and constantly mocked me about my efforts in getting it to move, to disappear into nothingness.

Any change of status since the last time I had checked? The answer was always no. Do we find meaning in life through death? Through hanging on to memories? The answer to those questions was: No. After a while, some memories become second rate, vulgar, like buying a used car tire—not much tread left on it.

Recycling pain is not pretty or interesting. No insight gained from that exercise, for sure. I had read that once matter is caught in the vortex of a black hole it cannot escape. Nothing escapes, which is why this thing is called a black hole.

Nobody knows where or how the information disappears. Is that the ultimate death? In other words, we die but only to exist in limbo. I was inside a black hole, neither alive nor dead. It did not seem to make any difference. I had been there for God knew how long.

At one time, I thought I finally understood what Emily felt about her own loss, but I was kidding myself. I was no more able to distill her suffering than I could do the same with mine. Nobody has a monopoly on suffering. Or how to deal with it. Suffering is suffering.

The heart does not grade suffering. The heart does not know it is suffering. We, humans, do. The heart just keeps on pumping blood through it all. It does not recognize graves.

I had stopped thinking on a constant basis about Emily for some time now. Very often, I had tried to remember what she looked like and all I got was a fogged-in echo, a blurred sketch.

But there were also moments of such madness and intensity, of feeling so near her that when those moments were over I was left completely exhausted, mentally and physically.

Then, at other times, I would go without thinking or feeling anything, very empty, but still, questioning why I was not dead. Then one day, I woke up and I felt no urge to reflect on her, her life, her death, or on anything that had to do with our brief, but strange interlude.

But the urge to forget was fleeting. Maybe that was the secret to trying to understand this thing; its briefness—but who was I kidding?

I remember forcing myself to think that dealing with my past was just a waste of time and energy—worthless. What was the point? To come to terms with it, as people are fond of saying, to put it into some kind of perspective.

To accept it and learn from it? But learn what? That we have no control over our lives, our destinies, and the outcome. Hell, the final outcome is pretty much understood, really. We die, period—any ending.

Not much secret there. When I learned about Emily's death, the ridiculousness of living was pretty clear. Why are we here in the first place? Is this some kind of game that some demented mind has been playing all along? And all we have to do is respond like puppets on a string?

How come Emily had dealt with her tragedy and I had not? She had been so brave about her loss, but I had not been about my own.

Suddenly, I started thinking about my own family. I was not close to any of them. Two brothers and a set of divorced parents. Remarried to others, which increased the size of my extended family somewhat but did not make me a member of anything. We were all separated by an emptiness, a distance, and ultimately, by a choice made.

Death! Again—any ending.

Is it not a transformation into another dimension, unseen, obviously and totally beyond our control and understanding? So what the hell was I doing here? Searching for something, I suppose, but what? Paying a debt?

Maybe gain some insights? But, again, insights into what? Death? Life? Existence? Destiny? Love? What? Was this some kind of attempt at redemption, pay for my sins, atone, but atone for what? For having loved Emily? Man, nothing makes sense.

This whole notion of wanting to find meaning in life, or in the things that happen so that we learn some truths about who we are is for the shits. There ain't no significance to life.

The planets, the stars, the moon, the sun, the galaxies, they do not give a rat's ass about all of the mysteries we want to attach to them because we want to play the game. Our game does not mean a damn thing to them.

Yes, we can speculate about the impact those physical bodies have on us. The moon, after all causes the tides, and without the sun's heat we would not be around; but, around for what purpose? There ain't none. The whole thing is a con.

"Life," Shakespeare wrote, *"is a tale told by an idiot, full of sound and fury signifying nothing."*

Less than perfect.

He should have written: " . . .*signifying absolutely, fucking, nothing.*" That would have made it almost perfect.

I looked over to where Billy was standing. He had not moved at all. I wondered if he thought I was being a pain in the ass. His sister, brother-in-law and nephew were buried here. So for him there was a definite connection, real, human, honest, true, for being here.

But for me? I was never really part of their family. I had wanted to be, had planned on it, and in the end it had not happened. I was a total stranger, which was the reason why I had not made it a point of visiting the family when I first got to the town.

I had gotten Billy's phone number out of the phone book. When I called the number, a woman answered and she told me that Billy was at work, at the police station. She asked me who I was and I told her that I was an old acquaintance of the family and was just passing through town.

She did not seem interested in any further details as I seemed to have caught her dealing with a crying baby. She excused herself and I told her I understood.

I found out where the police station was and drove over, but I did not make an effort to get out of the car and go in. I sat in the car for a long time. After I finally went in and made the contact, we both came out and stood outside trying to make small talk. When he saw my Chevy Impala, we walked over and he stood looking at it.

"You still have it," he said.

"Yes. It is getting old. Some things needed to be replaced like the top, but it is still a good set of wheels. I put over two hundred thousand miles on it in the last few years."

"Lots of traveling you've done in this baby."

"Yes, been moving around a lot. Everywhere and nowhere."

"Long way from home," he said, this but he was not being cynical.

"Yeah," searching for a home I had hoped to get to a long time ago would have been a better sentiment.

"How did you find me?"

"I looked in the phone book and I saw your name. I figured not too many people with the same name. I called and a very nice female answered the phone. I wasn't sure what to say. And when she asked me who I was I just told her I was an old acquaintance just passing through town."

He was silently looking at the car.

"That's Mary, my wife. We've just had a baby."

"Yeah, I could hear the baby in the background."

"Six months."

"A boy, a girl?"

"A girl . . . we named her Emily, after her aunt."

"Oh, that's lovely."

"We're very happy and proud."

"And, the rest of the family?"

He looked away for a moment and I wondered if I had made a faux pas by asking. I could see that his face and eyes seemed distant, unfocussed.

"My dad passed away a couple of years ago. Mom's fine and Jimmy's got two boys."

"Oh, that's great."

"What about you?"

"Nothing."

I wanted to say I had no family. I had no life. It has been like waiting for the red light, at a stop light, to change to green so I could go. I had been a crazy zombie, but in the final analysis, my troubles were not his problem. A long silence ensued.

I did not know if my sharing that I had nothing going for me had caused the pause. I then asked if I could visit the cemetery and he said he would show me where it was. And here we were. Billy finally walked over to where I was standing by the graves. He was holding his dark glasses in his hand.

"So, what brought you back?"

"I loved your sister so much, so much."

"I know you did."

"It's taken me this long to have the courage to come and see where she's buried. Over the years, I have done just about anything not to make this trip. I really don't know why all of a sudden I found myself wanting to come."

"I understand."

"Do you?"

"Yes, I think I do."

"I was never able to tell you what I felt after I received your telegram with the bad news. I didn't know what to say, that's why I never wrote to you. The worst part was not being able to be with her at the last moments. I was smack in the middle of nowhere and with no way of getting back."

Yes, the telegram had reached me in Pleiku, South Vietnam. A vulgar piece of paper, now yellowed and falling apart, I had been carrying with me ever since. It was Jackson who had brought it to me. He was crying and could not talk. At first, I thought it had to with his own family.

He understood that I had misinterpreted why he was crying. Then, it hit me! I have no recollection of just when he handed me the telegram, or when I read it. The next thing that I remember was Cash standing right next to me, and crying. I have no idea if he came with Jackson, or afterward.

"Jonathan, I'm so fucking sorry, so fucking sorry." Cash said.

"There ain't no fucking God," said Jackson.

This from a guy who never swore, who was as religious as you would ever want to be. His foul language was very apropos. We held each other and cried.

The other GIs did not attempt to come near us, not because they did not care, but because they understood that something had happened to the three of us that was private and personal.

I remember when I first tried to read the telegram. The strangest of things was that even though my tears were blurring everything in front of me and the news had shocked me—where in one split of a second my own existence, my life, my heart, my soul, my destiny, had suddenly become nothing—I could still manage to read the words clearly:

Jonathan,

Emily is no longer, nor is the baby. She passed away this morning while delivering little Timmy. Both are now gone. I'm sorry, so damn sorry.

Billy.

I think I said that I had to get back to the States. Jackson then told me that because I was not next of kin there was no way the Army would allow me to go stateside. No way.

I had never felt so useless. I looked at Cash and Jackson and I tried to give them comfort. I thought, that is what Emily had done with me when I had gone to see her after Wilson died.

So much pain in my heart, so much.

For the next few weeks, I went around like a robot, in automatic. I did not give a shit whether I lived or died. I was volunteering for any dangerous assignment available. I begged the other guys to let me go instead of them.

Until, finally, the chaplain met me and tried to talk some sense into my poor soul. He was partially successful, and I was ordered to maintain my regular rotation. There would be no exceptions.

I followed the orders but always in a daze, until the morning when Cash and Jackson bought the farm, and I was injured, and my military service came to a halt, but not my life in hell.

Emily had never told me that she was having problems in her last weeks of her pregnancy. She never gave me a reason to be anxious. In the short phone conversations we had, and they were so few, filled with static, and crazy because of the time difference between Pennsylvania and Vietnam.

She was positive, full of optimism, looking forward to her baby and to us eventually getting together to form the family she so desperately wanted. But, alas, it was not to be.

"I'm sorry," Billy said, after a long silence.

"I wanted so much to desert my unit but I realized even in my fogged up spirits that it wouldn't have made any difference. Emily and the baby were gone and nothing that I could do would ever bring them back to me. So I did not . . ."

"Yeah, I understand."

"What I should have done was split when I got my orders to Nam. I had told Emily that if that ever happened, I would take her and the baby and we would leave the U.S."

"Yeah, she told me that."

"She did? Really?"

"The baby was breached and he got tangled up in the umbilical cord and stopped breathing, they could not revive him. Then Emily started bleeding and they could not stop it. She never knew that the baby was dead. They did everything they could to save them."

"I think it's my fault."

"Why do you say that?"

"I was a fucking coward. I should have taken her to Canada like I said I was going to do. Now all I have left is a life full of regrets. I hope she has forgiven me."

"Come on, Jonathan, it wasn't your fault."

"Man, it's so fucked."

"The doctors told us that as she was fading she would mumble Homer's name and then, yours. She would go back and forth. It almost seemed like both of you had become one and . . ."

He stopped. His face was somber. I saw how hard he was trying not to lose control. In fact, we were both trying hard not to lose control. Son of a bitch, it was tough.

"I should have been here."

"We buried Emily and the baby together, as you can see. My folks and Homer's folks wanted it that way."

In a flash, I saw a five-year old Emily taking care of Billy her baby brother, as she said she had done it.

"In all of these years, I've tried to make sense of this thing. I still don't know how to do it. I don't think that there is a God. Anyway, I've never been a religious person."

"I've got to get back to work."

"I'm sorry for taking you away from your job."

"It's fine. Do you want to drop by later? I can get my mom and Jimmy to the house."

"I'd rather not."

"I understand."

"I hope you won't hold it against me."

"Come on. Should I tell them I saw you?"

"It's up to you."

"OK."

"I think I'll stay a bit longer here it you don't mind."

"No, of course not."

We shook hands. Then he pulled me over, which surprised me, and gave me a hug. I hugged him back.

"I'm sorry," he said.

He turned around and walked back to his patrol car. During the time we had been standing by the graves, I could hear the police talk through the car's open speaker. Billy got in the car.

I faintly heard him reporting back to the dispatcher. He started the car, sat there for a few more moments, and then he looked back at me and waived. I waived back and watched as the car went down the road.

I looked around the deserted cemetery. I saw the flowers on the tombs and straightened a couple of them over Wilson's tomb. I was trying to remember what he looked like and I was having a hard time.

I also found myself having great difficulty remembering Emily's looks. I had moved so much these past years that I had lost the photos she had given me. Who of the two did the baby resemble?

I sat down on the grass and then hazy images of Emily while she sat and painted on her canvas came back. It seemed so long ago. So many years had passed and painful memories now came back in slow motion.

I wondered if she had ever finished the painting she had been working on. And for a moment, I regretted that I had not accepted Billy's offer to visit his family.

I do not know how long I sat there. I felt sleepy and weary. I walked over to a tree not far from the tombs and sat against it, in the shade. I could see crosses and mausoleums all around me.

I must have fallen sleep, when I suddenly woke up with a start. Billy was looking down at me and, for an instant, I did not know where I was. I was completely lost.

"Sorry, I woke you up."

"No, it's fine. I just wanted to sit here for a moment and I guess I got sleepy and conked out. What time is it?"

I looked at my watch. An hour had passed. I shook my head.

"I brought you something. I wasn't sure if you were still here."

He had a thick manila envelope, and also had the painting with him. It was now finished. I stood up and looked at it.

"I'm sure Emily would have liked for you to have it. She told me she had been working on it when you came to visit us that time and that you liked it."

"I can't take it."

"Why not?"

"It belongs to you guys."

"Well, in many ways you're right. But I really want you to have it. It would give me a great pleasure to know that now it will belong to you. I know the rest of the family would feel the same way."

"Are you sure?"

"Yes. Please, take it." He gave me a long and sad smile.

"Man, you're something else. Thank you."

"You're welcome. And if you change your mind about visiting us later please call me. I haven't told anybody about your visit, so if you don't want to do it there will be no harm done, OK?"

He handed me the painting, then, the manila folder. I could guess what was in it.

"Your letters. She kept them. We've never looked or read them. I sealed them in this envelope. At one time, I thought of burning them—I'm glad I didn't. They also belong to you."

"Jesus Christ, Billy . . ."

For a moment, I thought I was going to lose it. Man, oh, man.

We shook hands one more time and now it was my turn to pull him in for a hug. We both knew that I would never visit him or his family, that we would never see each other again. He walked back to his car.

He never told me nor did I ask what had been Emily's health problems. We knew and understood that it would not resolve anything. Silence was best. Did she know she was not going to make it? Did she? I wished I had been there with her . . .

The sun was going down and the shadows were playing hide and seek with the afternoon. I looked at the envelope and at the painting and my heart got flooded with the memories of one afternoon so long ago.

For a moment, I thought of going to see if I could find the spot where Emily and I had spent part of that afternoon when she was working on the painting, but I was not sure I could find it especially now that it was getting dark.

My dearest Emily, I don't really know what I'm doing here. You know, the last time I was here, I was paying my respects to Homer. Now, I'm back paying all three of you my last respect. Man, oh man. And Billy, that no good brother of yours, has just given me incredible gifts that stunned me completely: The painting and my letters to you, which he had kept all of these years.

How do I deal with that? Please, help me. I'm no longer able to think for myself at this moment. Where are you? Can you see me? Can you hear me? Are you now reunited with Homer and your baby? So the three of you are back together the way it should be. I feel that I'm just another body here. But I know that I'm not. I'm part of all of you and you are so much part of me.

I wish I could talk to you like in the old days. There is so much I want to tell you and I don't know how or where to begin. One thing I need to repeat to you right off the bat is that I loved you in my most innocent and purest way. I have no regrets and I hope you have none either. In some strange and weird way, I also feel that I can find new love again. Not in the same way that I loved before, but, love pure and simple, honest and true, nevertheless.

At least I hope so. I'm not asking for your permission to search again as you would have argued that it was silly, that we all have a right to love and be loved, that permission is not needed. I haven't looked for it to tell you the truth. Not that I was afraid. No, it just seemed pointless. Now, standing here, for some strange reason it feels different. I just wish I could see you and talk to you . . .

I came back here not because I owe a debt or anything like that, but I have regrets. So many, so many. I came to visit you because it made sense. Please forgive me for not having come sooner. It's so hard to try to figure out the whys and the other things that crowd our daily lives.

You would argue for me to love life. I'm trying—it's hard. Looking at your painting, I can see some subtle changes you told me you wanted to make. I'm glad that I kept you from destroying it. Remember?

I will treasure it for the rest of my life. I'm so sorry that I wasn't here to be with you in your last moments. Billy told me that in your delirium you mentioned Homer's name and mine at the same time. It was as if both of us had become one. And in a way, it makes sense.

We, Homer, and I, were part of your life and in the final analysis it does not matter who came first or second. I won't go and see the rest of your family. I don't think I can handle it. I hope you'll forgive me for this faux pas.

I'm sure if I were to show up long and painful memories would come back and I don't want to be the one who brought them about. I told Billy it was up to him to tell them about my visit. I'll leave that to his best judgment. Anyway, I hope that if he tells them they will forgive me for my lack of manners; actually, it is more for my lack of valor.

I was kind of surprised that he became a police officer, I don't know why. I remember that when I first met him he was working in the mines. He told me that he and his wife had just had a baby girl, and she was named after you . . . and that

211

Jimmy has two boys. I can well imagine that all of these grandchildren have probably made your mother very happy.

And your father passed away. But I'm sure you already know all of these things. I'm going to hit the road now. I'm on my way back to California. I've been living in New York City for the last couple of years. I don't really know what I did, or why I was living there.

I have lived in a world of anguish and shadows since you . . . since you were taken away from me. To tell you the truth, I don't know how I've survived. I've moved around a lot, here, there, everywhere, nowhere, so I wouldn't go crazy. But I wouldn't be able to tell you what I've done. Now, after so many years of thinking about it, I'm finally going to move to Paris.

Remember we talked about going there together? I've got my GI bill, a bit of a pension from the Army for an injury I suffered, and some inheritance from my grandmother, on my father's side, and that should hold me. I'll go back to Los Angeles, settle my affairs, sell my car, which will break my heart no doubt, then go to Paris.

I hear so much about the city that I want to see it. I want to live there. I have no idea what I will do, but for the time being, I'm not going to be worried about it. Maybe go to the Sorbonne and do some graduate work. History or French, or something.

I'm not good at making plans anymore, which is why it has taken me so long to make the decision to go to Paris and to come and see you. As I've said, I've got a few bucks and I hear that you can still live like a bohemian over there.

I have to make a confession to you. I hope you'll forgive me. Up until recently, I had always kept from getting serious about any other woman. I finally realized that it was pretty damn sad not to let my heart find joy in someone's love.

I'm sure you would be scolding me for having been such a coward up to now. I'm still fearful of what the future holds, you know me. But I think I have finally understood that the human heart is not a cold and distant organ in our bodies.

It is there beating its regular cycle and part of that cycle deals with giving and accepting love. Maybe I'm wrong here, but if I know anything about you, you would argue that love cannot be denied or prevented from happening. And you'd be right, as always. Look at us.

So, please stay warm and give my best regards to Homer and take care of him and of little Timmy.

So long, Emily.

I love you. I will, always!

I did not want to drive all night, so I got a motel and early the next morning I hit the road. I do not know what possessed me to want to drive into North Carolina. Instead of driving into Ohio, I drove into Virginia. I was going back to the west coast and in no hurry at all. I was free and I had all of the time in the world. Besides, I have always enjoyed driving by myself.

The madness of the traffic and its complexity had always held a fascinating attraction. I had once taken a trip in the same direction when I had first gone to visit Emily back in the days. So I guess, I was somewhat familiar with the road and before I knew it, I was back in Fayetteville, North Carolina arriving in the late afternoon.

There had been some physical changes in the town from what I remembered. I drove to Fort Bragg and, at the gate, I told the MPs that I just wanted to pay a brief visit—remembrance of the good old days, I explained.

We chatted briefly and the young GIs loved my car. It was somewhat humorous in that on the Impala's windshield, the 1964 Army's circulation vehicle permit was still glued to it.

The young MPs got a kick out of it. The permit was different now. I drove in and went to the theater where I had spent long and happy hours. It had not changed other than it had been painted a slightly different color.

It was deserted except for a young GI at the office who told me they were at the present working on a set of one-act plays. When I asked who the civilian director was, he mentioned a name that I did not recognize. He did not know anything about Andy Catz, the guy who had been in charge when I was there.

I told him that I had been a GI stationed at Bragg back in 1964 and that, in fact, I had once directed a couple of shows for the troops.

When I saw that one of the posters he had in his office was of *The Diary of Anne Frank* production, I pointed out who the director was, and showed him my driver's license as proof. He was impressed and he and I walked into the auditorium and stood there looking at the empty stage.

Memories!

What do they serve? What do they bring? Why do they exist? Of course, they exist if for no other reason than to drive us crazy with thoughts of the past. But do they enlighten us in any way? Do they show us the way?

Do they clarify for us things that looking back on them show them for what they were, or for what they were not? We live with our memories. We may not get them all at the same time, but we still live with them.

In some instances, they do help us clarify certain past facts, events, that took place and we have stored in our brains. But I also have to admit that very often what we select to remember is not quite the way things or events came about.

It seems normal that we are rather selective in what we want to remember, how we want to remember things. I am back in Bragg and what I want to remember now is what I have to remember.

Looking at the *Anne Frank* poster, Julie's name had stared back at me.

"You know, there was a girl who did *Anne Frank*, her name is Julie A. Douglas. Her father was stationed here. Her name is on the poster. Does it ring a bell?

"No. But I'm new here."

"Yeah, I see what you mean."

"I can call my boss and ask him. He's off today because he's got the flu. I know he knows a lot of people around."

"Could you give him a call? I'm just kind of curious."

"Absolutely."

I had no idea why I wanted him to find out any information about Julie. It was a spur of the moment thing. Maybe the poster of *Anne Frank* had prompted me to wonder. I did not know. He walked back to the office. While he was making the phone call, I walked toward the stage and climbed the stairs.

I have always loved empty stages. They sort of sit there quietly, yet full of expectancy for what is to be shown or be presented in a not so distant future. Then they suddenly convert themselves into places of dreams, magic and splendor. An empty stage contains memories galore.

As I stood there looking at the empty seats, I thought of Leggs. She had been the young woman who had done the choreography for *Carnival* the show that Andy had let me to direct when the first director was pulled out and sent to Vietnam. I wondered what had become of her.

Did she ever go back to Vegas? Was she still married to the guy who wanted to make the military his life? I had not thought about Leggs for ages. I guess my being back on the stage triggered those memories.

"You're in luck," the young GI said. He was smiling, as he walked down the aisle toward me.

"What did you find?"

"Well, Marty, my boss knows of a high school teacher in town who is supposed to have done some show here. He's not sure of her name, but he has heard that she was a young girl who did work here on a show some time ago."

"Do you know what high school that is?"

"Yes. I've got the phone number. Do you want me to call and find out if this girl is the same one?"

"Yes. That would be great."

I started to walk off the stage and toward him.

My hands suddenly started shaking. I was somewhat afraid. Wanting to know, yet also fearful of finding out that Julie was still around. But to be truthful I would have been shocked to find out she was still living here. I did not believe it.

I stood right next to the young GI as he started to make the phone call.

"What's your first name, anyway?"

"David, and yours?"

"Jonathan."

"Do you want me to tell them you're looking for Julie, if that's the same girl?"

"You know, part of me says yes, but the other part says no. I guess I'd like to surprise her. I mean, if it is the same person."

"Understood."

Someone answered the phone.

214

"Hi, sorry to bother you, but I'm trying to find out if by any chance you have a teacher by the name of Julie A. Douglas working at your school?"

The smile on his face was the answer that we were both looking for.

"You do? Oh, great."

He listened some more.

"Yes, this is Fort Bragg and I work for the theater office. I was looking at a poster of the production of *The Dairy of Anne Frank* that was done here some years ago, and Miss Douglas is listed as a member of the cast. I was just curious about who she was, that's all. Much obliged, ma'am."

The kid was some smooth talker—typical GI. I started to laugh. He gave me the thumbs up. He put the phone down and wrote something on a piece of paper.

"She's there every day. The lady said that Julie also teaches a dance class after regular school and the classes end at five p.m., and you can find her in the auditorium. Here's the address."

"Wow! Thank you for your help."

"No problem. Do you know how to get there?"

"I'll find it."

"Yeah, 'cause I don't know much about this town. I just got stationed here."

"It's OK. Anyway, it's getting late. I'll do it tomorrow." He gave me a big smile. We shook hands and I left.

I was in shock! Jesus Christ, now what?

It was not the result that I had expected. I had asked the guy just trying to make conversation, really. I had no reason to want to find Julie, no reason whatsoever.

But finding she was still around really threw me for a loop, a giant, incomprehensible, mysterious, loop. I went and sat in my car for a while. I needed to digest what I had just learned. It brought to mind what one of the most famous Greek playwrights wrote: Life has some sudden twists!

I am so skeptical of destinies, of stories about people finding themselves in some situation that eventually structures their lives and more. I do not know why I had decided to swing by Bragg, and even more strange my sudden desire to ask about Julie.

It came out of left field. I had not thought about her for a long time. It was the poster from *Anne Frank* that gave me the idea. But it was just idle curiosity. Something to pass the time, really.

There were other things that took priority in my life and Julie was certainly not one of them. I was not surprised she was still living in Fayetteville, though. I mean, most of us end up pretty much settling where we have lived all of our lives.

Was she married? What did she look like now? She was a rather attractive young girl ten years ago. I did remember thinking back then that she would turn into a lovely butterfly as soon as she got out of her cocoon. In the past, I had once in a while looked at the poem she had written for me.

I still had the original copy, and my initial reaction that she had written a great poem had not changed. I treasured the thing immensely. But it was a memory that had no priority in my life. I found a motel and I had a light dinner in the small restaurant right next to it. I thought that I would have some trouble sleeping. That had been my pattern for a long time.

So, I went to bed with my normal dread about waking up in the middle of the night but much to my own surprise when I next looked at my watch it was midmorning. I had slept soundly. I guess the driving and the other things in my mind had helped in getting some shuteye.

I had to figure out a way to meet Julie. I wanted to surprise her. But I also dreaded the encounter might be difficult, if not strange. I had never kept in touch with her by choice, obviously. So I was not sure how she would welcome me or if she would be happy to see me, again.

I only hoped she would still be the shy, sweet girl that I remembered. But if truth be told, I was apprehensive. I tried to figure out why that was and I had trouble being clear as to why I felt this way. Guilt, perhaps.

I looked at Emily's painting across the room from me. I had had no desire to look closely at it since Billy had given it to me. It was sitting on the chair and I tried to avoid looking directly at it.

Having the painting along with the letters was disconcerting and it brought me, again as if I needed it, my own sense of a great loss, an everlasting void. I felt very awkward to now be the keeper of such memories.

After Billy had given it to me, I had wrapped it in plastic that I had bought and was careful to put it in the car with me and not in the trunk. And at the motel, the previous evening, I made sure I took the painting and the envelope in with me.

Now for some reason it seemed right that I should start looking closely at it. It was a great landscape painting and even though I had seen Emily trying to destroy it, the final product was exactly the landscape I remembered.

The softness of the colors and the design were clear and without any pretensions. It had a kind of directness and honesty that made you reflect on what the painter had done. I had seen her doing it, and seeing the final result made me feel good.

I had been afraid of accepting it from Billy, but now I was very happy I had. It was mine and a great memento of someone I had loved purely and dearly. I did not dare open the envelope with my letters. That would have to wait. I will write Billy a letter later, I thought, to thank him once again for such thoughtful and lovely gifts.

I checked out of the motel, late in the afternoon. I was not planning on coming back. I figured if I found Julie that would be fine. It not, then I would get back on the road and keep on going. I drove by the house where Emily had lived. There was a tricycle and several children's toys scattered around the front yard. Other than that, the house seemed the same.

Maybe it had been painted. I could not be sure. Then I drove by the drive-in, it was still there. I thought of Emily, Jackson, and me coming here, though at different times. The young GIs sitting in their cars were similar to those I remembered. It made me laugh. The more things change the more they remain the same.

Julie's school was a series of low buildings, which spread over a plain terrain. I stood around the entrance and watched as some students were coming out. What surprised me a bit was that I saw several black kids coming out of the school. I had not kept up with the efforts to integrate the South.

But since the passage of the Civil Rights Act there had been some changes in how the South treated its black citizens. The fact that I saw some black students signaled that things had improved and I was glad to see it.

I debated as to how I was going to meet Julie. So I decided to go to the office and ask where I could find her. A woman there indicated where the auditorium was, and she inquired if she should send someone to find Julie. I politely told her that this was a surprise visit and that I would prefer to go and find her.

She was nice and did not make a big issue of my refusal. Part of my refusal had really more to do with the fact that I did not know just how I was going to present myself to Julie. I had no plan. I was playing it by ear.

I stood outside the auditorium. For an instant, I felt like maybe I should just turn around, get in my car, and hit the road. It really was tempting to do that. I started to laugh to myself and decided that, what the hell, I was here, and I might as well go in. It would not hurt me to say hello. Slowly, I walked in.

The place was a pretty good size. The stage was brightly lit, but where I sat in the back, it was dark and I saw Julie in the middle of the group of girls while she was showing them how to do some dance movements.

I must say that seeing her on the stage gave me a bit of a jolt. I was not sure what I was expecting to find. Julie had turned into a very attractive and lovely young woman. Slender, with very long, light, brown hair now in a ponytail. She moved with the elegance of a dancer and her svelte figure was also a surprising element.

Her movements, as she was showing her students what she wanted from them, were graceful and precise. I had a tough time seeing her now mixing the images and memories of a sixteen-year old that I remembered. No doubt about it. The change was a wonderful surprise.

But I felt apprehension, too. I must admit that I thought maybe I should get out of there and just keep on going and not meet her. Her presence on that stage made me think of Leggs, again. I watched Julie conduct her class. I was impressed by the command she had of what she was doing. I have always admired the beauty and elegance of women dancers.

I sat in the darkness, quietly enjoying what I saw. The class ended and her students all said good-bye to her and left the stage. She was the last one and as she started gathering her belongings, I got up and said to myself: it is now or never. So I walked down toward the stage.

As I approached, she saw me but did not recognize me and started to walk toward the back. Then, she stopped. I knew she knew it was me! At that moment, everything came to a halt.

She stood still and did not turn around immediately. I could sense she was trying to get over the shock, so I did not say anything or move toward her.

Slowly, she turned around and I could see her dark eyes were glistening and she gave me one of the loveliest smiles. She was shy and seemed unable to move.

I finally took the steps up and walked toward her. She kept looking at me and I could clearly see not the young girl of my past. I was now in front of a very attractive young woman who no longer seemed afraid of her own shortcomings.

I was seeing someone who had instantly changed in front of my very own eyes. It was like some kind of time-machine that in one fleeting moment had transformed Julie from the shy girl that I remembered into this strange beauty. That transformation in front of me was unique, mysterious, and magical.

It was how nature works. Julie had filled in the right places. I could also sense that, as she was looking at me, she was challenging me in the way that only females know how to challenge men. She had become a lovely and beautiful butterfly!

"Remember me . . .?" I foolishly did not know what else to say.

Time stopped. I felt a bit lost, which surprised me. I did not know why. She did not answer. She just walked toward me and embraced me. She held me close to her for what seemed a very long time.

I could smell her perspiration along with her perfume and for some reason this added a very attractive and almost animal-like effect to the situation. She then pulled herself away from me, looked at me, and was shaking her head.

"You almost gave me a heart attack. It felt like I had to pick my heart up off the floor—how could you ever ask that question," she said, and broke up in big smile that lit up her face with more wattage than the stage lights could ever have.

"You're right. It is a stupid question. But how are you? You've changed?"

"Not that much."

"Oh, yes. Much, so much. I'm floored by what I see. All I remember is this young, shy, girl who once acted in a play that I directed and who wrote me a poem and . . ."

"Do you still have it?"

"Yes! One of my few possessions that I have always treasured."

"How long?"

"Ten years."

"Ten years!" She said, softly.

She shook her head and hugged me once again. It felt funny, for it occurred to me that there might be people who saw us and I started to laugh at my own idiocy.

"Why are you laughing?"

"I was just remembering that once you and I sat on an empty stage much like this one, and we talked about many things. Remember?"

"Of course I do. It was also when I first told you that I was writing a poem for you."

"Yes, I remember that."

"But you, how are you?" She kept looking at me not completely sure of what was happening.

"Well, I'm OK."

"Only OK?"

"Well, once I'm over the shock of seeing you again I will be—I don't know, better, happier, less fearful."

"Fearful? Of what?" She seemed surprised.

"Of your reaction about seeing me, again. I thought that perhaps you might have forgotten me, or something—I mean it's been so long."

"Fear not. I will always remember you. But, what are you doing here?"

Yes, what was I doing here? It was the simplest of questions. And I found myself tongue-tied with no clear answer. None of the answers would make sense. None. I was there, that was all.

She was looking at me and seeing I was having a tough time clarifying within myself the reasons why I was now standing in front of her, she gave me a reassuring smile as if to say: That is a silly question of me to be asking you. So the truth would have to do even if it was insufficient and banal.

"I drove into town so I decided to visit the old theater. When I saw the poster of *Anne Frank,* I asked the GI there if he knew anything about you. He called his boss, and that led to finding out you were a teacher here. It was a wonderful surprise! Actually, a great shock! I really was not looking for you. I was just curious. And, here you are. It is fantastic to see you again!"

"Jonathan, oh, Jonathan. If you only knew how many times I thought about you and . . ."

She stopped. I detected a doubt in her eyes. And tears came to them. She did not try to hide them and I pulled out my handkerchief and gave it to her. She took it and dabbed her eyes a bit. And she laughed.

"I'm messing up your handkerchief with my mascara and I'm also making a fool of myself. I had promised that if I ever ran into you again—a totally unattainable and insane hope just a few moments ago—that I would not act this foolishly."

"Come on. You're not acting foolishly."

I took the handkerchief from her and softly touched her eyes.

"There, as good as before."

She laughed. And took the handkerchief back from me.

"I will wash it."

"Don't worry about it."

"Are you going to stay for a while? I mean . . ."

"Actually, I haven't thought much about that. I really have no plans of any kind."

"We have much to talk about."

"Yes, I think we do. Are you still singing, playing your guitar?"

"Less now. I'm so busy with other things. I think that in many ways, I prefer dancing to singing or playing the guitar."

"I didn't know you were into dancing."

"I was doing it back then, but for some reason the subject never came up when I talked to you. So I never said anything. Can I tell you a secret?"

"Sure."

"When I tried out for *Anne Frank,* I was afraid to tell you I was also interested in dancing. I was afraid you wouldn't cast me because I wasn't sure if for the part of *Anne Frank,* you'd prefer not to have a dancer. And I wanted the part in the worst possible way."

"Really? You know, thinking about it now, I'd probably not have cast you. Dancers can be, well, how can I put it?"

She made a face. I started to laugh. And she understood that I was joking.

"I'm just kidding. I would have cast you whether you were a dancer or a chimney sweeper. You were perfect for the part."

She started to laugh. I could well imagine then, the sixteen-year old fearful of making a big mistake for something that she wanted to do very badly.

"Anyway, from what I saw a while ago, I'd say that I loved seeing you doing it. It gave me another view of you. I discovered something I didn't know before. I was impressed."

"Thank you. I love dancing. It sort of allows me to express myself in a different way than through singing or playing the guitar or even acting. It also allows me to help others. I have also been back in the old theater at Fort Bragg. Some kids at school did a dance recital there once."

And her voice suddenly got very soft, it sort of faded into a whisper.

"Listen, I don't know how busy you are but if we can get together tonight, that is if you are free, maybe have some dinner before I hit the road . . . that would be fantastic."

"Is this a date?"

She was now making fun of me. We both laughed. But there was a slight hesitation on her part. Perhaps I should have been more careful about asking her to join me for dinner. After all, I had no idea what she was doing, how she was living. Did she have a boyfriend, a husband, somewhere? Her left hand had no ring of any kind. She could have taken it off for the class.

"Well, yeah, it is a date. I mean—"

I was suddenly tongue-tied. I realized that I might be imposing on her and I did not want to do that. She waited a few moments, as if thinking, and finally coming to a decision.

"It would be great. I have other things to do but they can wait. This is such a special occasion that everything else now seems less important."

"And your parents, your sister?"

"Only my mother—my father was killed in Vietnam."

She stopped and looked at me in a way that seemed distant, and painful. I knew her father had been a military man all of his adult life.

"I'm sorry to hear that."

She shrugged her shoulders in that unmistakable way we all have of not wanting to deal with unpleasant things, without wanting to wallow in our painful memories.

"My sister is fine. She turned out to be a nice person, after all."

"Come on she wasn't that bad, was she?"

"I love my sister. Well, only when she's not borrowing my clothes and I have to go after her to get them back." She smiled at the vagaries of sisterhood.

"Yeah, I hear that can be a problem."

"OK, I have to go home and get out of these clothes."

"Do you want me to wait for you somewhere?"

"No, you can come with me. I have my own place."

"Boy, you are a grown up."

"What did you expect to find after all of these years, still that silly young girl filled with crazy dreams?"

"To tell you the truth I didn't expect to find you. I wasn't looking for you. I saw the *Anne Frank* poster with your name at the theater in Fort Bragg. It was an amazing surprise to discover you still lived here. I'm so happy that it has turned out this way."

"Are you, really?"

"What kind of question is that? Of course I am. It's fantastic."

"Just checking," she said, and she laughed. "Anyway, I went away to school, but after I graduated I decided to come back and live near my mother and sister. I thought it would be good to be near them. I thought my mother would need me. It turns out that she is very independent and is quite busy with all kinds of activities and projects that she doesn't have time for me. Which is a good thing, really."

She laughed a great uninhibited laugh, which made her look fresh and so young. She seemed to be free with no hang ups. I had forgotten that people can still enjoy life.

"Come, just follow me and I'll show you where I live."

She took my hand and I followed her. I thought, boy this is turning into something that I had never expected. When I started reflecting on things, my life was always turning, twisting, up and down. Never in a nice and straight road. We walked out of the auditorium to the parking lot where I had left my car.

"You still have your convertible."

"Yeah."

"You never let me ride in it."

"Come on it's not true. We just never had the occasion, that's all."

"Will you let me drive it one day?"

"Never."
We both laughed. She stood watching the car for a moment in silence.
"OK, follow me."

-XIV-

I followed Julie to her place. As I was driving, what suddenly struck me was that Julie did not really seem surprised to see me showing up like this from out of nowhere. I mean, after the initial shock her attitude was calm, restrained, and shy, as if encounters of this kind were normal.

That there was no reason to believe that it could not happen. It was more like routine. Though there was nothing routine about someone showing up in your life ten years later after never having kept in touch.

Julie seemed more in tune with the strangeness of life than me.

I was always in admiration of those who can do that, and certainly of women who seem to deal with strange things in a more adult and intriguing way. Anyway, I have always felt that women in general have a better fix on things than most men do.

I then started to wonder what Emily would say about these thoughts of mine. She knew of Julie because I had told her about her. She had also said she understood the feelings Julie had professed for me.

Emily never gave me the impression she felt threatened by them or that she was jealous. These thoughts were now more confusing than ever.

Maybe I should never have come to Fort Bragg in the first place. When I started thinking about why I was here, I could not find any specific reason for that. It had been more like a whimsical idea.

I was not conscious of trying to go back and find something I had been missing all of these years—certainly not in these surroundings, and certainly not with Julie.

The past, my past, I had plenty of time to try to make peace with it. It had not been easy and to be frank there were still lots of hurt and pain that I could not completely get rid of, memories that still managed to overwhelm me.

Too many tragedies in my life had made me cynical about it. I am sure that Emily would have disagreed with me on that.

Her own life and pain had somehow made her stronger and, after the initial stages of desperation, she had come to some understanding and truth about life in general, and about her own life in particular.

Yes, she was gone but that did not diminish my great admiration for her strength of character and for the things she had taught me, which I relished with tenderness and sadness at the same time.

Man, I wished I could see her and talk to her. There had not been a day when I had not thought about her. But I had painfully come to accept that dwelling on sad memories had to stop, though, I still did not know how to make that happen.

It was not easy. While there had been times when I automatically did not think about her; nevertheless, she was hovering inside my brain and she would always be part of my life, my soul, my heart. I could not renounce her even if I wanted to.

Emily would know what to do. Every time that I had been confronted with some strange twists in my life these past long years, I had always talked to her. I derived a great deal of inspiration from thinking about what she would have said to me.

I was not being stupid or crazy when I found myself having this dialogue with her. But I did find the whole thing very comforting. It made me feel much closer to her even though my reality was rather stark: Emily was dead. She was not coming back!

I started to imagine what had taken place in Julie's life these past ten years. She had said that there was much to talk about and there was, but Julie and I had never been close. I had cast her to play the role of Anne Frank.

Yes, she had once told me she had a crush on me, had written me a lovely poem that was flattering to say the least. But I always attributed her attitude to being young. I always thought that as she grew older it would disappear. These things do. They fade out with time.

Yet from seeing her reaction and from what she had said about thinking of me, there was still a residue of that innocence that she had exhibited years ago. Boy, I thought, why in the hell am I here; what am I getting myself into?

The nagging feeling that life was about to turn one of her tricks on me made me wary. I had better be careful here, I thought. But I also had to admit that I had been very happy that I had found her!

To see in front of me the lovely young woman she had turned into gave me a great deal of pleasure but not without a hint of anxiety. I do not know why I was feeling this way.

Maybe it had to do with the fact that I was back in this familiar place—a place that had brought me both pain and pleasure. I was not sure just how to deal with it. Life in general was not something that I understood or was fond of.

And my own personal life was even more strange and confused than what I thought a normal life should be.

We were driving out of town a bit. The houses and apartment buildings were newer, and I could see a golf course in the distance and plenty of green spaces around. I wondered how much I had missed the first time I had been here. I did not remember that the topography of North Carolina had been this pleasant.

We finally came to a campus-like setting with different looking buildings with ponds and gardens around. It had the feeling of a rural setting, yet it was modern and stylish.

I was somewhat surprised as I always imagined that this part of the country was not as architecturally advanced as other parts. It was all rather immature of me, really. Old habits and stereotypes are hard to get rid of.

She stopped and I parked right next to her. She got out, opened the trunk of her car, and took out her sports bag.

"It's a nice place here."

"Yes, I like it. Come on up."

"Do you play golf?" I asked, remembering the only time I had played with Yoshi and had failed miserably.

"No, actually, I prefer tennis."

"Are you any good at it?"

"I'm not bad. What about you?"

"Yes, I, too, prefer tennis. I'm not very good at it, but I do have a wicked serve. If I can get the ball over the net on my first serve, look out. For some reason, and I don't know how it happens, I put a spin on the ball that my opponents have a hard time controlling. However, that's the extent of my game. Most of the time, I lose."

"My sister is the one to beat. She's fearless. She's lost a couple of boyfriends because they could not beat her. Those guys didn't have a sense of humor."

"I guess not."

We walked up to the second floor and stopped at the top of the stairs. Her apartment was on the left side on top of the garage.

"I must warn you that my place is in a bit of a mess. I wasn't expecting any visitors today."

"I'm sure you're exaggerating."

"Well, maybe a little."

She opened the door and walked in. I followed her. The first thing I noticed was the balcony that overlooked a large green area with a pond at the end. It felt peaceful and quiet. Her apartment was airy and bright and had comfortable feel about it.

There were several posters hanging on the walls. There was no mess as she had warned me earlier. In fact, all I saw and sensed was the apartment of a well-ordered person.

We both stood in the middle of the room not quite sure what to do next. She put her bag down.

"OK, I was thinking that if you don't mind we can perhaps stay in and I'll make us a cheese omelet and I have some greens."

"Are you sure?"

"What do you have against my cooking?"

"Nothing, I just thought that we can go out and, I mean," I said.

"I don't mind. I'm not a great chef but I can hold my own," she said, laughing as she went into the kitchen.

"Would you like something to drink? I have a bottle of wine that a mother of one of my students gave me. I always thought I would drink it on a special occasion."

"Oh, thank you. But maybe we should save it for dinner."

"Good idea. How about some coffee or soft drink?"

"No, I'm fine."

"Are you sure?"

"Yes."

"OK, let me take a shower and in the meantime you can look at my scrap book. It might give you an idea of what I've done and where I've been."

"That'll be great."

She went into her bedroom and came out a few moments later with a thick book, more like an album. She had titled it: Julie's Madness.

She gave it to me and smiled.

"My mother put it together. Given that you are here and after you leave most probably I won't see you again for another ten years, this might make you remember me a bit more."

She stopped and there was a wistful look in her eyes. I did not know what to say. In some strange way the manner of Julie's attitude made it seem very natural that I would be visiting her, on the spur of the moment, and she would share her ideas and thoughts as if no time had elapsed from the last time we had seen each other. Then we would say good night and go back to our own lives.

She went into her bedroom and soon I heard the water running in the shower. I sat down and opened her book. There was a photo of Julie and two other girls. I recognized one of them as being her sister as there was a strong resemblance.

This photo probably had been taken about the time when I first met Julie. There was a photo of Julie wearing braces and trying hard not to smile at the camera, but not having much success.

Then on the following page, she had glued the program from *The Diary of Anne Frank*. It was open and I found myself reading what I had written when she had asked me to write something in the program. Seeing it now took me back to the last day I had seen Julie, so many years ago.

I guess it had to do with the simple fact that these past years, I had tried as much as I could to avoid dealing with this particular period of my life. In the next few pages, there were many photos of Julie and others. I noticed a guy who seemed to appear in many of the photos. Probably her boyfriend, I thought.

Julie came out of her bedroom. She had changed clothes and was now wearing a pretty yellow dress, which did more than accentuate her good looks and great legs. She looked refreshed, innocent, natural, and her smile was beguiling.

I noticed she was not wearing much make-up, her hair fell on her shoulders, and she was bare footed with painted toenails—bright red. It is always interesting and fascinating the things that women have to do to make themselves attractive.

I often wonder that even with beautiful women the need to look feminine and attractive makes them sometimes abuse their own ideas of who they are, what they represent, and forces them go to extremes in order to meet the expectations of others.

But Julie did not seem to be insecure about her looks. Maybe she was. I think she intrinsically knew that she was very attractive and her general demeanor seemed natural and not forced.

"I love your dress."

"Thank you. It's one of my favorites. How about some tea?"

"OK, that'll be great."

She went into the kitchen while I continued looking at her scrapbook. I did not know if what I was looking at reflected a lot of the past long years. I glanced in her direction a couple of times, and she was looking at me with a look of curiosity and amusement as if she were contemplating a joke. She smiled at me.

"It is strange isn't it?" I said.

"Yes, it is, but in many ways it seems natural. I was thinking while taking the shower that it is as if I just saw you a couple of days ago, and here we are as if these long years had not passed. I find the whole thing somewhat normal, but of course it isn't."

"No, it isn't."

I turned the page and there was a photo of two little girls. I recognized them as being Julie and her sister Becky. They were both blonde.

"I didn't know you were blonde."

"Yes, my sister and I as kids were blonde but as we got older our hair color changed and it got darker."

Suddenly, the memory of me looking at another album with another lovely little girl came to me. It shook me up. It really did. I put the album down, got up, walked to the balcony, slid the door open, stepped outside, and stood in the small balcony looking at the sun slowly fading into the other side of the earth.

I was trying to breath normally. It was not easy. I had not been prepared for this. What the hell was I doing here?

I do not know if Julie had seen my face or something for the next thing I knew, she was standing right next to me. I could smell her perfume. I looked at her and smiled. But I could see that her face was serious. She had sensed my discomfort.

"Are you all right?"

"I think so. It will pass."

"The tea is ready."

She turned around and went back in. I followed her.

I sat on her small couch again and she sat across from me. She had put the teapot and the mugs on a tray, which she had placed on her coffee table. She poured the tea into a mug.

"Do you want milk, or sugar?"

"Just a little sugar, please."

She extended the sugar bowl and I took a single lump and put it in my tea.

"So how did you end up teaching?"

"When I came back from college, I needed a job and at the time the school district was looking for new people. I applied and since I had graduated from college they sort of gave me a pass on any teaching credentials, though, I did take a couple of courses just to give me a primer on what to do. I teach art history, and dancing classes after school. I like it."

"Where did you go school?"

"Ohio State."

"That's a long way from home."

"Well, it was a sort of a sentimental journey for me. My mother is originally from Ohio, and went to Ohio State. She then moved to D.C. where she met my dad. She worked at the Pentagon. I was born in D.C. We lived there for about eight years, and then my father got transferred to Fort Bragg. He was a complete Southerner. Perfect Southern manners, which I think wooed my mother from the start."

It was interesting that I neither knew nor suspected any of Julie's family history. I was never really curious about her background then, certainly not in that way. There had really been no reason for me to want to know of her personal history.

"You know now that I think about it, you don't have a real Southern accent."

"Maybe a little bit. I wasn't born in the South, though, I have lived here for many years. My upbringing, my culture, is mostly Southern because of my father. He was very proud of it, and so am I. I'm not a native Southern person, but I won't let anybody push me around on that issue."

"So why didn't you go to a Southern university to study?"

"Actually, I thought I would go to Chapel Hill, but they only offered law, business, medicine, and library science. I didn't want to study any of those things. Besides, I wanted to see other parts of the country. I got a scholarship at Ohio for music school and I went. Turned out that I liked art better.

"Then I spent my junior year in Florence, Italy, and that pretty much cemented what I wanted to do with my life. I'm through writing my masters' thesis. I want to be a museum curator."

"Wow, that's impressive, Julie."

"Do you think so?"

"Yes, absolutely."

"However, here in North Carolina there aren't that many opportunities for a museum curator. So, I'll have to go to some other place. Maybe Texas, Chicago, New York, San Francisco, or maybe back to Ohio, though the competition is very heavy everywhere."

"I think that wherever you go you will be great."

"Really?"

I could see that she was embarrassed, surprised, and kind of lost by my words.

"I would like to show you something, may I?" I asked her.

"What?"

"It's in my car. Let me go and get it."

"OK."

I had no idea what prompted me to want to show her Emily's painting. Maybe it was something to impress her, or more to impress me. To give me some comfort from what I was feeling. It was true that I was enjoying Julie's company but I started to feel lousy, depressed, and sad.

Emily's memory was never far from my heart and mind. I went to my car and sat there a couple of minutes. I was trying to compose myself. I did not want to create a spectacle and embarrass myself, or Julie. I was feeling a bit shaky. I needed to control myself.

Julie's presence had brought to me in stark terms how much I missed Emily. And yet in another sense, I also wanted not to miss Emily. I did not want my existence to continue being a shrine for someone who was not there, who would never be there.

She had been part of my life in real terms then she had disappeared. And even though I had pretty much managed to deal with my loss, once in a while it overwhelmed me completely when I least expected it. Today, it was one of those days. It was tough.

I took the painting out of the car and, after a moment's hesitation thinking that maybe I was tempting fate too damn much, I went back to the apartment. My hands were shaking. I was not afraid that Julie would make a negative comment about the painting yet at the same time I recognized I was taking a hell of a risk.

Emily meant so much in my life that a negative comment about the painting, thus about Emily herself, would be much too painful. I was really cutting it too close. I put the painting on the chair.

Julie turned a small lamp on and we both stood looking at it, studying it. There was no initial reaction from her. Then she started to talk softly, as if talking to herself.

"I like the colors and the design of the painting. It reflects that the painter took time to make sure that the contrast of the landscape and the small stream did not take away from each other. It is a sharp and interesting perspective. It is a well thought out plan for the painting.

"I love the shadows, the style, and the mixing of the colors. Whoever did this thing he knew what was needed. I see no hesitation on the strokes. Firm and direct. No ambiguity about what was on the mind of the artist."

Better than I could have expected. Hell, better than what I could have said myself. I started to smile and Julie had a strange look in her eyes. There was something that either my look or the actual painting telegraphed to Julie that she got very quiet and serious.

"Can I ask you something?" She said, after a long silence.

"What?"

I instinctively knew what her question was going to be. I had better prepare myself for this, I thought.

"A moment ago I said that the painter—a he—had done a masterful job. But on second thought, I would be willing to bet that, in fact, this painting was not done by a male artist, but a female one. Am I wrong?"

"How can you tell?"

"There is a kind of lyrical quality about the painting. A softness to it. It is what I'd like to think of as "feminine" softness, as opposed to the softness that male painters often exhibit in their work. Maybe it has to do with women not being physically as strong as men; it shows, I think. Then from looking at your face when I said 'he', and from the way you reacted when I made my initial comment."

"Yes, it was done by a female painter."

Suddenly, an immense sadness filled my whole being. At that moment, I found myself completely lost. I felt numb. Desperate. I felt out of place. I did not want to have to share my sorrows with Julie who had been so kind, open, and honest.

I fought desperately not to show how much I was hurting. The next thing I knew, she had moved closer and had her arms around me and held me against her. Boy, talk about losing one's cool, I sure as hell had lost mine.

"It's from Emily, isn't it?"

"Yes . . ."

"I could tell."

She pushed herself away from me. She seemed to be trying to come to some decision. She hesitated, and then spoke.

"I'm so sorry, Jonathan. I knew what happened."

"You mean about her dying? How?"

When I asked her I could barely find my voice.

"Life has strange ways of showing you things. The lady who had rented Emily the house while she lived here knows my mother. And one day while talking about other people, she told a story of a young couple whose husband was in the Army and who had been killed in Vietnam.

"She had kept in touch with the wife's family, and one day she received a short note from them explaining that the girl in question—Emily—had died during childbirth. And that the child had also died. I'm so sorry Jonathan, so sorry."

I had tears in my eyes and I did not hide them. I did not want to hide them. I was hurting and to pretend otherwise was dishonest and foolish. Julie reached into her pocket and pulled out my handkerchief and very gently wiped my eyes. She was a bit lost, too.

"I learned about her death from her kid brother. I was in Vietnam when, somehow, he had found where I was by looking at Emily's papers. He sent me a telegram. The Army had transferred me over there about a couple of months before she was due. I didn't want to go as I wanted to be with her when the baby was born. But my lousy luck did not give me a break.

"I had debated for a long time that if I got orders to Vietnam whether or not I would go. I thought I'd rather desert. But Emily thought it was too crazy and she begged me to go saying that things would work out OK. Then she died and the baby died—yeah, things worked out all right. I know that there was nothing I could have done to save her, but I would have been there to say goodbye—to hold her hand . . ."

Son of a bitch. Why had I ended up here discussing Emily with Julie? What scumbag destiny had caused me to be in a place where I did not belong; talking to someone who was a total stranger? We were silent for what seemed like a long time. I went back and sat on the couch.

The sun had given way to the early evening. Julie and I were left in the semidarkness of the room as the small lamp was not strong enough. She came and sat right next to me.

"Do you want more light?" she asked me.

"No."

"Yeah, me neither. I like the dark. I can become invisible in the dark. When I was a kid I was never afraid of the dark. My sister would go crazy if she was left in a room without lights. In fact, even today she has trouble going to sleep sometimes unless the room is brightly lit."

"Yeah, there are people like that."

"It's a great painting, Jonathan. You should be very proud to own it and the fact that she did it."

"I was shocked when Billy gave it to me. I went to see her grave, their grave actually. She's buried in the same grave with her baby. And her husband is right next to them—I'm sorry."

I felt lousy and so isolated from anything. So removed from the simple things in life because my life had been such a total moral and spiritual wreck for too damn long.

"Jonathan, it's OK. I know about death. I know about losing a loved one. My mother has a cemetery plot she bought as she wants to be buried right next to my father. The Army wanted to bury him in Arlington, but my mother said no. She wanted him to be buried in his native soil."

Was it normal that Julie and I were talking about dead people? People who had made a difference in our lives? I guess it was. For Julie, it was her father. I know she was very proud of him just as he was of her.

For me, it was Emily whom I had loved completely without any ambiguity. She came out of nowhere and had filled my life with so much tenderness and affection. Then, she disappeared. Gone! Dead—any ending.

Though we never really lived together—it was not possible. Nevertheless, we inhabited a world that was filled with magic, beauty and tenderness. In all of our phone conversations, Emily always insisted that life had to be lived to its fullest.

I also remembered when the tragedy of losing Homer struck, she had faced the uncertain future with dignity trying so hard to hang on to her sanity and desire to live a new life. It was a constant fight, but it had to be done.

She had said that to me regularly. There was no time to sit back and let the misery and pain conquer you. It was hard and sometimes the agonizing feelings were so overwhelming, but Emily never lost that sense of wanting her life to be better, lucid, and honest.

I had learned that from her, though, it seemed that I had forgotten most of it. No, it was not that. The truth was that I hated life. That I did not want to be here. I did not want to be anywhere. I wanted to be lost in the fog of life. I wanted to be forgotten in the nothingness of my existence.

For so many of those long and gone shitty years, I had spoken very little about anything that had to do with Emily, my Army days, Wilson, Cash, Jackson, Yoshi. I did not have the energy or desire.

"Have you kept in touch with any of your Army buddies? Like Leno or Cash?" She asked as if reading my mind.

"You remember them?"

"Yes."

"They both got killed. Cash is buried back in Alabama. And Jackson back in Chicago. I held him in my arms when he died. Cash never knew what hit him. He died instantly. One moment they had been alive, and the next they were gone. Puff. In fact, that was also the end of my tour.

"I got a large piece of metal in my back that has sort of replaced one of my kidneys. The doctors said to leave the metal there. It was too dangerous to try to pull it out. It doesn't bother me really, except on very cold days."

"I'm sorry to hear about Leno and Cash. They were good guys."

"Yes, they were. I miss them . . ."

A long silence ensued between us. I had talked about what had happened in Vietnam to very few people in the past. Most of the time, I preferred to keep the whole thing to myself. My experiences and memories of those days were not unique or special. It was what it was.

Julie kept looking at me with a shy and reserved look, perhaps afraid to offend me or just simply trying to respect my privacy. I kind of felt that I should not be polluting her life with my misery, and with my painful memories. I really felt lousy about everything, everything!

"What do you want to happen in your life?" She asked.

Yeah, what I was looking for? What had I been looking for these past ten years? To be confronted with such a question was not easy.

Come on, answer her, you shit brain—Cash would have said—*thing is, you don't know what you're looking for. Have some balls and answer her, Hollywood, and don't lie or pull some of the cheap shit on her the way you normally do on me and Jackson.*

"To find simple things," I finally managed to answer to Julie's question. "To find peace and harmony. Not to wake up still depressed from the previous night and the night before that. To be able to sleep like a normal human being. To look at a sunset and enjoy its beauty, its magnificence.

"Or to look up at the stars and wonder about their mystery, how magical they are, instead of dismissing them as simply points of light up in the sky. Not to feel so separated and remote from others. I'd like to believe that I can be loved, but more importantly that I can love just as innocently, pure, and honestly as I once did—it is a lot to ask for, isn't it?"

"No, it isn't."

"I have a tough time accepting my own humanity, to believe in my own sensibilities as I constantly deny them. I persistently fight with myself because I want to believe in pure things—in hope. To tell you the truth, I find it hard to believe in anything anymore.

"These past years have been a constant struggle to try to remain human. I don't think that life really gives a damn about me, or anybody."

"You have to keep on trying, not give up."

"It seems such an impossible task."

"It is, but I believe in the heart's resiliency."

I was surprised that I was talking like this. I had not done it in a very long time. I caught myself, once again, in my own stupid contradictions as to what I was seeking to achieve. And at the same time rejecting the possibilities, closing myself to feel things, new things; t was not easy.

"I've been thinking of perhaps going to Paris to live. It has always been one of my crazy dreams. I majored in French in school so maybe I can study it further and see what happens. I really don't have any plans."

"Paris! When I was going to school in Florence, many times I thought I'd like to go to Paris but there was so much to do and see in Italy that I never got around to checking it out. My loss," she said, wistfully.

Suddenly, the phone rang. Its shrill sound was offensive and unwelcome. I saw it on her face. She got up and went to the kitchen to answer it.

"Excuse me, please."

There was a kind of frustration in her due to the telephone suddenly intruding on us. It was not welcome. I understood her reaction. The damn phone was an ugly reminder that other things exist in our lives, and they can happen at inopportune moments. She picked up the phone.

"Hello? Oh, hi . . ."

She turned slightly away from me as if trying to keep me from either seeing her face or hearing what she was saying.

"Tonight? No, I'm sorry, not tonight. I've got some personal stuff I need to take care of, I am kind of behind. But let me call you later and we'll talk. OK. Thanks, bye." She put the phone down and stood quietly for a moment, thinking.

It suddenly occurred to me that I had been overstaying my visit.

"Julie if you need to do something please don't let me be in the way. I think it's lovely for you to give me your time but I don't want to interfere with things you need to take care of. I can be on my way."

"Jonathan if you want to leave, I can't keep you from doing it. I'd like you to stay as long as you want. Anyway, I promised to make you one of my famous omelets, remember?"

"We can do it some other time."

"When? Ten years from now? You're passing through and most likely after tonight, I'll never see or hear from you again."

She sounded despondent all of a sudden, and her face was filled with sadness and longings. She came and sat right next to me.

"Boy, why are things so tough?" I asked, but I was not asking her. I was asking the universe.

"Because we make them tough. Life should be simple and filled with good things. It should not give us so many heartaches and pain. It should be bursting with fantasy, love and good stuff. It should be open, full of laughter, happiness, and innocence, and not so cynical and jaded."

"So you're a fine chef?" I said, changing the tone of our conversation to something more pleasant. She smiled and seemed to understand my sentiments.

"I do OK. I learned about good, solid cooking when I lived in Italy. I stayed with a mad family, the Sargentis. You know how Italians are. Full of passion, humor, totally in tune with themselves with a deep understanding of life's idiosyncrasies. Not given to brooding, or depressive behavior. I think I never laughed so much and so freely as when I was there. A truly remarkable experience. We have so much to learn from the old countries."

"Did you ever visit Venice?"

Venezia? Yes. A fantastic place."

"So, which one do you prefer, Florence or Venice?"

"It sounds like you've never been to Italy."

"I haven't."

"They are both jewels. Each of them represents something unique, magical, and spiritual. There is no preference to be made. You simply love them both. As you probably know, Florence has the statue of *David*; magnificent! It takes your breath away. And Venice, a city built on water and amazingly charming and beautiful. You'd have to be a simpleton to want to pick one over the other. I know many Americans do that, but not me."

"We Americans want to simplify things, to cheapen them often, don't we?"

"Absolutely. The Sargentis, my Italian family, consisted of *la mama, il papa*, and three brothers and a sister, Carmela, who is the oldest. All of the brothers spoiled rotten. Nico, Luchino, Roberto. Nico and Luchino are both married. Nico to Anna, and Luchino to Maria. Roberto is the youngest of the three brothers, the baby. Wild, smart, good looking, full of himself. All of the girls were after him.

"And he knew how to play one against the others. He used to walk around the house, buck-naked. His mother would hit the ceiling whenever he did it. Needless to say, I was shocked by his bizarre behavior until I understood he was doing it to give me a hard time. I don't think it was sexual, as much as to show who the boss was around the house. I finally figured out how to tame this wild beast."

"How did you do it?"

"I started calling him Bobby. He hated it. He would yell at me reminding me that his name was Roberto, that 'Bobby' was American, for sissies. He walked naked around the house, he was Bobby. And when his mother figured out what was going on she also started calling him Bobby, and that cured him from walking around in his birthday suit."

"That was smart," I said, and started to laugh.

"It was. I didn't see much of Carmela as she lived in Rome. And what I found fascinating was that when I first arrived, mama Sargenti got all the three brothers, sat them down, and laid the law down to make sure they understood there would be no funny business regarding how they treated me. As far as she was concerned, they had suddenly inherited a sister—*la sorella Americana*—and that was that.

"Italian mothers have a lot of patience with their sons. But once mothers lay the law down, they are not to be messed with, let me tell you. Mama Sargenti made it clear to the brothers that they had to protect me from all of the predators, as brothers are supposed to do with their sisters."

"And did they?"

"And how? And not surprisingly, when I think about it, Roberto was the worst of the best. He explained to me, rather formally, how to dress, how not to pay attention to what he called: the *papagallos*, you know the guys who are always chasing women. How to look down on all of these guys, to put them in their place. To call them: *Cornutos*."

"To call them what?"

"That's what Italians call a man whose wife is cheating on him: *Cornuto*, you know, horns. And if by any chance one of those guys got too fresh with me, to tell him that all three brothers would make sure a landfill would not be big enough to bury the guilty one after they got through with him. Honor is crucial to have in *la famiglia*."

I started to laugh just imagining the three brothers doing a number on some unsuspecting guy because he was not respecting Julie—*la sorella Americana*.

"Are you serious?"

"Very. But the most important thing was: learn how to cook pasta. If I were going to be a good woman and a good wife, with plenty of bambinos, I had to know mama's kitchen secrets. It was interesting to me because here in the U.S. it is women who do most of the cooking. Over there, I found a lot of men doing the cooking."

"So you learned to speak Italian?"

"Yes, I do OK. The whole family spoke English, which was the reason why I had decided to stay with them. I figured it would make it easier for me. But I did learn lots of Italian especially from Roberto, who taught me the bad words.

"I'm going back. I have applied to the University of Bologna as I want to get a Ph.D. in Renaissance Art. Did you know that it was in Bologna that the French learned the art of the cuisine? Of course, the Frogs would deny it but it's true."

"Have you told your Italian family that you are going back?"

"Not yet. I want to surprise them. Florence is only about fifty miles from Bologna. I'm sure the Sargentis will insist; no, demand that I come and live with them, at least until I find; no, until *they* find me a place to rent in Bologna. I know them." She smiled to herself.

"I envy you."

"Why?"

"Because by listening to you share your adventures, your future plans, I realize how narrow and limited my life has been these past years. I never tried to find some way of looking at life with different eyes. It has been a constant brooding and feeling sorry for myself. My life has been filled with emptiness and pain since Emily's death."

There was a look of sadness and yet also one of understanding on her face. A long silence ensued and when she spoke, her words were soft and they gave me the impression that she was saying them more to herself than to me.

"I know what you're saying. After finding myself in love with you and with no hope of ever having you love me back, and after losing my father to an ugly war, I also found that I was feeling sorry for myself.

"My life seemed bleak and with no purpose. I had to overcome my own misery. I had to change if I hoped to survive. I looked around me and it was seeing others—black people—for example, and how terrible their lives had become.

"And yet there was also an element of joy, of honesty, of reality, of hope in them that deeply resonated with me. Racism is ugly and depressing. I know I'm from the South, but my travels have opened my eyes to the ugliness of discrimination and I decided to try to improve my life and help others who are not like me. Lots of grief I got from my white friends, let me tell you."

Her last words had been pronounced quietly, but with a strong conviction. I could tell from her voice. Yeah, Julie had grown up a lot. I had not.

"I still love you, Jonathan."

Wow! This was not something that I had come looking for. She had said she still loved me, after all of these years? Man, oh, man, how do you deal with that? I thought of Jackson and Cash and, at the moment, I wished we were all back in the good old days where they would explain things to me. But, alas, Cash and Jackson were dead.

"Julie, it's so beautiful but strange to hear you say that. I can't believe that in all of these years you haven't found someone to love and have him love you like crazy."

"I've had some boyfriends in my life, though not that many. In fact, that phone call was from a guy that I'm breaking up with."

"Really, why?"

"He wants to get married and I told him, no. I'm not ready. He has been insisting on talking more about it. I'm not interested. There are so many things to do, places to go, people to meet. In fact, do you want to know something: He's driving me so crazy with his demands that I thought of calling my Italian brothers and have them come over and have a nice 'chat' with him."

"Are you serious? Would they come?"

"In a minute, all three of them!" She said, as she busted out laughing.

"Oh, Julie you are crazy."

"Well, maybe a little."

We were both silent. I started thinking about Emily and my love for her. Yes, it had faded, how could it not? But I tried to imagine what she would say about what Julie had said a moment ago, about still being in love with me after so many years of silence. Man, oh, man.

Can a man, can anybody, cling to love memories? Can we survive as human beings hanging on to past dreams? Fading memories? No longer real, no longer alive, no longer present. It was my struggle. It had been now for too damn long.

"Do you want to know who I was thinking about when I had sex for the first time?"

What? Did I hear her right?

"Julie, please . . ."

"I thought about you. I had your picture in my head and it wasn't nice, not right, and not fair. I had sex with this boy only that one time, but I never made love to him. So maybe I'm still a virgin. I jokingly told my sister about it and she laughed and told me to get rid of this crazy idea, as it would keep me awake at night. So, maybe I'm crazy!" And she laughed.

Holly shit! Now, what? Strange the thoughts that take root within our brains.

Cash had once said that Southern women grow up very fast. Now trying to reflect on what had happened then; no, on what had *not* happened between Julie and me back then, I got shook up by hearing Julie's confession.

Her fixation with me, ten years ago, I took to be just that: a fixation of a young, innocent, and naïve girl. But I also remembered that one time I had had fleeting thoughts about her.

And, now, I was once again being forced to deal with the dark secrets of the heart. Julie was not a naïve girl anymore. She was a young, beautiful woman, and she was confronting me with her truth, which whether or not I wanted to hear, I had no choice but to accept. Easier said than done.

"Jonathan, please forgive me. I don't mean to cause you any discomfort or embarrassment. I wish I knew why I feel this way. Why I have felt that way ever since I met you. Maybe it had to do with me doing the role in *The Diary of Anne Frank*. You made it possible for me, and not only me, to see things differently, to think differently. Remember I once told you about a diary I was keeping?"

"Yes."

"It has grown to lots of pages. It is still my most intimate friend. So much of what I've felt over the years is written there. Anyone who were to read it would learn all about me. I have entered private thoughts and feelings and sometimes it's not a wise idea to show others who we really are. What drives us to think and do the things we do."

"Julie, you have always overwhelmed me with your honesty and directness."

"OK, do you think that now that I'm no longer a silly girl that life would give me, would give us a chance?"

I stood up just to try to control my own conflicting thoughts. Her words had been soft, but the question was direct and unambiguous. She was essentially saying that now that Emily was no longer around that we should look at our lives differently.

Julie was directly challenging me, without being mean, to face the fucking truth: Emily was dead! It was such a hard and ugly truth for me to accept. I thought this whole thing was turning into something that I did not have control over. It confused me to no end. Maybe I should get out while the getting out was OK.

She got up from the couch, faced me, and stood still. Even though it was semi dark in the apartment, other light filtered into the room from the outside. It was enough to see her face and her eyes shining softly and with a degree of loneliness, but she was also putting my feet to the fire.

Man, oh, man I had not come here looking for challenges. *Merde*, my whole existence was nothing but a giant challenge. I did not need more troubles in my life. How does one decide upon one's own destiny?

Slowly, she moved closer and put her arms around me and held me hard against her. It was not a sexual thing, really. It was the desire of one person to let the other person know that one cares. I thought, oh, boy, this is not what I needed. She clung to me fiercely, almost harshly.

Her physical proximity was both troubling and at the same time it had an element of honesty, purity, innocence. It also scared me to no end. I was trying to pretend that what was happening was just another obstacle that I could easily navigate around.

I had not been this close to a woman for a very long time, and I do not mean only in the physical sense. The warmth of her body against mine was not vulgar. The thought of her, ten years ago, when she had suddenly kissed me after I had refused to kiss her came to me.

Again, I thought, this is no good but I also understood that things had now changed. Julie was no longer a sixteen-year girl but a beautiful, grown up woman, filled with desires and needs. Not, good, Jonathan, not good at all, I thought.

"Julie, oh, Julie, you're something else. You know that?"

"Do I have a chance? Do we have a chance?"

"My life is so screwed up. I'm not sure of my own feelings about anything anymore. I'm afraid to feel anything."

"I will help you. I promise. I want to so much."

"Julie, what's happening to us? This wasn't supposed to be this way."

"OK, how was it supposed to be like? Are you afraid of what thoughts you will have about Emily? Is that it?"

She moved away from me, but she was still facing me. Some women can get to the point without any pretense. Julie had always been one of them.

"Yes, in many ways."

"Jonathan, I hope I haven't offended you. But Emily is no more. We are! I understand that given what happened you would feel threatened, fearful, to open your heart once again to feel wonderful things, pure sentiments. I do understand that.

"But, again, we are here and those other people who have been part of us can only exist in our memories. We can't live on memories forever. Life won't permit us to do so. Life demands that we take a leap of faith especially when the fates are willing to give us another chance."

"How in the hell do you know so much? You scare me."

"Good," she said smiling, and she moved close to me again. There was literally not much distance between our bodies.

"Actually, you are a dangerous young woman."

"Is that a compliment?"

"More than that. It is also an inevitable fact."

"Dangerous, ah."

"Yes. Very."

"OK, I like that."

Suddenly, I started getting a hard on. At first, I was embarrassed to be so close to her but, after a while, even my own reticence gave away to lust and excitement for her. I kissed her. She was surprised, but she kissed me back and soon both of us were completely lost in our desire and passion for each other that nothing else mattered anymore.

Julie was right. We had to stop dealing with our own ghosts and conflicting emotions and had to admit our human needs and not deny them. We had to accept our own fates without any reservations. Could I do that? I wished I knew the answer.

For an instant, I thought: what the hell am I doing here? I do not belong here. So where in this life do I belong? Emily's image came into my mind but I felt no longer any sense of guilt. For some strange reason, Julie was showing me, as only a woman can show a man, that love and happiness can survive.

Was life teaching me that I had survived all of my troubles these past long years to be where I was now, confronting a different reality—a new reality?

I started to fumble with the buttons of her dress. She did not move. She was watching me not in a judgmental way but it seemed more out of wonderment about what we were doing. Surprised, might be the right word, though, in a much larger sense surprise still hid the meaning of what was now taking place.

The dress dropped to the floor. She was not wearing a bra. I kissed her lovely breasts, the nipples stood erect, hard, pointy, luscious, filled with desire.

She started to unbuckle my belt. I helped her. She was looking at me in such a way that I had forgotten how a woman who loves a man can possibly look. She, then, stepped out of her panties as I did out of my pants and shorts, and we were both naked and pressed hard against one another while her kisses were soft, tender, and timeless. My erection was incredible, shameless.

Julie took my hand and slowly started walking ahead of me as we went into her bedroom. I ran my hand over her sex and she was very wet and moaning softly as I touched her, and seemed lost in our moment of passion and tenderness.

When I finally entered her, she had a moment of recoil, as if this was the instant that would bring her some truth that only she knew. Our lovemaking was slow, but passionate, as if we wanted it to last until the moon fell out of the sky. I had been celibate by choice for a while but now all of my misery, loneliness, and pain, were suddenly replaced by an amazing physical desire for Julie.

Julie did not hold back anything. She was all giver and more.

We did not say much afterward. We had been lost in a world of lust and physical pleasure, one that we both did not want to end, and one that we did not totally understand. This magical moment told immutable stories that words might have turned into complete banalities.

"Julie, there's so much I want to tell you."

"Jonathan, we have time. I think we should get something to eat. Aren't you hungry? I can make us my famous *frittata.*"

"A what?"

"An omelet, but an Italian omelet with all kinds of exotic herbs and tons of garlic."

"Garlic . . . tons of it?"

"It's great for your health and according to Luchino, Nico and Roberto, it also gives men what they euphemistically called: 'certain stability,' " and she laughed.

"And does it?"

"I'm not a man so I don't know. However, Maria and Anna were in full agreement with that. Even Dr. Sargenti agreed with it."

"And mama Sargenti?"

"Yeah, she also agreed. You know what, come to think of it; it may have been why Roberto was not too crazy about my, then, boy-friend who hates garlic."

"I love garlic, I dream of garlic," I said, and we both busted out laughing. "Yes, but also I'm hungry for you," I added.

"But that's for later."

"OK, get up and go and make us your famous *frittata* . . . with tons of garlic."

And maybe garlic does make the world go around.

"I want to turn the lights on. I want to see you in your birthday suit," she said.

She laughed as she said this. She leaned over and kissed me and got out of the bed and turned a small lamp by the bed on. Then she stood looking down at me. But what I ended up doing was looking at her lovely body. She moved with the lightness of a dancer.

Actually, she glided over the floor in careful measure steps. She had a body on her that would not quit. I could imagine the Italian *papagallos* going crazy over what she represented, letting their imaginations run wild.

She went into the kitchen and a few moments later she came back now wearing her panties and my shirt.

"Oh, that's no fun. I want to see you running around naked."

"Later, my love. I have better put something on while I'm cooking. Don't want to end up getting some hot grease all over my naked belly."

"Good thing I started wearing that shirt only a couple of hours ago."

"I like it. It has your smell on it."

"Aren't you worried what your neighbors will say if they saw what's going on?"

"The only neighbors that can see anything from the outside are the chipmunks running around on the grass picking up nuts from the trees. And they are more interested in that than in a couple of half-naked bodies."

"Are you sure?"

"Positive."

"And what am I going to wear?"

"Yeah, good question."

"Well, I can always try one of your dresses."

"Not a good idea."

She went into the bathroom and came out with a white bathrobe.

"It belonged to my mom. This should do the trick. It's big enough for two people, actually. So you should fit in nicely."

She came over, sat on the bed and looked at me with a wonderful smile on her face. She handed me the robe. She leaned over and put her head on my chest. I stroked her hair, long, lush, soft.

"I like that," she said, quietly.

"You're not too difficult to please."

"I'm not. My likes are simple and not complicated."

I kept touching her hair.

"Did you plan this?" I asked her just to give her a hard time.

"What?"

"This whole episode?"

"Oh, sure. I knew you were going to parachute into my life after so many years out in the wilderness. So I figured you would come by the school today, and then we would come straight home and make wild love like there was no tomorrow."

"OK, at least you're honest about it."

"It always works. OK, show me where you have this supposed piece of metal encrusted in your back."

"Didn't you feel it already?"

"No."

"Too busy with other things?"

"Yeah, that's it."

I turned around and lay flat on my belly.

"OK, I'll close my eyes. Don't tell me where it is. Let me find it."

She started to run her hand softly over my back. But she was doing it in such a manner that I started to get hard.

"Are you sure you're doing this to find out if it is true, or, do you have ulterior motives in running your hand on my back the way you're doing it?"

"My motives are pure and honest."

She was caressing me and I decided not to stop her. It was physically thrilling and innocent.

"I found it. Oh, my, I can feel it right next to your other kidney."

"Yeah, that's the reason why the butchers didn't want to pull it out."

"Good decision. No sense in messing up the only kidney you've got left."

"I know."

"For once let's trust the butchers, as you called them, to have made the right decision."

She pressed her fingers once again, but not hard. Very tenderly.

"Does it hurt?"

"No. It feels funny that's all."

"You have a nice scar. Clean. No wrinkles."

"It's about six inches long, right?"

"Yes, it is well hidden in the skin."

"Yeah, the doctors said that since mine was not on my side that the skin would eventually help hide it. Actually, he said fat and not skin."

"But, you're not fat."

She leaned over and kissed the spot where the scar was.

"OK, that should cure your pain forever." She laughed.

She got up and went to the kitchen.

I stayed in the bed for a few more moments. I looked around the room. It was neatly arranged. There was a desk sitting in one corner with several files and papers sitting on top of it. The curtains were pretty, feminine. There were two closets. One was partially opened and I could see her dresses hanging inside.

A small TV sat in another corner and on top of it there was some kind of TV guide. There was a photo of a family. I could guess they were the Sargentis. A very handsome family, indeed.

Roberto was the youngest and full of roguish charm in that unique Italian and European manner. Their clothes were very stylish. The young woman was dark, and exuded a kind of mysterious charm. It made me think of Sylvana Mangano, the Italian actress. They were looking at the camera and seemed to be enjoying posing for the photo.

Right next to it, there were two large photos, black and white, of Julie. One photo was very stylish, chic, with shadows, and Julie in a dancing pose. The other was of Julie in a Spanish, toreador outfit, with a hat, and it made her look exotic, mysterious, and sexy.

What the hell am I doing here? I am not supposed to be here. I am supposed to be somewhere in Arkansas by now on my way back to California. Instead, I am naked on the bed of a total stranger; well, not a total stranger really.

242

Nevertheless, someone I know very little about. I have just had a round of great, loving sex, tender, passionate, but it came mostly from her.

Is she just another piece of ass? This is insane, I thought. Jackson had once gotten on my case when I had asked the same question about Emily and he had been right to call me on it. I am sure if I were to ask the same thing about Julie he would have been just as pissed and would have called me all kinds of names.

He would have been right, as he usually was. And where is Emily in all of this? I had not thought about her for a little bit. Just two days ago, I had stood by her grave and it had been tough.

And here I am, two days later, in Julie's bed as if this whole thing was normal. What is going on here, Jonathan? What is the game plan here? Are the gods planning a dirty trick on you because you are tempting the fates?

I could hear Julie humming a song from the kitchen. I could not tell what the song was. OK, again, what am I doing here? Am I just doing a number on this lovely woman after which I will split and be on my way? Shit, this is not supposed to be this way. Man, oh, man.

You know what, I thought, I should get up, ask her to give me back my shirt, get dressed, shake her hand, thank her for her wonderful hospitality, promise to send her a postcard from Los Angeles, and leave. Be on my way.

"What are you doing?"

She stood in the door way. The light filtered from behind her, and I could see the shape of fine legs, a body that was young, strong, incredibly attractive, and flimsily covered by own shirt. *Yeah, it has been fun Julie Anne. But I've got to hit the road. Got places to see, people to meet. You know, stuff—go ahead, asshole, just ask her to give you back your shirt.*

"Thinking."

"Good or bad?"

"Both."

"About me?"

"Good about you. Bad about me."

She moved toward the bed and sat on it. She took my hand.

"Jonathan, stop thinking at least for the next few hours. It's no good to think on an empty stomach. That's what mama Sargenti would say. Nothing that we did or want to do next is bad, ugly, or forbidden. Do you feel guilty?"

She looked at me and there was that innocence and simplicity that I suddenly remembered about Julie. She had asked the question but she was not lost like I was.

There was a kind of serenity and security in her eyes. She was not having any second thoughts at all. She was who she was and I should be man enough to accept a human gift from a beautiful girl. No questions asked.

"No," I answered, and it was true. But it did not give me grounds for security either.

I looked at Julie's face. She had little make up on her. I had noticed it earlier. She was no doubt a beautiful girl. She exuded youth, tenderness, charm, femininity, yet there was a sense of mystery about her as well. I knew of her, but I did not know who she was.

She smiled and touched her lips with her index finger kissing it, then reached over and touched my lips softly with the same finger. And I found myself wanting her again. Take it easy, buddy. There is time for everything. I hoped so.

"Hey, can I use your bathroom?"

"You don't need permission to do that."

She got up and went back into the kitchen. I saw this great pair of legs, and sitting on top of them a great looking ass slowly gliding away from me. Come on, Jonathan, stop torturing yourself and go with the flow.

I got up and went into her bathroom. I am always fascinated by women's bathrooms. So many secrets. It was a female's bathroom no question about that. However, I noticed that there were not too many beauty products. And that was surprising. Her panty hose were draped over the shower frame.

There was a small razor, pink in color, by the bathtub. Yeah, women shave their legs. The towels were on a small rack nailed to the wall. Neatly arranged. Even the toilet paper had flowers printed on it. The soaps were of lovely fragrances. There was a pot of flowers. They seemed fresh and smelled as such.

A typical female's bathroom.

I came out, put on the bathrobe, which as she had said was big enough for two people and walked into the kitchen. She had set the table in the small kitchen with proper cloth napkins, which in a way was not surprising, but I was surprised.

She had also put out the bottle of wine. And a small rose in the middle of the table. I took the bottle and looked at it. It was an Italian wine, red. I stood watching her from behind. She seemed serious dealing with the kitchen chores. She turned around and I shook my head and laughed.

"What?"

"OK, here I'm wearing your mom's bathrobe with nothing under it. And you standing there half-naked, and cooking for me, a stranger, really. And yet this whole thing seems so natural. It does scare me, I must admit."

"Scares you? But why?"

"I don't know. It's been such a long time since I had a beautiful woman cooking for me. I had forgotten all about it."

"Did you have many girls cook for you?"

Her question was simple and direct. But there was not any guile, any sense of sick curiosity. It was what we ask people just to find more about them. No underhanded intention behind her words.

"I don't know how to answer your question."

"Why not?"

"I'm not used to those questions."

"Are you embarrassed by my question?"

"In a way I guess I am."

"Should there be any secrets between us, Jonathan?"

She was looking at me half-mocking me, half-serious. I was not sure how to respond to her, how to act to her directness. Julie had always been very direct. That was why I liked her. But it was also what made me reticent in how to deal with her.

"No secrets."

But of course, there are secrets in our lives. It is not that we want to have them, it is that they exist. More often than not the things we want to hide are things that may be too painful, too embarrassing, or too personal, for the world to see.

So, we set up a defending line of pretension, and the façade we impose on us is to defeat the curiosity of others. But it is mostly to hide our feelings, our vulnerabilities, and our sensibilities,

Because of the fear that once we show who we are, we are left at the mercy of the reactions of others, and we become defenseless to any slight, rumor, and gratuitous insults we get exposed to in our daily struggle to remain true to ourselves.

I did not want to be a total cynic and ignore what Julie had meant. Anyway, with no idea of what was going to happen next it was better to agree with her. But was it? It did not seem honest; in fact, it was not honest but given my present state of mind it was the best solution under the present circumstances. I felt guilty about it, no question.

She moved closer, put her arms around me and held me close to her.

"That's always the best."

She kissed me passionately.

"You know, I think we'd better eat now otherwise your omelet will get cold and it won't taste as good."

"You're no fun. Here, open the wine. It's always better to let the wine breath a bit before drinking it."

I started to shake my head at how sophisticated Julie seemed. Yes, she had changed, no doubt about it. She was now a young, grown up, beautiful woman, filled with life, with the fantasy of life. I felt lucky to be around her. However, deep down within me I was also feeling confused, apprehensive, and not sure.

I opened the bottle of wine for her and set it on the table. She had fried some potatoes and had made a salad. She took my plate, put half of the omelet on it plus some potatoes and handed me the plate. She did the same thing for herself and then put the salad bowl on the table.

"Shall we sit down and eat? I'm starving. In Italy, they eat the salad at the end of the meal."

"I knew that," I said, in my boldest lie of today. She laughed and ignored my fib.

I went around the table and pulled her chair and she was so surprised that for an instant she seemed lost. She sat and I pushed her chair toward the table. I leaned over and kissed her. We lingered a moment over the kiss.

"Sit down, otherwise my masterpiece *frittata* will get cold."

I sat down and poured the wine for us. I poured a small amount into my glass first, then I poured for her, I then filled my own glass. I was not a total savage, philistine, after all. I raised my glass. She did likewise. We clinked.

"To a beautiful girl who is very special."

"Thank you. And to you and I hope that life will bring you happiness and peace. Chin, chin."

I looked at Julie and understood that something had happened in the last few hours that was going to take some time to digest, comprehend, absorb, and perhaps ultimately accept. Did I have it in me?

"Do you like Frank Sinatra?" She asked.

"I love Frank Sinatra."

"OK, after dinner and while we're drinking our coffee, I'll put on a recent record of his," she said, with a wonderful smile.

-XV-

I suddenly woke up with a start. I was having a dream but I could not figure out what it was. I had been having dreams like this one for a while now. I would wake up knowing I had dreamt something but I had no memory of specific dreams afterward.

But the one thing I longed to have and had never had these past years, and that was a dream about Emily. It drove me crazy. Why can I not have a dream about her? Nothing doing, pal.

I was not sure how long I had been sleeping or where I was. The darkness that surrounded me was disconcerting and the bed was not oriented in the direction that I was used to. I moved and there was a body right next to me. Then, I remembered where I was.

Julie stirred. I had awoken her. She put her arm around me for a long silent moment, and then leaned on my chest.

"Are you OK?" she asked.

"Yeah, I woke up and for a moment I didn't know where I was."

"Well, you're here with me. In my own bed, which I had a terrible time getting you to come to. I had to drag you. We drank most of the bottle of wine and then we made love, remember?"

"Vaguely," I said, just to give her hard time. "Wait, now I remember. You fell asleep in the middle of this passionate love making on the floor, and I was the one who had to drag you into bed and in your slumber you kept on mumbling something about Florence, *frittatas*, garlic, *vino Italiano, and* Frank Sinatra.*"

"I did not."

"Yes, you did."

There was a long silence for a moment.

"Did you say we made love on the floor?" She said.

"Yes, we did."

"Is that why my back hurts a bit?" She smiled. She was paying me back in kind.

"I don't know. From what I remember, you were on top and I was the one whose back was on the floor."

"Oh, no. And your back injury?"

"Well, I kept telling you to take it easy but it didn't seem to make any difference to you."

"Liar."

"OK, maybe I'm exaggerating a bit."

"A bit? What time is it?"

I glanced at her alarm clock.

"It's almost three in the morning."

"Oh, no. I'm going to have to call in sick."

"Really? Will you get into trouble?"

"No. I mean I have a few days of sick leave, but they are going to be surprised."

"Why?"

"I never take sick leave."

"How many days can you take?"

"I think I have two or three days."

"Hey, do you want to go to Myrtle Beach?"

"Myrtle Beach. Do you want to go to Myrtle Beach?"

"Can we go? How far is it?"

"I think about a hundred miles or so."

"Do you want to go for a couple of days? After all, a sick person needs fresh air. The sea and some sun would do wonders to your health, don't you think?"

"Jonathan, you're evil. You not only want to turn me into a woman of loose morals but a criminal to boot."

She stretched herself and gave me a knowing and sneaky smile. I turned and kissed her lovely breasts. She wrapped her long legs around mine.

"Yes, I'm going to turn you into the lowest form of criminal that you can think of. I will teach you how to lie, how to sneak out of your work in the middle of the afternoon so you can meet me to make love. And how to go and have a great and wonderful time in Myrtle Beach."

I touched her and started rubbing between her legs. She looked at me and smiled.

"Oh, Jonathan, you are lovely," and she kissed me.

Morbidity is my motto. Yes, morbidity is my motto and my favorite shitty companion.

But here I was, in Julie's bed, thinking back of the lovely sixteen-year old beauty who ten years earlier had written me a poem. Who had sung of flowers, and young girls, and young men, and of death, and of long time passing. Who sang to another bunch of young people on a happy night eons ago.

When everyone knew that half of those in attendance would eventually end up going to war, and for whom the last moments of their existence would be pain and more pain. Did they remember the song they had heard from the lips of an innocent girl?

Did that song make any difference in their lives, that night? Did they make any comments about it afterward, when they were getting ready for bed after a night of music, dance, and dreams?

Yes, morbidity is also my walking companion. I had once loved another woman so strongly and yet I knew less of her than I knew of Julie. Most of my realities about Emily were based on non-proximity. Based on illusions. On thoughts that I wanted to turn into tangibles. My long phone conversations with her were dreamlike.

And with Julie, while we were doing the play, I had spent more time around her than my total time with Emily. Emily lived in my head. Yes, I had loved her and had so desperately wanted to become part of her life, of her baby's life, but it had not happened.

I had wanted to create a simple reality for me and all I ended up with was a broken heart and a void so deep that time had no meaning anymore. And I was not looking to replace Emily with Julie. How fair would that be? And if I could ask Emily what I should do now that she was gone out of my life; would she then tell me to find someone else?

Just before I left her that fateful evening when I went to see her after Wilson's death, she had said that she wished that I would find someone who would love me with all of her heart.

Never suspecting or knowing that we would eventually become a pair, even though we were never a pair in the classical sense of a man and a woman sharing their daily lives together, in unison.

But did Emily know or suspect that things were not going to go the way we had both envisioned? Why did she not tell me that she was having problems with her pregnancy? Why? That question had haunted me all of these years.

I had no explanation other than the obvious stupid platitudes of not wanting to worry others with the things that were taking place. If we do not have time to worry about those we love, then, what good are we?

"Jonathan, I don't want to replace Emily," Julie said, after a while.

I did not answer.

"Jonathan?"

"Yes."

"Did you hear what I said?"

"Yes."

"Am I, Jonathan?"

"No."

"Are you sure?"

"Yes," I wanted that to be the case, but I knew of the uncertainty of life.

"I'm glad."

Then, she started to recite her poem. I could not believe it. Her soft voice suddenly filled my ears and head and heart. In the darkness of the room and with her voice filling the empty space, the setting took on a surreal quality. It seemed like time had stopped and the sun and the moon had taken a break from their interminable voyage around the cosmos.

Time was taking a break from its changeless routine of traveling across space with no destination in sight, because for the galaxies, suns, and planets there is no final destination. They just keep on going, unlike us humans. We know our destinations: Death—any ending.

People say there is a time and a place.
But no one knows.
Only the stars know and the moon, too.
But they don't tell us.
Trees and leaves know. The sun knows.
Even the sea knows.
The clouds, the sky, the rain, the night.
The flowers.
But they don't tell us.
But death does come and it has a time.
The heart knows, but it is quiet and only
Speaks in riddles, and it whispers softly.
And if we are lucky, we hear things, but
It is still mysterious.
We appear to be. But we are not.
Are you the essence of life?
Are you my new spring?
To see the other is to see a torrent of golden sunlight.
We want to be us and we are others instead.
To be loved is to know the time and place.
It is clear, warm and it is safe.
And to love is to find, and it is
As honest as the rainbow for it shares
The time and place.
Water droplets kissed by the sun's rays.
Those turn into beauty and nobility.
And laughter.
Still, no one tells us the time and the place.
Or when?
And to love is like a new dawn, bright, magical, and eternal
The time as well as the place.
Then we know that we are we and not others.
I am muted by fate and know my cries are in vain.
My wings have been shorn.
And flightless and worn
I turn and weep.

The poem had overwhelmed me when she had first recited it. Now In the darkness of her room, her voice and her words were brighter than any light that I could possibly turned on.

Son of a bitch, I thought. Could my longing and lonely heart ever find love again? Could I hope to find it as pure and as honest and mysterious again, the way I had once experienced with Emily? Was that possible?

Could I get rid of my pain and cynicism that had lived within me for such a long time that I had come to accept that it was the normal state of affairs? I suddenly felt cold, distant, and afraid. I just could not accept that my life was now going to change so drastically, and for the better.

I had grown not to let my own fantasies invade my psyche. It had happened once and it had cost me dearly. It had nearly cost me my fucking life, which was the only truth that I knew.

Yes, I had survived, but that was not a prize to be envied. I only knew I had done it. But, I also knew that I was damaged goods. I was not sure if I could do it again. If the truth were told, I just did not think I had what it took anymore.

"Julie, you're so amazing. Your poem when I first heard you reciting it to me made such an impression that was just beyond anything that I had ever experienced. I told Emily about it. I was so afraid that somehow I was leading you on and I didn't want to give you such an idea and then break your heart. I would have been devastated if that had been the case."

"What did Emily say?"

"She told me that I had to accept what you had given me. It was your heart that had spoken and that it came from you as pure and as honest as very few of us are privileged to experience."

"Did you show her the poem?"

"No, and she never asked to see it. Why are you asking that?"

"I don't know. It wouldn't have bothered me if you had shown it to her. It came from my heart."

"Yeah, maybe that's why she didn't need to see it. She understood you far better than me. It was obvious."

"I wish I had met her."

"You know, at one time she also said she wanted to meet you."

She smiled savoring the very idea of two women meeting because for some strange reason both of them were in love with—well, with me.

"I would have liked to have met her. Yes, I would have been insanely jealous but I would have liked her because I would have understood her love for you was as real as my love for you. Of course, that wouldn't have prevented me from sticking pins in her photo if I had had one." She laughed, leaned over, and kissed me.

"Women. I wish I understood them. Would you have done that, really?"

"Yes! OK, do you want to make love?" She asked.

"Do you?"

And afterward, both of us had fallen into a deep, and satiated, sleep.

I finally woke up as the morning sun was filtering into the apartment through the partially opened curtains. I could hear the soft sounds of Vivaldi's *Four Seasons*, the spring segment of it, playing on her stereo. I lay in bed listening to it. I could barely hear the shower water running. It was past eight in the morning. It had been a long time since I had felt as much peace with myself.

I got up and opened the door to the bathroom.

"Hey can I join you?"

"What?"

"Can I join you?"

"OK, but only if you promise to scrub my back."

"Only your back?"

"I'll let you figure out other things. Do you like Vivaldi?"

"Beautiful. That's the Spring section."

"Wow. I'm impressed."

I slid open the shower door and got in. Her head was covered with shampoo. I stood under the showerhead and let the warm water run over me.

"Hey, do you know what we say in California?"

"What?"

"Take a shower with a friend and save water."

"Yeah, you guys are weird and you waste everything. Gas, water, food, all kinds of natural resources. Then, too many people and freeways filled with thousands upon thousands of cars, all going nowhere, while polluting the air. You know what my Italian family said about Los Angeles?"

"What?"

"That you guys live in your cars. There are no sidewalks in some parts of Los Angeles. Is that true?"

"Not true."

I started to rub her head with the shampoo while she started to soap me all over. She grabbed my cock, put her hands and soap around it very carefully. I started getting hard. She laughed.

"Look at it. Didn't it have enough?"

"I guess not."

Then it was my turn to soap her everywhere. I started teasing her between her legs. She closed her eyes and started swaying as I touched her. I turned her around, entered her from behind while we let the water fall on us and perhaps wash off all of our sins. Great communal shower it turned out to be.

We came out of the shower and she dried me. I dried her in turn.

"I could get used to this," she said.

"It could get old."

"Never. Do you still want to go to Myrtle Beach?"

"Do you?"

"Yes, it will be great fun."

"OK, let's get ready. We'll stop and have some breakfast on the way."

"I already had my breakfast," and she laughed as she said it.

After calling the school to say that she was sick and could not make it to work, and asking for her sick leave days—it turned out that she had more than two days of sick leave. She also left a message for Laura Buchanan, one her students, to make sure that the girls were to rehearse the new steps in their dance routine.

"We're in luck. I have two and three quarter days of sick leave. And today is Wednesday, then the weekend will be here. We can go to the end of the Milky Way and be back in that time."

"Who's Laura Buchanan?"

"She's my assistant with the dance group."

She then called her mother.

"Are you going to tell her about me?"

"Should I?"

"I don't know."

"Not now."

The conversation with her mother was short and sweet, just to inform her that she would be gone to visit some friends in Myrtle Beach and she would call her from there. Her mother wished her a happy and safe trip.

"That was easy."

"My mother is a cool lady. She trusts me. She has made it clear to me that I'm now an adult and whatever decision I make, I have to live with the consequences."

"She sounds like a smart lady."

"She is."

She prepared a small suitcase in which she put her own clothes and mine. Earlier, she had modeled a bikini. Her slim body radiating youth, mystery, and beauty. Her long legs extended forever. She had a beautiful body no doubt about it.

"Wow, with that thing on you, you're likely to get arrested by the morality cops in Myrtle Beach."

"What's wrong with it?"

"It does not leave much to the imagination."

"It's a bikini. These things are supposed to be this way."

"You sure you can parade around the beach with that thing on? Would the good city fathers in Myrtle Beach be happy when they see that?"

"We're going to the beach, Jonathan, where most of the people walk around half-naked. Come on."

We walked out to the cars. The weather was clear and the sun was strong. She got into her car and put it in the garage. I closed the door.

"OK, we'll take your car and I get to drive," she said.

"Can I trust you?"

"Been driving for about ten years. Got my permit after we did the play. That was my parents' gift to me because they were proud of what I had done."

"I keep thinking that you are still that crazy sixteen-year old I knew back then."

"Well, crazy I may be, but sixteen years old I'm definitely not."

"I'm glad."

"Are you?"

"Yes, otherwise I'd be risking jail time for corrupting innocent girls in this part of the world."

"Something to think about," she said, then kissed me and started our long drive to the Myrtle Beach.

She had her feet up on the dashboard and we had the top down. She had gotten tired of driving, so I took over. The wind was blowing her hair and we were listening to some country song on the radio about a woman who is pissed off and sad at the same time because her man is cheating on her, but she also wants him back and is willing to forgive him.

She switched to another radio station and it was Dean Martin singing: "*King of the Road,*" and she started to hum along with it.

"I love that song," I said. "It really is one of my favorites, but I think I prefer Roger Miller's version. It's his song, after all."

"It's a hillbilly song, you're right. But the way Martin does it only an Italian could do it and get away with it."

"You're a fan of Italians, aren't you?"

"I love Italy! That's why I want to go back. I learned so much from them. Mostly, it has to do with life's priorities."

"Aren't you idealizing them?"

"In a way, yes. Of course, they have their problems. Who doesn't? But there is also an understanding of life's complexity. That if things can go wrong they will go wrong. But it doesn't mean that your life is over. Mama Sargenti told me that she had lost a child: Salvatore.

"He had died about a year after he was born. He came before Roberto. In her heart and mind Salvatore had been a gift for the whole family. She referred to him sometimes in the present tense, but not with anger for her loss. It just was the way it was. Life is precarious, fragile, but you could never deny the other beautiful things about life—like love, happiness, innocence."

Was she trying to give me a message? No, did not think so. If she wanted to tell me something, I had the impression she would come to the point without hesitation. I had memories of her doing just that.

She leaned over me and put her head on my shoulder and we let the time and the sun carry us.

"Jonathan, can I tell you something?"

"What?"

"I'm so happy to be here with you. My heart is ready to burst. I mean, if someone had said to me yesterday that today we would be on our way to Myrtle Beach, just the two of us, I would have said they were certifiably nuts yet, here we are—it's cosmic." She took my right hand and kissed it.

"I'm happy, also. Very happy, I said."

"Is that true?"

"Yes, very true."

Dean Martin ended his version of the song.

"You have very pretty feet," I said.

"Really," as she wiggled her toes.

"Yes."

"They are not too big or ugly?"

"No, they're not. They're perfect. And with that red stuff you have on your toenails. It's very chic."

"Well, I'm glad because Trevor Hamilton, the third, thinks it makes me look like a floozy. Only floozies paint their toenails and to paint them in red is the ultimate sin."

"Who's Trevor Hamilton, the third?"

"The man who wants to marry me. My supposed fiancé."

"What, are you engaged?"

"Of course not."

"Then, why do you call him your 'fiancé'?"

"I don't call him that, he calls himself that."

"Tell me about him. Do you love him?"

"No. I mean, I like him a lot but I'm not in love with him, which obviously presents some problems. He's a gentleman farmer of tobacco, has a stable of race horses, is a member of the state bar, and has ancient relatives who fought in the Civil War."

"Wow, that's impressive."

"For other women, but not for me. Besides, my Italian brothers don't like him."

"He met them?"

"You have to understand that Ham—I call him that, which he hates—and I have known each other for ages. He came to visit me in Italy. Because he owns racehorses, he wanted to go to Siena, which is where the townspeople stage a horse race every year.

"He was looking to invest in horses. Now the Siena race is very famous. *Il Palio* is called. Total madness, pandemonium. Where riders are allowed not only to whip their own horses but other horses and riders as well. With guys falling off their horses as they go around the piazza, three times. Very dangerous.

"Ham was looking for a Derby-like event with mint juleps and women wearing comical hats. How can you expect Italians to have a horse race like that? Then he kept complaining about the food and about Italians not having soft toilet paper—it was a disaster."

I busted out laughing.

"Are you serious?"

"Oh, yes. Roberto hated him. *Signor Prosciutto*, he called him. And he informed me, in a rather Italian forceful way, that under *no* circumstance would he approve or give me his permission to marry Ham."

"This character, Roberto, sounds like a card. I like him already."

"Oh, Jonathan, I adore him. He's my favorite kid brother. Completely insane. And I suspect that once I introduce you to him, he would like you and approve of you."

"Really, what makes you say that?"

"I know Roberto."

Julie had said: "once I introduce you to him." She had used the present tense. It had been a long time since a woman had used a present tense when discussing her relationship with me. A very long time. I had not had too many affairs these last few years simply because I did not want any. I had avoided them like the plague.

I was battered, bruised, and felt completely devoid of any potential to develop romantic feelings for a woman. Life had seared my heart and, in some ways, I accepted such a state of affairs without question. That was my lot in life and I had better not question it.

I became a zombie after I learned of Emily's death. A total fucking zombie. Days, months, years of ineptitude, of total moral collapse. My tour in Vietnam in many ways became my salvation, as crazy and ridiculous as it sounds. I did not care if I lived or died.

At least I was existing for something even if it was an evil something. There was no real reason for me to worry about dodging bullets or guns every day. I was walking around like a dead man. I was deader than dead.

When I got injured, and was told that my tour was over I actually protested. I wanted to stay. Lots of other GIs, who hated the place, thought I was out of my gourde. What they did not understand was that there was no place in this world for me to go; where I would find peace, or joy, or laughter or relief of any kind.

Whereas most of them looked forward to getting letters and packages from home, other than the letters from Emily, I never received any correspondence. My family knew I was in Vietnam, of course, because I had informed them but the couple of letters I got from my brothers I answered with a postcard.

I thought I would end up dead anyway. What difference would my demise make to the universe? What difference would it make? None! I was just occupying space, that was all.

"I know how to fix breaks on cars," Julie said.

Her voice sounded distant, mumbled, as if she was talking in her sleep, or coming through some kind of fog.

"What?"

"Jonathan, where were you?"

"I'm sorry."

"You were gone."

"I'm sorry. I was thinking . . ."

"Do you want me to drive?"

"No, I'm sorry. I'm fine."

"Are you sure?"

"Well, I'm sure you're here with me, and we're going to Myrtle Beach where you will get arrested for wearing a tiny bikini. And I'll have to vouch that you're not a floozy, but an honest, God-fearing person, an outstanding member of the human race and present no danger to society."

"I'll buy that. Remember that not too long ago women burned their bras. We're supposed to be free to make our own decisions. Anyway, that was the idea."

"Has it worked?"

"Not totally. Jury's out on that."

"You were saying that you know how to fix the breaks on a car?"

"Yes."

"How did you learn that?"

"From my dad."

"Why?"

"I just wanted to do it."

She looked at me as if not wanting to learn how to fix car brakes was silly.

"Julie, do you mean to say that you can get under a car, get grease and gook all over your beautiful hands, and that you know how to fix and change car brakes, on top of knowing how to cook a great Italian *frittata*?"

"Well, you tasted it."

"That I did, and it was delicious. It is true."

I slowed down and turned my head, leaned over and kissed her lightly as a large truck blew his horn when it passed us. I looked and the truck driver had his left arm out and was pumping it in the air while blowing his horn.

Julie stood, and gave the driver the thumbs up while the driver kept blowing his horn. I started to accelerate.

"OK, Jimmy, don't get us killed," she said.

"Jimmy?"

"Jimmy Clark. You've never heard of Jimmy Clark, the race car driver?"

"Of course, I have."

"Poetry in speed, Roberto used to say about Clark. Italians love car racing. They are fanatics. They drive like there is no tomorrow. It's insanity. Once Roberto took me to Venice, which is about two hundred and fifty kilometers from Florence, and during that time my knuckles were white and I was hanging on for dear life. A complete maniac the way he drove."

"But you survived."

"But never did it again. Roberto kept reassuring me, saying '*va bene, cara, va bene*'. I've got things under control here. I know what I'm doing.' "

"How old is he?"

"He's four years younger than me."

"You talk about him more than the other guys."

"Yes, because they were married and did not live in the house. Though they lived just around the block. Italian families are tightly knit. The children don't move too far away from their parents. Nico, Luchino and their wives were wonderful, really. They were always visiting their mother. I was closer to Roberto because he still lived with his parents."

"And their father?"

"Doctor Sargenti is a quiet man, very gentle and was always busy making house calls. It was so tough on him when Salvatore died. As a doctor, he's supposed to save people, and he couldn't save his own baby."

"What did the baby die of?"

"Leukemia. You know, I understood about death. My father had died just about a year before I went to Italy. I understood pain."

"I'm sorry about your father."

"Thank you."

And she got very quiet and pulled away from me. I glanced at her and her face was very serious. Does the knowledge of death, its intimacy, give us a leg up on suffering? I knew very little about Julie, really. She was a mystery to me. Yes, we had been intimate without considering the consequences.

It had happened on the fly, as it were. Too fast. And to be truthful, I did not know if I had the human tools or the personal strength or conviction to stop and look at what was happening to me at this moment, and try to make sense out of it.

I had not really come to find Julie or to make love to her, however, lovely and wonderful it had been. I was not sure now what I needed to do. I did not want to give her any false hopes or lead her into something that was dishonest. I liked her. I liked her a lot. I always did. But she was not the woman of my life, had never been, and I was not sure if I even wanted a woman in life.

"Hey, whatever happened to Karen, the other Anne Frank?"

"Her father got transferred to the Pentagon and I never heard from her."

"Did you know that at one time I told Cash and Jackson that I wanted to cast a black girl to play Anne Frank?"

"Were you serious?"

"Not really. Jackson said that it was the most absurd idea he ever heard."

"And you say that I'm crazy."

"I was just giving them a hard time."

"Can you imagine? In North Carolina? You'd have created a revolution." She started to laugh, shaking her head. "Karen, she had a crush on you, you know."

"Come on."

"It's true."

"How do you know?"

"She told me, that hussy."

And she laughed. I loved the way she laughed. Very natural with no pretensions.

"And what did you tell her?"

"I told her that guys like you were a total waste of time. That you probably had a girl in every Army base there was. I warned her against falling for guys like you; they are the worst kind of man. I lied, of course."

"You didn't tell her about your own feelings?"

"No. Women are very jealous of each other. I didn't want her to gouge my eyes out."

"I thought she was a very nice girl. In fact, the whole cast was a bunch of great people. I liked them all."

"Me, too. But I had to keep an eye open for Karen. She had plans for you and I had to protect you from her evil designs. I didn't really trust that floozy." And she laughed.

"Julie, you are crazy."

"I'm crazy about you. Let me tell you something, mister. There isn't a floozy out there who loves you more than I do. I'm not saying that Emily was a floozy. But floozies like Karen, or any other floozy you may have hidden away somewhere, they don't come anywhere near to love you the way I do."

"But, why? Where does this come from?"

"Where does it come from? I don't know. The only thing I know is that I felt it everywhere in my body from day one. In my heart, my soul, my stomach, my elbows, my brain, my hands, my ears, my belly button, and everything below that, my spleen."

"Your spleen?"

"Yeah, even my spleen got in on the act. I love my spleen for loving you so much." And she laughed again.

Jesus Christ. I felt like I was watching, no, living a movie where everything will come out right at the end because love conquers all. But I knew better than that. Boy, did I know it.

I envied Julie for the manner in which she had dealt with and was dealing with her life. Her hang-ups did not prevent her from being open and honest about what she felt, and with her great sense of humor to boot.

I, as the recipient of her feelings, was, of course, flattered. But it also gave me feelings of inadequacy about my not being able to reciprocate such tender feelings. But, could I learn to do it? Could I learn to love again? Could I learn to love this wonderful, crazy, woman-child, filled with the fantasies of life, dreaming of things, maybe impossible things?

"Jonathan, what I say to you comes from my heart. I also know love is a strange thing and sometimes it is slow to come about and grow. You don't need to love me the same way I do. You just need to give it a chance and while we wait, my love is big enough for both of us."

"Julie, in these last twenty-four hours you have given me so much, and have demonstrated to me how love works. I know I don't have the same intense feelings that you have for me.

"I also know that for so damn long I closed myself to even think that I could ever be loved again, or that I could love again. I don't know what is going to happen, but I want you to know that I'm so happy to be with you. That we're together, and that is all that matters."

"Over and out," she said, and giggled.

-XVI-

We drove into Myrtle Beach. We stayed in the center of town. The traffic was a little heavy as I had heard it would be. The place had changed from what I remembered. It seemed that it had caught the wave of tourism and tourists. We did not have a hotel reservation—bad idea.

But at the tourist office, the woman was very nice and was able to find us a room at a hotel overlooking the beach. She kept looking at Julie's left hand searching for a ring. Both Julie and I noticed and we smiled a secret smile.

"And the name, please?" the woman asked.

"Put it under Miss Julie A. Douglas and her boyfriend, please."

The woman did a double take, but seeing that Julie was not about to back off, she put Julie's name on the reservation.

As we were leaving, Julie whispered to me; actually no, whisper was not true. She spoke loud enough for the woman to have heard it, but who chose to ignore what Julie said.

"Thank you for this pre-nuptial honeymoon trip, darling," Julie said. "You promised to marry me after this, right? I'm sure my parents trust you not to go back on your word."

I started to laugh and pushed Julie out of the office while she kept laughing. I stopped and kissed her.

"You will get us into trouble."

"Did you see the way she looked at my hand?"

"Yes."

"What business is it of hers?"

"Maybe it's the law."

"No, too much religion around here."

"Before we find the hotel, I need some swimming trunks," I said.

"Not to worry, plenty of shops around here."

We found a small store and I bought a set of swimming trunks. Julie insisted that they be blue.

The hotel was very nice. We did not have any troubles at the reception desk. We had an airy room with high ceilings that overlooked the beach. It was in the middle of the afternoon and it was warm. We opened the windows to let more air in. The bed was a large king-size bed.

"Wow, look at the size of this thing: *Letto famiglia*. Big enough for a large family," she said.

"What did you say? *Letto* . . ."

"Yes, family bed in Italian."

"Yeah, father, mother, kids, and the dog, don't forget the dog."

"OK, let me check the news about a hurricane coming our way," she said, and turned on the radio. Country music and from what I could tell no news about a hurricane. The weather was fine.

"Are you hungry?" She asked.

We had stopped at a country inn on the way in and had eaten a delicious breakfast.

"Yeah, we can get something. I hear that the fish around here is delicious."

We spent the rest of the afternoon and part of the evening just walking around the beach area, being tourists. She bought a straw hat and with her pretty summer outfit, open-toe sandals, and her shades she was the perfect tourist. We did not go swimming.

I noticed some of the bikinis worn by some women. Skimpy. Really skimpy. Julie looked at me and threw her arms in front of her shrugging her shoulders in a rather Italian way, I thought.

What was interesting to me as we strolled through the beach area was the people whom we saw. Lots of military type guys. Sort of reminded me of the time when Cash, Jackson and I had come here looking for some action. Now thinking about it, it all seemed so superficial and without any humility.

To call the people around us rednecks would be an insult really, but they were. When I made a remark to Julie about it, she reassured me that Southern people were the salt of the earth, except, of course, when it came to dealing with black people.

"We didn't come here to judge these people, did we?" She said.

"You're right."

"Why did you want to come here in the first place?"

We were sitting by the beach. The warm night was pleasant. The dinner we had had along with some excellent white wine had mellowed me, but not totally.

"Cash, Jackson and I came here a couple of times."

"How was it?"

"Okay. We were just like all of those guys you see."

"Looking for action."

"Kind of."

"It's OK, Jonathan. I know all about soldiers. After all, I'm an Army brat and was warned by both my parents about soldiers on the prowl."

I looked at her. She was wearing a skirt, a nice summer blouse open at the neck. She was a very attractive girl, no doubt about. I had caught guys looking at her and at me with a disgusted look that said: Hey, girl, what are you doing with this bozo?

Yeah, why had I come here?

I wanted to get away from Fort Bragg. Actually, I wanted to get away from long ago memories, really, but instead my behavior had brought me back some painful ones. I had not thought out the whole thing. It had been a whim. It seemed like a good idea. And now that we were here; I did not want to be here. I really did not know where I wanted to be. I, once again, tried to understand why I had come to Fort Bragg in the first place and could not figure that out. Reflex, maybe?

The more I thought about it the more depressed I became. It was not Julie's fault. It was my own fault. I had not been around a woman for a long time and there were moments of deep regret that Emily was not with me. I thought, this is dishonest. I cannot do this to Julie. She does not merit it.

She is completely innocent in this whole ordeal.

Son of a bitch, I should be grateful that there was this lovely, beautiful, girl, telling me that she loved me with all of her heart and here I am sinking into deeper and deeper despair. What was wrong with me, anyway? Face it, I am being a total asshole. I am for the shits.

Emily will never come back. Face it, you jerk Yes, she brought you something unique and she loved you. But what if she had just said that because she wanted to make me feel good?

What kind of shit are you now thinking about, Jonathan? And Jackson, what would he have said? And Cash? He would have treated me like a shithead for the way I was now acting.

I loved those two crazy guys. I really did. And Yoshi, whatever happened to him? I had once driven to Canada to try to find him. Spent a couple of weeks looking for him. He was not enrolled in any university or medical school as he had said. Maybe he had gone back to Japan. And that racist moron, what was his name—well, whatever his name was, a real prick, a loser.

Julie took my hand and held it.

"I'm here, Jonathan. Don't forget."

How could she tell? What is it that makes some women have a sixth sense about things? Is it because of what they have between their legs? Their vagina, their ovaries, their whatever; intuition, some people say. I was acting like a piece of garbage and I hated myself for it.

For so long, I had rejected the idea of finding myself loved by another woman. I mean, I had thought about it but I did everything to keep away from it. Yes, I had had my one-night stands. But it was obvious that I had done everything not to let it go more than a few nights at the most.

Good night, thank you, and have a happy life.

Cash had asked one night as we were sitting in our tent, we had just arrived in Vietnam. "So, what are you gonna call the baby,"

"I don't know. It's Emily's baby. She'll decide."

"Yeah, but you gonna be his father. That gives you something to say. Right Jackson?"

"I'd say."

"You know, whatever she decides is OK by me. The main thing is to have a healthy baby. She can call him aspirin and as long as he's healthy I'm cool with that."

262

They both busted out laughing.

"Aspirin?" Jackson said.

"Hollywood, you're nuts." Cash said, using his cackling voice.

Why had Emily not told me there were problems with her pregnancy? Why? Why? We could have faced the thing together. True, I could not have done anything, but at least she would have known that I was there for her even though I could not be right next to her. Now I wished I had had the guts to ask Billy, back at the cemetery, what had really happened.

But, I had not. A coward I was. Her letters never said that things were wrong. I believed her. I never suspected anything. Was she afraid I would go crazy and do something I would regret later? Was that how she showed me that she loved me? By keeping silent about what she was facing?

I wanted to hear her voice again. Even if only once more. All of these past years, my only longing had been that if I could just talk to her that was all I asked, just to find out that she knew I loved her and still do. I hope she will forgive me for what I did with Julie. Did I betray her? Did I betray us? Did I betray her love?

I had tried to understand, since the day I found out she was gone, what she had gone through when she had lost Homer. I thought I had understood, but the real truth is I had not understood a fucking thing. I was being a phony, a coward.

What did I know then what it was to lose someone you love deeply, with total abandon? How do we learn to deal with that? Some people do deal with such loss and misery with grace. I was not one of them.

I do not know about love, I do not know a goddamn thing about anything. And now, here I am with another woman who has professed her love for me without any pre-conditions. Who has said that she has enough love for both of us until I learn to love her.

But what if I cannot learn to love her? What if my heart is so dead, shriveled to nothing, that I cannot feel anything anymore? Why after all of these years am I, once again, agonizing, driving myself crazy?

I had gone to see Jack when I came back from Vietnam. He saw me and he knew. He held me in his arms and I cried like a baby. I could not talk. Man, life is so heartless. Did she suffer? Did she know that she was dying?

Billy had told me that they did not tell her that the baby was dead. She would not have understood. But, maybe she would have understood and would have given her something to take with her but what, peace of mind? This is totally insane, I thought.

Oh, God, oh, God, please help me. Please. I who do not believe in anything, please help me. I've been in this fix for too long. I want to stop the pain. I want to stop the hurt and the darkness in my heart—Please, help me.

"Jonathan, did you just say, 'please help me?' "

"What?"

"I heard you say it."

"Did I?"

"Yes, you did. You were talking to yourself?"

"Are you sure?" I knew I was playing for time.

"I'm sitting right next to you. I distinctly heard you say it."

She looked at me and her face was in shock. I was crying. I was crying with tears rolling down my cheeks, like a baby.

"You're crying."

"No, I'm not."

"Yes, you are, talk to me, please, please."

"Julie, please, I don't wish to talk. Just let me be, OK."

"Oh, Jonathan, tell me what's bothering you. I love you. I want to help you so much. If you are suffering, my heart cannot stand seeing you like this. Do you want me go away?"

I must have made some kind of grimace that she took as a rejection, perhaps a sign of indifference about her going away from me, that hurt her in a terrible way. I did not mean to hurt her. But, I had. Son of a bitch, I thought, when will this darkness in my heart end? When?

She started to cry openly, and I saw her despair and I could hear all of that in her sobs. Then suddenly, she got up and started to walk away and I was stunned by her action. She started to run. It took me a few moments to realize she was running away from me and toward the dark beach. I took off after her.

"Julie, please, please."

I caught up with her and grabbed her and tried to keep her close to me, but she fought me.

"Julie, please, I'm sorry. Please forgive me, Julie, please."

"Leave me alone."

"Julie, please don't say that. I need you, I want to be with you."

"Jonathan, you don't need me. I don't know who you need, or what. And you don't want me. And please don't touch me."

Her voice was so sad and distant as she was crying. She was choking and not trying to hide her tears. I was also crying and at that moment I felt like dying. I felt so helpless and so fucking bad.

"I should have died in Vietnam. That's what should have happened. The wrong guys got killed. It should have been me."

I sat on the warm sand. I did not give a shit whatever happened to me anymore. My life had been over for many years now and I had not been willing to face it.

"And Emily, why did she die? And Cash and Jackson? Yeah, the wrong guys got blown away. What a sick joke. I deserved it more than they did."

Julie kneeled right next to me and took me in her arms.

"Don't say that, please. I love you, Jonathan. I don't know why, but I do. I wish I could create a miracle and make your life the way it was. I'd give anything. I'd give my life to make you happy again. To make you whole. To bring her back to you. If I could I'd trade places with Emily in a second, and I would not regret it one single moment. But I can't. But, boy how do I wish it."

Then through her tears she started to sing the words of the song: *"Where Have All the Flowers Gone."* She was choking but she kept on doing it, sweetly, softly, sad, sadder than I could ever imagine a voice could sound.

Everything was gone! Flowers, young girls, young men, soldiers, life, and even graves and everyone had disappeared so long ago because time had passed and there was nothing left but emptiness, sadness, and tears—what was left was a life barren, bleak, and empty because we humans never learn anything.

Through my own tears, I saw Julie's angelic face singing the words with such desperation that suddenly it made me terribly afraid. It was a desperate moment for me as well. I had never heard anyone singing anything with such sadness and melancholy. It was the most surreal experience that I could remember going through. Almost like an out of body experience.

Julie was not there with me. She was in another dimension dealing with things that were not her fault. Things of such misery and pain that it appeared as if she were in a trance. Her whole universe was now being sucked into a black hole where nothing escapes to see the brightness of life again.

I had been the source of such pain for Julie. I had brought it to her. She was a bystander. She had nothing to do with my life, with Emily's life, with what had happened. She was innocent and she was now suffering in a way that showed me, once again, that life does not give a shit for her, for me, for anybody. It just dumps on you, and good luck.

Her voice sounded like it was coming from a source that was just so disjointed, distant, and toneless. She stopped and held her head down as if in shame. I reached for her and held her close to me. There was no reaction from her. I might as well have been holding a rag doll, lifeless, totally devoid of any human energy. She was empty.

I do not know how long we sat there. It seemed like an eternity. I looked toward the walkway and there were few people ambling around. Time had stopped for us but not in a good way. I wished so much, so much, not to have been the source of Julie's misery and sadness.

That was all I had carried with me for so long and now I was giving her this terrible disease of mine and she was not prepared to deal with it. It was not her problem. It was not her fault. There are moments in life when the truth of who we are is clear and we cannot make any more excuses. I was a miserable prick—full of self-pity and self-righteousness—a regular jerk.

"Let's go home," she finally whispered.

"You mean back to Fayetteville?"

"No, back to the hotel, please."

"OK."

I held her close to me because she walked in a kind of stupor. Like some drunken person. She had no energy and I guided her as if she had no force, no desire about anything—spent. I thought, man, oh, man what have I done? What the hell have I done to her? How could I have been such a worthless piece of garbage? Is that what I had become? A miserable piece of human garbage?

We got back to the hotel. Julie had regained some control by now, but her look was still vacant, and distant. It was the look of someone so lost and in total despair. I thought I had seen that look before.

It was the look that Emily had shown when she had wanted to destroy the painting, when she had told me that our love was never going to work. I had not hurt Emily, but now I had hurt Julie in the worst possible way!

Julie sat on the floor in a corner of the room. She started to wipe some sand off her feet in a mechanical way. I sat right next to her and helped. She did have pretty feet. I had read somewhere that for some men a woman's foot is a source of sexual turn on. And I could see how that happens. It seems primitive, but sex is the most primitive aspect of our lives.

I was not sure if I would ever be able to reach her, to explain things to her. To have her understand my own misery and pain, and not have her become overwhelmed by my totally unhappy self. To have her forgive me for causing her so much pain and despair.

I was desperately searching for words, for phrases, that would reach her heart so she would not carry the burden I had brought to her. I fought against my own despair but the darkness in my heart, at this moment, was so hard, so hard. It had invaded me and converted me into a complete jerk.

My own desperation had not allowed me to understand Julie's lovely, innocent, and pure sentiments of love she had for me. I had been acting like she owed me. She did not owe me anything. She did not even owe me her sweet love. I had not acted with wisdom. I felt that I misguided her and that was the last thing I had ever intended to do to her.

An immense sense of sadness invaded my heart, my soul. I felt like a failure and a burden to this lovely, beautiful, girl who had loved me for so long that it was incomprehensible. And yet the beauty of Julie's feelings for me was so incredible and mysterious.

How does love happen? I had loved Emily and never understood why. Julie loves me, and I still do not understand the nature of love. Does anybody?

"Julie, I'm so sorry I brought you so much pain, that I broke your heart. I didn't want to. You had nothing to do with my life becoming so meaningless. You have been so incredibly strong and honest. I don't deserve nothing but pity from you. I don't know why you have come into my life. Like everything else, I want to stop asking those questions.

"I don't know anything. I don't know. It's not fair for you. I wish I hadn't polluted your life. I wish that everything would go back to the way it was last night. Beautiful, innocent, magical, and so full of your love, honesty and tenderness. I'm completely in the dark as to what my life is supposed to be like.

"I need to change my life. I can't continue to just survive from one day to the next. It is not sane. I had no reason to want to redo my life before. I have rejected any and all forms of attachment to other women. I want to become human again.

"I desperately need to change. To hang on to some fading memory, however lovely it was, is not healthy. I saw your beautiful face on the beach and I recognize how lucky I am, that you are here still willing to love me in spite of my shortcomings, my stupidity, and ignorance.

"I wish I could tell you that I love you the same way you love me. But tonight, I also understood that in order for me to learn to love you, I need to be less of a coward and stop hiding behind the impossible.

"I don't want to do that. Please, help me. Please, I realize that I need you more than you could possibly imagine. Please, give me a chance, don't give up on me, please, please forgive me. . . "

"Jonathan, help me take my clothes off, please."

"OK."

There were still a few grains of sand on her feet and I wiped them clean and kissed them. I felt her reaction more than I saw it. I then took her top off, followed by her skirt, the bra, and her panties. She seemed to have regained some strength. I started to take my clothes off. She was watching me quietly, as a young girl about to make love for the first time.

It was a ritual that went back to time immemorial. It was so primitive, beautiful, pure and innocent. Julie did not need me to help her take her clothes off. She wanted me to share in something so intimate and timeless. Something that was allowing me, as if for the first time, to share with her and discover some profound truth not only about her but about life and its delicate beauty.

I did not know if what she had said to me before about still being a virgin had something to do with what she was requesting. I was not about to ask her why she had asked me to help her. It was her secret and would remain in her heart because she owned it and nobody, least of all me, could intrude and make it banal and unworthy of her.

I felt like she had invited me into her very private world, and I only had to accept what was taking place without any stupid questions. It was what it was and any questions or reasons expressed aloud would only show me to be a vulgar man without any sensibilities and humbleness. She was not fixed on embarrassing me, making herself to be superior.

She was showing me that in certain matters of life, one has to accept them with love, humility, and human dignity. It was a moment that she had initiated, but it was a moment that she was allowing me to share as if to say: *Take a look not at my nakedness but to what my heart is giving you. Please, do not destroy it. I am now yours if you want me, but even if you do not want me I will always be yours until the end of time . . .*

Was I wise enough to overcome all of my stupid barriers and see Julie for who she was, for what she represented to me? Was I man enough? In many ways what she was showing me was, that in the game of life one had to be fearless. One could not be afraid to confront it.

I thought of the Julie of so many years ago. The lovely young girl who had once kissed me in such a shy way. A stolen kiss, really, because I had refused to kiss her when she had asked me to. I remembered her lost look the last time I saw her, when she had brought me the poem and had read it for me, and then walked away.

In my state of mind at that time, due to my relationship with Emily, Julie's heart had not been of much concern to me. I felt guilty and sorry now, but it had not been my fault. I do not know whose fault it was that she had fallen in love with me. Is that what she was now doing, trying to recoup from those most sad memories?

I lay next to her and she embraced me. I started to kiss her breasts and to touch her lovely mound. At first, she did not respond but, slowly, timidly at first, she responded to my kissing and touching her. There was no hurry, no rush. I kissed her everywhere. I went down and slowly opened her legs and she tasted warm and sweet. I did not hurry. I took my time.

I moved my hand to fondle her breasts, ran my hand over her stomach, her thighs. I could tell from the sound of her moans that she was getting closer to her orgasm. I inserted two fingers in her while gently caressing and licking her clitoris. Then I began lick harder while going in and out with my fingers.

"Oh, please, don't stop, please," she was moaning.

Her pleasure was intense and she was gasping. She moaned softly and the more I licked her the more excited she got. Soon she was holding my head and guiding me to where she would get the highest pleasure.

When her orgasm finally came, she was shaking and her physical surrender was incredible and so complete. But it spoke of something far deeper than just a physical pleasure. It was the emotion of pure love that we spend so much time trying to find and that very few of us are lucky to find. I touched her belly and it was like she was on fire.

Her skin was so sensitive to my touch that it got goose pimples all over. Julie was now transported into a world of mystery and magic that was amazing to see, and to feel. There was this sense of raw passion and abandon. Her pleasure was so intense that she was now in a decisive moment of innocence and love. She was not holding anything back.

"Please, now, please," she moaned.

She was immensely wet but I still waited some more. I kissed her belly, her breasts, and mounted her and was inside of her and my world and hers become one. Now it was her turn to move, to sway, to wrap her legs around me and she was holding me so hard against her that there could be no closer bodies than the two of us at that moment.

From the ashes of my previous universe perhaps another was being created that would be pure, blameless, and honest. When my turn came, I was completely overtaken by my desire for her. It was physical, but it was also deeper than that.

I knew that things had changed and that nothing was going to be the same as before. I was consciously surrendering who I was to her. I was not trying to hide anymore.

I wanted to be untainted and innocent as she was. I wanted her to feel me deep inside of her with a sense of truth and honesty. But more than that, I wanted her to feel that I was hers and that nothing but absolutely nothing would ever come between us. No more memories and excuses.

Julie, in the magical way when a woman surrenders to the man she loves, was also rescuing me from the abyss and had pulled me back. I only hoped that it was the beginning. I so desperately wanted that to be case. I needed her so badly.

It was as total loving moment as I had ever experienced with any other woman. I was surrendering myself to her the same way she had surrendered herself to me earlier. I lay right next to her, both of us exhausted, but satiated with our physical and spiritual needs now in complete harmony—harmony that I had sought and had found.

I hoped and prayed that no dissonance would ever be permitted between us. It was now our world. But I was scared of the unknown. Emily's memory was being slowly put away in the recesses of my mind and spirit, to take its place where it belonged, where it would now reside, and where it would not overwhelm me much longer. And it was a good thing that I urgently hoped for.

"Jonathan."

"Yes."

"Thank you. I love you!" She whispered.

Perhaps the fates had spoken. And if they had, I prayed them to be kind to lovely, innocent and beautiful Julie. To protect her. Not make her suffer for something that she had nothing to do with. And if they needed to punish anybody, they could punish me.

We drifted in and out from our sleep. At one time, I woke up and she was holding me. I looked at her and she had her eyes closed but I could tell she was awake, considering something. She turned her head toward me and gave this great and wonderful smile. Then, she draped her legs around me and started to stroke me gently, softly.

I was not going to remain neutral about such activity. I got hard. She changed position and started to kiss me as she went down my chest, my belly, and finally she took me in her mouth. There was something so ultimately tender about what Julie was doing, revealing another of the universe's mysteries. And sex is most definitely one of them.

I exploded and she did not recoil from the onslaught. She lay there looking at what was coming out of me and touched me with her tongue. What was surprising to me is that I had never thought that sperm would be such a mystery to a woman.

And yet in so many ways the mystery went beyond tasting it. It was trying to understand what it revealed, as if somehow she would find the untold secrets of the universe.

"I wonder how they count the sperm," she said.

"Oh, Julie, you're amazing!"

She looked at me, gave me a wonderful smile, and I saw that the trauma of the previous hours on the beach had not damaged her spirit, and that beautiful innocence that I had so much feared had been lost due to my stupidity and the darkness in my heart. Julie had not disappeared. And I was glad.

She got up and went into the bathroom. A few minutes later she came out and had a damp towel and she then proceeded to clean me. I do not know but there was something so incredibly primitive about what she was doing. So basic. It went beyond her desire to clean me. She really humbled me, but I do not think that it was her intention.

She put the towel on the night table, put her head on my belly and continued to play with my dick. Not intending on making me hard again, but more in wanting to bring comfort to a rather tired member of my body.

"Are you sore?" she asked.

"A little bit."

"I'm sorry."

"Why?"

"Well," and she started to laugh, stopped, moved right next to me, and kissed me.

"If he is as sore as I am, it's best to give him a break."

It was funny that she was referring to my sex as a "he", instead of as an "it."

We had made love literally all night. It was not a sprint; it was a marathon. We hardly ever spoke. I would wake up, reach for her and, then she would wake up and reach for me.

Now the day was up and the morning light was filtering through the curtains into the room. At one moment, I could imagine what the sheets on the bed would look like. Most probably, the hotel would charge us extra for cleaning them. I started to laugh.

"What's so funny?"

"I was thinking that the sheets are going to be rather messy."

"Jonathan, it's a hotel. People know what happens if they rent a room to a hungry man and a woman. It's part of the deal."

"Do you think?"

"Yes, of course."

I looked at her and there was a kind of aura to her. As if something had been found and fulfilled, no double meaning meant here.

"Jonathan, I'm sorry about last night."

"Which part?"

I was giving her a hard time.

"I mean about what happened on the beach."

"Oh, I was kind of afraid there for a moment."

"I will never be sorry for what happened afterwards." And she smiled.

"Yeah, on the beach. Sometimes, I have such a hard time dealing with my own misery and it infects those around me. Please forgive me. I know I hurt you a lot. You did not deserve that.

"You have brought me something priceless, something that I thought I had lost. I have been looking for it and was convinced that I would never find again. And now I know that it is still there just waiting, and I think the waiting is over."

"I'm glad." she said. "I'm so happy to be here with you. You have no idea. It isn't just for this instant. It is much more complicated than that. You may not suspect it but I was also lost in this jungle of horrible ideas and thoughts.

"It's all clear now. I don't have to make excuses either. You were not the only one making excuses, you know. I've made them, too. I'm free of that and it's a good thing."

She leaned over me and held me against her and kept looking at me with those wonderful eyes of hers.

"You know, I think you're right about getting some shades for your eyes. They give you away," I said.

"But in this instance, I don't mind if they do. OK, what are we going to do?"

"You mean now?"

"No, forever?"

"Wow, that's a long time."

"Yes. It's a long time. Do you think people love forever?"

"No. You read about that in cheap romantic novels written mostly by guys who don't know their asses from a hole in the ground."

"Do you think we're a couple of nymphomaniacs?"

"Men aren't nymphomaniacs."

"Oh, so only women are nymphos."

"Yes."

"What are men?"

"I don't know, oversexed, horny, sex fiends, take your pick."

"Women are all of those things, too."

"However, that's called Nymphomania."

"I love the way men try to control these things. Do you think that's fair?"

"What does that have to do with it?"

There was a knock on the door. We looked at each and automatically she pulled the sheet over us and started to giggle. I was trying like crazy not to laugh too loud.

"Who is it?" she finally asked.

A voice from the outside informed us that it was the maid wanting to come in to clean up the room.

"Could you please come back later?" Julie, asked.

"OK, miss. You can call downstairs to tell them when I can come back to take care of the room."

"Yes, that's fine."

We giggled. She got up, went to the window and pulled the curtains apart to take a look outside.

"Oh, no, it's cloudy and raining."

"Do you think we're going to have a hurricane?"

She came back to bed.

"I don't know. I love the sound of the rain. It's even more beautiful and delicious now that I'm in this bed with you. In my wildest dreams, that could not have happened to me. But if it's raining when am I going to wear my bikini?"

"You can't wear it in the rain?"

"Yeah, but it's not the same. Not too many guys will be outside watching girls in bikinis."

"It's a good thing."

"Yeah, I saw you yesterday watching those girls and I could tell that you wanted it to rain so I wouldn't be prancing around in my bikini. You were jealous of what the other guys would see."

"Not true."

"Course it is. Don't you want to show those guys what you've got at home?"

"Boy, what an ego."

"OK, how many times have we made love since you came back?"

"I don't know. Are you keeping track?"

"No, but . . ."

"Well, if we keep going this way, at the end of the day when the maid comes in to clean up the room, all she would find would be these two shriveled bodies with nothing left in them. They'll take us to some research lab to study what's left of us and help determine a corrective course of action."

"I want you to make love to me in every hole in my body. Even through my nose and ears."

"Pretty hard to do. It won't fit."

"You can try."

"Right."

"OK, we'll excuse the nose and ears, but everything else is game."

She was looking at me. She was serious, and at the same time she was teasing me.

"I thought we tried it in every which way, last night. Boy, after all of my efforts to be creative, it turns out I didn't do the right thing."

"Yes, you did. You were the champion penetrator—" and she let out a great laugh, primitive, natural, human.

"Oh, that's a good one. I have never thought of myself as the 'champion' of anything, let alone 'penetrator', but come to think of it, it does fit the bill."

"Doesn't it, though?"

What makes a woman and a man bring down all of the barriers that society imposes on us in terms of our normal, human, sexual behavior? It seems to me that curiosity about our sexuality should not be limited to the obvious, to the missionary position, as it were.

Whatever mystery and pleasure both sexes are supposed to have, it cannot be ruled by fiat or done by some legislative body that thinks that it is only protecting the American Way of Life!

Dishonesty about our bodies, our needs, and our curiosity need to be allowed to run their course. After all, why do children play doctor?

She took my hand and put it on her breast.

"Do you like my boobies?"

"I love your boobies, they are majestic."

"What about my legs?"

"They are beautiful."

"So, which are you? A boobies guy or a leg guy?"

"Tough call."

She laughed. And put her hand on top of my hand.

"Majestic! I like that. But I thought majestic was something like Mount Everest or Kilimanjaro."

"They are too, but your boobies leave them behind, way behind." I kissed them.

"I wonder why men are so keen on boobies."

"I don't know. I mean, we come out of the womb and we're given the boobies right off the bat."

"Girls are given the boobies right off the bat also, but we don't spend our adolescent and beyond years fixated on them."

"Ah, the mysteries of the universe. But I want to ask you something."

"What?

"Why do you want to be a museum curator?"

"Because of what art brings to my heart, to my soul. It keeps me innocent, intact. It does not depress me. You talk about something being majestic. Art is majestic. It appeals to what is best in the human. Yes, it sometimes represents violence as for example the *Guernica* by Picasso.

"Yet, it remains such a powerful symbol of what not to do that in the end it achieves its purpose, which is that by so graphically showing what is worse in us it challenges us to get rid of such brutality. That it has no place in our lives, that we are better than that, and that we must fight against our worse instincts.

"Then, Degas' paintings of dancers. How beautiful, delicate and lovely they are represented. His stuff is majestic, too. The mystery of the human body, how it moves, how it composes itself through the dance and through music. Michelangelo's *David* is another example of such clarity, purity and beauty. When I lived in Florence, I went to see it just about every week.

"I could never get enough of seeing the result of his passion, his creativity, his innocence. Or if you look at a Monet or a Cezanne, they have an amazing effect on our impression of their impression. Art should keep us all innocent. It should protect us from life's ugliness—and life can be and often is ugly."

"Hearing the way you talk about what you love and what you want to do seems so removed from my own reality," I said. "I saw the *Guernica* when I lived in New York. It disturbed me so much. I tried to put it into the context of what we have done in Vietnam, Cambodia, and I found the whole thing both depressing and an exercise in futility. We don't seem to learn much about preventing wars."

"That is why we must never give in to our worst instincts. Why did you ask me about my wanting to be a curator?"

"Because I'm in awe of people like you wanting to do it. It seems so complicated, and mysterious."

"Yes, it is both. OK, let's settle the question," and she turned around and wrapped her legs around me. "Are you a boobies man or a leg man?"

"Yesterday, you argued that to make a choice between Florence and Venice was a false choice. They are both jewels."

"OK, so you were paying attention to what I was saying."

"Hey, I'm a fast learner. I love your boobies and I love your legs. I don't have to make a false choice."

"Are you hungry?"

It is always intriguing and interesting, at least to me, how often a woman can make an existential leap in a conversation with deep meaning to something practical like eating or having to feed the baby, or whether legs are more attractive than boobs or vice versa.

While the man is thinking of the results of a score of a football game, or what is the batting average of a baseball player. Men and women are different.

"You seem to always be hungry and you eat like a horse. Where does all that food go? You're so slim."

"My dancing keeps me in good shape."

"OK, let's call room service, what time is it?" I looked at the clock. "Perfect. We'll have a wonderful brunch."

"With a bottle of their finest champagne?"

"Absolutely."

"But it has to be French."

They brought us a wonderful brunch. We chose French toast, sausages, fruits and a bottle of French champagne. We sat on the floor naked, as she did not want crumbs on the bed, and proceeded to enjoy a well-deserved break from the other activities.

"OK, I want to ask you something but you have to promise that you won't laugh and make fun of me," she said.

"OK. Shoot."

She hesitated. She seemed very serious. I wondered what she wanted to know. I hoped I could answer her question.

"You promise it won't upset you?"

"It won't."

"OK, you were with Emily when she was pregnant, right?"

"Yes?"

"So a pregnant woman has a big belly. Well, how does the man manage to make love to her?"

I started to laugh. And fell on my back, and spilled some champagne on my belly. Our human curiosity never ceases to amuse me.

"See, now you're laughing at me."

"No, I'm not. But to answer your question: In the usual way."

"No, it cannot be the usual way. She has an increased-size belly with a baby inside. You get on top of her and you risk crushing the baby."

"Well, there are ways. But why do you want to know?"

"I want to be prepared for when our turn comes."

"You're planning on having babies?"

"Aren't you?"

"You mean walking around like a duck, with swollen feet, and gaining a ton of extra weight in that beautiful body of yours?"

"So?"

"So? It doesn't bother you?"

"No!"

"Women, are so weird."

"Well, someone has to think about these things."

I knew about a woman being pregnant. Emily looked so striking in her pregnancy. Julie most likely would look just as striking if not more. Take it easy, old buddy, I thought. This thing can get out of control.

The universal rule about humanity and eventual reproduction. The continuance of the race: the offspring. One of the most basic reasons, if not the only reason, to have sex. Well, one of the reasons, anyway.

"So, how do you do it?" She asked.

"Well, rear entry."

"Rear entry?"

"No, I don't mean that kind of rear entry."

I started to laugh, again. I was looking up at Julie and trying to picture the sixteen year old girl of ten years ago asking those questions. She seemed to be lost by my reaction.

"No, what I meant was doing it from behind."

"Like you did it when we were taking the shower?"

"Yes."

"OK, now I understand."

And I could see her wheels turning, visualizing strange but human things.

"But you know, the strangest thing for me is to think of my parents making love," she said, after a moment of silence.

"Why?"

"I don't know."

"Excuse me Miss Douglas, but how do you suppose you got here?"

"I don't know, immaculate conception?" And she busted out laughing.

"Right. It's supposed to have happened once, so I guess it could have happened again."

"Affirmative on that."

"Julie, you're something else."

"God, there is so much that I don't know. I want to learn. I want to be a good woman for you Jonathan, that's if you help me, teach me and let me. Will you let me?"

"Yes."

She got on her knees scooted over, leaned over and kissed me. Her mouth tasted of French toast and champagne. Then, she started licking the champagne from my belly. Slowly, like a cat, though her tongue was not raspy, but sweet. I got hard. I kissed her majestic breasts, hard, expecting, and ran my hand over her beautiful legs. She climbed over me, found me, and guided me into her.

We took a shower later. Straight shower with no further calisthenics. She put on her bikini and she looked absolutely delicious. It was still raining when I looked out the window.

"Come on, let's go out and walk in the rain," I said.

"We just took a shower."

"So?"

"I thought you didn't want to go outside."

"Never said that."

"OK, let's do it."

Even though it was raining the temperature outside was high. Maybe not as high as it had been in the room, but still warm. The rain was warm, too. We waded into the ocean but the water seemed kind of dirty, so we got out. There were some hardy souls doing the same thing we were doing. It was a time to have fun, to be.

"What would you think if I got a tattoo?" she suddenly asked me.

"No."

"Why not? Look at all these guys and some women, they have nice ones. Come on be a sport. In fact, let's each get one."

"No."

"You're no fun."

"I hate tattoos."

"I'll get your name on me and you'll get my name on you."

"And where do you intend to put this tattoo?"

"I don't know, on my arm, or shoulder, or my belly, I suppose."

"A future museum curator walking around with a tattoo."

"Well, I can always cover it."

"So if you are going to have a hidden tattoo what's the point? The whole idea is to walk around half-naked showing your tattoo the way these people do."

"If I had your name tattooed on me I would never take it off. It would be there forever."

"That always makes me laugh. A guy gets a tattoo: 'I love Cindy'. Then he breaks up with her and now he has a problem because his present girlfriend is called Lisa. He has to scramble and get the thing off, which has to be painful, so he can put Lisa's name where Cindy's name used to be. While I was in the Army, I saw plenty of guys doing that. Not for me. I think only rednecks get tattoos."

"Not true."

"You're right. One of my professors at school—excuse me he hates to be called 'professor' he prefers teacher—did have a tattoo now that I think about it."

"See. Who is he?"

"His name is Jack. You'd like him. He's also insane. A great teacher, and one of the best friends a man could hope to have."

"I like him already, and if he has a tattoo he is no redneck. I want to meet him. Maybe he can give me a few pointers as to how to become a good teacher. Yeah, let's go meet him."

"He lives in California."

"Aren't we going to California?"

She caught me by surprise. I stopped and she kept on walking ahead of me. We were completely soaked. She kept looking for seashells. I was looking at her ass. Great looking ass, sitting on top of great looking legs.

The image of Julie's legs all wrapped around my waist came to me. Jonathan, you oversexed, depraved creature, do you not have better things to think about? I laughed. A couple of half-naked GIs walked the other way, and I could see the horny look on their faces as they glanced at her. Bastards.

She stopped, picked up a shell and brought it to me.

"Isn't it pretty?"

The rain seemed to have slacked off and I could see that some clouds were beginning to drift away, as if wanting to give the sun a chance to shine again.

"You didn't answer my question."

"About the shell?"

"No, about California?"

Man, oh, man. This thing was perhaps going too fast for me. Yet in a much larger sense Julie had waited ten long years. Was it fair for me to stand in the way of her happiness? Of her search for who she was? Of wanting to catch up and live or at least try to live a normal life?

Jack had not said much when I went to see him on my return from Vietnam and I told him the news about Emily. Normally, Jack always had a retort, an answer to anything, but I could see that he was at a loss for words.

He just hugged and held me as if I were a child seeking comfort, and in a larger sense I was looking for human comfort.

"I'm so sorry, Jonathan," Jack said. "These are times when I'm at a loss to try to figure out the business of the cosmos, of religion. This puts me in a frame of mind that if there is a God, He does not a give a damn for us. In fact, this proves to me that there ain't no God.

"It's all bullshit and so many of us keep on believing the line from the mumble-jumbo-bible-beating-bum-bastards who want to make us believe there is a larger, greater design for mankind. I think that if there is a God, He just forgot about us."

Yes. He had forgotten about us, idiots.

We kept walking on the beach in the rain. Julie was quiet and looking at the waves in the distance. She glanced once in a while in my direction and just smiled.

"So, you want to go to California?" I asked her.

"Might as well, we can't dance."

"That's a funny expression, where did you get it?"

"I don't know. I think Ham uses it all the time."

Ham. We hadn't talked about—what did Roberto called him: *Mr. Prosciutto.*

"Let's talk about Ham for a moment."

"Why?"

"Well, it seems to me that he's in the middle of a situation."

"He's not in the middle of anything. Ham wants a trophy wife, a country club wife. Prim, proper, who does not paint her toenails, let alone red. God forbid. As for sex, the missionary position is probably still kind of daring for him.

"I don't know what he'll do when the woman he marries gets pregnant. Maybe he'll invent something, a new way. I'm not in love with Ham. Yes, I did have sex with him, once, that's all, and it was a kind of accident if you really want to know."

"I wasn't asking for any particulars."

"Yes, but that's for the record. I'm not interested in Ham. I'm not interested in high society with dancing balls, gowns, or expensive foreign cars, and especially not cars with a woman's name on them. Black servants, frills and private jets. Yes, Ham wants to get his own jet. That he is poisoning others causing them to die with the stuff he grows in his private domain so he can get his jet, is not on his radar.

"Ham is the plantation mentality that is still pervasive in the South. He's not a mean person, really. He's nice, actually. But, he is a kind of a throwback to civil-war times. Being married to Ham would be purgatory for me. Maybe for other women he's perfect. I'd like a little bit of dirt under the fingernails as you've probably noticed. So, Ham is not part of the equation. No, thank you very much."

"I didn't mean to get you upset about this."

"I'm not upset. I think you have got to understand what the deal is here, mister. I belong to you whether you like it or not, period. In fact, you have nothing to say about this matter. It has been decided by higher echelons than you or me. Thus, you'd be wiser to get on with the program, as my dad used to say, and conquer your objective."

I started to laugh. Julie was soaked. Her hair stringy, with rainwater all over her. But she still looked amazingly beautiful. The water running down her body, glistening, caressing her body. I started thinking about other things.

"You know, it's good thing we're on the beach, otherwise I'd be jumping all over your bones," I said.

"What's keeping you from doing it 'Mr. King of the Road.' Don't tell me a few rednecks are going to keep you from getting what you want. If it were the exact opposite, I'd never hesitate to go after what I wanted."

She laughed and stood legs apart challenging me, while the rain kept on falling. She looked like some kind of exotic mermaid who has just come out of the ocean. I started to laugh.

"No, let's go back to the hotel."

"Chicken."

"Oh, it's chicken now? OK, let's see."

I started to chase her down the beach and she started to run toward the hotel, laughing. The people at the reception desk did not appreciate our hilarity and the fact that we were, well, a bit wet, though we had left our towels just outside the entrance door and managed to dry ourselves off a little before entering the lobby.

We hardly got back into our room and I was ripping the bikini off her. It was not too difficult, really.

And Julie, this lovely, mysterious, mermaid, did not hesitate to give herself to me with everything that she was worth. The floor got a little wet, but, what the hell, it would dry by tomorrow. We took another shower, afterward. The sheets on the bed had been changed.

"We take showers and make love, or we make love and take showers." I said.

"Are you complaining?"

"Who's complaining?"

-XVII-

We woke up in the early evening from a sex nap. The sun had gone down and the rain had given way to a starry sky. I could see the stars through the open window.

"Now, I'm hungry," I said.

"Me, too. How about some lobster and an excellent bottle of white wine, château Montcontour, 1968."

"I thought that kind of life was not really your cup of tea."

"I never said I'm against the great pleasures of life. I'm just against false choices, that's all."

"Where did you learn about these things?"

"Jonathan, I told you I spent a year living with an Italian family of impeccable taste, great tradition and fine old European manners. Well, except when Roberto walked around stark naked."

I laughed.

"Who would have thought that Julie, this little shy, *signorina,* would turn out to be a hussy of great taste and education, worldly, wise, and romantic?"

"I'd prefer to be romantic than to be sentimental."

"With plenty of sexual appetite."

"Look who's talking. Are we back to the nymphomaniac thingy?"

"You know, a play that I wanted to do back in the days was *Lysistrata.* Are you familiar with it?" I asked.

"Yes! That's when the women go on a sex strike because the men are always going to war."

"Yes."

"I read it. It's by Aristophanes."

"After *Anne Frank* I wanted to do it but Andy, you remember him, said that it would cause a riot."

"Probably would have."

"Did you do any more acting while at Ohio State?"

"Yes, I did *Antigone*, by Sophocles, in a school production."

"You did? Wow, I'm impressed."

"Well, thanks to you."

"Thanks to me? How?"

"I showed the drama teacher the program of *Anne Frank* and the review of the play by the Fayetteville newspaper, and after auditioning I got the part. I love *Antigone.*"

We were now sitting at a very nice and chic restaurant. We had oysters, fresh lobster, but no château Montcontour. So we settled on a Riesling from Germany. It was not bad, according to my number one wine expert.

Even though we had not gotten much sun, the sea air and the other things we had done had given Julie a wonderful and elegant look. She was wearing a white, soft dress, open toe sandals, bright red toenails, I had retouched them and her finger nails as well. She thought I was cool to be doing her nails.

She said that doing her nails would keep me from touching other parts of her anatomy. I complained, of course, and said it was not fair. She smiled, kissed me, and said we would take care of that later. Julie always seemed attractive and fresh without trying. She was a lovely girl, no doubt.

Earlier, she had called her mom and told her that everything was fine. That she would call her back when she was ready to come home.

She did not call Ham.

"Tell me about *Antigone*."

"A remarkable young woman. She fights for the right to bury her brother but Creon, the King, rules against her. But she goes ahead and does it anyway knowing that she will pay the ultimate price."

"How did you relate to her. When you played Anne Frank, you were both about the same age, and Anne was dealing with the emotional impact of growing up in a hostile world."

"Surprisingly enough, I found both women similar in their strength of character. It's true that *Anne* was based on a real story and she also paid the ultimate price. *Antigone* was not based in a vacuum. The ancient Greeks had some issues and the powers of the government had to be challenged.

"Sophocles understood that. We don't do that in this country today. The Greeks wrote great women plays: *Electra, Antigone, the Trojan Women, the Suppliants, Andromache, Lysistrata, Medea, Hecabe, Phaedra, and The Oracle of Delphi.* Amazing! You had mentioned them. I read them all.

"My parents drove all the way to Ohio to see me in *Antigone*. My father had missed seeing *The Diary of Anne Frank*, which he always regretted. We talked about you, wondering where you were. It made me sad to think I had no idea where you were."

She looked at me and smiled a half-sad, half-happy smile.

"Antigone has a beautiful speech that summarizes the meaning of the whole play. I was terrified I would blow my lines. Remember how worried I was about Anne's lines. Well, with *Antigone*, it was murder. I nearly went out of my mind. I thought about you and how you'd have told me what to do. I tried to get in touch with you by telepathy."

"Yeah, I do remember getting some strange vibrations one day."

"That was me calling you to come and help me," she said, laughing.

"Do you remember that speech?"

"Let me see."

"Not for my children, if I had been a mother, nor for my husband, if his dead body were rotting before me, would I have chosen to suffer like this in violent defiance of the citizens. For the sake of what law do I say this?"

She stopped. She was not sure of what came next. Then she continued after a moment's hesitation.

"If my husband had died, there would have been another man for me; I could have had a child from another husband if I had lost my first child. But with my mother and father both hidden away in Hades, no other brother could ever have come into being for me . . ."

Julie was lost in the moment. I saw her face and there was something mystic, far away, and hidden. I felt like I was intruding upon a world that was hers alone. She had the right to have interior thoughts.

And I had to accept that even though she had said that there should be no secrets between us, secrets between a man and woman are facts of life. I guess part of getting to know the other person was respecting their private inner thoughts.

"I love that speech." She regained her control.

"Nixon is not Creon. Do you think Nixon will resign over this Watergate debacle?" I asked her after a while.

"I'm not a gambling person but if I had to bet, I'd put my money on his resignation. Our country cannot afford to continue with the status quo. Ham thinks that Nixon should stick it out, fight against these liberals, communists, pinkos, fellow travelers. He's raised bucks for Nixon's election before. He's willing to put up his own money and help Nixon stay in office."

This fucking war had been going on for too long. Thousands of people getting killed. And not just GIs, but Vietnamese and Cambodian civilians after we bombed the hell out of their country. It was ugly, sick.

What corrupts mankind? I thought our country was better than this. I had not thought about the war while I was with Julie, but it was the war that incongruously had led me to Emily and to here.

I often wonder if I had been less of a coward, if I had taken Emily and the baby to Canada would we be there now living like a normal family. Nonsense. If she was going to die whether we were in Canada, Timbuktu or in Siberia, it would have been the same. Geographic location really had very little to do with it for when your time comes, it comes, that is all—any ending.

Yet, I had not been able to deal with this nagging question. There had been times when that question was the only thing that occupied my mind. I found myself with days of total despair, blaming myself, questioning myself, always ready to put all the guilt on me.

Even when I had gone to see Jack, he tried to make me see that I had nothing to do with Emily's death. That I should have been grateful I had known her, even if for a few days.

And again, I had only spent a week with Emily. Days, actually, as if that made me a hero. *Gee, Jonathan, you only spent nearly a week with Emily that time, you know, when you went to visit her?*

Screw you, world!

As I am watching Julie talking about her experiences during her university days, hearing her, but not really paying attention, feeling her touch me with her foot under the table teasing me, again, strange thoughts flood my mind, heart.

"Jonathan, you're gone again."

"What?"

"Where were you?"

"I'm here."

"No, you're not."

"Ask me what you were saying last."

"OK, what was it?"

"You were talking about not being a betting person and that Ham was trying to help Nixon stay in power."

She laughed. And she rubbed her foot against my leg.

"OK, you're sneaky."

"I'm not."

"Yes, you are."

"I'm smart, that's all."

"If you are so smart how come you haven't made a comment about the way I look, tonight? I did it for you."

"You look beautiful," and she did. "I love your hair and the way you did it tonight. Your white dress. I think your feet are sexy with those great looking sandals you are wearing. I love the smell of the perfume. I love the speech of *Antigone* that you just did. I love your smile, your eyes, and your sense of humor. I love so many things about you, I always did."

"How come I had to wait ten years to hear you say that?"

"You were too young back then. I didn't want to give you false ideas that would go to your head and you would become unbearable."

She looked at me and a sudden shadow crossed her eyes. But, it was instantly gone.

"I just saw something in your eyes. What was it?"

"There was nothing."

"Yes, there was."

"So only you are allowed to have interior thoughts?"

"I never said that."

"You're right. So do I look OK?"

"Yes. Julie A. Douglas, you're a most desirable, beautiful woman. Dangerous, of course, but still very beautiful."

"You want to know how dangerous I am? I also played *Lola* in the musical: *Damn Yankees*. That was in my senior year. I figured I'd go out in a blaze of lights, music and fun."

"Is that the photo I saw in your bedroom in that Spanish costume?"

"Yes. I danced and sang that great song: "*Whatever Lola Wants, Lola Gets.*"

"You did? You look so stunning and exotic in that photo. You never told me that!"

"You never ask me anything."

"You have played: *Anne Frank, Antigone and Lola*, and read all of those great Greek plays. What made you want to read them?"

"Because you talked about them when we were doing *Anne Frank*. I remember so much of what you said, the way you looked, and the way you sat. I remember everything about you." Her look and her smile were soft.

Is this what love is all about? Memories, good, great, wonderful memories?

"Lean over, I want to kiss you."

"Here, now?" She was surprised.

"Yes."

"No, you won't."

"Funny thing. If I remember correctly, not a few hours ago, you challenged me that if you wanted something rednecks would not have prevented you from getting what you wanted. Now I want to get what I want and you're squeamish.

"Didn't you call me 'King of the Road'? Yeah, do like I say but don't do like I do, typical female. And from someone who played *Lola*, the demonic seductress. *Lola* would have understood and gotten on top of the table and started dancing."

"OK," she said, shyly looking around the room.

She leaned across the table and I kissed her. Not a long kiss. Some GIs at another table started applauding. She got red in the face and she sat down, a bit embarrassed.

"Serves me right," she said, laughing at the whole situation.

"You're delicious."

"Is that true?"

"Yes!"

"I loved playing *Lola*. It was a fun role. You're right, she was the demonic seductress but she loses Joe at the end. He goes back to his wife."

She made a sad face.

"But what about you? You're such a great director. Have you done any theater work?"

"We're not talking about me."

"You have never attempted to do any theater work?"

"Yes, I did some."

"Like, off-Broadway?"

"If you want to call off-Broadway doing a couple of shows in Bakersfield, California."

"Bakersfield? That's not off-Broadway."

"That's my point."

She wanted to laugh, but was not sure if I was joking or serious. Yes, I had done a couple of shows in Bakersfield, California—unforgettable forgettables.

I had not become involved with any drama group since my release from the Army, other than those two shows in Bakersfield, which I did as a favor to a guy I met. I had more than enough drama in my personal life.

My whole stupid life had become a giant, painful, maddening, tragedy. Emily had been so impressed when she found out I was doing *Anne Frank*. She had told me that she had read the play.

I did go back to school to work on my masters. It was either that or go crazy. So I did the work. Actually sleep-walked through the whole thing. It took me longer than should have been the case. But, I did finish it.

Jack got me a job as his TA—teacher's assistant—I did enjoy the work and it helped me pay for my tuition, which in itself was not too shabby. But I did not get seriously involved in theater work. I was just too bummed out and I had to go to the VA hospital for many weeks due to the piece of metal inside my back.

Should they take it out? Should it wait for more tests? If it was not giving me a hard time, and considering its location, maybe it would be better to keep an eye on it and not mess with it. Questions and more questions. In the end, I was the one who made the decision and said: Screw it, just leave it where it is. I could see the quacks were relieved when I told them that.

Jack thought it was a good idea not to mess with it, as he never trusted military doctors, anyway. Eventually, the military gave me a small disability pension and along with my GI Bill, and with a small inheritance from my grandmother, I had managed to scrape by.

I had drifted here and there with no specific destination or idea. I had done a great deal of just driving my car all over the place, which was why I had told Billy that I had put over two hundred thousand miles on it.

I just lived from day to day. No plan. No vision. Not trying to get involved with life or anybody. I had a couple of affairs, but nothing of substance and the women finally gave up on me. Who could blame them?

Then I had ended up in New York City, where I had lived for the last couple of years and did try to find some work in the off, off, off, off, Broadway but had not been successful. My own fault. I did not try hard enough.

Julie had been quiet for a while. I guess she was matching my silence.

"Hey, do you want to walk around a bit?" She asked.

"OK."

I paid and as we were walking out, Julie was walking slightly ahead, we passed the GIs who had applauded when I had kissed her. One of them guys spoke loud enough that I heard.

"Great poontang, look at them legs. Lucky bastard. What the hell is she doing with him?"

I glanced back at him and started to give him a dirty look but then I remembered I had once been in their shoes, so I smiled and he smiled back.

The boardwalk was filled with people. Half of the women were wearing bikinis as the weather was balmy and the cloudy sky had given way to lots of stars that were still visible even with the brightness of the area.

Again, many of the guys walking around were GIs on the prowl. Julie had her arm around my waste and I was enjoying rubbing my side against hers. She was humming the song: *"Whatever Lola Wants, Lola Gets."*

"I can't believe you did *Lola*. I wish I had been there to see it."

"You would have liked it. The director was good, but you would have been better."

How do women end up creating this amazing belief in the men they love? I guess that is how Mother Nature works. It creates an intangible thing that makes women believe in the impossible, sometimes. Actually, it makes all of us believe in the impossible.

Just a few days ago, hell, a few hours ago, really, who would have thought that I would be walking in Myrtle Beach with a lovely young woman while she hums a song about *Lola* and what she wants? How do these things come about? Who is pulling the strings?

I had not thought about Emily for a little while and I felt somewhat guilty about it. My whole being had been invaded with her images for so long that I had never contemplated thinking about not thinking about her.

I resented Jack when one day he had gently suggested that thinking and getting stuck on such thoughts was not healthy. I had argued that he did not know a fucking thing of what I was going through. And he agreed with me. But he also said that suffering for its own sake did not resolve anything.

"I never met Emily, but based on what you've told me about her, I bet you she would get on your case for doing this to yourself."

That evening, we had gotten a little drunk. Well, actually a lot drunk. His wife and kids had gone to see her mother's parents, and Jack and I had spent the whole evening together talking and drinking. He had barbequed some steaks and we were sitting out in the back yard.

"Yeah, she'd probably agree with you."

"Listen, buster, you had her love. Whether it was just for a short time or a long time, in the final analysis it don't matter shit. The main thing was that you had it. It filled you with magic and poetry. You should be grateful for that."

"OK, explain to me why I should be damn grateful when she was taken away from me. Explain that."

"Who knows? All I'm repeating is what you told me. Emily was unique and, again, from what you told me, she understood life a little bit better than you did. Give her credit for that."

"Jack, I loved her. I worshipped her. We were making plans. We were going to make a life together. I think with her everything would have been possible. She believed in me. You know how it feels when you wake up one day and you find yourself wondering where it all went? It's all fucked, man."

I had never talked to Jack about Julie. There was no reason to say anything. I had forgotten all about her. But, now, life had gotten into the act again and here I'm walking in Myrtle Beach, South Carolina, with her.

And I was desperately wondering if she had come into my life to replace Emily—no, that was a bad choice of words—no, she had come into my life to give me another chance. And was I man enough to accept the challenge, for it was a challenge. Julie had nothing to do with my sad past; it belonged to me, and not to her.

Should I give Jack another call and talk to him about Julie? Knowing him, he would probably call me an ungrateful bastard for refusing to accept how lucky I was and to stop torturing myself.

That it was time to get my act together and live instead of acting like I was the only person in the whole stinking world who had suffered such a tragic loss.

I stopped, grabbed and kissed Julie hard on the mouth. She responded, but was surprised.

"What was that all about?"

"What?"

"The brutal kiss?"

"That wasn't a brutal kiss."

"Oh, yes it was."

"OK, maybe it was a bit robust."

"No, I know about your robust kisses. That wasn't one of them."

"Are you complaining?"

"No, just curious, that's all."

She was looking at me with a bemused look on her face.

"OK, it was a hard kiss, but I felt like kissing you."

"Any particular reason?"

"Do I have to have a 'particular' reason?"

"No."

"OK. I just want to let all these horny GIs know that are looking at you with those nasty, horny, thoughts, that you're off limits."

She laughed.

"What did the guy say to you as we were leaving the restaurant?"

"Oh, something silly."

"I couldn't understand it, but I know he said something."

"Don't worry about it, it was GI talk."

"Let's go walk on the pier."

It was crowded. As we walked further onto the pier, she held my hand and started to laugh nervously while looking down at the wooden planks. As one walks over the pier, the water under it, especially when waves come in and recede, sometimes gives people a sense of vertigo, a kind of insecurity.

"I love to walk on these things, but I remember when I was a kid I was always afraid. It felt like I was going to fall into the water."

"And here you tell me you are not afraid of the dark, which most kids are. But this little motion makes you act like a scared kid."

"I can't help it."

"Well, you wanted to do it."

"I know. Just stay with me and hold me if I start to fall in the water."

"You won't fall. Come on."

But she kept holding my hand very hard, while looking down and giggling. We got to the end of the pier. Lots of people were leaning over the railing and looking down at the water, laughing, talking. There were some others sitting quietly with their fishing lines patiently waiting for the fish to bite.

There were kids running around having the time of their lives. But what I saw mostly were packs of young guys, GIs on the loose for the most part, just hanging about. Waiting their turn to face bullets that other young guys were shooting at them.

GIs whose fathers had probably served or were still serving in the military, and who were now the next batch of bodies that would be needed to replace the ones who were being killed. And would continue to be killed because in this country war is a necessity that defines our society. A strange, domestic, and national industry. Just like our gun laws' industry.

A national manufacturing process that never stops, that continually designs, produces and distributes its final product: death. Yes, this was the newest generation of killers and victims all tied together with one simple goal: Kill the other guy before he kills you.

"Remember the night when you sang for the officer's club and I was working the lights?"

"Yes, I was so nervous but I think I did all right."

"You were great."

"Really?"

"Come on you knew that."

"Are you thinking about that night because of all the guys we see around, and whose haircuts tell us they are soldiers?"

"Yes. I hate military haircuts."

"On some guys they look fine."

"I want to ask you something."

"What?"

"Did Andy ever say anything to you about that evening, after you sang at the club?"

She looked at me surprised.

"He mentioned something but I didn't understand. Why do you ask?"

Now I was caught up in my own silly memories. *Stupid jerk always looking for trouble.*

"I was curious that's all."

"Was there something?"

"It wasn't important."

"What was it?"

"It was just something silly. You don't need to concern your pretty little head with false memories."

Suddenly, the sound of a trumpet drifted our way. I looked over where the sound was coming from and I saw this white guy playing the trumpet. He was wearing an Army jacket. He had by his feet, in the typical fashion of street musicians, a hat to collect money from the public. The guy was young or at least seemed to be from where we stood.

The sound of the music was longing, mournful, but it was clear and as it drifted our way, I could not help but be reminded of Cash and his trumpet. The guy was riffing on *Porgy and Bess,* one of the best pieces of music that Miles Davis had made famous for the way he played it.

I reached into my pocket, and pulled the mouthpiece of the trumpet that I had kept with me since the day when Cash got killed. I had always carried it with me. It was a kind of bridge, more like a spiritual bridge that I had to him and to my past.

"Let me show you something," and I handed the mouthpiece to her. She looked at it not quite sure what it was.

"What is it?"

"It's the mouthpiece of Cash's trumpet. I've kept it all of these years."

"Where did you get it?"

"One of the medics who tried to save Cash gave it to me afterward because he knew we were close."

"That was nice. And you've had it this long?"

"Yeah, a memento from my buddy's life snuffed out so pointlessly."

She took it and looked at it. Then, she leaned over and put her head on my shoulder.

"I thought of finding out where his family lives and sending it to them," I said.

"That would be great. I'm sure they'd appreciate it."

"OK, can I tell you something but promise you won't make fun of it?" I said.

"No, I can't promise something if I don't know what it is."

"You asked me to promise you something earlier and I did it without asking you what it was."

"Maybe you should learn to negotiate better."

"OK, I won't tell you what mine is, but it has to do with you."

"It does?"

"It sure does."

"Tell me what it is."

"No."

"Fine."

She pretended that she did not care but I could tell she was dying of curiosity. OK, I thought, I am going to show her that two can play the game. Finally, she could not stand it any longer.

"OK, I promise," she said.

"Too late. I've changed my mind."

"That's not nice."

"Well, you should have agreed to it earlier."

"OK, then, I won't tell you my own secret."

"You have one?"

"Yes."

"But, I thought we weren't going to have any secrets between us."

"Well, I've changed my mind."

"OK, too bad for you."

"If I tell my secret you *will* laugh at me," she said.

"It's a chance you'll have to take."

I turned my attention to the music. The guy was good. Jazz is so American, black in its origin, and seemed to have come about, as other types of black music like gospel or church music, out of human desperation, misery, injury and pain. A deep and personal injury to people whose innocence and integrity were destroyed because they were black.

Who found themselves crammed in the holds of cargo ships, being transported thousands of miles away from where they had lived for untold generations, and made into slaves for the masters of the new world.

"Hey, this guy is good," she said.

"Give me the mouthpiece. Come on."

She handed it back to me. I took her hand and we started to walk toward the guy playing the music. Julie was startled by my sudden move. The guy was probably my age. He had a beard and looked like he could use some nourishment. But his eyes were merry, shiny, and they seemed to be looking at the world with a sense of irony not distant but more like the joke was on the rest of the world. He stopped playing.

"Look," I said, to him, "your playing reminds me of a buddy of mine—from many years ago. He used to play the trumpet just like you. I don't know if this will make any sense to you, but when he died in Vietnam, I took the mouthpiece from his trumpet and have kept it as a personal souvenir, possession, actually. I hope I won't be offending you by offering you this piece instead of some cash."

I handed him the piece. He took it, examined it very carefully, turned it over, put it up against the light and I saw a look of surprise.

"Man, this is an HTC2. Are you serious?"

"What's an HTC2?" I had no idea what the hell he was talking about.

"It's the mouth pieces that Miles Davis had specially made for him. Wow! They made about a dozen of them. I've seen it in museums, man. This is dynamite. Where did he get it?"

"I don't know. Knowing Cash, he probably stole it, or got it in some gambling game."

I started to laugh and Julie gave me a look of disapproval, and the guy let out a guffaw louder than the waves crashing below us.

"My buddy used to worship Miles, though, he was always saying that he had better chops than Davis."

"Man, thank you, I'm honored. Your buddy must have had some great chops to say that. I got another trumpet at home and this baby will fit into it very nicely."

He put the mouthpiece in his mouth and blew through it. It brought back when Cash used to do it and drove everybody crazy around the barracks.

He looked at Julie with the eyes of a man who also appreciates female beauty.

"Beautiful lady."

Julie was surprised but rewarded him with a warm smile.

"Thanks, brother," he added. "I'll treasure this baby until my time is up to go and play for the big man up in the sky. God bless both you and your lady."

"Thank you," Julie said.

Julie and I shook hands with him. We walked back to the barrier.

"Jonathan, that was a lovely thing to do. I like it better than sending it back to his family. They probably have lots of other things to remember him by."

"Do you think?"

"Come on, and did you look at the guy's face? I bet you he'll carry that thing with him everywhere he goes."

"Cash used to do the same."

"You're full of surprises, you know that?"

"Here's one for you. OK, what I wanted to tell you was that one day, while we were doing *Anne Frank*, Cash told me that you had a crush on me."

"He said that?"

"Yes."

"Get out of here. You're making that up."

"No, it's true."

"How did he know? I never told him or anybody anything."

"Well, he said it and he was serious."

She started to laugh and to shake her head.

"This is crazy. I wonder just how many people realized that. And here I was walking around, thinking that my secret was safe, that I was cool and stuff, when probably everybody knew.

"Oh, and remember I told you that I had run into Jackson one day and I asked him about you and, come to think of it, he seemed slightly uneasy. I thought I might have said something wrong but I was sure I hadn't. He eventually told me about Emily and that you had gone to see her."

"He probably didn't want to upset you because he knew or sensed what your feelings were. In fact, those two bozos used to harangue me about it all of the time, but in a nice way."

"How come they knew or sensed or guessed it, and you didn't?"

"The story of my life. I'm always behind the eight ball."

"Don't feel bad. I was also a dummy. I wonder if my mother saw it. And Karen, that hussy, she probably saw it, too."

She stopped and silently contemplated what I had just revealed to her.

291

"Julie, did you ever wonder what your eyes reveal? They betray you all of the time."

She thought about this for a moment.

"OK, no more Mr. nice guy. I'm getting me some dark shades from here on end and I'll wear them even when I go to bed—my eyes, I'm never going to trust them."

"You have beautiful eyes."

"Is that true?"

"Yes, I love your eyes."

She gave me a lovely smiled and leaned against me and we were quiet for a while. The guy went back to playing his music.

I turned around and looked at the people who were there. They did not look like monsters or racists, they looked like everyone else. The white people, that is. But, in fact, lots of them, millions of them, were racists.

And yet, when you met Southern white people in a normal course of a day's activity, they were polite, kind, open, friendly, and always wishing you a good day. That is if you were also white like they were. The contradiction was impossible to understand.

"OK, I am going to tell you my secret," she said.

The sound of her voice was very serious and it rather surprised me. Her look was clear and soft. Julie's eyes were always the windows to her soul. All you had to do was look at her eyes and you could learn things about her, about where she stood in the scheme of things.

I was learning to watch her, to sense her, to guess less things about her. We had been together just a few short days—three actually. Yet the one thing that was pretty obvious to me now, was the sense of security she exhibited. It had to be this way.

It was as if this whole adventure had its roots back in time when the whole universe had been born. Her destiny she understood, accepted it, and did not have to worry about its origin or final outcome. It had had a beginning, it had now a middle, and would end where it was supposed to end in the first place.

I thought of Emily again, for the billionth time; and she had also had this strange insight on things. That is why I had had such a terrible time wondering if she had known all along that she would die young. Did she know?

That somehow, the secret world she had wanted for her and her baby, for us, after Wilson's death, would disappear into nothing? I had been troubled with that thought because it would deny that she ever loved me like she said she did.

I was just a stopgap until, no, this is crazy I thought. I am now taking away her humanity. Cannot do that. My dark thoughts were too stupid, really. I could not lower me to that level of nastiness, meanness. No matter how much I hurt, and that hurt was always present.

I cannot turn into a piece of garbage and question Emily's attitude and love toward me. This is no good, Jonathan, this is no good. You are better than this, much better. Do not let life screw you up in that way. You will never make it. You do not want to go there. No way!

"I'm no longer a virgin," Julie said, softly, quietly.

I looked at her and this was the ultimate confession from her. She had been holding on to some idea about herself that had nothing to do with having sex with some guy. In her mind, the act had done nothing to break that psychological and spiritual barrier that women want to keep until the day when it arrives, and they give themselves to the man they truly love. I know it sounds crazy, but I could understand that idea.

Now, here was Julie saying that the barrier had been broken, as it were, whereas before the act had had no meaning for her. But I think that it was far more complex than the image of losing her virginity. It was a realization of some profound truth about who she was in life, independent of anybody else in the scheme of things,

Julie had now became whole in her definition of who she was. The physical act had been replaced by something far more significant and deeper, and I had better be wise enough to understand it and appreciate it. Couple relationships are always complicated.

"Julie, you're really something else. I want to learn from you. So many hidden things in people's hearts and souls that I don't know anything about. I've been hiding from my own pain and have tried to replace it with platitudes.

"I'm tired and I don't want to keep on pretending that I don't want a better life for me. A life not filled with superficial feelings and phony attitudes. A life of endless nothingness, if that's a proper sentence. I want to see things, feel things, that aren't misguiding me in my search for me. I don't want to continue being rootless, empty, and indifferent.

"That's why as I look at you I feel dishonest because you're proving to me in so many ways that love can exist and it doesn't have to become some kind of charade. And I'm not sure yet that I can reciprocate your love. I don't know."

"Oh, Jonathan I now belong to you in a way that I didn't just a couple of days ago. And only love made that possible. I don't know what's going to happen tomorrow, or the day after or the day after that.

"If you leave me behind, I want you to know that I'll hurt but I won't hate you. I'll always love you. I'll never change my mind even if you reject me and don't want anything to do with me."

I kissed her. She had tears in her eyes.

"Oh, Julie. I hope that I'm not the cause of your tears."

"No, but there are so many things that make me sad, that make me insecure, afraid, lost, and I try to fight against such feelings. It isn't easy, but I try."

Sometimes, I wonder if the night betrays us all. Or, in fact, it is because the night with its darkness allows us to pull back from the other ordinary things we have to do in the glaring light of the day.

And thus, it is the darkness that brings on some clarity to our spirits that helps us understand more. I can see why the night speaks loudly for some people.

We kept on walking and watching the other people.

The guy's music wafted over the noise of the crowd. It was sad, and yearning.

Cash, that crazy son of a bitch. A guy whose idea of life was just simply playing his music day in and day out. And Jackson, a preacher's son, a kid who would never hurt a fly. Both of these guys who had wanted to be godfathers of Emily's baby. And, now, all of them, all of them, were gone. Fucking gone!

OK, what am I doing here? Leading a lovely and beautiful girl into a world of nothingness. She doesn't deserve any of the bad shit that may come out of this. A couple of days ago her life was fine. I wasn't in the picture, though, she now says that she had never forgotten me. The simple fact of the matter is that she was doing fine in her life. Content with the world around her.

Now because I show up her whole world is all upside down, and she's in the hole deeper than I am. Man, even her "fiancé" was there for her. I don't know if she would have married him but, at least, I wouldn't be around to add another layer of confusion.

What chance does she have with me? Zero, nada, nothing, or niente as the Italians say it. Shee-it, I even know that word. Niente. Man, why didn't I leave well enough alone? Why? The story of my life. Screwing things up. What kind of love can I provide for her? I ain't got any. I'm dead. My heart is dead. My soul is dead.

Man, she deserves more than a jerk who only pretends. Well, I like Julie immensely. It's not that maybe, just maybe I could learn to love her. But, there ain't no guarantee in that.

I had been banking on my own bitterness and loneliness for too long only to discover that my account was overdrawn; my reserve had dwindled to nothing. I was broke spiritually as well as in my own heart. I had to replenish that emptiness with which I had lived so goddamn long, somehow. I had to. Could I do it? Could I do it?

My love had been Emily, but she was gone. Gone! And I was not even around when it happened. Shit, I was out there in the middle of nowhere trying to kill people who had done nothing to me, absolutely nothing! I should have told the Army to go and screw themselves the way Yoshi did.

I wonder what became of him? Yoshi, a sweet kid. And his girl dumps him because she says that he is going to kill other Asians. And Yoshi is left holding the bag. Man, I should have taken Emily as pregnant as she was and split. I was going to be a father . . .

I wanted so much to know just what Emily felt at the end. So damn much. Did she know she was dying? Jesus Christ, I'll never have an answer to that question. Never! And Jackson, he had been there when the news of Emily's death got to me. Both, him and Cash, the best friends a man can ask for in this chicken shit world.

Both of them had cried with me. I had never seen them cry and those two crazies fell apart as if they were mourning someone from their own families. Cash and Jackson crying for some white woman. They loved her because she was so fine, because of who she was, so sweet, and so full of life. Fuck life.

Jackson, before he faded forever, had grabbed me by my blood-soaked Army fatigues and told me to take care of myself, to love life. He said I had to promise him. That he would keep an eye on me and that I had better not screw it up. That he would know if I did, and that he would get on my case as he always did.

And I promised him that I would, but the question was: how? I told him, begged him, not to leave me behind. I needed him so bad, and he gave me his sweet smile and he was gone!. And some guys took him away from me and I almost killed them for touching him.

"Greene, you're bleeding like a fucking pig. You've got to get out of here before you bleed to death. Come on, man, stop being the fucking hero and get yourself into the emergency tent, and we'll take care of Jackson."

"Fuck you. You're not touching my buddy. You do not touch him, you hear. I will fucking kill you if you touch him. You fucking assholes. Leave him the hell alone. Leave him be . . ."

I had not realized that Cash was gone, too. He had been point man, the guy who walks ahead of the others in a combat operation. Then, an explosion, confusion, bullets flying, I felt this incredible jolt in my back and I went down, too. I saw Jackson double up and fall to the ground right next to me.

I managed to crawl to him and I saw him trying to breath and he could not do it; blood was coming out of this mouth. I had been paying all my attention to Jackson that I had not noticed that Cash was not there.

"Where is Cash, where's Cash?"

I could hear my voice but it seemed like it was coming from under some water tunnel. I thought I was yelling at the top of my lungs, but no one could hear me. They were deaf. Shadows moving noiselessly in front of my eyes.

"Where is that bastard? Cash, you prick, answer me you piece of useless shit, answer, please, answer me, stop playing your stupid games. Fuck you, Cash. Answer me, please, please, answer me . . ."

There would never again be the usual come back to my words. I would never hear: "Thank you, Mr. Greene, " from those two crazy bums.

I had never felt so alone and lonely in my whole life. I felt so cold. I did not have anybody left to keep me straight. Did they not know I needed them badly? Did they not know? They left me behind. The ungrateful, worthless pricks. Now I had nobody. Nobody. Did they not understand that was not part of the deal?

We were all going to make it together, or none at all. Did they not fucking know that? Later, I was told that I had drifted in and out of consciousness. According to one of the nurses, they thought I was not going to make it. I barely remember being transported to the emergency room. I was in great pain. My back was killing me.

I do not have much recollection of what happened afterward. I really did not give a shit if I lived or died. I mean, who cared? I was in the hospital when they took Cash and Jackson's bodies back to the States. I never even had a chance to say good-bye to them either.

I can never say good-bye to people who die on me. The story of my worthless, piece of shit life. They flew me to Hawaii and I hated the place. Too much goddamn paradise. All I did was stay in the hospital and brood.

I was finally sent back to California and discharged from the Army. The piece of metal would live with me until my demise. The doctors had finally agreed that it was safer to leave it where it was.

They told me it would move and go deeper into my body, but that eventually my flesh would cement it in place. But if I had any kind of discomfort and pain to come in and they would check it out to make sure that it did not present any danger. Danger, right.

Now here I am with Julie and I fear I will only bring pain and sorrow to her. I have done it to others who were close to me before. So why should she be any different? And she loves me. I can see it. So sweet, so open, so honest, and so true. Maybe I should be grateful that in this miserable life I have been loved by two great and wonderful women.

I mean, how many assholes like me luck out? How many? I do not know if by asking why things happen we eventually get an insight on things. I doubt it. Fucking life happens without any reason. I mean, why things happen? Who in the living hell orders them? Who?

"Jonathan, I want you to read my diary."

The beach was now less crowded than earlier. We had taken a long walk, both of us lost in our thoughts, fears. We had not said much and now we were going back to the hotel.

"What?"

"I want you to read my diary."

"Julie, I can't do that."

"Why not?"

"Well . . ."

I could not think of any specific reason.

"You're asking me to do something that I find very difficult. Not to say impossible."

"Why is it impossible?"

"Well, it's your diary. I have no right to look at it. It'd be like sneaking into your privacy and I'm not so sure if I can do it."

"I'm not begging you to do it. I'm asking you point blank. I need for you to read it. When we get back home, I'll give it to you."

"Julie, please don't do this to me."

"Are you afraid?"

"Well, yes."

"Why?"

"It's just too delicate."

"I have nothing to hide."

"But, it's your whole life."

"So?"

"Why are you doing this to me? What did I do to you?"

"Jonathan, it's not going to kill you."

"It might."

"That's silly. If you had a diary like mine and if you asked me to read it, I'd do it."

"Well, you're not me."

"What do you think you'll find in it?"

"Look, I don't know what I will find in it. I don't want to find whatever it is you have written."

"That's the most ridiculous thing I've heard."

"Maybe it is, but I'd rather not."

"Jonathan, you are being stubborn for no reason. I can't believe what I'm hearing from you. It's almost childish."

"Call it what you want. I'm not in a position to argue with you."

"I can't believe you're against it. Why, Jonathan? Why?"

"I don't know."

"Are you afraid that by reading it you will fall in love with me?"

"I don't need to read your diary or not read your diary to either fall or not fall in love with you."

"Jonathan, too many negatives in your sentence."

"So now you're correcting my syntax?"

"Well, someone has to."

"OK. I'll read it but I don't want you around when I do."

"Finally, we're getting somewhere. When I'm at work, you'll have the whole day to read it. Is that a deal?"

"OK, but I can't promise that I'll have read it before you come home."

"I'll call you before I come home just to make sure."

She looked at me as if she were dealing with an unruly child. And maybe she was. But to be honest, I wanted to read her diary, but I also did not want to read it. Be dammed if you do and dammed if you do not. Take your pick.

"Why are you being difficult?" She asked, mystified.

I had no answer to give her, really. I knew it was ridiculous.

"So, you can love me better and longer," I finally said, and gave her a hug.

"You don't need to go to such extremes for me to love you better and longer. I'm not sure I can love you any better. And longer? How about until the sun dies, is that long enough for you?"

We walked in silence a bit more.

"What am I going to do with him," she said, softly to herself.

"What did you just say?"

"You heard me."

"What if I don't want to know all there is to know about you?"

"You mean through my diary?"

"For example."

"You don't have to read the whole thing. Pick to read whatever date or entry you want."

"Sure, then you'll be asking me about some entry that I've overlooked and I'll look like a fool, and you'll get upset because I missed some interesting or important stuff."

"Everything in that diary is both important and interesting," and she laughed.

"See, now I'm going to have to read tons of pages."

"OK, what else are you doing with your life at this moment that you don't have the time to read what I wrote?"

"Lots of stuff. People to see, places to go. You haven't had anybody, according to you, who has ever read it."

"You're not 'anybody.' You're going to be the father of our children and asking you to do this is part of the deal."

"Kids?"

"Yes, kids. Or are you planning on getting a different woman pregnant?"

"I'm not planning on getting any woman pregnant."

"You'd better not, otherwise, I suggest you'd better sleep with one eye open." She laughed.

"One eye open? You're crazy," I said, and hugged her and kissed her. "However, with what we've been doing in these past couple of days, I wouldn't rule it out."

"So, I guess we'd better stop, check, and see how things develop."

"Who said anything about stopping? Maybe you're pregnant already. All it takes is a quick shot."

" 'Quick shot,' typical male talk."

"Do you want to get pregnant?"

"Not now, but we'll have to figure out when."

"What in the hell am I doing here, at nearly midnight, walking around Myrtle Beach talking about pregnancy, kids, and soon you're going to talk about diapers, runny noses and . . ."

"And what's wrong with that?"

"I'm too young to be a father."

She broke up in laughter.

"Jonathan, you are thirty-two-years old. I'm twenty-six-years old. We're the perfect specimens to have children and raise them."

There was something incongruous about me rejecting the notion of fatherhood. I was not being honest, and I knew it. I wanted to be a father to Emily's child. I was looking forward to it. It made perfect sense, but the fates had ruled against me.

We got back to the hotel. Our lovemaking was less frantic than the previous night's but just as intense. We could not get enough of each other. It was a good thing we were leaving the next morning as the sheets would have to be changed, again.

"I think we should leave a nice tip for the maid," she said.

"For changing the sheets so often?"

"Don't you think we should?"

We made love and drifted off into after-sex slumber. Satiated, happy, exhausted. Then, we would wake up and start over again. We were not going to get much sleep, it seemed. We would cuddle up and drift into some kind of magical world.

Actually, to make love and to talk and drift off in a slumber before starting over again is what a man and a woman do, when they are sharing a bed for the first time. Julie's tenderness was complete without ambiguities.

And she was not replacing anything or anybody. She was just a wonderful young woman being herself, when love is permitted to those lucky enough to have grace and beauty. It had been such a long time since a woman had made me confront what was important, had shown me the amazing degree of love and closeness only a woman in love can give a man, whom she loves without any conditions.

"Jonathan."

"What?"

"I want you inside of me."

"My love, really?"

"Yes, oh, so much, so much."

And I did what she wanted. And soon, once again, we were in a world of complete surrender and complete physical harmony. Where no barriers existed to hurt us or menace us with horrible and unpleasant things. Where Julie's love was my salvation from my own private hell.

And where my own tears about how much I wanted to be lost in her would be revealed to her, and she would know that she was erasing my sadness and bitterness. Where we would be in such a magical place and even ugly memories could not interfere and make us sad.

"Jonathan, you have tears in your eyes."

"Yes, I'm sorry."

"It's OK, my love. I know your struggle and I'm so happy we're one. I love you so damn much. I want to be one with you, now, tomorrow, and for always."

OK. Italy? It had become more than a passing thought for Julie. It had metamorphosed into a reality that was hard to ignore. I had to make a decision and it scared me.

"Jonathan, what are you thinking?"

"Stuff and stuff."

"Like what?"

"Like why after all of these years you're still beautiful and still in love with me. I mean, how do I explain those things?"

"No need to explain. Just accept it."

Just accept it. Easier said than done. Acceptance is not one of my strongest points.

OK, Greene, what's your problem, Jackson would have asked? *What the hell do you want? You've got nothing going for you—face it. You've got this fantastic, beautiful broad, and totally crazy about your ass. No holds barred. And here you are acting like a jerk. What's the matter with you?*

I was afraid, no question about it.

I was not afraid of what Julie said about me, but I was afraid that this whole thing would turn into another fucking, ugly nightmare, again. I had no reason to believe something bad could *not* happen. My previous life had not given me much hope to say: Thank you, life; it's been great to have you around. Yeah. Right, fuck you life! Man, I wish I knew what was what.

Hey, shithead, what about Italy?

She's going back, she told you so. Yeah, come to think of it, a good and perfect excuse for your sorry ass to get you off the hook as it were. Well, it ain't gonna be easy, Mr. Greene. You're now dealing with some rather interesting facts. Facts that you can't just ignore.

They may deceive you, but the truth never does. And you can't pretend seeing her go ain't gonna have some deep effect on your reptile brain. It will, my friend. It will and you're being a total asshole if you think you can ignore it.

Face it, Julie has shown you the possibility of what could happen to you, but you've got to act your age and act with courage. Do you have it, asshole? Do you? Face it, you're no longer some crazy, lost, son of a bitch out there hiding behind your pain.

Yes, your pain is real and has ruled you for so damn long that you've become dependent on it. Like some kind of pain-junky who has to have his pain-fix on a regular basis.

Yeah, that's you. A regular, immature, piece of shit junky for spiritual garbage that has sustained you these past ten years. You like it. You, thrive on it. You couldn't get out of a paper sack if your miserable life depended on it. Boy, you're a real head case.

I bet you, Cash and Jackson are laughing their assess off because they have seen this shit from you before. Remember? Yeah, they may not be around the way they were back in the days. But they know, they know your game. They ain't stupid.

Jackson told you to love life. Didn't he? And if Cash didn't have a chance to tell you the same thing it wasn't because he wouldn't have thought the same thing. This shitty life got in on the act and kept him from telling it to your own ugly mug.

Neither of these two guys would be proud and happy to see you acting like Julie owes you something. Jonathan, you're a miserable, low-life prick. She don't owe you a thing, shithead. She don't even owe you her love. No, you owe her stuff and don't you ever forget it!

And do you know something else, even Emily would not accept that you want to deny a bit of happiness in your life. She would be horrified at seeing you act this way.

Yes, Emily loved your sorry ass, but she wasn't a dummy and she understood better than you will ever understand in a million years that one cannot, one must not, get stuck in the misery of it all.

Yes, deal with your pain. Recognize it. Respect it. But, don't, repeat, don't, let it rule and decide what you need to do next. It ain't part of the deal, my friend.

"Don't mess this up, Hollywood. It ain't allowed," Jackson would have said. "You've got what few jerks like you ever get, and twice! Make sure you follow through. The last thing you want is to have me and Jackson pissed off at you. You ain't gonna like it old buddy. You ain't gonna like it one bit . . . you cool with that, Jackson?"

"You've got it, brother."

"Screw you both."

"Thank you, Mr. Greene."

"You're welcome Mr. McCall, you're welcome Mr. Jackson."

And Italy? It scared me to no end. I guess it was that I could not hide behind nonsense anymore. This was the end of the road.

"So, you're going back to Italy?"

"Yes, come with me, Jonathan."

"When are you going back?"

"This coming August. Come with me."

"I don't know. I've got some things to do in Los Angeles."

"We'll go there first. We can fly to Rome from there."

"You want to come to California with me?"

"Yes, I want to parade on Malibu Beach in my bikini."

"I don't live in Malibu."

"Or wherever. Maybe I'll get discovered, like Lana Turner." She giggled.

"But, if you do, you won't go to Italy, then."

"No, I wouldn't like that. Italy comes first."

"You make it sound so simple."

"It is."

"What would I do in Italy?"

"You can to go to Bologna University and study there."

"I don't speak Italian."

"I didn't either."

"Yeah, but you're better at that stuff than I am."

"It's just a matter of wanting to do it. You love languages. Don't you want to be with me?"

"What kind of question is that?"

"OK, then. Bologna University is one of the oldest universities in Europe. Since the tenth century. Don't you think that in those hundreds of years, Italians haven't figured out ways to help those who didn't speak their language learn it? Italians are practical and masters of their own house."

"But what would I study?"

"You can study how to become a great theater director."

"They have better guys than me over there."

"You're just making excuses, that's all."

"Julie, it's not true."

"Please come. The Sargentis would welcome you with open arms. I know it."

"Won't Roberto be jealous?"

"No. You know, when I left it was tough. Boy, really tough. And Roberto, the craziest of the Sargentis, the guy who gave me so much hard time did not want me to leave. He kept saying that I was family, that I had no right to abandon him. That I could not do that to him! He kept calling me: *Bruta, bruta*, which you can translate as being mean. He was so emotional.

"When I told him that I had my mother and my sister back home, he said to bring them over, that their house was large for everyone. And they do have a very large house. Plenty of rooms. He kept arguing that I could not marry *Il Prosciutto*, as he called Ham.

"That he'd prefer I marry the garbage man than to see me married to him. He was so upset. I love him. I love the whole Sargenti clan. They are the salt of the earth."

"It sounds so wonderful, Julie. But I don't know if I can do it?"

"Why not? What's keeping you in the States? Memories? We've talked about that already. Come. I know you'll find peace, happiness, balance and harmony over there. We'll be together. We can make a new life for us. Isn't that important?"

"Course it is. What if the Sargentis don't like me?"

"Jonathan, they'll love you. They'll be crazy about you. I can see mama Sargenti already making special dishes just for you. You'll get along with the three brothers, and Marcella will most likely fall in love with you. I'd definitely keep a jaundiced eye on that Italian hussy. No funny games. She's married, but still. . . "

She started to laugh.

"You're crazy."

"Jonathan, come with me, please."

"What about money?"

I've got a Guggenheim Grant to study there. It's good for my Ph. D. studies. It is enough money for both of us. Besides, I've been saving all of my money these past years and my father, God bless his soul, left Becky and me a small inheritance that I've never touched. And if your back hurts, there is Dr. Sargenti. I know he would take care of you as if you were one of his own sons."

"It sounds like you've got this whole thing mapped out pretty well."

302

"I have. What's wrong with making plans?"

"Julie, just a few days ago I wasn't even in the horizon. Now, your whole life seems to be centered around me, and that scares me."

"It's not centered on you. It's centered on us. You and me. You'll love Italy. You said you wanted to go to Paris. Well, Bologna isn't very far from Paris. We could go there on weekends and visit Paris. I've always wanted to see Paris. Now, we'll get to see it together. There is so much to see in Europe. Jonathan, please."

"Would you still go if I didn't go with you?"

"That's not a fair question to ask."

I knew it was not. I did not ask it to be mean. In fact, it came out of nowhere. I had not thought about it ahead of time. It just came out. I saw her reaction.

You're doing great, Jonathan, Cash would say. *Just great. Sheet-it. If there was a prize awarded for being the greatest asshole in this world; no, in this universe, Jonathan Alexandre Greene would get it hands down. Here you've got an amazing woman, willing to love your ass until the sun dies and you're acting like a regular shithead. Typical. It seems to be the story of your life. What are you waiting for? For whom? For what?*

I was being a coward and I hated myself for it. I had asked her about money but, in fact, I was not that poor. I knew it. When confronted with the reality of someone to love me without any conditions, I really had no tools, no fallback position. The only thing that appealed to me was to run.

With Emily it had been the same story. Jackson had gotten on my case for exactly the same reasons. In fact, both Cash and Jackson had been very critical of my immature behavior. I remember how upset they had been about my fears and tribulations regarding Emily.

At one time, both of these bozos had said that they were jealous of me for having someone like Emily fall in love with me. And, what would they say of Julie? Probably that, once again, I was being a regular jerk, big time loser! I had a woman crazy about me and I was acting like a big shit.

I could now see Cash just razzing my ass for now admitting that he was right when he told me that Julie had a crush on me. Though, he did not use those words, of course. But, being a GI your words can and do become rather flowery.

And Julie's mother? Man, oh, man. She met me ten years ago and I do not think I ever gave her any reason to suspect that anything untoward was taking place because there simply was not. Julie was for me a lovely young girl, then, who was talented and whom I had cast as Anne Frank because she deserved to get the role.

And, her mother, did she suspect and not say anything because she knew that these crushes happen to most of us. We eventually grow out of them. But Julie had not. And now what will happen when her mother and I meet again? Man, what if I do not pass muster? What then? What would, could I say to her?

How do you do, Mrs. Douglas. You look lovely as ever. I can see where your two lovely daughters get their charm, their poise, their good looks; from you! I hope things are going well with you. I know that you now know I have spent several days with your lovely daughter having, well, sharing a common bed—letto de famiglia—as Julie would put it.

Please, do not judge her. And I hope that you will not hold it against me, or, worse, against her. If I understand correctly, you had some idea, hope I may say, that Julie would agree to marry Ham. Oh excuse me, Trevor Hamilton, the third, gentleman farmer, scion of a noble North Carolinian family.

I hope that your disappointment will not be such that when we finally meet, again, you will not be tempted to slam your door in my face. Confession, Mrs. Douglas. I have no idea why this beautiful daughter of yours ended up loving me in such a way and for such a long time. It is a total mystery to me.

Being a woman, perhaps, you can help me understand the female psyche. I think only women can be such believers in guys like me. Believe me, back in the days when I became aware of Julie's sentiments toward me, I did everything within my powers to discourage that. I mean I was terrified of the whole situation.

And Cash, you might remember him. He was one of the guys who helped with the show. When he told me, at that time, that Julie had, well, a bit of a crush on me, I thought he was harassing me. I wanted to beat him up for inventing something that I thought was pure bunk. Little did I know that he was right.

And just for the record, ma'am. I did not come back here looking for your daughter; repeat, I did not come looking for her. I had no idea she would be here. And if the thought had occurred to me that I would run into her, I would have expected to find her married and taking care of your grandchildren.

OK, now that I have found her and single and free, yes, I have to admit that things have changed tremendously. She is lovely, beautiful, smart, with a great sense of humor, which I like to believe she inherited from you. And, apparently, still with strong feelings for me.

I must say that I am humbled by that. If you want to know the truth, Julie has always humbled me by who she is. She is a remarkable young woman. You should be very proud of her and what she has accomplished, and who she has become.

And if you really want to know the truth, I am having a tough time resisting what she has in mind for me and her. Tough time. I would like to ask for your honest opinion about this whole situation, if you are willing to unravel this great mystery called: Julie.

To be truthful, Italy scared the hell out of me.

-XVIII-

As we were rolling into her parking lot, there was a guy leaning against a new shiny silver color Mercedes. He was smoking and staring at us from the distance. Julie looked at me and I saw a look of confusion in her eyes. She was driving.

The door to her garage was open showing her car parked inside. The guy threw the cigarette down and crushed it with his foot. This doesn't look too swift, I thought.

"That's Ham," she said, quietly.

"Trouble in paradise," I said, trying to make light of what might turn into an ugly scene.

"Is he the violent type?" I added because I was concerned about her safety.

"No." She did not give me the impression she was afraid. Embarrassed? Yes.

"Do you think I should leave?"

"No."

"But, Julie?"

"But, Julie nothing."

"Look, it's a bit awkward don't you think?"

"Yes, it is."

She drove and parked the car not quite right next to his. But I did have a closer look at Ham. He was not a bad looking guy. Athletic, short dark hair. Dressed like a man of means, but not flashy at all—understated.

He had a serious look on his face. He did not come to greet us. Julie got out of the car and went around to greet him. I stayed in the car a few seconds and got out.

"Ham, what are you doing here?"

She kissed him on the cheek. He half responded and looked at me but not in a threatening manner, but just curious—curiously hostile.

"I've been looking for you. I called your mom and she told me you were on your way back from Myrtle Beach."

He glanced at me, but, again, not with a menacing look more like perhaps the look that he used when looking at a horse he is thinking of buying, then decides the beast is not worth a single penny—*hey, Ham, would you like to look at my teeth?*

"Ham, I'd like you to meet, Jonathan, you might remember I talked about him . . ."

"Yeah, the theater guy."

His voice was distant and dismissive. Breeding and self-control were pretty obvious.

We shook hands.

"Hey, how is it going," I said.

"My pleasure," he said, though his whole demeanor was showing exactly the contrary. His "pleasure" probably meant for him to strap me on a giant cartwheel and stretch my body into strands of spaghetti.

I wanted to laugh. "My pleasure," my ass. Right—*For the last three days, you have been boinking my beloved, you worthless piece of shit. I should knock your fucking teeth out . . .*

He turned to Julie.

"Julie, I'd like to have a word with you in private, if I may."

He sounded so damn formal. His self-control was interesting and somewhat comical, I thought. On the other hand, I had never experienced what he was experiencing now.

"Julie, maybe . . ." I started to say.

"Jonathan, could you excuse us for a moment."

She still had the keys to my car in her hand and I saw her opening her bag and putting them inside. Well, I thought, it looks like if I want to get my keys back and leave, I would have a fight in my hands.

Was she showing him that it was futile, or she just acted without thinking? Or was she showing *me* what was up? With women, we, men, are always behind the eight ball.

I saw the control she had and, in some humorous way, I understood it. I just hoped that Ham would also see the humorous side to the whole scene, as well. So I walked toward the building but sat on the stairs and waited. I could see them but I could not hear what they were saying. Both seemed to be in complete control of themselves.

They took a few steps away from the cars, but I could still see them. I do not think that Julie was trying to hide from me. They were facing each other. Ham's body language was rigid. From where I was sitting, there was no way for me to know what he was saying.

I could guess, of course. To beg a woman who does not want you hanging around is damn depressing and humiliating. I had seen guys in the Army when they got the "Dear John" letters. It was ugly.

Julie was also rigid, but much less than he was. At one time, he put his hand on her left arm, softly, gently, and she never recoiled from his touch. I now remembered that it was the guy I had seen in some of Julie's scrapbook photos.

Then, she touched his face, again, gently, like trying to give him comfort. But, can a woman give comfort to a guy she is essentially telling to get lost, that she wants nothing to do with him?

Rejection is such a bummer, really. Especially love's rejection. I did feel sorry for him. I thought that maybe I should not have been there to watch what was obviously an embarrassing and painful moment for him. And in another crazy way, it seemed that if I had to root for anybody I would root for him! Male natural bonding against the common enemy . . . the female of the species. I chuckled, softly.

Again, I had nothing to do with this situation, really. Though, if I had not shown up this scene probably would have eventually taken place anyway based on what Julie had said to me, but at least I would not have been there to witness it.

They stood still for a few more moments. Then, he took her hand and very gallantly kissed it, held it for a few moments, and then walked back to his car.

I could see that he was trying to hang on to his dignity. He got in then he got out, walked to the garage, brought the door down without slamming it, and closed it. He walked back to his car, got in, and drove away, slowly.

She waved at him. She stood watching him go. The image of me watching Emily drive away one early morning, long ago, suddenly flashed in my mind.

Julie walked to the back of my car, opened the trunk and took out her suitcase. I did not go join her. She walked toward the building. I took the suitcase from her, silently walked upstairs behind her, she opened the door and we got into the apartment.

"I think he understands," she said, quietly. She had a sad face.

"Can't be easy."

"It's not."

"Look," I said, "maybe you need to be alone for a while."

"Where would you go?"

"I can get me a motel, somewhere, I mean. . ."

"Jonathan, don't do this to me."

"Now, you are being difficult."

"I'm not. I told Ham I didn't want to hurt him, but that what he wanted was not possible, not now, not ever. That there were plenty of girls who deserved him. I wasn't one of them. I asked him to forgive me, but I needed to live my life the way I saw it. And he could never be part of it, other than as a wonderful friend. I know the truth hurt him, but it was best for both of us."

She went into the kitchen and drank some water.

"I told him that I loved him as the wonderful friend that he has been. At one time, he said that I had had sex with him not because I had wanted it but because maybe it had been a game with me. I told him that it wasn't true, but that it had not meant, at least for me, something that would continue."

"Do you think he'll bother you?"

"Not directly, he's more subtle than that. What he'll do is look for reinforcements to bear, bring in the artillery, the heavy guns, and maybe even call in the Calvary."

"And who would that be?"

"My mother for starts. She loves Ham. He has never been mean to her or to me for that matter. He was wonderful when my dad got killed. Really great. My sister likes him a lot. Once, jokingly, I suggested that he should go after Becky, but he responded that it would amount to some kind of incestuous thing."

"He said that?"

"Yeah," and she laughed softly, while reflecting on the word.

"I thought his closing the garage door was a bit melodramatic, but upon further reflection it did give him some kind of dignity. I mean, I thought."

"Yeah, he told me he had been waiting for a long while. He understood when he saw my car in the garage, then we drove up and he had talked to my mother earlier and she told him I was away in Myrtle Beach. Now he knows I was there with you, and I think things are going to become interesting shortly."

I did not believe she was taking the whole situation lightly, really. I did not believe that Julie was that kind of person. But it was obvious that neither she, nor I for that matter, had given any thought to something like this happening.

I guess she had not considered that Ham would show up at her place only to discover that something had changed, and now he found himself holding the short end of the stick. No pun intended here. I could see that Julie was trying to deal with the present situation as best as she could. It was not easy for her.

"Are you going to be in trouble with your mom?"

"Jonathan, I'm an adult now. I'm capable of making my own decisions. Have been making them for a while. It's now my life. It has been for a long time. She knows it and she also knows that interfering in my life isn't a good idea at all.

"I love and respect my mother, of course. She has been an amazing mother. She may not agree with my decisions, but she also knows better than to obstruct. It won't get her anywhere."

She walked over and gave me a hug. What she had said about her mother seemed normal and reasonable. Still, I was now the foreign element in the situation. The dynamics had changed. Parents and children. At least Julie was talking to her mother, whereas me—well, that is another story.

The phone rang. Julie gave me a knowing look before answering it; she walked over and picked it up.

"Hello, oh, hi, mom."

She put her hand over the mouthpiece and mouthed off the words—speaking of the devil.

She listened.

"Mom, it was inevitable. You know that I don't want to marry Ham. He has known this forever. I don't love him. I like him as a friend. I don't want to lie to him."

She listened some more. Then, she pointed to me and to the phone. She smiled. It is simply the old classic story between generations and children and parents. Her mother was obviously talking about me. So old Ham had gone to higher authorities to look for reinforcements, as Julie had said earlier.

"Mom, negative on that. Yes, of course, it has been years, yes, mom . . . mom, I understand. You and dad raised me to make my own decisions. You have always said that I had to live with my mistakes. I was to be responsible for my own actions, please . . . listen, can I call you back a little later with the status? OK, yes, of course mom, I love you."

She put the phone down. She took another drink.

"You sound like you're in the Army."

"I'm an Army brat. I told you. Words like: negative, downrange, CEO, TDY, old man, check with the brass, field of fire, check out your perimeter. I mean, come on."

She started to smile and I felt a little bit better. In the final analysis, we all have to deal with our own imponderables, every day. I considered that I had never had that kind of family problem in my own life. Man, life is sure screwy. She looked like a little kid having to now deal in a world of grownups. Not an easy thing to do.

"I told you that Ham would do his number. That was my mother, as if you couldn't tell. He told her about you. She was kind of upset, but now she wants to meet you."

"Oh, boy. Am I in trouble?"

"You had nothing to do with this. You just happened to come by. "

"Rather inconvenient time, for Ham," I interrupted her.

"Well, yes, but again, unless you planned for this whole thing to happen it's not really your concern."

"Are you sure? I mean, I don't want your mother to think of me as being some kind of carpetbagger, I mean spiritually speaking. A guy who just drops in, and plucks one of the most beautiful flowers in this whole South, and takes her with him to unknown destinations."

She walked over and put her arms around me.

"Oh, 'unknown destinations' I see. And would I be too insensitive or too inquisitive to ask just where these places might be?"

"Top secret."

"I know about top secrets."

"There you go."

"OK, what are your immediate plans, mister?"

"I don't know."

"OK, not to worry. I'm going to dust off all the operational plans that I had hatched back in the days and bring them up to date."

"Operational plans?"

"Lots."

"Did those plans involve me by any chance?"

"Not all of them—only about ninety-nine percent."

"Oh, I wasn't meeting one hundred per cent of the world's expectations, I gather."

"Well yes, but one has to consider contingencies where you hold something back in reserve in case, you know, to make sure your objective is obtained."

She was making fun of me because earlier I had said she sounded like she was in the Army. I was getting a kick out of her, and she was not above having some fun at my expense.

So, what are my plans? I did not have any. Yes, I was going back to the west coast, sell my car, and go to Paris. I had wanted to do it for a very long time. But I had never found or looked, for that matter, for the necessary energy to do it.

I procrastinated all of the time. At certain moments, I would think I had better get going, but the next thing I knew weeks, months, and years had passed and I was still procrastinating.

The phone rang again. She picked it up.

"Hello, oh, hi honey. How are you?"

She put her hand over the phone again, and whispered: Becky. She listened to her sister.

"Yes, of course. He did? And what did you say to him?" She listened some more.

"No, you know that's not true. He told you I would live to regret my imprudence? Boy, I thought Ham knew me better than that. What does he know? . . . who, Jonathan? Yes, he is here, you want to say hello? OK, let me put him on the phone."

And without any preamble, she handed me the phone. I hesitated, but took the phone from her.

"Hello?"

"Hi, Jonathan. Do you remember me?"

"Yes, Becky, pig tails, pretty dress, lovely smile. Of course, I remember you."

"I only met you once," Becky said.

"Really? I could have sworn it was more than that, come on."

"You probably are saying that just to make me feel good."

"Not true."

"So, how long are you going to be in town?"

Her question was not mean or obnoxious. I was a total stranger who had suddenly shown up out of nowhere and, like in any normal family, siblings do constitute the first line of defense against possible enemies.

"I don't know yet."

"Well, I hope we have a chance to visit before you leave." The accent was on the word "leave."

"Absolutely."

"OK, bye, and please pass me back to Julie."

"Bye, Becky, nice talking with you."

"Likewise."

She seemed to have a stronger Southern accent than Julie did.

I gave the phone back to Julie. She listened.

"Well, a little thin, longer hair, but otherwise the same," Julie looked at me, then back to the phone and listened. "Of course honey, yes, of course. Can I get back to you—need to work out the logistics. OK, bye, I love you."

She smiled as she put the phone down.

"I told you Ham would bring on reinforcements. She was curious to know if you still looked the same."

"Do I?"

"Like I told her, a little thinner, but not much changed. She wants to get together."

"I'd gathered that much. How old is she?"

"She's four years younger than me. She was twelve when you last saw her. She is now a lovely girl. Really has filled in the right places.

"Just like you. What does she do?"

"Works for a local bank. She wants to go to graduate school and study economics. She wants one day to head the World Bank. She's a whiz when it comes to numbers."

The world did not seem so nice and calm any more. I stood looking at Julie and wondering but not really wondering what was going through her pretty head.

"Would you like some coffee," she asked.

"That'd be great."

She started to prepare it. I looked at Julie and, once again, the thought of that young girl flashed in front of my eyes. Grownups, we sometimes do things in a sort of mechanical way. Automatic, especially when we are confronted with unhappy things. It is a way to push aside, at least for the moment, that which we do not wish to deal with at the precise instant.

We walked into the bedroom while the coffee was being made. The bed still unmade. She stood in the middle of the room as if looking for something; she knew what it was, but still had to come to terms with it.

Maybe it had to do with trying to understand where her life was leading her. We both sat on the bed. She looked at me trying to read what I was thinking. I really was not thinking about anything in particular.

Then she got up, walked to the closet, opened it, and took out a rather thick book. I knew what it was: Her diary. She came back to the bed and handed it to me. I did not take it from her. She looked at me and had a smile on her face. She put the book on the bed.

She was now going to make me share her life in a way that seemed to please her. She knew that I was not keen on the idea of reading her diary, but she had made up her mind and what I also sensed was that I had no other choice. It was the same Julie who had faced Ham earlier, but this time the opposite was taking place.

Julie was not rejecting me but making me an accomplice to who she was, to her dreams, to her life, to her destiny. I do not know how to fight her on this, I thought.

"Here it is, as I had promised you last night."

"Julie, please, you can't do this to me. This is your private domain. I have no desire to invade it. I told you that. Please, don't do this to me. I can't do it."

I got up from the bed and at that moment, I really wanted to grab my stuff, get in my car and keep going. I felt like she was making me an accessory in some kind of crime. I know it was stupid, but that is how I felt. She propped some pillows on the bed and lay holding on to them.

I looked at her and she had a look of tolerance, willing to deal with a recalcitrant person whom she knew would eventually come around to her point of view, as there was no other choice. How do women get away with this?

"Jonathan, everything that is written here is the truth, however ugly, and painful it was. I have never wanted to hide behind any kind of veil and pretend that what was happening around me I could ignore. Maybe in many instances, I didn't understand what was going on around me. But, everything in this diary is my life.

"I want you to read it. I want you to become my life's partner, my love, my destiny, and my future . . . everything. Please, you need to understand that I'm not making you into some kind of peeping Tom into my life.

"No, I belong to you, my love. I'm not ashamed of what you will find there. I have nothing to hide. My life is yours. Please don't be afraid that you'll discover in this narrative something ugly and unseemly about me.

"What I have become is, in some strange way, because of you. You don't have to read it now. You don't have to read the whole thing. You'd probably be mostly bored by it."

Julie was challenging and changing in front of me in such a way that I was not used to. That, in fact, had never occurred to me these past few days, hours, really. But there was no question that she was laying it on the line, and I was not prepared to deal with it.

I thought, old bud, you have been moonlighting in your life for too damn long. This might turn out to be your comeuppance. Get with the program or the train is going to leave you at the train station holding the bag.

"It is my long road," she continued. "My journey has brought me to be here with you. I don't know what the future holds for us. I don't know. I only wish it to be good, honest, wonderful, magical, full of fantasy; full of life, dreams, hopes, sex, laughter, love, tenderness, and no doubt tears . . . it's how all of us should try to live by.

"I'm not trying to set myself up as some kind of moral standard, higher than others around me. Or that if I let you read this, you have to view me as the most perfect specimen of a human being. No, I'm not seeking any tit for tat. I humbly ask you to discover me as life has made me.

"Not the most wonderful person there is. Not the most perfect woman that you'll ever meet. Not the most glorious human being that ever lived. I want you to see me as I see myself. Full of contradictions, fears, frustrations, angst, imperfect, full of warts, so lonely many times, but someone who loves you without any reticence.

"I'm not seeking for you to validate me in order for me to show you my moral superiority so that you will be prepared and less disappointed in me when the shit hits the fan, and you know and I know that it will."

Julie had never used any gross language in the last few days when we had been together. In fact, at one time, she said that though sometimes language needs to be colorful, and humorous, she always tried to find a different way to express what she saw and felt.

She had lived surrounded by soldiers, who in most moments of perhaps frustration used vulgar language as a matter of routine. The fact that others did, did not mean that she had to, also do it.

Dealing with others, and especially with complicated women is never easy. Sometimes, I think that we, men, would rather face an angry mob than deal with a woman who puts everything on the line the way Julie was now doing.

I was not sure if I were up to the task. I walked back to the bed and lay next to her, leaned over, held her close, and kissed her. So many hidden secrets in the human heart.

I took the diary from her and I felt like a doomed man. I had no idea why I had this strange feeling. It was most likely some kind of modesty on my part. Maybe it was false modesty; nevertheless, there it was. But it had more to do with her than with me.

I was still resisting the notion of reading her diary. It was something she had kept up for so many years and it did not seem right for me, even with her permission, to read it. Yet I wanted to do it, and I did not want to do it.

Suddenly, there was a knock on the front door. She looked at me wondering. I shrugged my shoulders. We both got up and we went to the front door. She opened it.

A man's voice.

"Miss Julie Douglas."

"Yes?"

Julie stepped aside and a guy walked in holding a beautiful bouquet of red roses inside a very expensive crystal-looking vase.

"Just put them on the table, thank you," she said.

I could see that she was really very surprised. She looked at me seeking some explanation as if I knew what was going on. I was just as surprised as she was, though it did not take a genius to guess who the sender of the flowers was.

The deliveryman put them on the table and extended a clipboard to Julie. She signed the receipt.

"Here, let me get you something for you troubles," she said, looking for her purse.

"It's all been taken care of, miss. Thank you."

He turned around, tipped his cap off to me and left. Julie closed the door.

"They are beautiful," I said.

"Yes, lovely."

She took the card off the flowers, opened the envelope and read it. She smiled and handed the card to me. I was not sure if I should look at it.

"You can read it. It's very nice."

The handwriting was solid. I read:

Dearest Julie:

You may not believe this, but I have always dreaded this moment when your past would catch up with us. I always hoped that your

313

destiny would be with me. But I also knew it was a crazy dream and in many ways stupid, but you cannot blame me for hanging on to it all of this time.

Even though I believe you're making a huge mistake, I do wish you the very best and please remain sure that if you ever need a friend, I will always be here.

Love,

Trevor

I handed the small card back to her. Her eyes were moist. I took her in my arms and she leaned onto me and was holding me tight.

"He knew about you. I never hid it. He didn't know all of the details but like me, I never thought that you would ever come back."

"Are you sad?"

"Yes, but not in the same way as when you left. I'm sad more for Ham than I am for me, obviously. I do care for him, but just not in the same way that I care for you. Life is so incomprehensible, isn't?"

"Yes. Tell me about it. I think he's a true son of the South with his manners even if he grows poison that kills people."

As she stood with the light of the afternoon filtering through the windows, I could understand how Julie had been able to play *Anne Frank, Antigone,* and *Lola*—three tough broads. I laughed. Not one of them would have appreciated such a description, I was sure. I laughed quietly at my daring to call them that.

Nevertheless, female characters who did not just fade away by the vicissitudes of life. They all faced it and dealt with it, within their means when confronted with what life had brought them. For some reason, the thought of my girlfriend in college came to me. I had not thought about Pamela for ages.

I did not know why the thought came to me at that instant. I often wondered what had become of her. This is weird, I thought. I am dealing with a complicated woman presently, have dealt with another complicated woman in a not too recent past: Emily.

And here I am thinking of Pamela, who from my memory was not tough, though, at the end of our relationship she had been the one to split. And here, once again, life was testing me as I was now contemplating getting further into a new relationship that was intriguing, mysterious, and maybe even dangerous.

Julie went back to the bedroom, I followed her. Again, she propped herself against the pillows and kept looking at me searching for my reaction to what she had said, to her giving me the diary, to the flowers being delivered, to everything happening to us.

Man, oh, man. I wish I could talk to Jackson and Cash about this.

Cash had made fun of me when he had told me that Julie had a crush on me. That crazy bastard! He never knew the level of discomfort that his words had produced in me. I had never shared anything about Julie with either him or Jackson. It would have brought me all kinds of grief.

"Why is it that my luck would always be to run into complex women? Why is that?" I said, to her.

"I'm not complex," and she smiled a look that said: That is the truth. Truth—right.

"No, of course, you're not. You're only the most levelheaded individual around. Clear, concise, focused, direct, smart, well organized, not a slacker, bright, well-educated, resourceful, great sense of humor. Able to look at life and its ridiculousness. Able to think for herself. Take command gal. No bull shitter.

"Has her masters and on her way to a Ph. D. in Renaissance Art. Calls them as she sees them. Sexy. Great ass, and fantastic looking legs. A body that won't quit. Knows what she wants and isn't afraid to go get it. Let's see, did I leave something out?"

"And totally, and ashamedly in love with Jonathan, don't forget that."

"Sorry, small detail."

"Small detail?"

"OK, big detail. I'm not used to dealing with your kind of woman. My fault."

"Mister, you have better get on with the program here. Times have changed. I'd counsel you that it's in your best interest to get to know this female specimen better."

I got on top of her and started kissing her and she responded.

"Haven't I made some progress along those lines?"

"Yes, my darling. I'd say that your efforts have been outstanding. But, like anything else in life, you can't rest on your laurels. This is for keeps."

The phone rang, again. Damned phone. She reached over and picked it up.

"Hello? Oh, hi mom, OK, OK, in one hour? Give me another extra thirty minutes. OK? You need anything, all right, see you then." She put the phone back on the night table.

"The commander-in-chief requests my presence."

"Bad news?"

"No, this is like the Douglas's War Council. All hands on deck. Becky's presence has also being requested."

"Boy, you have lived your life in the military."

"True. Though you must remember that with top down institutions there is always a way of dealing with the powers that be. You know, messages get misdirected, personnel is out to lunch, supplies get lost, orders get confused, stuff like that. We've got an extra half hour—now, where were we?"

And she started to undo my shirt.

Afterward, while she was in the bathroom, I put on the robe, went to the kitchen to get some coffee, stepped out on the balcony and looked at the pond in the distance. I could see some ducks gliding in the water.

She came out and was wearing tennis shorts, sneakers, a T-shirt, and no bra. Looking at her, I thought that if I had to play tennis against such a beautiful broad, my wicked serve would fail me miserably, as I would most probably spend my time looking at her ass and not paying attention to where the tennis ball would land.

The one thing I had noticed about Julie, was her almost innocent way of dressing. No, innocent is the wrong word. Studied carelessness would be the perfect term. Everything matched but not in a blatant way. The whole only added sexiness to her as a woman, and in many ways, it also managed to exude exquisite femininity and good taste.

"OK, here's my mother's phone number and address," and she handed me a piece of paper, "in case you go out and some extra-terrestrial hussy tries to kidnap you and wants to take you with her to unknown destinations. You can call for reinforcements. There is also an extra key to the apartment in the kitchen drawer, center drawer."

"How long will you be?"

"I don't know. Maybe a couple of hours or a bit less. On the boob tube, they are showing: *All about Eve*, tonight. I love the movie. I think Betty Davis is great in it, and Anne Baxter is so wickedly and deliciously evil. I don't want to miss it. Do you want some Chinese food? I can pick it up on the way back."

"They have Chinese restaurants here? I thought it was all meat and potatoes, greasy ribs, and stuff like that people eat around here."

"Times have changed, my love. It may come as a surprise to you but we have finally joined the world. Thank God."

"OK, *All about Eve*, Chinese food, and who knows wicked things may happen . . ."

"The night is long . . ."

She leaned over to kiss me. I kissed her and ran my hand over her lovely breast. She gave me a wonderful smile. Looked at me both with desire, and to some extent with a sexy tolerance.

"Will you miss me when I'm gone?"

"Nope."

"OK, be that way, see if I care."

She grabbed her purse, and out she went. I missed her already.

-XIX-

I waited two whole days before I started reading her diary. Those two days felt like I was in some kind of purgatory. I was afraid. I do not know why. She had insisted that I read it, but I still felt like some kind of intruder.

Her diary was as clear, intimate and as complex as Julie was herself, but sparse. I thought that Julie would be more detailed in what she wrote. The entries were not long or detailed. It was more like impressions.

I did not read it in its chronological order. I decided to open it at random. I really did not want to see the progression as much as wanting to catch Julie at different times unaware as it were.

I was not interested in the time sequence directly, as much as kind of dropping into one entry, or date, reading, and then continue leafing through the pages and read some other entry. I was not even sure that I would read the whole thing at all. I read when . . .

She had her first period. How magical and troubling the whole event was. The crushes she had over the years. She even had a crush on a girl, but it was not sexual or physical, she noted. It was that she looked at this girl—no name had been entered but an initial L., as someone so mature and so sophisticated that Julie felt like an ugly duckling and she wanted to imitate this girl.

Her greatest surprise and joy was to find out that I had selected her to play Anne Frank. Her first discovery of finding herself thinking about me. She was also delighted that Karen had also been selected. She thought that Karen was just a fine choice, but she also feared that she, Julie, was not good enough. She went to the library and read as much as she could on Anne Frank herself and WW II. She did not understand a lot of that history.

Her parents had come to see her do Antigone, in Ohio, early in 1968. They all reminisced about me. She was sad because of that for a few days. She wondered how I was doing? Was I warm? Did I remember her? Where was I? Then receiving the terrible news that her father had been killed in Vietnam at the end of 1968.

She only thought of her mother and of her sister and she wished to have spared them such pain and sorrow when her father had died. The details of her father's death were not clear. The phone call at school. Her sense of loss and pain. Her flight back to North Carolina. The long drive home from Raleigh with Trevor who had come to pick her up. She was grateful that her father had come to see her act in Antigone.

The funeral, the folding of the U.S. flag that was given to her mother. How empty the house had become and she heard her mother crying and so disconsolate.

She noted with tiny hearts around a page when she realized that she was falling in love with me. How she had found herself not wanting to understand what she was feeling because she did not want to believe that what she was feeling was true and real. She fought against it, but she also noted she had no will power. That it was stronger than anything she had ever felt.

The memory of when she kissed me when I last saw her. It was a sad, bitter, kiss that filled her with dread, sorrow, yet also with a feeling of happiness and well-being. The touch of her lips to mine would always remained fresh in her memory. She wondered if she ever kissed another boy, if that new kiss would erase what she was now feeling. She hoped that it would not. She would allow me to kiss her—everywhere! She would kiss me everywhere, even . . .

She had written the poem in her diary. It showed how she started it. How she struggled to find the right words that would describe what she felt. And even after she had finished it and gave it to me, she still thought that she had not done as good a job as she imagined she was capable of doing. She felt she had failed in her project. And even after I had told her that I loved the poem, her doubts were intense and overwhelming. She would go to California to try to find me.

In her senior year in college, in a kind of a lark, she had auditioned for Lola in the musical Damn Yankees, and had gotten the part. She understood Lola. She got to sing: "Whatever Lola Wants, Lola Gets," which brought the house down. Everyone said that she was great. The passage of the Civil Rights Act was not very welcome in the South, but she supported the effort.

And among her friends, the anger and disgust was palpable. Ham had been livid and, though she understood his anger, she was also saddened by the attitude he and his own family had expressed. She did not blame them, never called them racists, but she also tried to keep away from that subject-matter. It was not easy.

The death of both Bobby Kennedy and Martin Luther King Jr., had thrown her into panic and extreme sadness. She wondered about their families and how totally senseless it was that they had been killed by murderous and uncaring people. Her views of black people were complex and confused. She agreed that black people had a right to live normal lives like anybody else. On the other hand, she had no black friends and she accepted this state of affairs without much question.

She went to the library to investigate what Pete Seeger had done and why the government turned against him, after I had told her about Seeger. She was deeply disappointed that other kids had few ideas who this guy was. All they could say was that he was anti-American and a communist. She had argued that it was not true, but nobody believed her. For a while, she had been ostracized by her classmates. She also did some research on the ACLU and the NAACP.

After Anne Frank, she had always wanted to do another show but it did not happen. She had run into me and was disappointed that I may not be the one directing it. She loved me more than she thought possible or prudent.

She had read the play Hedda Gabler by Ibsen, and thought it was great play and she wondered if she could ever do it? But she thought no; unless, I would direct it as she trusted me to help her guide her.

The Democratic National Convention had kept her awake not because she considered herself a democrat; she was not. In fact, considered herself apolitical. It was that she felt totally helpless as to what she could do as a single citizen, seeing the chaos and madness of our political system.

The Beatles' music was a great discovery for her and she loved McCartney's songs, and her favorite was "Yesterday." She wondered how someone so young could write such wonderful lyrics and music.

She loved the madness of the famous quartet, and she thought it was ridiculous that people had broken long-playing albums when Lennon had said that they were more famous than Jesus was. She did not agree with what Lennon had said but she thought he had a right to say it.

Then one day, she found Trevor not quite crying but despondent. His father had been caught with one of the black maids in what she wrote: 'flagrant delict.' She could not console Trevor, who kept saying that he would prefer to die of shame than to face his father. And Trevor wondered about his mother, and what she would do because she knew what his father had done—sex is all men want.

It was all strange to her about a white man and a black woman "doing it." Her own quote. But, she also expressed what she called: Sick curiosity as to why this "event" had taken place. She thought of asking her mother, then her father, but in the end she thought best to keep quiet about it. Trevor was then sorry he had told her, but she promised him that she would never talk to anybody about it.

Trevor then had said that he "loved" her. And she agreed to consider what that meant. She was upset when the school administration was not keen on having black girls participate in a musical show she wanted to put together. She even threatened to quit. They relented, but things were not easy now between her and some of the other teachers. She would learn to cook just for me. She wanted to have all of my babies!

She worried about her sister for always acting silly, and not thinking before speaking. But in the end, she knew there was nothing to do. Becky was like that, period. Her mother was, of course, upset whenever Becky got into trouble. But she loved her sister also. So she questioned why she got angry with her sister. Her friends at school said that they also hated their siblings. It was not only natural but to be expected. Someone had said that little sisters were nice pets.

In college, she had stayed in the dorm for the first year and had had two roommates: Natasha and Wendy. Natasha came from Boston and was a rebel from way back. Smoked, swore like a sailor, was always wearing outlandish outfits and had lived in Europe for a couple of years. She was also on the pill. Apparently, her parents did not want a surprise so they had accepted that it was a practical

319

choice to allow her to do this. Julie thought of asking her parents about the pill, but thought it best to be careful about sex. The drug scene did not attract her so she kept away from it.

Natasha's father was a diplomat. Wendy came from Montana, grew up on a farm, with horses, and vast distances, was part of a large family and was, in contrast to Natasha, studious and serious. You could always count on her being on time, doing her homework on time, and lending a hand. Julie was intrigued, however, that of the two girls Wendy was the most promiscuous. Julie thought that it did not make any sense. She regretted she had not kept in touch with them at all after graduation.

She kept the diary under lock both at home and at school, where she was constantly making sure nobody had access to it. And nobody did. In her sophomore year, she found her own set of digs and was happy she no longer had to share bathrooms with anybody. It was then she acquired her first boyfriend. Anthony was a senior and was majoring in political science. Funny, smart, but a complete jerk of a republican. Totally committed to their philosophy.

Wendy introduced her to him. Natasha did not like him because of his political views. Natasha was a flaming liberal opposed to the Vietnam War, and it had led to some heavy clashes of will and political views in their all night discussions. In the end, Julie had decided that politics was not for her and she kept away from any point of view until her father got killed. From that moment on, she opposed the war.

She read, voraciously, the Greek plays about women because I had talked about them. She even thought to change her major to Classical Greek, especially after playing the role of Antigone. But, then, changed her mind. Her thoughts about the first time she had sex.

I must confess that already knowing about it, I was not that curious about what she had written. I had to laugh a bit because it occurred to me, that maybe that would be the entry she would ask me about later. Just to test me, to see if I had read the diary.

Her trip and stay in Italy. How marvelous the exposure to the culture was for her. Her discovery of amazingly long and rich Italian history and tradition. She struggled with the language at first, though she had taken an accelerated course before making the trip. And she was not afraid of making syntax mistakes. She wanted to take advantage of her visit as much as possible.

Then, when Ham had come to visit. It was a catastrophe! She preferred not to dwell on it. But she loved the openness of the Sargenti family with her from day one. And, of course, her shock at finding herself looking at Roberto's naked ass. At first, she was completely confused about it. But it did not take long to realize that it had more do with her presence.

Roberto had been the baby of the family, pampered, allowed all of his teenage caprices. Suddenly, his whole family seemed to be more interested in Julie, and she understood that Roberto resented it. She came up with the idea of calling him Bobby, when he walked around bare-ass, and that did the trick. She loved the whole family. And was mortified when she left to see Roberto, this mad half-man-child, begging her not to leave him. She adored Roberto!

She thought about me very often, especially during her lone walks around Florence. She thought I would love Florence. However, she had to accept that life was that way. She also felt terribly sad about me when she found out that Emily had died. She never told her mother what she had learned from Jackson about Emily and me. And she wished that she could meet me and talk to me, perhaps help me with my pain. She imagined how much pain I was in. She thought of her own pain when her father had died.

She had wanted to write postcards to me. Things she wanted to share with me. But, of course, she did not know where I was. So she only wrote that it was a good idea. At one time, she thought I was dead, which she recognized made things easier for her. She often thought that perhaps her mother should become interested in another relationship with a man. But was then ashamed that she thought about that. She felt guilty because she had loved her father so much.

She had kept up her dancing lessons and had become quite good at it. She loved the big band sounds. She had not kept up her singing, and she regretted it. But now dancing replaced her need to be creative. She missed me, and her little hearts on the margins of the pages appeared on many of them. They always had an arrow across them. And she would write: Sad, right next to the hearts.

She knew about Corby Johnston, a choreographer, and she had contacted him about helping her put on a final show for the school. He was game and she had been impressed with his artistic sensibilities. She loved learning about cooking from mama Sargenti. She missed them a lot. She wrote about the first time she wore a bra. It seemed strange to her.

It was not comfortable. Her mother had insisted that she buy a size larger than what she thought she should have. At first, she was embarrassed as she did not want to have big breasts. One day, she was caught without tampons when her period suddenly "showed up" as she put it. But one of the other girls at school had a spare and gave it to Julie. From that day on, she was careful to make sure she carried a couple of extra ones, especially when her period was near.

One day, she looked at herself in the mirror and decided that her breasts were nice looking, after all. She wondered how it would feel if I kissed and caressed them. She fantasized a lot about that. She now regretted having had sex with Ham. It happened during the senior prom dance night. It really did not mean to her what it meant to him.

Again, I skipped that part. I was not being prudish; it was that those details held no interest to me, as she had already told me about them.

Her curiosity also included the whole thing about "orgasm." Many girls talked about that and said that they have had "amazing ones," but she could also tell that it was less than candid. Most of them had no idea what they were talking about. She asked her father to show her how to fix brakes on cars. It was a whim on her part. Her father indulged her. Becky wanted no part in it.

She was surprised when she first heard the audience's reaction to The Diary of Anne Frank. It had never occurred to her that the reaction would be so positive. She and Karen were both shocked and giddy about it. She had watched Karen from backstage and she thought that Karen had done a better job. Though, everyone else, including me, told her it was not true. In the end, she had been happy with her performance.

The school integration had been traumatic even for her. She had not expected to be so confused about it, but she was. At one time, she even thought that black people might have been abusing the system. All of her friends had been dead set against it. She had accompanied Ham to a demonstration against the law that allowed black kids in school, and it had not been a pleasant event.

At one time, Ham accused her of "loving the niggers." In, fact, he even accused her of wanting to have sex—"to fuck the niggers"—she had written. They had a huge argument over his accusation. Eventually, they made up. Ham apologized for the words he used, but not for the idea behind them.

The rain and the seasons she looked forward to. She wondered if she should ask her sister about her own sexual "indiscretions" but decided against it. She framed a copy of the program for Anne Frank along with a poster of the Beatles. Religion was not as strong as she had hoped. And she tried to avoid it. She wondered what it would feel like to be married to me. But then decided that I was probably like a bee going from flower to flower. But, she still loved me.

She was scared of not being able to teach the kids anything of importance in her class. So she read voraciously. Ohio State was big, with lots of students, and some of them from foreign countries. This she found fascinating. She, then, changed majors from music to art. She complained that sometimes her diary entries were too long in between. She thought she would marry Ham, but did not look forward to it.

One day, she decided to tell him that she "had had an abortion," which was not true so he would not think of marrying her anymore, as he was religious. She thought it would be hysterical to tell him that, but understood that Ham did not have a sense of humor. And he would most probably end up demanding that they get married just so he could make a decent woman out of her!

The Vietnam War was hopeless and she decided that politics and religion were for the birds. She wondered if I had been killed in Vietnam. Did I remember her? Was I warm? Of course, in California the weather was always sunny.

She wondered about me and Emily making love, and was depressed for many days thinking about it. She missed her father a lot. His sense of humor, his gentleness, but she also wondered about him becoming a soldier. Soldiers kill people.

She was troubled by that idea for weeks and weeks, especially after her father died. How many people did he kill? The whole scene of Jack Ruby shooting Lee Oswald was beyond anything she imagined. She remembered John Kennedy, Junior, saluting his father as the casket went by. Some kids at school thought it was humorous. She found their attitude revolting.

After a while, I stopped reading, made myself another cup of coffee, and decided to call Jack. I had debated long and hard about calling him. But in the end, he was the only friend I had who could throw some light on the whole situation. He had known what had happened with Emily.

And, in fact, when I came back from the Army, I had stayed with him and his family sharing a bedroom with Red, his son. Great kid who was nuts about baseball. I had taken Red to a couple of baseball games in the past. I had not talked to Jack for a couple of months. He answered the phone.

"Jack, it's Jonathan."

"Hey, Nathan," he was the only one who had ever called me that. "What's going on buddy? I called your place in New York and the phone has been disconnected."

"Well, yeah I'm on my way back to California. I forwarded my mail to your house."

"OK, no problem."

"I finally decided to go to Paris."

"Good for you. So where are you?"

"Well, that's why I'm calling you . . ."

"You're not behind bars, are you?"

"No, not yet."

I had told him about my escapade with the MPs back in my Army days. I could tell that Jack, who knew me better than anybody, immediately knew that something was up. That bastard could read my voice like there was no tomorrow. He waited.

"Well, you see there is this girl . . ."

He busted out laughing.

"Greene, whenever you call me like this it has always to do with a girl. Man, the time I have spent talking with you about your women. If I had been a marriage counselor, I'd be sitting pretty with all of the dough I could have made from you!"

"Well, this thing is kind of different. I mean, totally unexpected. It's kind of freaking me out."

"So you call Uncle Jack and he'll make things clear for you."

"Jack, come on. This thing is really out of my range. I mean, you know what I mean, kind of complicated."

"Anything that has to do with women is always complicated. Do you want to give me the particulars about this girl? For starters, what's her name?"

"Julie."

"Why does that name ring a bell?"

"I might have talked to you about her."

He was silent and I told him the whole story. From when I had first met Julie while doing *Anne Frank*, back in 1964. To her declaration of her love for me when she was only sixteen years old. To the poem, she had written to me ten years ago. To having Cash and Jackson, he knew about them because I had often talked about them, making fun of me about Julie.

To the fact that Emily had also known about Julie because I had told her about Julie's crush on me. To the fact that Julie had written a poem and I had told Emily about that. And that Emily had thought that it was all innocent and lovely. To the fact that I had finally stopped to see where Emily and her baby had been buried. I told him they were both in the same grave.

"It was brutal, Jack."

"I can understand that. I'm glad you did it."

"You know, Julie knew about Emily. Which I didn't know she knew. One of my buddies, Jackson, told her about Emily and me. Julie spent her junior year in Florence. She's going back to get her Ph.D. in Renaissance Art, and wants me to go with her. She has also forced me to read the diary she has kept these long years . . . I'm reading it right now. She's working, and I'm at her place."

"What do you mean 'forced' you?"

"Well, she didn't put a gun to my head or anything like that. I just didn't seem to have any choice in the matter. I didn't want to do it. In fact, the reason why I'm calling you is that I'm now reading it. And it is just an amazing narrative of the things she has felt and thought, especially the things about me through all of these years. I'm floored and humbled that someone could have such strong feelings for me. It's disconcerting."

"Why?"

"Well, to tell you the truth, I don't know why."

"Nathan, are you by any chance related to some deity out there that is protecting your ass, while the rest of us only dream of the things that happen to you?"

"Jack, this is no joke."

"Who said it was? So what do you want from me?"

"You know I loved Emily. You told me not to hesitate when I talked to you about her that time. You thought it was just amazing what happened between us that night when I went to see her after her husband died, and everything that came later. And she died on me, Jack. She and the baby died on me. This fucking, piece of shit life took them away from me . . ."

I stopped. The whole situation was a total insane. I started to choke. Why could I not have a simple life?

"I drove by her town and met her kid brother. And it was mighty tough. Man, oh, man. Since the day when I learned Emily had died, I've been a fucking mess. I total wreck, emotionally, spiritually, and morally. A total mental wreck! You've seen me, Jack.

"Now I'm confronted with Julie, this beautiful, funny, innocent, amazing girl. No, young woman. Totally committed to me. To my happiness, and my fear is that I won't be able to reciprocate her feelings. That I'm still wondering around in this sick hell of mine not completely out of it, really."

"Are you afraid that the memories of Emily are going to screw up your new situation?"

"Yes."

"It's understandable."

"But what I wanted to tell you is that Emily's memory has been receding from my head, from my heart, and I feel guilty about it. I feel as if I'm letting her down. I feel as if I'm betraying her. I feel like a piece of shit really because I think of her less, and think about Julie more."

"Take it easy, buddy."

"I saw Emily's grave. As I've said, she's buried with her baby. It was one of the loneliest, emptiest, and saddest feelings I have encountered. And as you know, I've had my share of them. I wanted so much to feel something, something more and I didn't. The whole experience revealed nothing new to me. People, died, that's all."

"No surprise there."

"Emily had been working on a painting back then and I was able to talk her out of destroying it, which she wanted to do. She later told me, she had found something in it, and was glad I had kept her from destroying it. I was kind of shocked when her brother gave it to me. I could never have imagined that I would end up with the painting. I didn't want to take it, but Billy insisted. I showed it to Julie and she was impressed by it. She really meant it."

"Women painters. They're not that many."

"That's what Julie said. The painting is great. I was with Emily one afternoon while she was working on it . . ."

I stopped. Man, what was I trying to prove? What?

Jack knew I was really struggling with all of the stuff that I was confronting, that I had been confronting all of these years. He had had a first row seat to the whole circus of my life.

"So how did you end up in North Carolina?"

"I don't know. I don't know."

"Hell, you must have had some idea, however crazy, to drive into North Carolina after all of these years, and have all of this happen to you. It had to have crossed your mind."

"It didn't. I swear to you it didn't. I mean, after I saw where Emily and her baby were buried, I just kept on driving. I have no idea what drove me here and not even what prompted me to try to find Julie. It was just out of the blue that I asked some kid at Fort Bragg's playhouse if he knew about Julie. And bigger than hell, she is living here. I'm calling you from her place. I had no idea that I would find her. I wasn't looking for her. I didn't come back to look for her.

"She went to Ohio State and spent her junior year in Italy. She told me that after she graduated she came back here to be close to her mother and her sister. Her father was killed in Vietnam. She's going back to Italy in the fall to Bologna to be exact. She has a Guggenheim Grant to finish her Ph. D. Listen, had you said to me that I would find myself here and calling you from her place, after ten years, I would have called you a totally ignorant and crazy man. I would have."

"Bologna has a great university. Good choice. You could go there and perhaps learn a few things."

"Julie argues that."

"How old is she, again?"

"Twenty-six."

"Julie has loved you since she was sixteen years old?"

"That's what she says and I believe her."

"You're a lucky bastard do you know that. I don't know of anybody, I mean nobody, that could find himself loved by two great broads. Where do you find these women? To what deity do you pray so you can find these women?"

"Man, I don't pray to anybody."

"Well, it seems that Aphrodite loves your ass, but Athena ain't too keen on you. In either case, don't piss them Goddesses off at the same time."

"OK, but what about Emily?"

"What about her?"

"You know I loved her. You know . . ."

"Let me stop you right there. I hate to be the bearer of sad news for you, Nathan, but Emily is dead. She has been dead for ten long years! You've been through hell. It was an immense tragedy in your life. Would not wish it on anybody not even my worst enemies and you know I've got a few of those.

"But if I know anything about the Emily that you described to me and loved you, and if she could communicate with you from the other side, she'd probably be mighty be pissed at you for not understanding what's going on now . . . she would not allow any crap from you, old buddy."

Jack was right. Cash was right. Jackson was right. The pricks. Who in the hell do they think they are? Who?

"What does Julie do?"

"She teaches art history and dance at the high school. In fact, when I told her about you and that you're a teacher and not a 'professor', she said she wanted to come to California so you can coach her on a few pointers about teaching."

"Shit, she could probably teach *me* a few things based on what you've said about her. Is she coming with you?"

I let that question hang in midair.

And that was the crux of the matter. In a way, that was the reason I was calling Jack. Not that I wanted him to make the decision for me. He was the only friend I had left around and I had nobody else that I could talk to.

"I don't know, man, I don't know."

"Do you need any money?"

"No, it's not that."

"OK, I understand, even though I don't understand you. But it is your decision that will count and not what I think, and not even what Julie wants."

"I guess not."

326

"So, again, what do you want me to 'suggest' to you, shall we say?"

"I don't know. I want to be free again, and to be able to love again. I don't want to feel his emptiness in my heart, my guts, my soul, anymore. I don't think I deserved what I got. Nobody needs to go through the shit I've been through.

"I'm not in love with Julie, not yet anyway. I do like her a lot, I mean a lot, always have. Though, I have never been in love with her, I want to be and perhaps with time I will be. In the meantime, Julie argues that her love is big enough for both of us for now."

"Wow. You know, Greene, there ain't too many broads like the one you are now describing to me. Emily came from the same mold. I don't know where in the hell these women come from. And I hear all of the time they are not around anymore. Not true. Not true. They are there and if you're lucky enough to end up with one you had better hang on to her."

He had said the same thing to me before regarding Emily. The fact is there was a special link—a cosmic link—call it what you will, between Julie and Emily. I did not understand it, but it was there. Maybe Jack was right and I had some deity looking after my sorry ass, after all.

"But Jack, what if something bad happens? Like Julie gets pregnant and dies during childbirth, man . . ."

"Stop right there. You have no grounds to think that way. None whatsoever."

"It did happen to me before, man. It did. Why should I not be afraid of that?"

"You're right, but you are making it impossible for you to have a life. Come on."

"Jack, I never thought that I would lose Emily. Not in a trillion fucking years would it have occurred to me. Yet, I ended up losing her and the baby. I was going to be a father, remember?"

"Nathan, listen, if you want to drive yourself crazy there isn't a damn thing I can do or tell you that will make your life any better, simpler. I wish I could tell what the future holds, but I can't."

"Shit, people I have loved have died on me. Man, the only one who has not gone is you, and . . ."

"I've got news for you, old buddy. I'm such an ornery bastard that I'm going to be around for a long time. The Man upstairs don't want my ass showing up and messing things up for Him."

And he laughed.

Jack was never a religious guy. He was pretty lucid about it. Yet, I also knew that Jack had been raised Catholic, that his wife was also Catholic, that there were times when religion was not far from his spirit. I loved this guy. He was a crazy man, but I loved him! The same way I had loved Cash and Jackson.

"Man, I'm not ready for this."

"Ready for what?"

"To take up with Julie and stuff."

"Greene, it's your choice. But let me remind you that for the last ten years your life has stood still. You put it on hold. You have been here, there, nowhere, and everywhere, not only in actual physical terms, as you are fond of pointing out how many miles you've put on that car of yours, but also in your heart and spirit.

"Now, something has come up and it scares the hell out of you. You can't ignore it. And from Julie's point of view, she is serious and she is real. So all of your wonderings have come to a halt and you're scared. You can't fathom that your life could change. I hate to tell you this, but you don't owe anything to Emily. Nothing!

"I'm almost sure she would tell you the same thing. Your life is here, now, not in the dark past that has enveloped you and invaded your heart and soul. It's about time that the beauty of life and love comes back to occupy your heart, once again.

"You need to open up that vault of yours, where you've ensconced yourself and air it out. You cannot recoup the wonderful feelings you had for Emily and what she then represented to you. Cannot be done.

"On the other hand, the sources of those feelings have not disappeared from your existence. They have just simply been put aside and now Julie shows up and they are forcing you to unearth them.

"Yes, it is the time to dust them feelings and emotions, to clean them, make them shiny and whole as they once were and put them to their proper use. If you sit by and wait and wait and wait, you'll find yourself getting deeper and deeper in this black shitty hole of yours that you always talk about.

"Nothing will ever replace what you felt for Emily. But, on the other hand, nothing can exist that will deny what Julie feels for you. She may end up telling you to go jump in the lake, and she would be right and it will be your loss.

"Nobody can force you to have or to even develop feelings for her. Though, based on what you've said, you ain't neutral about her. She will not replace Emily. She knows that. I'm sure she does not want to replace Emily!

"And, again, I'm sure Emily would be horrified to think, that is what you intend to do. She'd tell you it is phony, crass, and dishonest, not worthy of you. Julie does not deserve that and you would be unworthy of her. You need to know that. But by the same token, Emily cannot continue to rule your life.

"She is gone. She loved you. You loved her. And that's that. But Julie is now. She's not a fantasy. She is real. She is present, and she loves your ass. And that my friend is worth a lot for all of the misery you've been through these past long years. Don't blow it."

We talked about a few other things and I promised to keep in touch with him before hanging up. I went back to browsing through her diary. The writing was neat, clean, cursive style. I could see that she had re-read her entries because there would be underlining in some of them, and notes to the side to refer back to an earlier entry. Her last entry was about me. *It simply said: Jonathan is back!*

The next thing I knew, there was Julie coming into the apartment. I was surprised and also wondered if she was coming back to check if I were still there. Stupid, thought, really. She had not asked me if I had started reading her diary. She knew she had me over the barrel and was probably getting a kick of seeing me squirm.

"Are you checking up on me?"

"Yes."

"That's what I thought."

"Boy, your ego is larger than all of my Italian brothers put together."

She came and sat on my lap and embraced me.

"I missed you." I said.

"Really?"

"Yes. From here to the end of the galaxy."

"Wow, that big, ah?"

"Yes, that big. But what are you doing here. Aren't you supposed to be working?"

"Lunch hour. Besides, I need to take my dirty laundry and go by my mother's and put it in the machine. I didn't take it Sunday when I went to the Douglas powwow."

"Your mother does your laundry?"

"No. I do it. I put it in the washing machine, it runs, and then, I come back, later, hang it out in the yard, the way the Italians dry their laundry, and my mother eventually takes it into the house, leaves it in the basket. I come by later, fold the stuff, have a cup of coffee and we talk. It's nice. Do you need to do some laundry?"

"Yes, but I can go to the Laundromat and take care of it."

"Why?"

"Well, I mean . . ."

"No."

"Julie, come on don't you think that . . ."

She interrupted and looked at me as if I was some kind of idiot who was behind the times.

"Jonathan, I will do your laundry. My mother won't do it if that's what worrying you. No, this is my job. She'll understand. I usually go early in the morning to drop the stuff before going to work, but it seems my schedule got thrown off, for some reason, this morning . . ."

"Yes, for some 'reason'."

"I'm going to have to re-think some things." She laughed and hugged me. "Besides, you re-retouched my nails with red so it's only fair that I pay you in kind. We can make a deal: I do your laundry, you do my nails."

"I don't know. Doing your nails requires some deep concentration and certain artistic sensibilities. Doing the laundry is pretty much a mechanical task. I feel that I'm getting cheated here."

"Well, there will be other 'things' that will come into play."

"Really?"

"Oh, yes."

Yes, to everything. Right. I had woken up with an erection that would not quit. Julie saw it, and she simply suggested that we should not let it go to waste. And we did not.

"Something else, too, I'm going to be coming home late today and for the next three days."

"What's going on? You're going back to your wicked ways. You don't care for me anymore?"

"I care for you more than you will ever know. OK, I've been putting together a dance show with the kids you saw the other day. It is the last show of the school year. And this is our last week of classes. It's my last project as a teacher. We've been rehearsing and rehearsing and now we are putting on the last touches. Of course, I was absent for two days—apparently I was ill. Do you know anything about that?"

"Well, I heard rumors, but you know how it is."

"I think so. Anyway, this coming Saturday evening is the show. The kids are all excited and terrified. I think they'll do great. So you can well imagine the level of excitement. Also, they had wanted me to do a couple of dance numbers and I foolishly agreed. I can't let them down."

"OK."

"Will you come to see the show?"

"You mean, living with you and stuff for another five days."

"Yes, and stuff."

"OK, I will sacrifice myself."

"I was afraid you'd say no, and tell me that you'd be on your way back to Los Angeles within the next few hours."

"I did consider it."

"Jonathan, what am I going to do with you? OK, I don't want you to come to the rehearsals. I want you to see the actual performance, what the kids and I have done. You won't be so bored here in this apartment in the meantime, will you?"

"I'll stay in bed for the next few days."

"In bed, without me?"

"You're too damn busy."

"Oh, you're right—my lousy luck."

"When you see your mom next, will you be talking about *the* dinner last night?"

"I won't have time, but I'm sure a complete debriefing will be presented to the troops later in the week."

Army lingo was never very far from Julie's vocabulary, which always made me laugh.

We had been to her mother's house the night before for dinner. The dinner had been scheduled when the Douglas's War Council had been called into session Sunday evening—Julie and Becky had been summoned.

"Maybe I should have gotten a motel or something," I said, as we were getting ready to go to her mother's house.

"Why?"

"Julie, don't you think that we're playing with fire here when it comes to me staying here and having to face your mother tonight?"

"I hate to tell you, mister, but the cat's out of the bag. What do you suppose my mother and my sister have imagined we were doing in Myrtle Beach at night or even in the day time? Looking at the waves and collecting sea shells?"

"OK, but I do feel awkward about it. In fact, awkward is really a mild term."

"Should have thought of that before don't you think?"

"I don't want to appear to have a cavalier attitude about this whole thing that's all."

"Again, what's to be done?"

"Look, try to see it from my point of view. I come here, find you as beautiful as ever. I end up with, well, in—flagrant delict, with you."

"You mean sharing some bodily fluids," and she let out a laugh filled with total freedom. No hang-ups with her that's for sure.

"Julie, that's . . ."

"Sorry, yes, that's a bit crass, but that's what Becky would say."

"Yeah, you and your sister are something else."

I started to laugh seeing that the whole thing did have its comical side. Still, how many mothers would appreciate their unmarried daughters doing, well, doing things that in the scheme of things were not exactly kosher.

" 'Exchanging bodily fluids'. Does Becky really say that?"

"You don't know my little sister. She's fearless. You think that I'm bad. You haven't been around Becky at all. She will say whatever comes into her mind and if you're not comfortable with that, that is your problem."

"Is she likely to come up with something tonight?"

"OK, I'll have a talk with her. She owes me one. But I'm not promising you anything. Just be prepared."

Prepared for what? How in the hell can I be prepared? How? It was too ridiculous to even contemplate it in a normal situation. And this was sure as hell not normal.

I had not asked her about the result of the previous visit to her mother, about the "War Council" as she called it. I understood that family matters are private affairs, and I was not family. It all seemed unreal and too damn easy, as I thought back of my previous life. I was simply preparing myself for when the other shoe dropped. I was in a survival mode when it came right down to it.

Julie was getting dressed. She looked splendid. She was sitting on the bed and putting on her panty hose. I stood by the side of the bed and looked at this most lovely and sexiest of females to come along in my life for a long time.

I moved over to her, pushed her back on the bed, and got on top of her. She was game. And soon her panty hose were coming off as fast as I could peel them off her without tearing them up, and my other concern was not her mother or her sister, anymore, but how fast I could step out of my shorts.

Boy, oh, boy. I was praying that Mrs. Douglas would be thinking about other things and not wondering about what her daughter and I might be doing.

We ended up laughing after it was over. When you make love in such a hurried manner, it always strikes me as more for the humor than because it happens so fast.

"What if I just stay here and not go?"

"Negative."

"Why?"

"I promised my mother that I would bring you with me, and that's exactly what the operational plan calls for." And she laughed.

"OK, let's say that your father were still around: Would we do this?"

"Probably not. But, here's the thing: My father is not around. So get on with the program, get dressed and let's go. We don't want to be late."

"Where in the hell did you come from, anyway?"

"Who knows? But you need to understand that I won't hide my love for you. I did it for many years and it wasn't easy. Now I don't have to pretend anymore. You have come back into my life; thus, *ergo e finito* with pretending."

Julie was now dressed very elegantly. She was wearing high heels, a black dress, with those spaghetti straps, very chic, that clung to her. Her rich, radiant, loose mane cascaded down her naked shoulders. Again, she was not wearing a bra. Her lovely breasts sort of stood at attention pointing outward. I thought of what I had read in her diary about her breasts.

How do some women manage to have such dexterity with their breast muscles? We, guys, are always marveling at how they do it. The way she was dressed, it seemed like we were going to the opera. But do you go to the opera wearing no bra?

Forget the opera. We were going to be collectively interviewed for the position. The Army would call it: Passing muster. It was more like a torture chamber for me. Julie did not say anything as to how I should dress.

I did forego my regular jeans and tried to make myself presentable by wearing the only decent pair of pants I had with me, and a nice set of cowboy boots that always impressed other males, even rednecks, whenever I wore them. Jeans were my lifeline but they would not do for tonight.

"How should I dress?"

"Anyway you like."

I had with me a rather nice corduroy jacket that I had not worn for a while. I had taken it out of my suitcase and it was hanging in Julie's closet. I put it on and I could see a smile of approval on her face.

Hey, I was hoping that only one of my knees would get busted during the evening, and also hoping that my other functioning kidney would be spared.

"Very handsome," she said.

"Julie you look beautiful. So how are you going to cook without getting tomato sauce, cheese, flour, onions, and garlic all over your dress?"

"Not to worry. Mama Sargenti showed me how to do it, and my mother has all of the aprons necessary to protect this dress. Do you like it?"

"It's so lovely. I like it not only because it fits you so great, but you're not wearing a bra."

"Oh, you've noticed?"

Only a blind man would not notice it. And I was not blind.

-XX-

Mother and sister were waiting for us. Both women were wearing very chic clothes. Becky was also wearing high heels. In fact, all three women were wearing high heels. There was a kind of formality about the whole scene, but not overwhelmingly so.

I did, however, feel as if I were going in front of a court martial hearing. Julie had made that comment before we got there. I had insisted that we—that is to say, I—buy flowers for her mother. I wanted to buy some wine, but she said that her mother had already done it.

"I'm impressed," Julie said, and kissed me.

"Well, I don't want to appear to be some kind of philistine."

"You're not."

The house was very comfortable. Nothing extra fancy, but stuff with good taste. For an instant, I imagined little Julie growing up here. There was a large back yard. A flower garden. Her mother was pretty much as I remembered her. Still attractive. Her hair, however, was nearly all gray, which gave her a distinguished look.

She gave me a nice smile, polite, and shook my hand. I wanted to embrace her but decided not to. I wondered if her charm was just a mask. I did not know her. So I had to keep looking for that extra tick that would tell me things were not what they appeared to be.

"Thank you for the lovely flowers. It's very thoughtful of you."

"You're welcome."

She took the flowers, went into the kitchen, found a vase, put them in some water and brought them back into the living room. Becky was a little more reserved. She was a very good looking girl. There was a kind of guarded attitude about her, however.

She was measuring me, no doubt about it. She gave me a great smile, and it was not phony. I was somewhat relieved. We also shook hands. Looking at the three women, I could see the genes had not done a lousy job.

"Mrs. Douglas, I can see where both Julie and Becky get their great looks. You brought two lovely daughters into this world."

Looking for brownie points are you, asshole? Yes, damn it, I am. I need them in the worst possible way.

"Well, thank you very much," Julie's mother said.

I could see she was touched by both the flowers and the compliment. We all laughed. The three women were a bit embarrassed. Julie held my hand. The questions would not take long to come, I thought.

I could sense that Julie had most probably briefed them as to how far or deep to go. We were all doing this strange version of the *dance macabre* to keep from stepping on each other's sensibilities. Not easy. I had to be on my guard. I could not afford to make a *faux pas*.

We all reminisced about the play, *Anne Frank*, for that was what had brought us all together in the first place. I glanced at Julie, and she had a most radiant look on her face. It was almost as if she had imagined this scene and now that it was taking place, she could not contain her happiness and well-being; she could not believe it was actually happening.

I also noticed that mother and sister, seeing how elated Julie was, were intrigued, and also seemed to be willing to share in the feelings that Julie was obviously showing, at least for the evening.

My original fear was slowly giving way to also wanting to be part of the scene. Becky and Mrs. Douglas were doing everything in their power not to be churlish or exclusionary. If anyone was not feeling human and real, it was yours truly.

"Mom, did you buy what I've asked you to?" Julie asked.

"Yes, honey. Everything you gave me on that list I was able to find."

"*Pasta, a la Sargenti*," Becky said. "You always keep promising to teach me how to do it, but you never do."

"OK, this is as good a time as any. Come on, let's get started."

Both women got up and went into the kitchen.

"Do you need any help?" Mrs. Douglas asked.

"No, mom," Julie answered. "Just sit there and visit with Jonathan, I'm sure you guys have plenty of memories to talk about . . ."

If this was the signal for the daughters to leave their mother and me to ourselves, it sure as hell could not be otherwise. I guess it was time to present arms, salute smartly, and go capture the hill. I laughed to myself.

Both of us sat, awkwardly, in silence for a few moments.

"Let me show you where Julie and Becky wanted to dig up half of the garden to make a pool when they were kids," their mother said, suddenly. She stood up. I did the same. Classy, lady, I thought.

Becky walked back into the living room carrying two glasses of red wine. She handed one to her mother and the other to me.

"Thank you, honey," her mother said.

"Thank you," I said.

Holding our wine glasses, I followed Mrs. Douglas out of the door. It was a great evening, not too humid, and the sun was now on its last phase before going to sleep. We walked to the end of the yard and stood watching the sunset. She pointed out to a place at the end of the yard where you could still see remnants of a hole in the ground.

"They drove their father crazy. Of course, we ended up buying them one of those plastic, portable pools. I think they saw that it was more practical than trying to dig a hole here."

"Yes, I can see that."

"May I be frank with you, Jonathan?" She said, after a long pause.

Not surprising to think that the source of Julie's directness was standing in front of me. Here it comes, I thought. *OK, Mrs. Douglas, let us lay the cards out on the table and let us take our best shot.*

"Of course."

"I love my daughter with the pride that only a mother can have for a child that has demonstrated time and again that she's a unique, and an amazing human being."

"I'd like to think that you had a lot to do with that."

"Thank you. It's lovely of you to say that."

My compliment took her a bit by surprise. But it was obvious that we were fencing, sparring, thrusting, around the other. Not necessarily trying to injure or offend the other, but more like establishing our perimeters. Again, I laughed internally thinking that Julie would have been pleased to have me think Army. Cash and Jackson would have appreciated it, I thought.

"Sunday night when she came by to the 'Douglas's War Council'—oh, I know what these children of mine say about meeting with me—and suggested we get together tonight, I must confess that I had never seen or heard Julie sound so positive, so happy, so relaxed, so full of life, in such a long time. So in tune with her feelings, thoughts, ideas. Filled with enthusiasm and tenderness. Looking to a great and wonderful future.

"And I must also add, upon further reflection, that most if not all of that has to do with you being here. She's always been the dreamer. The one who could go to her room and I would not hear from her. I thought of her as this little mouse just quietly thinking of things, trying to unravel the mystery of her life, her feelings, and her emotions. She has always been very direct about them."

"I have experienced that part of her already."

"I'm sure you have."

She laughed and I could sense that the awkwardness of the earlier moments was slowly giving way to a more relaxed attitude. Maybe it was the wine.

"She has always lived in her own world, full of fantasy, and to some extent a bit mysterious. I think that she got that from her father. . ."

She stopped, looked at the sunset, drank some wine, and looked back at me. Her look was both painful and serious.

I looked back to the house. Through the glass door, I could see Julie and Becky busy with the preparations, drinking wine, whispering to each other, looking in our direction, and giggling. They were both now wearing white aprons. I wondered what secrets they were sharing and what crazy ideas they were discussing. Did Julie collect her debt and tell Becky to be cool?

I was apprehensive thinking that Becky might later decide to lower the boom on me. Julie had once mentioned something about a new boyfriend Becky had, though not a tennis player, but he was not joining us. So tonight, it was only the Douglas firing squad and me standing in front of it. Again, it was Julie who had said it.

"But I love you," Julie had added. "And that is enough armor to keep you protected and safe."

"I guess, what I'm trying to say is: What are your plans?" Her mother, continued.

Boy, no ambiguity about her concern; cut to the chase.

"Mrs. Douglas, I don't know exactly how to answer you. My life these past long years has been something that I don't wish on anybody. I was in love with a lovely woman and she died—yes, she died in childbirth along with her baby—it was not my child. So many years ago.

"I understand from what Julie told me that you had accidentally found out about Emily. I was in Vietnam when I received the tragic news. Since that time, my life has been this dark world where pain and misery had reigned and controlled so much of who I am . . ."

I stopped.

What in the name of hell was I doing explaining deep and intimate sentiments to a total stranger? Yes, she was Julie's mother, but she was not my mother. She was nothing to me.

"Now that you mention it, yes. I did find out about a young woman who had lost her husband in Vietnam. And who went back to live in her hometown and who had eventually died in childbirth along with her new born. I shared the news with Julie, but what you now are telling me comes as a total surprise to me."

"Yes, that was Emily."

"I'm so sorry about your loss," she said.

She was looking at me now in a different way.

"I hope that we keep this conversation between ourselves," I said.

She touched my arm and smiled.

"Not to worry. It's done!"

"Thank you."

She had a different look in her eyes now. Maybe what I had just revealed to her, showed that I was not just another ordinary schmuck who had sprung out of nowhere. Now, both of us were sharing deep, painful, family secrets that would remain sealed in our hearts until we died.

"I know about your personal loss. Julie told me about losing her father, your husband. I'm sorry, too."

"It seems that we are both bound by immense tragedies and losses," she said.

"You might remember two guys who helped with the *Anne Frank* play, Cash and Jackson. I, well, I lost both of them in Vietnam within a matter of seconds."

And I suddenly began to feel lousy, again. She saw it in my eyes and, in that instant, I felt that something had changed between the two of us. I do not know if the tragedies of our mutual loses had done the trick, but the heaviness of the previous moments did seem to be less menacing.

"I understand. I also have lost many dear friends. It's a constant emptiness in my heart, I must admit."

What ties people together? Their common experiences? Their common pain? Their common humanness, their common hate of others? What?

"Now, through some kind of miracle I'm here with Julie and I don't really understand what is happening, or why. I didn't come back looking for her. If I told you otherwise it would be the boldest lie that you have ever heard.

"I had no idea I would find her here. It had never occurred to me. It was only when I went by the playhouse at Bragg that I saw the poster from *Anne Frank*, and there was Julie's name staring back at me.

"I asked the kid at the office if he knew anything about Julie. And I was so surprised, shocked, actually, when I discovered she was still living here. But it was a question, I hate to say this, a gratuitous question to him because I had no idea I would find her."

"I do appreciate your candidness, Jonathan. I have always known about Julie's feelings for you. Her father also knew. We went to see her do the role of *Antigone* in Ohio, and we talked of *Anne Frank*, and of you, of course. I saw Julie's face, and I understood. After all mothers know things about their children that children think we don't know. But we do.

"And I have never read her diary. I had always thought it was just a passing fancy, something that happens to all of us at such an early age. I also know that Julie has suffered a lot for those feelings she had for you.

"It isn't easy for a parent to know that a child is suffering and there isn't a damn thing you can do about it. I remember the crush I once had on Mark, a boy in my freshman year in high school. You see, I still remember his name."

She laughed a rich, deep, laugh. I guessed the source of Julie's own laugh.

"Jonathan, you knew about her feelings didn't you?"

"Yes, but believe me I did nothing to encourage them. I couldn't."

"I believe you. Julie never told me about them, but I knew."

"You have no idea how uncomfortable I was. I was in a panic, actually. But I must also tell you that I was flattered very much so. I mean, here was this lovely, young, innocent, beauty, telling me to my face what she felt. I really didn't know what to say or how to act. It has also been my precious secret all along."

"But now you are back, and you seem to have caused a bit of a revolution in our neighborhood."

It was obvious that she was referring to Ham. How should I handle that? What can I say? What should I say: Tough shit for Ham. However, in the final analysis it really was not any of my damn business. She could see that it was not a comfortable position for me, nevertheless.

"But you needn't be concerned. It's Julie's decision to make and you shouldn't feel guilty about it."

"I don't."

"Good. You know, we raised our daughters to become responsible adults. We taught them that whatever decision they made, once they became adults, they had to live with the consequences. Yes, times have changed in our world today.

"We see it around us all of the time. The things that young people, especially young women have to contend with, can be overwhelming. But I have no reproach to make for either one of my daughters."

Was she referring to the new and more open sexual attitudes, to a bit more tolerance regarding those matters. To Myrtle Beach, perhaps? She was looking directly at me. She was challenging me and I held her look. It was not easy. She was a classy lady, all right.

"She wants me to go with her to Italy. Should I go?"

She started to laugh. This was not the reaction I expected. But to be fair, I had no idea what to expect. My question had just popped into my head. I was even surprised, I had asked it.

"Jonathan, I'm flattered you ask for my opinion. I mean, I'm after all the mother of this lovely, mad, enchanting young woman, but I'm afraid I'm biased and it wouldn't be proper for me to tell you what to do. But why do you ask?"

"You are much wiser than me and . . . I don't know. I'm sorry."

"Don't be. But if I know anything about Julie, I'd only counsel you not to bet against her."

And she gave me the loveliest smile that I had seen on her face tonight. I guess her words were sealing something. My fate? My destiny? My past? I thought that this was the strangest conversation I have ever had in my whole stinking life. What did it all mean?

"Jonathan, do you love her?"

That, briefly, was the crux of the matter. She was confronting me with the core of the whole situation. I could lie or spout bullshit, or I could tell her the truth as it stood. Take your pick, old buddy, as Jack would say it.

"Before I answer that. May I share something with you that I have never told anyone. I think you as a woman would understand it."

"I hope you're not going to ask me for a judgment?"

"I don't think so. I hope not, anyway."

I hesitated for a moment. Since I had been with Julie, Emily's words had come back to me. I could not get rid of them. The mystery of the universe is as confusing and impenetrable as trying to make sense of what I was about to share with Julie's mother.

"I had told Emily about Julie, and about something that I want you to never repeat to Julie, please."

Mrs. Douglas' look told me that whatever I was about to say would never be repeated to anyone, period.

"Julie had written a poem for me. A beautiful poem. I still have it with me. It's one of my most precious possessions. Nobody has read it only Julie and me. And I intend to keep it that way. I told Emily about it and I also told her I was terrified that I might have been misleading Julie without wanting to. Her response was that Julie was just a lovely, special person, and that I should not fear that.

"She also said and, these few past days those words have come back to me about Julie. Emily said: 'With time, Julie will find a man worthy of her, of her love, her passion, her affections, her poetry, of who she is—it's inevitable, she will, trust me.' I'm quoting her directly."

I stopped. Emily's words overwhelmed me suddenly. What was even stranger, if not bizarre, I was sharing them with Julie's mother, as if wanting to find some kind of approval to Emily's words, and to Julie being the beneficiary of those words. I mean, talk about the gods screwing with your head.

"And you want to be that man."

"I don't know that I can. Too much has happened to me that I feel kind of abandoned by life, empty, and unable to imagine another woman loving me, or me loving her. I feel terrified by that thought. Yet in some weird way, what Emily said about Julie, so many years ago, gives me hope and that's why I'm telling you this. You're a woman. I always think women know a hell of a lot more than us guys do."

"Sometimes, though, like men, we often fail pretty badly. Jonathan, I don't know much about you. But as a mother and as a woman and, that is what you want to know, I believe and trust that this wonderful young woman has chosen wisely."

Her smile was wistful, but not distant. I think she understood that I was not looking for her approval, or her acceptance, or her blessing. I really was not. The gulf that had divided us just a few moments ago now seemed to have narrowed a bit. I could see that on her face.

She was looking at me in such a manner that I seemed to have broken a barrier and, in a much larger sense, it brought to me in no uncertain terms that I needed no longer fear love or its aftermath. That I had to trust my own being, my guts. That I should not be so afraid to be human again. What does it all mean? What?

"Now regarding your question of whether I love Julie? I don't know. For so long, I have rejected the notion that I could love someone again. Purely, simply, with honesty and with all of the love that a heart can muster. The answer is not so simple as a yes or a no. One thing is true, Julie has forced me to confront what is essential in life and to stop rejecting becoming human again.

"And to tell you the truth, it scares me. I don't want to deceive her, but I don't want to continue suffering. It has been too damn long. I want a new life. It's not easy, but I'm trying my best. I guess the short answer to your question is, that I want to participate in Julie's life. I want to be part of her life! I want to have her feel proud of me. I want to make her happy. Yes, I want to love her. I need to love her for my own sake that's all."

"Thank you, Jonathan. I believe you and I appreciate your honesty."

Honesty. Boy, oh boy, I thought. Cash and Jackson would be rolling over in their graves laughing their heads off upon hearing Julie's mother calling me: Honest! Those bums never gave me credit for anything. Will someone tell 'em to get lost.

340

Becky stepped out of the kitchen and walked over to join us. She was holding a glass of wine.

"You guys seem too serious from where we can see you. Anything shaking?"

I did not know just how much Becky was in on the secret. I imagined that there were few individual secrets to each sister. On the other hand, maybe there were none. I chose to remain silent.

"Nothing shaking honey. Just two people reminiscing about past sins and history," her mother said.

"Oh, boy, I'd like to hear about those 'sins,' " Becky said.

"Not from me," I said to her, and all three of us had a bit of a laugh.

"So how's the pasta going?" I continued.

"Julie is amazing. She knows how to make that sauce. It's out of this world. I'm going to miss *la pasta Sargenti* when she goes back to Italy."

Becky looked at me and gave me a sneaky smile, I thought.

"So, Jonathan, are you joining her in Italy?"

Man, oh man, the question came out of left field. I was looking at Becky totally in shock. I guess the debt that Julie had hoped to settle had been done but on what appeared to be half measures. Becky looked at me with a look that said:

We are not dummies here, buddy. We know what the score is. After all, Jonathan, you have spent almost a whole week jumping on my sister's bones. Some truth and honesty is not totally out of line here.

I could see Mrs. Douglas wincing and looking a bit alarmed, and embarrassed.

"Honey, that's not polite. It's . . ."

She was out of words. Becky looked at me and I knew she was challenging me directly. I was not sure how to answer her. On the other hand, her mother was right. If it had been just Becky and me talking, I probably would have told her it was none of her goddamn business.

I started to laugh. Becky started to laugh with me and even her mother found a bit of levity in the whole situation.

"The answer is that there are no known defenses in this world if Julie has plans for you. It'll be a losing war." I said.

"OK, I think we both agree that whatever Lola wants, Lola gets," Becky said.

I really busted out laughing this time. I put my arm around her and hugged her. Boy, oh boy, the Douglas's Army was not to be messed with. Lesson learned, I thought.

"Never a dull moment with these two," her mother said, and gave me a wonderful smile.

"I guess not," I said.

"Will someone come up here and finish setting up the table?" Julie said, from the house.

"I'll do it. Mothers, after all, have to be good for something." Mrs. Douglas said.

And she went back to the house. I laughed inside. Very clever, I thought. Now, I am to be examined by team A. Team B had set the ball rolling, had softened up the opposition a bit. Now it was team A's turn to come to deliver the *coup de grace,* if necessary.

"Julie says that you may go to Paris."

"I'm thinking about it."

"Not far from Bologna, is it?"

"No, it isn't."

"Did you come looking for her?"

Not wasting any time are you, my dear Becky.

"No. I had no idea Julie was living here."

"What did you imagine?"

"I didn't. I've been asking myself why I ended up here. I don't know."

"Do you regret it?"

"No, on the contrary."

"It's good to know. I think you know you have made my sister gloriously happy, but you have also made a whole bunch of other people unhappy."

"Are you including yourself in that bunch?"

She did not answer me right away. She was considering what not to say, I think, much more than what to say.

"No. I like Ham and I also like his family. They have been great to all of us, especially after my father died."

"Yeah, Julie told me."

"It's delicate."

"I imagine it is. Are we talking about some kind of family feud here? I understand Southern folks hang on to grudges for a very long time."

"Not that kind of grudge, at least I don't think so. In any event, this only concerns Julie. She's an adult."

Right. Jonathan, just be careful not to walk into the swamps at night by yourself, and remember to keep a fully loaded shotgun with you at all times.

"There are not many secrets between Julie and me. I want you to know that."

Oh, boy. Did Julie describe in detail just what she and I had been doing these past few days? Man, oh, man. What if Becky decides to ask more direct questions from me? What then? How can I cut her off at the pass? Am I looking at female jealousy, sister resentment?

Julie had said that women can gouge the eyes of another female. There is no reason for Becky to feel jealous, is there? Professional female jealousy, perhaps? Or is she simply trying to wish her sister and me the best of what we each had to offer the other?

Buddy, careful how you tread on this treacherous terrain.

"Can I ask you a question, Becky?"

"Please."

"Are you worried about what your sister and I are doing, have done, and most likely intend to do for the foreseeable future?"

"And what is that?"

Oh, boy. She was not going to let me off the hook that easy. I got me a lively one here in my hands. I thought. OK, hot babe you asked for it.

"Well, in the realm of people exchanging bodily fluids, for example?"

If she was expecting this from me, she held her ground. She just looked at me and for a second I thought I had put one over on her. But she was not about to concede the point. If I was going to win it, I had to bring my own heavy artillery into the game we were playing.

She started to laugh, a great, unadulterated laugh. No embarrassment coming from her that I could tell. Tough broads these Douglas sisters.

"That's just one aspect of the equation."

"Julie told me that you are a whiz in math."

"Oh, I don't know about that. But I can read the credits and the debits on a balance sheet."

I decided that I was going to like Becky. There was no phoniness about her. You got what you got.

"I hope that my balance sheet has some credits. I'd prefer that to debits."

"Reviewing where you are at the moment, I'd say you're looking pretty solid. I wouldn't suggest an audit, at this time; furthermore, the climate for heavy investing is propitious."

Touché. I started to laugh; I hugged her and clinked our glasses. She was laughing and I could see that Becky was now looking at me with a different set of eyes.

It seemed that I had cleared the first hurdle, and probably the highest and the most important one. That my stock had increased in value.

"Becky, you're something else. I wouldn't want to bet against you either. Your mom has already said to be careful when betting against Julie. I think that having the two of you on the opposing team, I sure would lose in no time. I'd rather have you on my team."

"Jonathan, just remember that I love my sister. That she *is* my family. And that neither my mom nor I want to sell her short. She's lovely, she's smart, and she loves you. Always keep that in mind. It'll carry you through all of the peripheral stuff that we all have to deal with every day."

"Thank you. I hope to be worthy of your sister's love."

"If she has chosen you, you already are."

She took my hand and we both walked back to the house. I had not done so bad so far. Jack, Cash and Jackson would have been proud of me, I thought.

When we walked back, Becky and her mother went into the other room, which left me and Julie in the kitchen alone for a few precious seconds. Her chef's apron actually looked rather chic on her.

She had on the tip of her nose a smidgen of flour. I leaned over and licked it off her nose. She got a kick out of it. She gave me a quick kiss in case her mother suddenly came back into the kitchen.

She dipped the large wooden spoon in the sauce, and handed it to me. I tasted it. It was damn delicious.

"Do you like it?"

"It's great. And you know how to do this?"

"Yes. Not bad, ah."

"Not bad at all."

"And the pasta is freshly made. Just like mama Sargenti likes it."

"Are you sure you don't have any Italian ancestry in your family?"

"Not that I know of. I will have to check it out."

"And you did all this for me?"

"Yes, especially for you, but also for my mother and for my sister. For all of you because I love you all."

Yes, we do things for others because we love them. Because without them we perish. Because to be part of a group that loves us is to belong, to feel safe, protected, with no fears of what the future will bring. I thought that Emily had once said something like that. And seeing me in this strange and yet familiar setting, I wanted to feel safe, protected, and loved.

It was a marvelous evening. Full of stories about both girls. However, no photo albums were shown. I had told Julie about Emily's mother showing me photos of Emily. I thought how lovely and tactful Julie was in not showing any photos.

It was just a verbal recounting of their lives. Their trajectory during the perennial cycles of life; its vicissitudes. Once in a while, Julie would reach over and touch my hand without any embarrassment or fear. She was as free as anybody could possibly be.

Her sister and her mother were both completely comfortable in how they acted toward her, and toward me. I thought that maybe times had really changed. After all, I was not married to Julie, and Myrtle Beach had been a reality. Just a couple of days ago, I had not existed in their lives.

Our collective reality was based on one individual: Julie. I had to stop once in a while and take stock of the whole thing. I had once spent another great afternoon with another family, with another lovely woman, in another universe, and its outcome had been less than perfect.

Tonight, it was a kind of mutual discovery of known facts for all of us there. After all, Julie's mother had known about her daughter's feelings for me. She had known it for years, really. I wondered about the secrets the heart holds.

The pasta, the sauce and the wine were outstanding. I am not much of a food critic, let alone Italian food, but it was obvious I was tasting something delicious.

As I ate and watched the three women, the ghost of another young woman came back to me, again. But I noticed that it was not as sharp and as

344

desperate as it had been in the past. It was hovering around my own consciousness but the heaviness was not so apparent.

There was less sharpness of pain in what I felt. For a second, a sense of guilt came out, but it was only for a moment. Julie saw my face, reached under the table, touched my leg, rubbed it softly, and gave me a warm smile to reassure me.

"What did you talk about with my mom?" She asked, as we were driving back to her place.

"Stuff."

"Like what?"

"Like the weather."

"Sure thing. Why is it that you're not a good liar?"

"My mother would be happy to hear that."

"Your parents back in California?"

"Yes."

She did not go any further about my parents. She sensed it was not a subject that was close to my heart.

"OK, do you want to know what both your mother and your sister said about you?"

"Absolutely."

"That you were the strangest human being around. Your mom said that she had no idea where you came from. Furthermore, that being in love with you would be the worst thing to happen to me. That I should run now before it's too late, that . . ."

"OK, now I know for certain that you're the biggest liar in this whole wide universe."

"Oh, you don't believe me?"

"No. I'm beginning to know you. I can sense your game."

"And what is that game?"

"To be difficult."

"Not as difficult as you."

"Worse than me."

"I told your mom that I feared falling in love with you because you didn't deserve it. I told your sister pretty much the same thing."

"And what did they say?"

"That they had never seen such a fool as me."

She let out a big laugh. And she leaned over and kissed me on the cheek. I was driving.

"Good for them."

I pulled over and stopped the car on the side of the road.

"What's wrong?"

I leaned over and started kissing her.

"I want to make love to you now, here, right now."

"I was wondering how long it would take you to get going," she said.

She gave me what I can only call the: Mona Lisa look and smile. Suddenly, I saw her pulling down one of the spaghetti straps of her dress from her left shoulder and I thought, oh, boy, I really got what I deserve. She slowly pulled my head toward her and offered me her beautiful breast. I kissed it. It was firm.

However, what we were doing was insane, and the last thing I wanted was to make love to Julie in the middle of the road and have someone come by and catch us. I did not think these rednecks would have a sense of humor.

I had challenged her and she was not about to back down. And we both started to laugh. She was teaching me a good lesson; that I had better measure up to her, that she would give as good as she got.

I kissed her breast again, and got back on the road. She was laughing and as she was putting her strap back up, she reached over and touched me.

"Stop it."

"Boy, you're no fun. And he keeps calling himself 'King of the Road,' " she said.

And she laughed but kept her hand on my thigh, rubbing it.

Needless to say, I drove back to her place like a maniac. Roberto could not have competed with me in how fast I was going. 'King of the Road' I was not. King of other things I sure as hell was trying to give it a shot. No pun intended.

The rest, as they say, is history.

After making sure that all of the dirty laundry, mine included, was inside the laundry bag. "I've got to get back to work," she said.

"I called my friend Jack in California this morning. I think your phone bill took a pretty big hit."

"OK, we'll share the cost."

"No, I'll pay for it."

"Did you talk about me?"

"No."

She came and sat on my lap again. Some things just simply cannot be hidden from others.

"So, what did he say?" She continued.

"The usual pabulum."

She stared to laugh. She knew better than listen to my silly talk.

"So he told you to love me like crazy and to make sure to take me to California with you so I can meet him. Right?"

"Were you listening in? Are you tapping the phone?"

"No, no need to."

"Boy, what an ego."

"Mister, you had better understand that things are happening and it would be wiser for you to join the forces of progress."

"OK, before you go, I want to ask you something. Last night, on the road, were you disappointed that I wasn't 'King of the Road?' "

"No, because after we got home, I seem to remember you recovered very nicely; actually, your recovery was outstanding!"

She kissed me, got the laundry bag, walked out of the apartment and back to her car. I followed her to the door and watched her walk downstairs.

"If I'm not here when you come back, please, ship my laundry, clean, and well folded back to me in California."

"Will do."

She stopped, threw me a kiss, got in her car, and drove off.

This was Tuesday. So I was pretty much stuck in staying until the end of the week. The idea of leaving was not completely forgotten by me. Stuck is not the right word. I just could not make up my mind as to what my next step should be. Stay. Leave.

There was nothing in between. Maybe I should not have so readily agreed to stay. I had not really thought about what I was going to do. I was playing it by ear. But playing it by ear was not too swift when dealing with someone else's feelings—and life. You cannot do that. It ain't recommended.

I went back to Julie's diary. After I got out of the Army, I had also kept a diary, but I found the whole thing very depressing as I always ended up writing about Emily. And only about Emily and how much I missed her, and how fucked up my life was.

It was not a diary as much as a written tribute to the woman I had loved like crazy, and whom I had lost forever. After a while, I just simply stopped doing any writing. I understood the intellectual aspect of the ordeal but emotionally it was a losing proposition.

Yes, it was a desperate attempt to try to gain some kind of perspective, but the truth was that I hated the idea of reducing Emily's impact on me to lines on a piece of paper. I wanted Emily to still be alive and with me. I found the whole exercise of keeping a diary just too painful. I was not gaining anything.

I thought that people who talk about doing something to gain "perspective" were full of shit. You cannot gain "perspective" when your whole lousy life is down the toilet. When your reality is forcing you into nothingness. What I had wanted more than anything else was to get Emily back, period. Was that too much to ask of this shitty life? Man, who was I kidding?

After I was discharged from the Army, I rented an apartment and spent most of the time inside not doing a damn thing. Even the routine of going to buy food I found irrelevant, ridiculous. I started to go out only at night. My bedroom had no windows so whenever I shut the door I was in complete darkness. I did not connect a phone line. I did not want anything to do with any aspect of daily living.

Because I had problems with the kidney, the only time that I ventured outside during the day was simply to go to the doctors. In many instances, I did not even make it to the hospital. It would not have made any difference if I had died. I mean, I was unnecessary.

I did not try to get in touch with my old school buddies. I hated the whole fucking world! I attempted to go to church one day, and the whole thing was so obnoxious to my fragile emotional state that I simply walked out and never went back.

My own family after a few attempts to get in touch—and the only way they could do that would be to either write me or come by and knock on my door—they decided to leave me alone.

I never responded to any door knocking. There had been days of absolute anger. And I realized it would eventually drain me emotionally so much so that I would get sick, but I could not help it. I was in a state of stasis.

One evening, and it was an evening that later I came to regret immensely and cried over many times, I started to re-read her letters. I had not done it before. I had avoided it like the plague. Then as I continued reading, I got so desperate and so angry that I lost it, and before I knew it I set all of her letters on fire.

I could not stop. I was completely out of control. I was crying. I was throwing the letters in the fire and my heart felt like it was going to explode. I was choking and I could not breathe.

The piece of metal in my back was also causing pain, but I did not give a damn. My miserable life had come to mean absolutely nothing! That was a night when thoughts of suicide were not far from my mind. I do not know by what miracle I survived the ordeal. I do not know.

Perhaps, Emily's spirit was hovering over me, and protecting me. I do not know what saved me from doing away with myself. The pile of ashes from the letters stayed on the floor of my living room for days. My whole stinking life had turned into a nightmare. I eventually swept the ashes away.

Now that I am reading Julie's diary and also looking back to those years of meaningless existence, I regretted that I had not kept writing the diary, but the emotional cost and effort were just too damn much for my battered soul at that time.

As I leafed through Julie's diary, I realized that my life was now changing. Once in a while, I felt that Julie was putting pressure on me to come around and commit to her. I wanted to. But I did not want to.

Julie had several classic books, *War and Peace,* and *The Idiot* among them, that I tried to read. Not recommend for a beaten soul. She also had two James Bond books, by Ian Fleming, *Gold Finger* and *From Russia with Love*. I had read them before. That was surprising.

One afternoon, I decided to take a drive around the town. But when I found myself sitting in a parking lot and not knowing just what I was supposed to do and having a hard time remembering where Julie's place was. I knew the shit was going to hit the fan.

I had not called Jack because I did not know what else to tell him. I knew I had to do something. It had been years and years of total absence from the world. Julie had now presented me with some obvious facts. She loved me. She wanted to make a life with me.

She had committed to making a life with me. I had to either shit or get off the pot. I was getting restless. Reflecting and thinking but ignoring what my reality was, did not make me happy. I drove by Emily's house, her old house, many times.

Julie was coming home late, and she was tired. I found myself not only anxious as to when she would get back, but when she finally arrived, I would grab her and hold on to her like I was afraid I would never see her again. She understood my anxiety but never asked what I had done that particular day.

Her wonderful smile was such a welcome sight for me. Once in a while, she would call me. And she would whisper: "Obscene phone call: I love you," without telling me it was she, and would hang up. It made me laugh especially when I needed it.

I went back to her scrapbook and spent long hours looking at the photos she had glued on the pages. What I also found curious was that in reading her diary more often than not, I would spend more time just re-reading what I had already read. And her thoughts about me throughout the years had little variation on them. I was so overwhelmed by her love for me.

I really had no idea if I would ever love her the way she loved me. Her love was beautiful, tender, innocent, magical, and mysterious. I thought how bitter my life had been and it brought me, once again, a sense of confusion and darkness. Man, how long would this kind of life last?

I mean, I was sick of what I had become. It was not my fault, originally, but to keep on acting like my world had ended with Emily's death was not healthy. Jack was right, Julie was right. Emily was dead. She was not coming back. Maybe a bullet through my head would end the whole thing, not in a glorious end, but it would at least put me in a place where the questions would be buried for good.

I had once considered suicide and that was on the night when I had burned all of Emily's letters. Now the whole episode seemed kind of humorous. Sick humor it goes without saying. I know this sounds incoherent and maybe there was a kind of sick humor to the whole idea.

I needed a formula. I needed a guideline. I needed a paradigm shift; I needed those two bozos, Cash and Jackson, to talk things over; I needed a new life; I needed to make a decision; I needed to reclaim who I used to be. There was one simple reality staring back at me. I had to think fast and hard back to what Emily always said: Tragedy and pain could not rule our lives.

She did not allow her immense suffering to get in the way of what was important to her—to live her life with hope. She found me and had fallen in love with me not to replace Wilson, but to give herself another chance. She believed she deserved it. In the process, she showed me that I also deserved to be at her side. She was no longer around, but what she said still existed.

In my own misery, I had always rejected those ideas. It was not because I did not see the truth in them. It felt so inadequate to live up to those ideals. I just did not believe that my life could ever get better. I had really given up. I also resented that I had not been able to balance my pain and agony and had ended up not respecting and protecting Emily's memory, but instead I had become my own jailer.

In my darkest moments, deep in my guts and heart, I knew Emily would not have accepted my failure to understand and not fight against giving up. And now that I was confronted with another chance, I was just being a shithead and not only would I end up rejecting Emily's love and memory, but I would also end up denying Julie's love, honesty and innocence.

Jack was right, I could not blow it. Man, it was tough. But I had to do it. My love and my memories of Emily, in a much larger sense, were being tested. I was not sure if I would ever be able to understand my own stupid contradictions in the face of what life was now offering me.

I felt like I was betraying Emily. Jack had said that Emily was dead. I did not owe her anything. I was free. I had always been free except that now I was confronting that reality. For too long, I had denied my own capacity to control my own destiny. I had to get out of this damn hole. I could not continue to deny the truth, and still remain human. Either, I would permanently become a loser, or something had to change.

-XXI-

And so it was that for the next few days, Julie would come home late, tired, but elated. And not only because the school year was just about over, but excited about what her class was planning to do.

I knew all about technical rehearsals when everything that could go wrong, often did. She never asked what I had done in her absence and I never volunteered any information. I was used to living alone so the present situation was not new to me.

Julie had rushed out of the apartment sometime around noon. Today was Saturday, the fateful day. She was full of beans. Excited. Fearful. Concerned with the last minute details. We took a long shower together before she left. Needless to say, while taking the shower there were some activities that had nothing to do with taking a shower.

In the previous nights, we had explored, touched, and tasted our bodies from one end to the other. We could not get enough of each other. I knew not only her physical body but also much of what she thought. Her plans, her sense of humor, her dreams, and her desires to please me.

When, in fact, just sharing her life such as it was, was more than enough for me. Was I falling in love with her? It was probably closer to the truth than I was willing to admit. To say that I was enthralled with this lovely creature would be to deny that she was now part of my life!.

You might be a lucky bastard, Jonathan. After all, you're still doing her nails, right.

"You should open a pedicure shop for women," Julie said.

"Hey, great idea—interesting possibilities."

She saw my enthusiasm, which I was faking, of course.

"On second thought," she said. "It's too risky so we'll table that," and she busted out laughing.

Her mother and her sister came by to pick me up this evening. I had not seen them or talked to them since the night of the dinner. I had asked Julie if there had been a "briefing" as she had said. But, due to what was going on, it had been postponed until further notice.

"I want to go in your car. Will you let me drive it?" Becky said. It sounded more like an order to me. But, what the hell."

What was it with these women wanting to drive my car? I was going to say no, but I decided that Becky had earned her shot. So I handed her the keys and bowed. I got in the back while her mother sat right next to Becky.

"You know, I hardly ever sit back here. I really don't remember that I ever sat here and had a pretty chauffer drive me around. I can easily get used to this."

Both women were amused. Becky was a little more like Roberto when she took off. Her mother did not say anything. Neither of the two women seemed to find it unusual that I was occupying half of the bed in Julie's apartment. Or if they were, they had resigned themselves to the inevitable.

When an adult wants to do what she wants to do and you are her parent, you have two choices: Fight her and risk losing her, or ignore it. When you think about it, neither choice is the best choice.

The auditorium was filled. Students and parents. I saw black parents, not too many, but they were there. The buzzing was loud and the atmosphere was charged with interest, excitement and, I thought, of ideas of what the summer vacation would bring.

Not without a vague sense of regret, I thought about when we had done *The Diary of Anne Frank,* at the Army post, back in the days. Her mother leaned over and whispered. Obviously, she was also thinking about the same thing.

"Remember?"

"And how? I'm thinking about the old saying that the more things change the more they remain the same."

"Yes, it is true." She gave my hand a nice squeeze. I was sitting between her and Becky who turned and gave me a nice smile. Not, bad, I thought.

The lights went down and a spot light came on. There was applause from the audience. A middle-aged man came on the stage and walked to the microphone.

"Good evening ladies and gentlemen, and welcome to our last school show. This is also a very special occasion because our magnificent dance-teacher won't be coming back next year. This is her last year with us. She's preparing for her journey back to Italy where, I'm told, she'll be pursuing her Ph.D. in Renaissance Art, at the University of Bologna. How lucky can one be? Ladies and gentlemen, it is my pleasure, and honor to introduce Miss Julie Anne Douglas."

There was a loud applause. Julie appeared and the people were cheering and whistling, mostly the guys. Julie looked radiant in her costume. I hated those rednecks. I laughed thinking of my sudden jealousy.

"Thank you so much. We have prepared something very musical and very American for tonight. The group thought that jazz, big band sounds, and swing are such an integral part of who we are as a nation that we must honor such culture.

"And even though our musical tastes have evolved, the music that you'll hear tonight has been with us and will be with us for years to come, even as other types of popular music also grow and become part of our musical culture and heritage. Please, enjoy the show, and come fly with us."

Another round of applause.

The lights went down.

And suddenly the auditorium was filled with the introduction of "*Come Fly with Me,*" a rendition by the great band of Count Basie in upbeat tempo, followed by Frank Sinatra's voice coming through the speakers singing one of his most famous signature songs. It was electrifying. The lights on the stage came back on, again.

I suddenly remembered that Julie had played the song on the first night we were together. She had never mentioned the show. As the music started, we saw the dancers, all girls, probably a dozen or so, glide onto the stage while keeping the rhythm.

There were three black girls in the dance troupe. It was not surprising to see the response of the black audience. It was pride, but also unsure as to how to react to what they were witnessing, especially from the white audience.

In a way, it was the South being confronted with its own ugly history, its own racist past, but now perhaps with a degree of tolerance that was not seen in this part of the country that often. I marveled at Julie nudging it along. I had no doubt that she knew what she was doing.

Her diary had made a pointed reference to it. The lights were moody and, with the dancers, the music, and how the girls were moving, it took us back to an era of fantasy and innocence.

Boy, I thought, this is really a remarkable statement that all of the kids on that stage were making. Look at us, they were saying. Look how we move to the music. We love this music. It is gay. It is filled with a great beat and we know that at this moment we are all the same.

The music makes us all the same: Human beings. Yes, we are different in our skin color but not in what we feel in our hearts for this fantastic music. It belongs to us all.

Son of a bitch, I was really touched by the scene we were watching. I could see that both Becky and her mother were also very moved by what we were seeing. But more importantly, by the fact that it was a member of their own family who had dared do this.

I do not know much about dancing, choreography, or rhythm but the whole opening was just great, exciting, enchanting.

And the opening of the show, once again, brought me the memories of past experiences. The time I had been arrested with Cash and Jackson in the restaurant all because Cash was hungry and he wanted something to eat.

The group of kids, not much older and not much different from the ones at the restaurant, but now sitting in the audience swaying to the music, and I wondered how old they were then when the shit at the restaurant took place.

Were they related to the ones we had encountered then? OK, Jonathan, take it easy, do not be such a damn cynic. OK, OK, look at it as the glass half full. Cash and Jackson would have simply been shocked and delighted not only to hear the music, but to see black girls dancing in the group.

The number ended and the round of applause was loud, and long. The dancers had conquered us and they would take us with them wherever they wanted to go. We had no other choice but to follow them. The other numbers remain a kind of blur in my mind.

353

I was familiar with them, of course. The whole ensemble worked as a team. These girls were giving everything they had and I am sure the memories of this evening would remain with them for a long time, a very long time. I knew about such things.

Then Julie's first dance number came in the middle of the show. It was a song from a film: *Daddy Long Legs*: "Something's Got to Give." I loved the song. Now I had to take a few moments to think about this one because Julie had a partner dancing with her! She had never said anything about dancing with a guy. That hussy! I looked at her mother and she had one of those looks that said: Guilty as charged!

Both dancers were dressed in black with white shirts. It made me think of something from an old style film of the 30s or 40s. I watched the guy closely. I wanted to make sure the schmuck was doing his part to make her look good. It was, of course, silly, petty jealousy on my part.

But it was just fabulous to see the couple in step never missing a beat, not concerned about any mistakes. I do not know if there were any. Again, I do not know a damn thing about dancing.

All I saw was these two people enjoying themselves and making us believe in the beauty of artistic sensibilities, physical grace, and of the lyrics of the song. About people, like me, refusing to accept the inevitability of love. The whole presentation timed to perfection.

It was a strange sentiment to see Julie doing what she was doing and a shock for me to realize so clearly that I was no longer looking at a teenage girl, filled with the fantasy of her teenage years, but at a complete young woman who was whole, independent, sure of herself, and giving her heart and love not only to the music but to us, the audience.

I was the person who would not accept the reality of her love for me and she was the person who would not walk away from it. The lyrics of the song were so apropos to what was happening between her and me.

Man, she could not have known that I was showing up. She could not have known she was preparing a song that would speak with such frankness about her and me. And me still refusing to accept the unavoidable, the obvious.

When love rules and dictates what will happen, one cannot simply ignore the evident. One has to accept the inevitable. She was only stating what she knew to be real about her, about me, and about us.

She was giving me a glimpse; no, she was giving me a frontal view of life when all of the barriers are pushed aside and we are left with what is essential and true.

Son of a bitch. What is going on? My life was being given a lesson in humility.

The applause was deafening.

I found myself being transported into a world of pure joy and fantasy. Of course, I would have to have a serious talk with this wild hussy, afterward. She could not think she could just get away with this type of behavior, and in public no less. No, sir. The law would have to be laid down. Who in the hell does she think she is?

Then, a couple of other songs and her solo number came on: *"This Love of Mine."* And I was in for another shocker, I mean a real down to goodness shocker! The music started, soft, with that lovely melodic tempo, slow, with lots of strings. The next thing I knew was the sound of Julie's voice coming through the speakers.

She was dancing to the music and to her own voice! I was floored. Her voice was deeper; she was using the lower registers. The voice was so amazingly dramatic. The longing for the loved one was so powerful and honest. The heart was broken. You could see it!

This song was diametrically opposite of the previous one. Yet, in that mysterious way that life sometimes affects us, the performance by Julie showed us the inevitable—the sadness of a love that one longs for so damn much—and one that can break one's heart in the process.

I had goose pimples all over me. Julie was not hiding behind a barrier. It was raw, naked. I thought, holy shit, this is unreal. She is exposing herself. It was all guts. She was giving it everything she had! Not afraid. She was not holding anything back. Man, oh, man.

The image of Julie when she had asked me to help her take her clothes off flashed in my head. Whereas then there had been a physical nakedness, her nakedness now was spiritual, and without any ambiguity. Julie could never go back to what she had been before she sang the song. Her life had changed, too.

She was not just interpreting the song, the lyrics; she was living it! There was such a sentiment of something missing, of dreams unfulfilled. With her voice, with her being, she was lamenting a love that may be lost. Incredibly yearning for it; perhaps with very little hope of ever finding it.

She was wearing a long, soft pinkish gown, and the combination of the lights, music, her voice, the lyrics, and her dancing was just beautiful. Her whole performance had been so incredibly on the money that it left me completely dazed!

Love can be so overwhelming that sometimes it borders on triteness. I thought, son of a bitch, this is simply striking, and amazing.

The song and her voice faded out slowly as did the lights. At the end of the number, she was left in the middle of the stage, her head down with a soft spot light bathing her that slowly faded away into complete darkness.

The image of Julie in Myrtle Beach the night when the whole thing went to hell and she had tearfully sung *"Where Have All the Flowers Gone"* was nothing compared to this.

This thing was electrifying! I saw the immense power of the heart's honesty. There was no place to hide. This was a moment of total grace! For a moment, there was dead silence in the audience, which soon gave way to a thunderous applause. It was just a stunner.

Again, I had to wonder why she had selected these songs. If she had wanted to send a message to me, I had to stop and think that she had no idea I would be showing up. She could not have known. I could not have known. I know it takes a hell of a lot of rehearsals to get the dance right. Through the songs she had done, the universe was giving me a message and I had better fucking listen, as Cash would say it.

Then, a couple of other songs danced by the girls, and the final song. Again, another surprise. The tempo was up, fast, and as the lights came on we were inside a casino with gambling tables and people sitting around. They had recruited some guys, the gamblers, for the number. And the music suddenly crashed on us. It was from the musical *Guys and Dolls: "Luck be a Lady Tonight."*

And *Lady Luck* was Julie and the gambler was her dancing partner. And as *Lady Luck* moved among the gambling tables, she would blow on a guy's dice and there would be a throw of the dice and the reactions from the gamblers after either losing or winning. Great show stopper.

The whole cast got in on the act, and there was a rousing ending with everyone moving to the front of the stage with the whole cast throwing cardboard chips to the audience. The choreography and staging were just outstanding!

Many people in my life, throughout these past years, had tried to bring me back to a sane life. But they had not succeeded. They had ultimately run out of patience, or just simply got too tired to deal with me. They had their own problems to deal with, after all. But not Julie. She had not. She had kept something in her heart and had not given up.

She, of course, had no idea that I would ever appear again. But the flame in her heart was still burning, had not been extinguished. She had demonstrated it in these last few days. And the sudden realization that she knew better than me that to fight for love and one's own destiny was not easy or a one shot deal; it was both sobering and real. It had to be an everyday thing. You could not put it aside as a piece of stale bread to be thrown away because it was useless to keep stored.

I was fighting against the obvious. I did not want to do it anymore. I thought of Emily, yes, lovely, beautiful, kind, sweet, Emily. A woman who had loved me. I knew. Did she still love me? Was she about to give up on me because I did not want to carry this heavy burden in my soul anymore? Would she remember me the way I remembered her? Would she forgive me?

The show ended and there was a roar from the audience. I sat stunned by what Julie had done. The response from the audience would not stop. We did not want the dancing or the music to die on us.

We did not want to walk out of the theater and go back to the mundane things that in so many instances did not bring us joy, peace, good will, happiness, and love, as the show had brought us tonight. In fact, so much of what we all experience in our daily lives was pain, sorrow, dishonesty, vulgarity . . .

People stood and applauded and applauded. Julie and her partner bowed to each other and then to the audience. People were whistling, applauding, and whooping it up and carrying on. And at that instant, the whole notion of racism revealed, as if needed be, that it was fucking bullshit, so much of it self-inflicted and worthless.

Nothing would unite us more than to be a witness to a wonderful, innocent, and happy spectacle of people enjoying themselves with a much beloved American music. At that moment, we were all in tune with our own grace. I had experienced that sentiment in my past, with the shows I had done back in college and even here at Fort Bragg, Fayetteville, North Carolina.

Suddenly, the music of *"Dancing in the Dark"* came on for an encore, and then some of the kids in the audience started to dance in the aisles. And the dancers on the stage came back and also started dancing.

Soon, just about the whole auditorium was dancing to some terrific music. The faces showed that this was just a great moment in our dreary lives. This was their curtain call.

And Julie was dancing with all of the girls, and I could see that some of the girls were crying and hugging each other both in groups and individually. Black and white. I thought about Cash and Jackson; they would not have believed it. But, it was there. My eyes were not lying.

It was a great moment. Man, oh man, everyone having a grand old time. I sat back and looked around me. All of these red necks, people who hated others who were not like them, who had different skin color, at that moment, they were all the same.

Did not the white people know better than to hate those who were not like them? And yet, the sentiment of joy, and happiness was not absent from that audience. If only . . .

I turned to her mother and her sister and to say that pride was in their hearts would be poorly put. Both had tears in their eyes. It was one of their own who had managed to move us so deeply. Some people behind Becky started talking to her, and it gave her mother and me a chance to have a few moments to ourselves.

"Did you know about any of this?" I asked.

"This is the first time we have seen it. We were expressly forbidden to come to any rehearsals, or to ask questions. I'm beyond words. You love your children so much and want so damn much for them to succeed in life. And Julie has just done what she has always done: surprise me. I thought I was going to faint," she said, with a wonderful, soft, laugh.

"I love my sister." Becky simply said.

"I'm speechless," I said, and I was.

Julie, and the others, in those minutes, had demonstrated the quality of the human. She had thrown all caution to the wind and what she had done—along with her students—with so much love and artistic integrity had captured us completely.

But more importantly, it made us if only for a few moments, free, believers in the immense capacity of the human to connect with everyone else because we are all the same! Son of a bitch, I thought; now, what is next?

Her mother and her sister got up, and I followed them. We slowly started to move through the throng down toward the stage. Some people recognized both women, embraced them, expressed appreciation, and congratulations to both of them.

I could see how Becky was affected by what she had seen and at one moment, she held my hand and would not let go. I guess afraid that the moment would disappear and we would never again be together like this.

However, it would remain with us long after the music was silent. And the earth would go around the sun, the sun would travel around the Milky Way, and life would move around this strange universe.

And, Julie, Becky, Mrs. Douglas, I, and the rest of the audience, would remember that all it takes is a bit of good will and a bit of effort to be human, even if only for one lousy, stinking hour, out of our miserable existence.

Julie saw us. I could see she was trying to find us through the crowd. Her mother and her sister walked up to the stage. I stood back. This moment really belonged to them. But, after embracing them, I could see that Julie was asking about me. Mrs. Douglas looked back and pointed to me.

Julie excused herself from people who wished to congratulate her, and she came to me. I opened my arms and she buried herself against my chest, and she was crying without shame.

"I guess I have to carry a clean handkerchief with me from now on," I said.

I gave her my handkerchief. She smiled, and started dabbing on her eyes. There were traces of make up when she got through. We both laughed. I took the handkerchief from her.

I kissed her softly on her lips. I could see some people looking at us with big question marks on their faces. Well, screw them, or as Julie would say: Too much religion around here.

"Did you like it, did you really like it? I did it for you. All the time I was dancing I thought of you . . ."

She was just like a kid seeking approval and wanting to please those whom she loved.

"Were you proud of me?" She asked, softly.

"No, of course not. In your solo dance, you missed a couple of steps there, but otherwise . . ."

"Oh, no, you did notice?"

"Julie, had you missed all of your steps I wouldn't have noticed it in a million years. You were just absolutely beautiful! You took my breath away especially with your singing and dancing of 'This Love of Mine.' "

"Does that mean you are falling in love with me?"

"Let's not get carried away here. On the other hand, you know, I'm going to be very careful, this falling in love business . . .you're a very dangerous woman."

She hugged me again.

Two of the black girls, their faces both bathed in sweat, came by and hugged Julie and me, and I found myself hugging three women at once who were crying. It made for a rather peculiar sight. But, who gives a shit about such inconveniences.

"Thank you, Miss Douglas. We will never forget you. Never!" One of the girls said. Julie embraced them, again.

Her dancing partner came by. He was also bathed in perspiration. I guessed he was in his early thirties. He was shy when he came over but gave me a warm smile.

"I know who are," he said.

Julie turned around and gave him a hug.

"She has told me so much about you."

"Jonathan, this is Corby Johnston."

We shook hands. There was a kind of shyness about him. At first, I was not sure what I was feeling. I had been around theater people before. Male dancers are often the victims of sick jokes about their sexuality. I thought that Corby was probably one of those people who had suffered such offensive and crass behavior.

I often wonder why we should not let people live their own lives. While in the Army, I had heard words that had always offended me to no end. "Southern faggot" was something that was so despicable and ugly, and I had heard it said often enough to know how vile it was. I got into trouble more than once for telling the shit heads who said it, to shut the fuck up!

"You guys were great. Absolutely. I'm in awe of what you both did. You moved with such elegance and style. It was a fabulous show. Really, fantastic." I told him.

He gave me a wonderful smile.

"Thank you. When you're paired with a talented dancer, you always end up looking your best. I trusted Julie. I trusted her implicitly. I wasn't afraid. She is the one who made me look good and kept me honest."

Julie gave him another hug. I could see that they were both in high heaven from how the whole audience had responded to their great artistic effort.

"Jonathan, Corby was the one who did most of the choreography for the dances. The girls just simply adore him. I just followed him, that's all."

"She's the best. I'm going to miss you," he said, and took her hand and kissed it. Very cool guy, I thought. Someone came by and pulled him away from us.

It was a night when we did not want to go home.

"I need to get out of these sweaty clothes. Come with me."

"Want help to get undressed?"

"Absolutely." We both looked at each other remembering another magical night.

"You *are* crazy."

"Yes, and I'm drunk with happiness and I want you to jump on my sweaty bones and who cares what the school principal says."

"In front of all of these people?"

"Why not?"

"Boy, I'd hate to see you really drunk."

"I giggle a lot. I'm a cheap drunk, really."

Her mother, Becky, and Julie holding my hand, started walking toward the dressing rooms to one side of the stage.

I saw Ham before he saw us. I do not know why I squeezed Julie's hand a little harder than I should have and she looked in the direction I was looking and saw Ham. Her mother and sister were a bit ahead of us so they did not see him immediately.

What was interesting about Ham was that people stopped him to say hello, but he kept moving toward us ignoring them. I also noticed that he was being followed by three other guys younger than he was, but the resemblance was immediate. His brothers.

And right behind them there was a man and woman, the parents. No doubt. I was more interested in the mother considering what I had read in Julie's diary about Ham's father and a black maid. But it was not prurient curiosity on my end.

The father was a bit heavy and was also glad-handing people as well. It was obvious they were part of the privileged social class in the town. You do not raise thoroughbred horses, and plant a killer weed that others crave without becoming notorious. Julie held my hand tightly. I looked at her and there was a bit of discomfort on her face. Still, she was going to play the game.

"Julie, that was just sensational. I was so proud of you," Ham said.

He kissed her on the cheek and ignored me but, of course. It was somewhat awkward seeing that she was right next to me and holding my hand.

The rest of his posse stopped just behind him. He was obviously the heir, the designated hitter—waiting in the wings.

Her mother and sister turned around and saw Ham and his family. Greetings were exchanged and they were all very gracious to each other. Good public behavior was imperative. They knew that they would be here tomorrow, the day after, and had been around long enough to know what proper protocol demanded.

Still, no one seemed to want to know who I was. I was laughing inside. I did not give a shit what their game was. I could not care less.

"Ham, thank you for the flowers. They were lovely. You remember Jonathan," she said.

I had to hand it to her. Nothing was going to trip her. Man, who in the hell is this broad, where does she come from?

"Yes, of course. How are you?"

"Very well, thank you and yourself?"

"Fine."

Julie let go of my hand and went over to greet Ham's parents and the rest of his family. His mother, like any mother of a child who is now out of the game, glanced at me, but again no move was made to approach me.

Then it occurred to me that it was Julie who was actually doing the ignoring. She did not want to introduce me. I could really see it now. Boy, I thought, she will not take crap from anybody. Again, I was getting a kick out of the whole scene.

Then I noticed an attractive blonde girl working her way toward us. Ham saw her and extended his hand to her. Proprietary rights? The girl was no slouch. She was kind of pouting and very much affected by her good looks. A spoiled brat, I thought. It occurred to me that there might have been a signal from Ham to have her join us, and now she was there.

"May I please introduce Candace?"

"Please to meet you," she said. She had a kind of girlish voice. Somehow, her looks did not go with her voice. I thought of those Southern beauties that Southern writers are fond of writing about: Another Blanche DuBois. She was not unpleasant, but it seemed more like she was not totally in her element because she was not really the center of attention. Julie came back to our group.

"Julie, I really loved your show. It was just stupendous. Isn't that right, Trevor?"

For some reason, hearing his name and her rather thick Southern accent when she spoke made me smile. I would have guessed Candace was what people call a Southern Belle. Her mannerisms and body language also made me think of a windup doll. I thought, what the hell is Ham doing with her? Was he trying to make Julie jealous? Bad bet, my friend. Very bad bet.

"Thank you, Candace, very kind of you to say that."

They kissed each other on the cheek without feelings. It was for the form. The other people, Julie's mother, sister and Ham's family were talking behind us, I could hear them but I could not make out what they were saying. Though, I did hear someone, maybe it was Ham's mother, make a comment about the black girls. She thought they were very talented.

"So, you're going back to Italy?" Ham said, and he looked at me, again, as if I were the horse he did not want to buy because it had bad teeth.

"Yes."

"I was sorry that I wasn't able to enjoy it as much as I had hoped when I went to visit you," he said, and he glanced at me.

Was this guy trying to inform me that I had not been the guy who first had sex with Julie, that there were certain rights—*les droits du grand seigneur*—that could not be ignored? Old friend, that is the second bad bet you have made tonight, I thought.

"Italy is difficult especially if you don't know the language," she said.

And if you do not like their scratchy toilet paper, I wanted to add. The crowd was thinning by now.

"OK, come with me, I want to show you how tiny the dressing rooms are," she said to me.

She was not about to lose control. Tough, cookie, this one.

"Julie, may I have a word with you?"

I could see that he wanted to pull Julie away from me. Candace was patently embarrassed. I was just curious. I glanced in the direction of Ham's mother and I could see that she was eyeing them. There is nothing like a mother hawk keeping an eye on her offspring. I wondered what she was thinking: About her husband having sex with a black maid, or about Julie and me?

Ham and Julie moved away from us where we could not hear what they were saying. Candace and I just stood like a couple of statues, waiting. I was not about to engage her in any kind of conversation. Maybe it was impolite of me, but I really had no desire to play their games. The conversation only took a couple of minutes. They turned around and joined us.

"I think we'd better run along," Ham said to Candace.

"Yes, darling."

I stole a glance in Julie's direction and I could see that she was trying her best not to laugh.

I shook hands with Candace, then with Ham, and Julie took my hand and I started to follow her. Again, no effort had been made to introduce me to Ham's family neither by Julie's mom, nor by Ham. And no further effort had been made to wish Julie *bon voyage,* and good luck with your studies. I did not ask her what Ham wanted, and she did not volunteer anything.

Strange episode, this whole thing, I thought.

We walked backstage and Julie embraced a couple of the dancers as we ambled our way to the dressing rooms. Julie's mother and her sister were behind us. I ain't gonna be able to jump on her sweaty bones, I thought, and laughed. Julie looked at me but did not ask why I was laughing.

Later, after getting out of her sweaty clothes, taking a quick shower— the dressing rooms did have small showers stalls, after all—and scrapping off the make-up; without make-up was the Julie that I preferred, all witnessed by her mom and her sister while I stood outside the dressing room, we walked out of the theater. There were a few people standing around, talking. I did not see any black people. Julie was now wearing her pretty yellow dress.

It was always interesting to see that she seemed to favor dresses rather than pants. Maybe it was to show off her great looking legs. Female vanity? Sure, why the hell not? She was still excited and hugging people as she went around the groups. They were probably her colleagues.

It would take some time for her to come down to earth. I noticed the woman whom I had seen when I first came looking for Julie at the school. She gave me a half-friendly nod.

The school principal approached us. He was the guy who had done the introduction of the show earlier.

"Miss Douglas, thank you so very much. It was just wonderful. The school board is grateful for everything that you accomplished here with us. You will not be so easily replaced. We will never forget you. And on behalf of all of the teachers and students, we wish you a most successful sojourn in Italy and with your studies. We know you will be a fine representative of our fine state and of our country."

Is this guy looking for votes, or what? Jackson would probably have asked.

"Thank you, Mr. Phillips. I enjoyed working at the school."

"Well, then. Good luck and I bid you all a good night," and I assumed he was including me as, again, he bowed ceremoniously and walked away from us.

Becky had a kind of smirk on her face. Julie's mother was the model of graciousness and good upbringing. Julie had not made an effort to introduce me. I was kind of curious about it, but, then, I am not from this part of the world.

I could only guess what gossip had been circulating in their community.

I drove back to Julie's place where her mother and sister had left their car. We were all quiet, privately savoring the lingering feelings of the evening. I was a bit surprised that no additional comments were made by Becky or her mother. Julie was sitting right next to me in the front seat and we were holding hands.

We got out of the car. The night sky was filled with stars. Julie kissed her sister and then hugged her mother, all three women were beaming.

"Thank you, honey. I was so proud of you. Your father would have been very proud. I love you." It was bittersweet moment for all of them.

There was a pause and I took it to mean I could embrace Mrs. Douglas, which I did. Becky embraced me in turn.

"Good night, mom, I love you. And thank you for coming," Julie said.

"Good night, honey. You were just great, isn't that right, Jonathan?"

"Absolutely!"

"Good night, Beca," Julie said.

"Good night, Jul."

"Good night," I said.

They got in their car. Becky was driving and we watched them drive away into the night. Julie leaned over to me and put her arm around my waist.

"I want to drive over to Bragg, by the theater," she said.

"Now?"

After the usual preemptory questions from the guards at the gate and, again, surprised to see the old Army decal still on the windshield of the car, they let us drive in. The side parking lot was empty. No cars.

The old theater seemed to have settled in for the night. We got out of the car and walked to the front entrance. I tried the door and it was locked, which I knew it would be.

"I wish we could go in," I said.

"Me, too."

"Let's break the lock."

"You are crazy," she said.

"What can they do to me? Put me in the Army? I only have one kidney left thanks to them."

She smiled and looked around the empty surroundings. And suddenly I understood why Julie had asked to come here tonight. She wanted to make sure, as she looked around, that the innocent feelings her heart discovered many years ago and was now relishing again were true, real, and would remain so for the rest of her life.

"I suddenly feel strange," she said. She hugged me and held me close to her.

"But are you happy?"

"Oh, yes! And how. My heart is so full of you, of love, of happiness, because we're together." She turned around and took in the whole place.

"It's here where the whole thing started," she added. Her eyes were radiant.

"What whole thing?" I asked just to give her a hard time.

"You, and me," she said, and she kissed me softly. She was exhilarated.

"Yeah. I was so innocent then," I said. "All I wanted was to do my military service, go back to California and . . ."

"Instead, you ended up with me." She made a funny, sad face like a clown.

"Yeah, didn't do very well, did I?"

"I think you're right."

"Yeah, all I got me was this hussy who dances half-naked in front of those high school boys filled with plenty of testosterone, whooping it up, carrying on, and imagining things, while I sat in the audience trying like crazy to keep my cool."

"Was it that bad? Were you jealous?"

I saw that she wanted me to tell her I was jealous; well, why not?

"You've no idea. The way you danced with Corby, so sensuous, so daring, so suggestive, and soooooo shameless. And your *Lady Luck* number was something else. Boy, *Lady Luck* was so amazingly erotic. I felt sorry for your mom and your sister sitting there probably sliding down their seats trying to hide from people looking at them."

"Yep, hussy with no shame."

"You've got it."

"So what are you going to do about her?"

"That's the problem. You got any ideas?"

"Well, you can take her with you to California and try to stuff some good sense in that empty head of hers."

"Hey, that's a thought."

She walked away from me and started dancing by herself. Whatever music she was listening to, I had no part in.

I sat on a small bench and there was Julie dancing and dancing. If the MPs happen to drive by, I thought, it will be the repeat of something that happened to me ten years ago except that this time there ain't going to be a Captain Rove to bail us out. She came back and sat right next to me.

"Was it you who selected the songs?"

"We sat around and had to go over what to put in and what to leave out. It was hard for everyone."

"And your solo?"

"It was Corby. We were talking one day about love, life, and stuff. And I mentioned about someone in my life. At first, I was reluctant to name you, but he wanted to know. I saw no harm. He told me about having been in love once some time ago. He didn't go into details, and I never asked him. The conversation happened at the beginning of the production, weeks ago.

"Then, one day he said that he had selected the solo song for me and that he was choreographing it in his head, and that I had to sing it. It would be my own voice over the dancing. Boy, talk about getting the willies.

"Then, he told me what it was. I didn't want to do it. I felt so naked and vulnerable. He said that I owed it to myself. He insisted. He wasn't about to change his mind. I was freaked out. I finally agreed to do it.

"We recorded the song some time back and Cory, that slave-demon-driver-genius-mad-man, told me that I had to record the song on the first take. No second take on this one. Even if I sounded flat. The song had to be from the guts. It had to be the truest thing I had ever done. I was a nervous wreck. Boy, talk about a taskmaster. And tonight, before I came on stage, I almost threw up."

"Why?"

"Why? You were sitting in the audience! In all of my fantasies having you sitting in the audience was like saying that there are oceans on Mars. Cannot happen. I had totally rejected the idea of ever seeing you again that I'm still waiting to wake up and find that it has been a hoax. Jonathan, my life has been a crazy mixture of incomprehensible things.

"I don't even think the gods, that rule this universe, had any idea of what was happening. Before "*This Love of Mine*" started, I blanked out. I forgot the steps. I forgot where I was supposed to be. I forgot where I was supposed to make the transitions. I forgot my movements. I couldn't think of how the music went. I couldn't remember anything.

"I really got panicky. Corby saw it. He took my hand and said. 'Listen, nobody would ever believe what is going on in your life at this very moment. Nobody. You can't chicken out now. You worked your heart and soul on this number. You have to do it. Yes, Jonathan is in the audience, and that's real.

"It's more, much more, than us working so hard on this number. Go out there and show this man that you mean business, sweetheart. Break a leg.' That's what you said to me when we did *Anne Frank*, remember?"

"Break a leg—I wonder who invented that expression? You know what the French say?"

"What?"

"They don't say: Break a leg. They say: *Merde*."

"What's that?"

"Shit, in French." We both laughed.

"Leave it to the Frogs," she said.

Another long moment of silence. She took my hand, she usually kissed it. This time I kissed her hand. She looked at me as if she were discovering a secret. She smiled and kissed me softly.

"Just before the curtain went up I thought breaking my leg would have been less painful than what I was now facing," she said, after a while.

"You were absolutely beautiful. Just stunning. That solo when you were singing. I don't know, it was scary. No, that's the wrong word. Transcendental is more apropos. You know, if you had been looking for a way for me to fall in love with you, that came close."

"How close?"

"Pretty damn close."

"Wow! Should do it more often, then," and she hugged me.

OK, Hollywood, Cash would have said. *What do you want? What? Don't you think that it is about time you give up this crown of thorns you've been wearing and stop driving yourself nuts? This absurd world ain't perfect my friend. You know we loved Emily like she was our own kid sister. You know that. And me and Jackson wanted to be the godfathers of her baby. You know that. So, don't chicken out on us. Don't be a jerk. Julie ain't no ghost.*

"Ham wants me to meet him for dinner."

"OK."

"Only OK?"

"I mean, what do you want me to say?"

"Jonathan, you're back in my life. I could never dream of that happening to me. Never! It was something out of fairy tales and I'm somewhat old for that. Yes, I often romanticized about it at the beginning, but it soon became obvious that it wasn't going to happen. I never heard from you not that I expected it. It was over. *Finito.* But now it's no longer *finito.* And there are loose ends. Ham is one of them."

"I thought you have made it clear to him."

"I did. But, well, it's hard to explain."

"You don't owe me any explanation."

"I know. Should I go and meet him?"

"Julie, I don't know how to answer your question."

"You don't care?"

"I do, and I don't."

"OK, let's take the do first."

"Simple. As you say: I'm back in your life and things can't be the same as before."

"OK, what about the don't?"

"You're an adult. You don't need me to tell what to do. I can't tell you what to do. I don't want to tell you what to do."

"Sounds fair. I won't do it. And it isn't because of you. It's because I know how these things go, and on top of that he wants me to come to his house and have dinner. It will be the equivalent of the Spanish Inquisition, and in the final analysis, I don't owe them that kind of loyalty.

"I love Ham, but only as a friend. He knows that. It's just his way of putting pressure on me. Like Candace earlier tonight. She's a lovely girl. Has been in love with him since God knows when. He should marry her."

366

Julie kissed me again, stood, and went back to dancing by herself.

How simple life was back in the days. I directed *The Diary of Anne Frank*, found Emily, Julie fell in love with me, which, again, was pretty damn flattering. I had three best buddies, Cash, Jackson and Yoshi. Cash and Jackson are dead, and I have no idea where Yoshi is.

And, now, I am back where this whole thing started and feeling good. I have not felt like this in a long time, and I have to make a decision about what do to next.

I could simply tell Julie that it cannot work, that there is still a lot of baggage I am carrying. That I really need more time—time for what? To continue for another ten years longing, sad, pissed off, my poor heart bleeding, and my soul shriveled to a shadow of its previous self?

I do not owe anything to Julie, really. Fact is, I do not owe anything to anybody but myself. I never promised Julie anything. Never. That she is a remarkable person does not change that equation.

So what the hell am I looking for? Or, worse, running away from? What?

These past few days, while Julie was at work, I found myself restless but not depressed; that is, until one late afternoon I drove around the town. It had increased in size and there seemed to be lots of GIs walking around in civilian clothes.

I drove, again, by Emily's old place. The toys and the tricycle were still on the front lawn. I parked my car on the same spot where I had parked before, sat, and watched the house.

Why was I torturing myself this way? What was I trying to prove?

OK, I now had had more time with Julie than the five days I had spent with Emily. Yes, Emily and I had had plenty of phone conversations, but we were not sharing digs the way I am now sharing with Julie. But, does that make any difference?

Would I still be with Emily if she had lived? Is that a fair question to be asking of myself at this moment? Was I now hedging my own bet on what I needed to do with my life?

What kind of future would Julie and I have?

I mean, I wanted to go to Paris and, as Julie said, Paris is not that far from Bologna. I go to Paris, and she goes to Bologna. Call it a compromise. But just what kind of a compromise is that? I go to Bologna two weekends a month. Julie comes to Paris the other two weekends. So we set up alternate weekends. Odds for me, even for her.

Man, this is so stupid. It is insane. Wholesale insanity!

My own fears have not been included in that scenario. Julie gets pregnant and nine months, for nine months, I suffer. I fear. I die. I drive her crazy. I drive myself crazy. I drive her mother and her sister crazy. Not that I would say anything to them, but they would know. Especially, her mom.

And in the meantime, this lovely, beautiful, hussy, as she calls herself, also knows that I am in the shits with the whole thing. And what does she do? What does she do to cope with all the *merde* I am piling up on her? How does she cope? How?

You know, something, Jonathan. I suspect all the musings and bullshit just mean that you are a worthless coward. Not willing to face your life. Yes, it has been miserable, painful, and somehow you got stuck in this time warp and you cannot get out of it.

Julie is real. She is willing to sacrifice even her own happiness if you want to split and not ever see her again, you're free. She said that to you. Did she not say that to you, dickhead?

OK, here is what I am going to do: I will take Emily's painting along with Julie's poem, and I will fade into obscurity but I will have two great gifts from them. One from each. Shit, that should do it. I do not have to be in the moment. I can once in a while look at the painting and the poem and think of myself as a big shot hero.

Typical Hollywood jerk, Cash would say. *Yeah, our friend wants to be a big hero. Big time, Charlie. Jackson, please, excuse my language: Fuck you, Hollywood. Shee-it . . .*

-XXII-

My orders to Vietnam had come in the middle of the night. It was shortly after Jackson had gotten his orders. He was still with us. I knew there had been heavy talk about what our company was waiting for. We had prepared our equipment; the medics shot the hell out of our arms with all kinds of anti-vermin. Were there any vaccines to protect your ass against Vietnamese bullets?

But when the orders came that we were going to ship out within three days, my life went to hell. Three days! I could not ask for a leave of absence. The Army would not have given it to me. No way. My first thought, my only thought, was for Emily. Man, oh man, the Army was doing a number on her, on me, on us. Son of a bitch!

So how am I going to tell her? Shit. What am I going to say? How am I going to break the news to her? Gee, babe, guess what, I am leaving for Vietnam in three days. Sorry, but I cannot get these bastards to give me time off. It seems that they do not understand the situation with you.

Fact is, they do not give a shit about you or me. All they care about is to haul my ass over there and start shooting people. Our whole company is shipping out. We are flying to Oakland, then on to Saigon.

But, get a hold of this. Our orders are to ship out forthwith, which would follow logically that we should fly all the way. But, no, a ship crossing the ocean for fourteen days is what they mean by forthwith. I hate all of this. You know what, I am going to split, swing by your place, pack you, and we will drive to Canada.

We will make a life for ourselves and we will not ever have to worry about wars, military, killing. The Canadians are smarter than we are. It is their official policy not to start wars. Got to hand it to them.

I am not going to tell anybody what I intend to do. Not even Cash or Jackson. It is every man for himself now. You and I have talked about this for a long time. I know you are afraid, but do not be. I know what I am doing. I want you with me. You promised me that we would face thick and thin together. I know we can make it. I know it.

Do not tell your family anything. Let us act as if we are going for a short vacation to the Great Lakes. Not far. On second thought, let us tell them we are going to Boston. It is closer. You know, clam chowder, fresh ocean air, sun, and stuff, plus as I have said it is closer.

Then, we split to Canada. And once we get there, we will call them. What can they do? The baby will be born there. They have great medical facilities. And the U.S. cannot touch me. I am out of their paws.

I know that this is pretty sudden but I was not given much of a leeway. So please prepare your suitcase. Pack light as if you are coming back. And it is good-bye, Charlie.

But, she did not want to do it.

I could tell that she was so frightened. She was confused. It was not that she did not understand what was going on. We had talked long enough these past few weeks for both of us to be clear as to what we needed to do.

I did everything within my powers of persuasion to get her to come with me. She did not want us to do it. I, then, suggested that I would go ahead and she could wait for the baby to be born in the U.S., and then she could join me. I begged her. I got angry thinking that it would do the trick. I used every stinking argument I could think of, but to no avail.

I told her that I did not want her to be looking forward to another telegram advising her of my being blown away by a mortar. I asked her to find a lawyer who could help us get married right away. That she was a widow and there had to be some way of us getting married as soon as possible.

I wanted to put her in my will, as the Army was ordering us to make our wills. The pricks knew that many of us would not be coming back. She finally agreed to that. And she was crying.

My poor, lovely, Emily. The woman who had shown me something that very few of us males ever get a chance to experience in life. She had not agreed to my plans, demands, to my begging. She said that she believed that life would not be so mean, again. She trusted this worthless universe to not do that to her.

I finally realized that she would not come with me. She would not do it. She kept saying that life could not be so cruel to her again. She had paid her dues. She was now overdue on a great future for us—a great life for us . . . what a sick joke.

I can still remember Emily's words: "Jonathan, God will protect you, my love. I know. I have faith that He will. Yes, He was once cruel to me. But I trust Him that He will not do terrible things to you or to me." She was so scared, so scared and I could not protect her from life's ugliness and pain—son of a bitch.

God, fucking phony . . .

I was in Vietnam less than two months and in that time I wrote every day. I called her whenever it was possible. All of my paychecks went to call her. To hear her sweet voice. To know that everything was going just great was worth the long waits to get to a phone. The baby was now moving like crazy. She had picked a name already: Timothy. I loved the name. I asked her what if it was a girl?

Had she thought about that? She said that Beth was a name she liked. It had been her grandmother's on her father's side. I liked the name. I saw myself taking Beth to the park, and buying her pretty dresses and teaching her about animals and stuff. Watching her grow up to be a beautiful lady just like her mother.

It was funny, because I thought how crazy it was not to know whether it would be a boy or a girl. But in the final analysis, what was important was to have a healthy baby. She told me she trusted her doctor. He was a good guy. She trusted him, I trusted him, also.

I have tried so many times to remember when I had gotten the telegram from Billy. It was early evening where I was, that is the only fact that I still remember. I have always tried to take the moment apart.

Like a scientist searching for the one set of clues about one of nature's secrets that he is been trying so hard to unravel. I have difficulty recollecting the exact moment. All I have remembered for so long was me holding this piece of paper that simply said:

Jonathan,

Emily is no longer, nor is the baby. She passed away this morning while delivering little Timmy. Both are now gone. I'm sorry, so damn sorry.

Billy

I had memorized the words. But that is all it said. No explanation as to how it happened. Nothing. Did he want me to call him back? Did he want me to, what? No, no other word. Nothing. And that would be my life for so many stinking, rotten, fucking, years: Nothing!

Julie stopped her dancing, looked in my direction and continued. I imagined Julie dancing by herself as a little girl as she was growing up. There was an amazing degree of innocence that she represented that I had so sorely missed in these last lousy years of my life.

I wanted to stop and regain some of it. I knew it would not be possible unless I accepted the reality I was now watching. I reached into my back pocket and pulled the telegram out. It had now faded and the yellowish color of the paper had been slowly fading away.

I had touched that paper a dozen times, a hundred times, a thousand times, ten thousand times, a hundred thousand times, a million times. I could hardly read what had been written on it now. And it was not because the light was poor where I was sitting.

It was because the essence of its meaning had also faded. It was not that what it had said had not been crucial to my life. It had been, boy, it had, but it could no longer remain part of my life. I thought that maybe I should show Julie the telegram.

But, then, another thought suddenly got clear in my head: What was I gaining by keeping the copy of the telegram in my pocket? What will it gain me? What? The answer was obvious: Only misery!

Yes, it was true that it had been my link to a distant past. But that past no longer existed. It had now been replaced by the now. By a lovely, innocent, beautiful creature, who was now dancing in front of me in the middle of an empty parking lot totally blameless of the other things that had come to crowd my life and made it bitter. The telegram was just a piece of paper that no longer held the truth of how my life had been. Its message was also fading.

Yes, it would be part of me for as long as I lived but it could no longer rule my life anymore. I thought of the manila envelope with my letters to Emily that Billy had given me. I knew that I would also have to destroy them as soon as I could, as I had destroyed her letters to me.

I appreciated that Billy had kept them, but I also knew they no longer served any purpose. Billy would understand the truth of my sentiments if he knew what I was going to do.

Something about there is time for everything. The final stage had finally arrived and as I watched Julie, I knew what I had to do. Slowly, I tore the telegram into small pieces, and then stood and threw them away one by one in all four directions. I do not think that Julie saw me doing it.

Not that it would have made any difference. I saw the night breeze get a hold of the tiny pieces of paper as they slowly drifted away into the night and beyond. Emily had been right all along. Life cannot remain dark forever.

I felt sad, but I also felt a new sense of curiosity about what I was doing. And the other thing that surprised me greatly was that I had not thought of Emily as I was tearing up the paper. I smiled and felt solid, and good. Not completely happy as I thought this state of affairs had not yet arrived, but I could also feel it on its way.

I looked up at the sky and even with the streetlights, I could see stars and they were not just tiny lights fixed up in the firmament, but they seemed more than that. I thought; screw it, that is how it is. Finish writing this saga, buddy. It has been a long time passing, but you now have to do it.

Jack had not used those exact words, but he had pretty much said to either shit or get off the pot. The truth was brutal. But enough was enough.

And looking at my lovely Julie still doing pirouettes by herself, on an empty parking lot, I knew that Cash and Jackson had also been right about this beautiful child-woman having the "hots" for me.

They were probably laughing their heads off now remembering how upset I had been when they first told me about it. Shee-it, I did not know. I really did not know. How come those bastards had understood and I had not?

"Hey, come here," I said, to Julie.

"What?"

"I want to show you something."

She walked over and stood right next to me. I hugged her and kissed her.

"You know, I think the back door may be open. That gives us access to the boiler room and I bet you that it is not locked. Come on."

We quietly walked around the building. It was not as well lit as in the front. I remembered the times when we had to come back and stoke up the boiler to give us some heat. And for convenience, the door was always kept unlocked. And bigger than sin there was no lock on the door.

I opened it slowly. It was dark inside, but the lights from across the street gave us enough illumination. Julie was holding my hand and a bit fearful about what we were doing.

One thing that the Army insisted then, and I was sure it had not changed, everything had to be clean. Inspection was something that we all had to be concerned with.

I grabbed Julie and started kissing her and she was giggling. But much to my own surprise, my member did not seem to be in the mood. I was rubbing myself against her. Maybe, I was about to be taught a lesson in humility by my own body.

"You're crazy," she said.

"Well, the other night it was me who didn't want to make love to you on the side of the road. So, let's take up where we left off."

"What if the MPs—Military Police—come by?"

"They won't. They never come around here."

I put my hand under her dress and started to pull down her panties. She resisted, well, only a tiny bit, then, the next thing I know, Julie was pulling down her panties and giggling. I lowered my pants, my shorts. My erection—that I was somewhat concerned about earlier because Julie might be right about the MPs—was suddenly taking shape from its slumber and on its way to stretch out in its full splendor.

"Oh, my goodness," Julie said, and she touched me.

She stepped out of her panties and held them in her left hand. I lifted Julie up to my waist and she wrapped her legs around me. She kept kissing me and hanging on to me while I was holding her, then she guided me into her.

There was something very primitive and yet innocent in what was taking place between us that went beyond the physical act we were engaged in.

It was not the best position, but we managed to connect and in the boiler room of the old playhouse, the place where we had met ten years ago, I made love to Julie.

"Can you imagine if we had done this ten years ago," she whispered afterward giving me her wonderful smile.

"I'd still be in Fort Leavenworth on a diet of bread and water," I said.

"The Army has no sense of humor."

"Hey, let's leave your panties behind."

"Negative."

"Come on, somebody will find them and they will wonder for the rest of their lives who they belong to? Who was the GI who got lucky? Come on."

"No," she said, but she was giggling. I am sure if I had insisted a bit more, she probably would have left them.

"You're no fun."

Then, as we were walking out of the boiler room, the whole thing became clear. There was no more reason to struggle with what life had given me. I now had to take the damn thing by the horns, as it were, and wrestle it to the ground.

There was something strange in my no longer feeling guilty concerning what had happened to Emily and me. She was gone. She was the past. I had known that for years and years. I just did not want to accept it.

I had felt too inadequate to accept it. And there was something else that also struck me, now. I was not replacing Emily. Julie was not replacing Emily. No way. She had once asked me if she were replacing Emily and I had not been certain.

What I had failed fully to understand was that Julie was not replacing Emily. Julie was giving me a second chance. I was not sure if she would understand it that way. My previous life with Emily was ending. Wherever she was, she would know, understand it, and approve of it.

"Come on, hurry up."

"Why, is somebody coming?" Julie whispered.

She looked around the dark room and toward the outside and back at me, not sure as to why I was now pressing her to hurry, suddenly. We kept whispering.

"No, but we're late," I said.

"Late? Late for what?"

"I'll show you."

I was pulling her and she kept resisting.

"Wait, I have to put my panties back on."

"OK, but hurry up."

She struggled to put her panties back on. She kept looking at me without comprehending why I was in such a hurry. We came out of the building, and I started to walk fast toward the car while pulling her behind me. There was not a soul in sight.

"Hurry up."

"Jonathan, what is the problem?"

"There is no problem."

"Why are you acting this way, then?"

"You don't know?"

"Know what?"

We got to the car and I jumped in. She got in after me. And she kept looking around and at me. Completely lost as to what I was doing.

"We're leaving," I was now back to using a normal tone of voice.

"What?"

"You heard me."

"What do you mean, 'leaving'?"

"That's right."

"You mean going back home?"

"You don't get it, do you?

"I guess I don't."

"We're hitting the road. We're leaving for California this very minute."

"What?"

"You heard me right."

"Wait a second. I don't understand."

"You don't have to. When we get back to your place, you'll have exactly eleven and half minutes to pack your suitcase."

"Eleven and half minutes?"

"That's right."

"Wait a second, you're saying we're leaving for California this very night eleven and half minutes after we get back to my place?"

"That's the idea."

"Jonathan, you're mad."

"Yes, I am. You said you wanted to go to California didn't you?"

I started to drive fast. She kept looking at me trying to figure out if I had taken leave of my senses.

"But not like this. You can't do this to me."

"Can't be helped."

"This is total insanity."

"OK, it appears that I've failed miserably in articulating what we're going to do. So let me put it to you as simply and as succinctly as I can: Once we get inside your apartment you'll have exactly eleven and a half minutes to get your suitcase, pack up some clean underwear, your favorite shoes, dresses, your diary, your tooth brush, your passport and whatever cash you have in the apartment and we're leaving."

"What if I don't want to go with you?"

"Excuse me, I'm not bargaining with you. You'll come even if I have to do like the ancient cavemen did to their recalcitrant women: bump you on the head a couple of times with a club. OK, no club, a frying pan will do the trick. Grab you by your hair and drag you and put you in the car."

"Jonathan, I think you have confused me with your other floozies."

It was interesting to watch Julie trying to come to the realization that life sometimes takes sudden twists and forces you to confront some existential choices. She wanted to have control and now it appeared as if she was losing it. I could see that she was not quite prepared to accept it. Yet, the lure of the unknown was also present.

She had also lived on the edge for years and years. The reality that was now facing her was something else. In many ways, I was confronting her with what I had been confronting myself with for too damn long. It was time to cut the Gordian knot for her, and for me.

"You're not a floozy. You've never been a floozy and you'll never be a floozy. You're not smart enough to be a floozy."

She was looking at me and I could see a glint of a smile on her face. She was trying to figure out if I were just joking, or if I were serious—I was. I was going to teach this hussy a few things.

"I just can't pick up and go. What about the stuff in my apartment?"

"Small potatoes."

"It's my stuff, my . . ."

"What? Fine, have your sister and your mother set up a garage sale and get rid of it. There's only so much my Chevy can carry and I don't want to load it with 'stuff.' I want to keep the top down as we're barreling down the road. I don't want your stuff flying out of the back seat."

"Jonathan, you're like the plague, insidious, malevolent. You're like some boil that needs to be lanced."

"Fine. Lance the boil and nature will take care of the rest."

"You know, I haven't agreed to this madness of yours."

"True. But it doesn't change one simple fact: and that is that any moron would have understood what you have said and the way you have acted these past few days. So being the moron than I am, I grant you, I didn't understand it.

"And for the record, I will remain a moron but this time around, I will understand it. Don't ask me how because that becomes an oxymoron and my life without you would be an oxymoron. It ain't gonna happen."

"You're speaking like some of the rednecks around here."

"What have you got against rednecks? I love rednecks. Yes, their music is for the birds about men and women who cheat on each other and go back to their places to drink hard whiskey or their moonshine, shoot their guns, hate the government, and want no part of it. How can you not love these guys?"

"And you think because I love you that I'll agree to sneak out of town in the middle of the night?"

"OK, you should thank me for keeping you from having to go to a dinner, a kind of Spanish Inquisition dinner, to quote you directly, with Ham. Send him a postcard if you must."

She leaned over and kissed me on my right cheek.

"Will you finally love me one day even when I'm old and decrepit?"

"No," I said, "who do you take me for?"

"What am I going to do with you?"

"Hey, come on, I'm easy."

"Right. Again, what about my stuff, my apartment, my car, my . . ."

"What? Your dishes, your towels, your toilet paper, your what?"

"I can't just take off in the middle of the night like this."

"Why not?"

I could see that she was now fighting to make sense of what I was saying. She started to laugh. A great lovely laugh. A combination of fear and total elation.

"You're completely insane."

"No, I'm not. I have been, yes, but no more. Enough of my unhappiness, my pain, enough of my life being a total mess. I ain't interested in that anymore."

"What if I don't want to go with you?"

"Sorry, too late. I have a debt to collect."

"A debt? What debt?"

"You know, the other night when we went to your mom's house. When I was talking to her outside, she said something to me that made perfect sense. She said and I quote: 'Jonathan, please take her with you. She has become unbearable. A total pain in the, well you know where.' She was too polite to say it.

"Then, she added, 'Julie is not the lovable child I raised.' I told her that for me to carry out the mission she was proposing that I didn't come cheap. And she said: 'I will give you a five figure check. I just want her out of my hair', can you imagine your own mother saying that?"

She started to laugh and laugh until she had tears in her eyes.

"My own mother selling me to the cheapest bidder in the land! I would have asked for all of the gold in Fort Knox."

"I guess I'm not a good negotiator."

"No, you *are* not, mister."

"Yeah, I think you're right. And she also warned me about your stubborn streak."

"Stubborn streak?"

"That's what she said. Even your own sister agreed. I'm telling you, now a days you can't even trust your own family."

"As soon as we get home, I'm going to call and have a serious talk with these two women."

"No, not enough time."

"Jonathan, I can't just leave without telling my mom anything."

"You'll call her from the road, tomorrow, or next week, or next year."

"She's going to be worried about us if she doesn't hear from me."

"No, she won't."

"You're so sure of yourself, aren't you?"

"Yes, more than you can possibly imagine."

We got to her place and I slammed on the breaks and jumped out of the car.

"Hurry up. Remember, once I open the door to that apartment you'll have exactly eleven and half minutes to get your stuff. As I've said, a couple of sets of clean underwear, your tooth brush, your pretty yellow dress which you already have on you, your favorite shoes, your lovely black gown you wore the other night, your diary, we mustn't forget that, your razor blade to shave your legs, your nail polish, your passport, whatever money you have in the house. Oh, yeah, all of the documents about your grant and for Bologna. Let's see did I forget anything?"

"Yes, whether or not I'm going with you because you haven't asked me."

"I thought I already did that at Bragg?"

"No, you simply told me to get in the car, to hurry up, and that we're leaving."

"That's as good as asking, in my view."

"OK, I want to understand this."

"There is nothing to it. I finally figured things out. That all I have done these past few years was getting ready to come by here and stake my claim."

"Stake your claim? You didn't even know I still existed. You didn't even care to send me a lousy postcard, like you know: 'Hi Julie, hope things are well with you; now, get lost.' "

"You're right. How inconsiderate of me for not having thought of that."

"So you agree that you weren't too swift?"

"You've got me on that one, babe."

"I think you're doing this because you feel guilty about the way you ignored me all of these years."

"Not true. My love, as you have called me, I've got some strong feelings for you. I can't deny them. I don't know where they came from. I know they're there. What you have brought to me these past few days can't be distilled in any kind of term paper. It'll take a lifetime for me to write it and for you to read it and find out what's there."

There was a long pause. Julie knew that I was putting her feet to the fire. She had imagined me in all of these past years. Now, she was confronting a reality that even I had trouble understanding.

"Can I ask you a question, if you don't mind?" She said, after a long pause.

"Shoot."

"Why eleven and a half minutes?"

"Don't know. It sounded good. I don't like the number nine because it's a bastardized right side up of number six, and thirteen, well, you know how people feel about that number, come on."

I opened the door. She got out, started to laugh again, and before I knew it she was running up to the apartment while I chased her up the stairs. I put my hand up her dress and grabbed her ass. She could not stop laughing. I opened the door.

"The eleven and a half minutes start," I looked at my watch, "Now!"

Julie stood in the middle of the room kind of lost.

"I have to take a shower."

"You already took one."

"Jonathan, I know, but . . . "

"But, nothing. Hey, it is now eleven minutes and fifteen seconds, exactly, " I said, while looking at my watch.

I could see that this whole thing, whatever she had hoped for, thought, felt, or even considered, was far from what she could have imagined taking place in her life. What she did not see was that it was also something I could not have imagined happening to me, either.

"How could you do this to me? Why?"

"Because, I had suddenly found myself not thinking about my past, but about you, my present, my future, my afterlife. I couldn't ignore the obvious. I would have been a complete moron not to read the tealeaves. It was pretty clear. And I must confess that it's a great moral sacrifice to want to take you with me, after I discovered you like James Bond books. How shameful."

"They are not mine. They are Becky's. Though, I can see the whole fantasy of this immoral guy, bedding women, gambling, drinking dry martinis, shaken not stirred, and shooting the bad guys."

She busted out laughing.

I had no idea where this mad idea of mine of just packing up and leaving came from. The only thing that I knew was that it felt good. Yes, it was crazy, but good crazy.

"You're the most devious, sneaky, human being that ever was. You're going to pay for this. Yes mister, you're going to pay for this. I promise you that. I'll never forgive you for what you're doing to me. Never!"

"Ten minutes and counting. You're wasting time."

She stood looking at me. Then, it suddenly became clear to her, and I saw it in her eyes, that her life was about to take a direction that she only dreamed about. And it was not just me. It also involved others: Emily, me, Ham, her mother, her sister— everyone. We had to carry the whole thing to its inevitable end.

She rushed into her bedroom, grabbed her suitcase, opened it, and started to throw stuff in while laughing her head off. But her laughter now had a serious under tone. She understood that it was no longer a joke. She was muttering to herself.

She went into the bathroom. I could see her putting on a new set of panties while she balled up the ones she took off, put them in a plastic bag that she then threw in her suitcase. I laughed.

"Cannot believe this mad man, cannot believe it. What's worse is that I'm agreeing to his foolishness like some wanton hussy. Won't even let me call my mom, won't let me take a shower. I cannot believe it."

"OK, let's take a shower and catch a quickie."

"We've already had our quickie for the night. Don't have no time for no more quickies, not now, mister."

"Too many negatives in your sentence."

I busted out laughing and fell on the bed. She threw herself on top of me and started kissing me

"You *are* insane," she said.

I looked at my watch. "Eight and a half minutes and time is running."

She stood and went into her closet and started looking for her shoes. She opened a set of drawers and pulled out her bikini and her undies, threw them inside the suitcase. Went into the bathroom again, grabbed her stuff, came out, and threw it inside her suitcase with her other stuff.

She was now going full bore. And laughing in a glorious way. She went into the living room and grabbed her diary that I had left on the kitchen counter and brought it in the room and, very carefully, she put it in the suitcase. She also put the scrapbook her mother had made for her right next to her diary.

"For our kids," she said, softly.

I stood up and opened my own duffel bag, threw in all my clothes and in fell swoop—did not have too many to begin with—sat on the bed watching her. She gave me a dirty look.

"What am I going to tell my mother about my stuff here?"

"I told you: Tell her to set up a garage sale, and to send you the money later. She has a key to your place, right?"

"And my books, school papers and my notes?"

I stood and went to the other closet, threw open the doors and just inside there were two big, fat, envelopes. I pointed them out to her.

"What's that?"

"Your books, school papers, your notes, miscellaneous stuff."

She looked like, had she been able to do it, she would have thrown me out of the window.

"You are sly one, aren't you? You have a criminal mind, insidious, shady, and sneaky. You have been planning this whole thing all along haven't you?"

"Not true."

But to be honest about it, I had packed all of that stuff a couple of days earlier because they seemed to be all over the place, which was very unlike Julie as she seemed to be rather neat with her belongings. The envelopes had been sitting in a corner of the room, empty.

"Then, why is my stuff packed in these envelopes?"

"Hey, they were there. I just thought you hadn't had time to put the stuff away with how busy you have been. I was just trying to be helpful, that's all."

"Helpful . . ."

"Hey, now, it'll be easier for your mom to ship them over."

She pulled two large folders from one box and put them in her suitcase. It was the stuff for Bologna University and her Guggenheim Grant.

"And my paycheck?"

"You can write and have them send it to you care of the Sargentis. I bet you the people at your school have never sent a letter to Italy."

"I have a lease on this place for another two more months."

"So let 'em sue you."

"What about my car?"

"Garage sale, or give it to your sister."

"I love my Datsun. It's a good thing it's all paid for."

"There you go."

I looked at my watch. "Hey, we're ahead of schedule," I told her just to tease her.

"OK, I get to drive, which direction?"

"Do you see where the sun sinks? That's due west."

"California. Los Angeles, St. Monica, Malibu, Hollywood, earthquakes, pollution, freeways, floods, wild fires, no sidewalks, too many cars, the land of plenty of nothing, and people who do not walk; they forgot how."

"You got it. But they also say to take a shower with a friend and save water, I mean . . ."

"Yeah, I grant you it isn't bad, it has merit," we both knew what she meant.

380

"I'd like to request that on our way we stop in Alabama and find out where Cash is buried."

"Can do. Pay your last respects?"

"Are you kidding? Cash would kill me if I did that. No, I'm going to dance on his grave, piss on it, and call him all kinds of names . . . that bastard. I will teach him a lesson he will never forget. He knew before I did that you had the 'hots' for me. The words he used. I never believed him. He wasn't guessing. He knew!

"Cash would never forgive me if I didn't call him dirty names and I know that bastard has been laughing his head off ever since because he has had one over me. I can't let him get away with this. He called me 'dog breath'. He thinks I forgot. No, I will piss on his grave to even the score."

She started to laugh.

"You will not do that."

"Julie, you don't understand what's at stake here. I don't piss on his grave, he'll haunt me, and he'll laugh his ass off. He'll give me no peace. He'll call me a sissy. I know the guy. He is the most ruthless, sneaky, opinionated, double crossing skunk that ever lived. He has no shame.

"There is no way that I would let him get away with what he pulled on me that time. And now I have you with me, and that we're together, he's having the last laugh.

"Yeah, Mr. Know It All. I've got to go toe to toe with Cash to show him I ain't afraid. That my pain for the loss I suffered when he went ahead and died on me is over. That I ain't no wimp. He expects that from me. He'll appreciate it. And knowing that I know he's watching me, I had better get with the program.

"Show him my love for him isn't with platitudes and phoniness, which he hated because he was never a phony, but with something as elegant and true as dancing and pissing on his grave because he expects it from me—that rotten bastard."

I started to have tears in my eyes. She hugged me.

"Jonathan, I love you out of this world but you belong in an insane asylum. In fact, I belong in an insane asylum myself for agreeing to let you do this. And Jackson?"

"About pissing on his grave?"

"For example?"

"Don't worry, his turn will come. Boy, I loved those bums. I miss them. . ."

I was trying like mad not to let her see my eyes. She just held me closer to her and kissed away my tears.

She sat right next to me and held me in her arms. She was shaking her head and looking at me with such a wonderful soft, look; and it was true, her eyes always gave her away.

Is there a time when the scales of life finally bring equilibrium to our beings, when we do not have to carry emotional burdens with us every minute of our putrid existence, when we can breathe freely without having to worry about looking over our shoulders to make sure we are not being followed? Can we ever be free? When one reflects on what we see around us the answer appears to be, no.

We seem to burden ourselves with nonsense constantly. And in the process the essentials are forgotten or pushed aside. Our primitive and pure senses are corrupted not by the rain, the sun, or the stars, but by us.

Were we to let the sun, the stars, the moon show us the way, if that were possible, we would most likely reject them and we would go back to our lousy, rotten ways, because to do or think otherwise amounts to rejecting that we are children still pure and innocent.

If only we could always remember the purity of who we are. Julie then took the photo of the Sargentis and her great photos from the wall and she stood looking around the room.

"I'm good to go," she said, but she stopped, and suddenly a panicky look came to her eyes. I thought, oh, man, she is not going to go through with it. What the hell do I do now if she changes her mind? How do I convince her? If she says no dice, I am in the shits.

Then, the next thing I saw was so funny, so completely outrageous, and unimaginable.

After handing me the photos, she threw the covers off the bed and started to pull the sheets from the bed. I started to laugh my head off. It was so unreal. I knew why she was doing it. We had not changed sheets for a day or so.

She got the laundry bag with the dirty clothes, put the sheets inside it, opened my duffel bag, which was half-empty, stuffed the laundry bag inside, and shut the duffel bag again, while I was bending over, in pain, from laughing so hard.

Not a word came from her. I knew she was trying like crazy not to laugh. She gave the bedroom one more look, took the photos back from me, and then she walked to the living room. Julie looked at her surroundings. I do not know how long she had lived in that place. She had never told me.

I brought her suitcase and my duffel bag with me. She took Emily's painting with her. Julie, I think in the last half an hour, had suddenly realized that life has no interest in getting you from point A to point B.

You have to do it yourself. What was also interesting to me was the fact that she had been instrumental in what had changed me. In what was now taking place.

I do not think that she had put two and two together, not yet. But I also knew—as certain as the sun would come up and find us on the way—that what she had brought to me would become very clear to her soon enough.

"You've got everything you need?"

"Jonathan, all I need is you with me. The other stuff can easily be replaced."

"That's what I thought."

I did not make any comments about the sheet incident. Time would come and later we would have a few laughs, drink champagne, and make love on the same sheets that were now inside my duffel bag; clean, of course, she would say. Incidentally, we had left a nice tip for the maid at the hotel back in Myrtle Beach.

Julie hesitated for a moment, looked around, and followed me. She turned the lights off, and locked the door. There was a moment of total silence. What we were doing seemed so strange but it was real.

Life had gotten into the picture and it no longer just represented an idea, a dream, and a plan. Julie did not yet really understand that she had made this whole thing possible.

One day it would come to her. And she would understand that nothing would have taken place, but for her love and a love poem she had written from her heart ten years ago.

The world is always better with poetry than with the other ugly things we humans are guilty of, like wars, and corrupting ourselves with cruelty and dishonesty.

We walked slowly to the car in silence. It was not because she or I were having second thoughts about what we were going to do. It was simply the realization that so much of what we fear in life is self-imposed. That what people often say is true.

You have to one day come to the full realization that you have control over your life, your destiny, that you cannot go on forever making up excuses, but that the truth is always within yourself. You just have to trust your own instincts and not get bogged down by petty details.

I put the suitcase, my bag, the painting, and the photos in the trunk and I looked at my watch.

"Hey, a whole minute to spare. The whole universe was born in less time than that."

"Can I tell you something?" she asked, while embracing me.

"What?"

"When you first came into the theater, just ten days ago, and the first thing you could say was: 'Remember me?' I thought, didn't he know that I have never stopped loving him, never. Didn't he know it?

"I wanted to kick you hard in the area that Becky said the 'Jewels of the Kingdom' are ensconced. But I immediately realized that I didn't want to take the risk on our future children, not that you wouldn't have merited a hard kick!"

I looked at her and she was dead serious. I did wonder if Julie would do it. But, then, I thought that I didn't want to take such a risk. I was trying like crazy not to laugh. "Jewels of the Kingdom."—leave it to Becky all right.

"Wise decision about the kick. Our kids would never have forgiven you for that. It would have been a crime against humanity, but I concur with your assessment," I said.

"Mister, you're a fool," she said, laughed, kissed me, and held me close to her for a long time. She smelled delicious even without another shower.

I handed her the car keys.

She got in the driver's seat while I sat right next to her. Julie was no longer living in her past. She was now confronting a future however uncertain it may appear.

But she seemed no longer that young woman I had found just ten days ago, or the lovely, shy, young sixteen-year old girl of my past. She was different.

There was a sense of destiny. That's the only thing I can think of. There was so much that I did not know about her. I thought: It is going to be a wonderful discovery!

Life was sure as hell imponderable. It had taken me ten years to get to these last ten days not only to confront the truth of what my life had been up to this moment, but to fully comprehend it. My buddy Jack had argued with me over the years to accept that life was not about to give anyone of us a break.

It did not happen that way. We had to fight and claim our share of the good things. They were there, but it was never a given. Some people, perhaps, had it easier but no one could claim to be victorious all of the time. Julie believed that. And so did Emily. Two great broads!

Like Cash had once said to me: "A bit of happiness don't hurt nobody none!"

Julie started the car, and made a fast U-turn that pushed me against my side of the car.

"Take it easy, Jimmy."

"Got you."

"Oil pressure?"

"Check."

"Engine temperature?"

"Check."

"Gas?"

"Check."

"Brakes?

"Check."

"Proper heading?"

"Due west. Check."

"All right, soldier, this is not a drill. Let's roll out and make sure you get us there in one piece."

"Check."

She thought for a moment, then turned and gave me a rather sneaky smile, and a smart salute. I returned the salute, not as smartly as hers.

"Now, I wish I had left my panties back at the theater."

"I told you. You want to go back?"

"Negative. That's tempting the devil. By the way, are we *eloping*, Jonathan?"

"Eloping? No, that's only for sissies and wimps."

"That's what I thought."

384

"We're, you know, going to the coast and beyond to check things out, see what I'm sayin?' "

"Absolutely!" She said, with that mysterious smile of women who know the score.

We, men, are so full of ourselves that we get lost in peripheral stuff, and it really takes women to figure things out for us and set us on the right road. I am sure Julie and Emily would both have agreed. Robert Frost had a poem: *The Road Not Taken*, and I had read some interpretation of it.

I did not know the poem. Something about our tendency to look back and blame events in our lives, or to add more significance to things that do not merit it. I have to find the poem and share it with Julie, I thought.

Yes, my life had been long time passing. I did not exactly know what I was now looking at, but I felt incredibly free of the burden that had weighed me down for such a long time. Perhaps, if I had been smarter and wiser, I would have done what I was about to do sooner.

I would never know what would have happened. The truth, though, was simple: Julie did not exist in my life then; and now, she did! In the final analysis, all of my crazy thoughts were ex post facto. I was through thinking of my past. It was over.

I could hear both Cash and Jackson, over the roar of the engine, getting on my case.

Hollywood, you piece of trash, shee-it. Talk about wimps. You still don't get it, do you? You loved Emily; we loved her, too, but she's gone. We've got news for you loser. Julie had your number all right just like we figured years ago. You're the luckiest bastard that ever lived. Tell her you love her, you wimp—shee-it.

I laughed aloud. She looked at me waiting for an explanation. But I was not about to give her one unlike my wish to find Frost's poem and share it with her. Some things are strictly reserved: for men only! Women are excluded.

Seeing that I was not about to give her any explanation; she shrugged her shoulders, then, turned on the headlights and slowly eased the car out of the parking lot and headed down the highway.

"Do you know where Gilroy is in California?" She asked.

"No, what's that?"

"The Garlic Capital of the whole world!"

"OK, we've got to check it out. California, you say?"

"Sure do."

"Let's go by there, buy a ton of the stuff and ship it to the Sargentis."

"Now, you're talking," she said, and I imagined what Roberto would say about that. Maybe garlic does make the world go around!

Then I turned the radio on, and I could not believe it but there was Ray Charles, bigger than life, singing: "*Hit the Road Jack*"—what the hell.

"OK, how cool is *that*?" she exclaimed!

"Did you order this?"

"Guilty as charged. Me and Ray go back a long way."

Julie then gave me a superb smile. And she started singing along with Charles, while letting the night air touch our faces softly and sweetly.

Your comments regarding this novel are most welcome, and I hope you have enjoyed reading it. Also, be sure to check out my other novel: *At the End of the Day* in its original English version, or in its French version: *A la Fin du Jour.*

www.edlevesko.com
edlevesko@gmail.com